By Laura Castoro

Love on the Line
Icing on the Cake
A New Lu
Crossing the Line

Love on the Line

A Novel

LAURA CASTORO

𝓌𝓂

WILLIAM MORROW

An Imprint of HarperCollinsPublishers

FIRST WILLIAM MORROW PAPERBACK EDITION PUBLISHED 2009.
SECOND WILLIAM MORROW PAPERBACK EDITION PUBLISHED 2021.

Designed by Diahann Sturge

The Library of Congress has catalogued a previous edition as follows:

Love on the line / Laura Castoro.—1st ed.
 p. cm.
Sequel to: Crossing the line.
ISBN 978-0-06-154276-3 (acid-free paper)   1. Racially mixed people—Fiction.   2. Widows—Fiction.   3. African American clergy—Fiction. 4. Mothers and daughters—Fiction. 5. Domestic fiction.   I. Title
PS3533.A8152L68   2009
813'. 54—dc22   2008043292

ISBN 978-0-06-309295-2 (pbk.)

21 22 23 24 25 LSC 10 9 8 7 6 5 4 3 2 1

To
David Parker Willis
And
Christopher Noble Willis

ACKNOWLEDGMENTS

So many wonderful people make my world go round.

Thank you, Carol Mackey, for first offering me the opportunity to continue Thea and Xavier's story.

Thank you, Alyndria Thompson, my smart, beautiful college student friend, for answering my questions about your generation's culture and college life, and instructing me in the more modern forms of communication like text messaging, Facebook, and YouTube. I predict that one day she will have her own books in print.

Mucho thanks to Sandy and Judi, who shared their home and hearts with me when the going got rough.

Thanks, Georgette, who read, edited, and offered on-the-money critiques at a critical time in my writing process.

Special tribute to my stepdad, Kenneth. His 24–7 dedication to my mother's health care made it possible for me to escape daily into the worlds of Thea, Xavier, and Jesse. Words can't give adequate thanks for all you've done.

To my husband, Chris. You're the hero in my life.

Chapter 1

"My beloved is mine, and I am his. . . .'" Thea turned back a page and ran her finger down the thin leaf of the old Bible until she found the passage she had flagged. "'Let him kiss me with the kisses of his mouth: for thy love is better than wine.'"

Xavier's response was quick. "'Thou hast ravished my heart, my sister, my spouse; Thou hast ravished my heart with one of thine eyes, with one chain of thy neck. How fair is thy love, my sister, my spouse! How much better is thy love than wine!'"

Thea's gaze lit on another passage from the *Song of Solomon*. "'By night on my bed I sought him whom my soul loveth: I sought him, but I found him not.'"

There was a moment of silence and then she heard Xavier's book snap shut. "I think we've studied enough for one night."

"Agreed." Thea shifted the mouthpiece of her phone. "When you suggested that we read the Bible together I didn't expect it would be quite so stimulating."

"Then you underestimate how much I miss you." Xavier's

voice sounded low and deep in her ear, as if only inches—not thousands of miles—separated them.

"And I you."

"Hm." She knew that when Xavier tempered his response with a thoughtful sound or even silence, he was thinking deeply. "So then, it's time we did something about that. What do you think?"

"What I think—" Thea broke off. *What I think is that eighteen months is a ridiculously long time to be engaged to a man who has spent most of that time as far from me as possible.* But she didn't want to sound unsure. "Are you ready to come home?"

"Are you ready to plan a wedding?"

"How about tomorrow?" The moment the words were out she wished she hadn't been so impulsive. They had talked often of marriage but had not yet set a date.

His chuckle reassured her. "The lady's anxious."

"The lady's forty-five years old, Xavier Thornton. A woman my age has only so many good years left."

"Oh, I plan to make best use of all those left, and quite a few of the lesser best years, besides."

Thea closed her eyes. "So then, I can make plans?"

"Plan away. But keep it simple." He paused. "I've had an answer from the letter I sent the bishop. I had asked him to find me a church placement as soon as possible and he has found one. So I'm coming home to check it out as well."

"Oh, Xavier, that's wonderful." Even if he didn't say he was coming home only to see her she was still happy he was coming back. She supposed she should be beyond such silly feminine sentiments but what woman in love ever was?

"I hope you will think so, Thea. I've asked for a modest appointment. There won't be a St. James Jubilee Crown of Heaven Tabernacle or sizable congregation or . . ."

Thea's thoughts strayed away from his explanation when she glanced down at the engagement ring on her finger. It represented a love that had survived greater odds than they had any right to expect. *Even I had my moments of doubt.*

When she tracked down Xavier in Cabo San Lucas last year, after he had disappeared following the renunciation of his wealth and his position as pastor of a powerful church in Atlanta, she wasn't at all certain that they had a future. She hadn't immediately opened the ring box Xavier had placed in her palm that weekend after they'd made love. Even after he'd asked her to marry him, and she'd said yes, she wasn't sure she was ready to wear a symbol that so conspicuously announced to the world her plans to make Xavier Thornton a permanent part of her life. A three-carat diamond elicited a lot of comments, especially from other women. And she was by nature a private person.

Not every couple that falls in love needs to marry. A lot could change in a year, even if she were certain. But now Xavier was coming home!

". . . all that aside"—Xavier's voice drew Thea back into their conversation—"I must have a job if I'm to provide, however simply, for a wife. Are you fine with that?"

As he fell silent, Thea realized she might have missed something important. Yet she wasn't about to admit she wasn't paying attention. Better she should try to finesse the moment. "Are you trying to tell me your prospects are limited?"

"Limited to what God will provide." His answer carried an abrupt seriousness.

She admired his ease in introducing God into conversations. She never felt completely comfortable doing that. It made her self-conscious, except when talking with him. But, at the moment, she was a bride-to-be teasing her groom.

"So then, it's a good thing that I have been a faithful contributor to my IRAs."

His familiar silence seemed suddenly tense. "I will not ask you to share my vow of poverty."

"Poverty?" She whispered the word.

"So, if you need more time or . . ."

"No." She took a breath instead of asking how small a stipend he was expecting. Xavier had placed his considerable fortune in a blind trust, yet she had assumed that he would eventually return to the life, if not the lifestyle, he had abandoned. Even if he didn't . . .

"How about an August wedding?" She crossed her fingers like a child. "You think you can be home by then?"

"I'm ready to come home to you for good." There was a smile in his voice again.

"Then it's settled. A wedding in two weeks!" She had a good career, savings, and investments; they would survive.

"You better call my sisters. You know how they like to be part of my life plans."

Did they ever! "I'll keep them informed."

But when they hung up, Thea didn't make any calls right away. She sat on the side of her bed holding the Bible that Xavier had given her just before he left. She was supposed to be studying it daily. But often she read it for only a few minutes before his weekly calls. If she were going to be a minister's wife, she supposed she should make it a habit.

A minister's wife! Me?

She rubbed her thumb over the gold foil lettering of her name on the front, wondering if she hadn't been better prepared to be a minister's wife the first time Xavier came into her life. But then, at sixteen, she had been young enough to adapt to almost any future that might have been placed before her.

From the back pages of the Bible, Thea slid out a fading photograph of a slender, fair-haired girl and a tall, broad-shouldered young man in a Maxwell-style 'fro and a soul patch. The photo was nearly three decades old. She squinted at it. Were she and Xavier ever that young?

They'd first met when Xavier was working at his uncle's law office between his freshman and sophomore years of college. She'd fallen mad bad in love with the smart, confident brother from Chi Town long before his name became a household word. He'd treated her as a kid sister until his last night, when hormones and desire pushed her to show him just how much of a woman she wanted to be to him.

Thea shook her head, thinking of her naïve young self. She was a kid doing what kids in love do, believing that nothing bad can happen because her love was so special. Reality had come crashing in on her after he went back home to Chicago.

She was pregnant. By then she knew Xavier had forgotten her. He never called or wrote. Silence. Shame and pride made her refuse to name her baby's father. Hoping to shield her from shame, her parents sent her to Aunt Della in New Orleans to have and then give up for adoption the son Xavier never knew he had.

Thea tucked the picture back in place. It was a hard way to learn that love doesn't conquer all.

Within a few years, Xavier was living a life that anyone who picked up a sports section, fanzine, or even a tabloid could follow. His physique, skills, and intelligence turned him into the professional basketball phenomenon known as The "X" Factor. Headlines traced his trajectory: "The 'X' Factor: Small Forward Sensation." "'X' Pro Shoots for Hollywood." "'X'-it Hollywood: 'X'-celling on Wall Street." "Entrepreneur 'X'-changes Shares for Souls." That kind of fame never went completely away even after a lifelong calling to the ministry finally won him over. His celebrity status quickly catapulted him into the very influential and coveted position of pastor of St. James, a mega-church in Atlanta, Georgia.

She had gone on to lead a good but unadventurous life, except for the fact that she had fallen in love with and married Evan Morgan, a wonderful man who happened to be white. She was certain that nothing would keep them from being happy into old age. Yet on a bright summer morning Evan dropped dead in his law office of an aneurysm.

Two years ago, just as she was getting comfortable coping with loneliness and single parenthood, Xavier reentered her life. The old pull between them erupted with surprising power, startling two sophisticated people in the prime of their lives. But they were no longer children and their baggage was considerable. Hard on the heels of her reunion with Xavier, David Greer, the son she'd given up for adoption, found her, and demanded to know not only why she gave him away but, more important to him, who his father was. The resultant explosion rocked all their worlds.

Thea stood up and set aside her Bible, her musings of happy topics derailed by other, harder memories.

Perhaps it was asking too much of fate to hope that all those she loved could learn to live in harmony. Despite a reconciliation of sorts between her children, Jesse and David, neither had tried independently to form a closer relationship. In fact, David had decided earlier in the year to leave Dallas and move back home to Biloxi, Mississippi. He told her that his harrowing experience as an activist for Black Lives Matter in Dallas had convinced him that she was partially right about the need to work within the system.

"All the laws in the world won't make the lives of the have-nots better unless black and brown men and women of all races are willing to dedicate their lives to making certain the laws are justly enforced," he'd told her as they parted. "That means taking and holding power. Political power."

David had gone home to set up a law practice and run for a city council seat.

Though she was proud of him, his moving from Dallas felt a bit like losing him all over again. If only she had—

No! She shook her head in defiance of useless what-ifs. *All that is behind us!*

She glanced down and smiled. The ring on her finger represented the power and grace of forgiveness. And a second chance at happiness. It was time to share the joy.

The first person she called was her aunt Della down in New Orleans. "Praise be! It's about time that man made an honest woman of you."

"I've always been honest, Aunt Della. And thrifty, loyal, and clean."

"Make your little jokes, Theadora, but you know God don't like ugly."

Thea chuckled. Aunt Della might have married and buried three husbands but she still believed in the proprieties. "I'll have you know, Aunt Della, I've been living a virtuous life for the past fifteen months."

"That may well be. But the man is coming home. While Xavier Thornton is a man of God, he also struck me as the kind of man who won't long be satisfied to simply hold the hand of the woman he's taking to wife. He will have expectations."

"And they will be met! Just as soon as the minister pronounces us married."

"Very fine. Now just where is this wedding going to take place?"

"I was thinking of a small, quiet service here in Dallas."

"You don't have any relatives in Dallas."

Thea gave a mental shrug. This was one thing she could always count on. Things needed to be done properly when Aunt Della was involved. "Xavier mentioned his sister in—"

"I'm not traveling up to Washington, D.C., to see you wed through the groom's relatives. Folks will think your family can't provide."

"I wouldn't expect Xavier's family to—"

"It will come up. I've met his sisters." Aunt Della clicked her tongue. "They will have you thinking you're a guest at your own wedding. Mark my words."

Thea couldn't argue. Xavier's sisters were an obstacle course she had already run, twice. Both times she had escaped intact, but not before they let it be known in no uncertain terms that she was not what they hoped for their brother: both as a black woman who could pass for white, and as a widow who had married a white man and produced a blond, blue-eyed daughter.

Come to think of it, Cherise, Pearl, and Liz, Xavier's sisters, had a lot in common with Aunt Della when it came to trying to run other people's lives.

As she hung up with her aunt, Thea glanced at the clock. Nine forty-five. Ten forty-five in Atlanta. Selma might still be up.

"Girl! I had begun to wonder. I was just saying to Elkeri that a man who loves a woman shouldn't be able to be away from her for a year."

"Thanks for the backup, sis."

There was a slight pause. "But, you know, I can be wrong."

A year ago Selma would never have backed down from cracking on her sister. A year ago Thea's guilt would have kept her silent when attacked, feeling she deserved her sister's attacks, even though Selma had not known the real source of her guilt. That old laundry had been aired. Today, things were different. And better.

"So, I need to put together a wedding in two weeks. Got any ideas?"

"Only a thousand!" Selma was one of Atlanta's top interior designers and event planners, specializing in Afro-centric influences. "First, you're coming to Atlanta to marry. It's Xavier's old stomping grounds. His former congregation alone will send the guest list into the thousands—"

"Small wedding, Selma. Xavier's stipulation."

"I hear you. You wouldn't be comfortable with the type of extravaganza I like to put on. Xavier's status demands it. But you wouldn't be up for the drama required."

"Nobody else but Diana Ross could have carried off the production you created when you married Elkeri. What did you do with your feather headpiece?"

"The live magnolia blossoms were dried for permanence and then I had the entire piece mounted under glass. It's on a pedestal in our bedroom."

Thea laughed. "You're too much."

"Hold on." Thea could hear her sister digging in her purse. "Okay, got my cell phone. You're lucky the third Saturday in August is open. How soon can you come to Atlanta? I need to get you on Elkeri's business calendar."

"Why?"

"So you and Xavier can house hunt. The quality of home a celebrity like Xavier requires doesn't come on the market that often. Don't expect miracles, even if Elkeri runs the largest black real estate business in town."

Thea sighed. "Xavier's new posting is not Atlanta. It's in a small town."

"Small? Do you mean a suburb like Alpharetta?"

"No, he's hoping for a small church in a small town."

"Say what? You've got to do something about that. Xavier is set to become the political and spiritual successor to Jesse Jackson. Everyone says so. Can't you see him helping Obama with his post-presidential dreams? He can't be doing that from a small-town pulpit."

"He's given up such ambitions."

"Like he gave up his wealth?" Selma's exasperation bristled through the phone. "Elkeri says it was a shrewd move, politically, for Xavier to separate himself from his fortune. Shows he's not addicted to the Benjamins. I still say it's crack-crazy thinking, even if it is temporary. There are plenty of wealthy preachers. It is temporary, right?"

Trust my sister to pounce on a tender spot. "I'm not sure."

"Oh, *hell* no! The man is thinking he can live poor? Married to you?"

Thea wished she hadn't opened her mouth. "I'm not high maintenance, like my sister."

"I own that. Proudly. But you're the one who is Ms. Big Bucks Corporate Attorney. You have an assistant to remind you of social occasions, Jesse's soccer games, and to pick up your laundry. You're going to ditch your six-figure job to become a poverty-stricken preacher's wife? I don't think so. You better talk him out of that foolishness now."

This conversation needed a change of topic. "So then, about the wedding."

Thea could feel her sister's attention switch gears. "I'm on it!"

"You'll have to deal with Xavier's sisters."

Selma expelled a breath through her nose. "Didn't I decorate Cherise's Arlington, Virginia, home? You think she can tell me anything about arranging a wedding?"

Thea smiled. If anyone could keep Aunt Della and the Thornton sisters in line it would be Selma.

"How's my beautiful niece?"

"A born diva if there ever was one." Selma paused as a baby's cry split the air. It was a fussy, impatient cry of a one-year-old who thought her needs weren't being met. "Can't get a minute's peace around here. Excuse me."

Thea jumped at the sound of Selma's cell phone hitting a hard surface. Then she heard through the line, "Elkeri! Put Andromeda down! You're exciting her and it's time for her bath. Dee! Dee! Where is that trifling girl? Oh, there you are. Bathe Andromeda now. No, before her bottle. You can finish your dinner later."

A moment later the phone was picked up again. "I don't know how you did it, raising Jesse and working. With Andromeda I'm tired from morning to evening and again when I wake up. She's got to be kept on a schedule or I can't get anything done."

"Well, you hardly slowed down after having her."

"Don't you start! I get enough of that from Elkeri. I have a business to run. Two, in fact. But I'm a good mother."

"Of course you are."

"A wonderful mother!"

Thea frowned. "Is everything all right?"

"What do you think? We're perfect. Perfect!"

Knowing when to retreat was also part of negotiating a better relationship with her sister. "Wonderful. I'll call you in a day or two and we can make definitive plans."

"I'm taking you shopping for your bridal ensemble. You'll just choose any old thing—*Elkeri!* Didn't I tell you not to excite that child? I don't care! Put her down. She's naked. Oh, look—she's wetting herself. Thea, I got to go!"

Thea smiled and shook her head when she had hung up. Selma was addicted to drama. A baby was built-in daily drama.

Selma named her daughter Andromeda, "because the ancient Ethiopians believe that Perseus and Andromeda are the progenitors of the black race." She certainly treated her daughter like royalty. From the moment Andromeda arrived, a perfect sloe-eyed angel, Selma had a "mini me" to dress and adore.

From a grouping of pictures on her dresser, Thea picked up a photo of Selma, Elkeri, and Andromeda from their baby's christening six months ago. They made a cute family, though as usual, Selma dominated the photo. At thirty-five, she was still that beautiful. Who would ever have thought she had inferiority issues?

Selma inherited her father's coloring, a shade or two deeper than Halle Berry's with thick, long black hair and cat's eyes the color of pralines. "They may not know I'm black but even strangers on the street know I'm some kinda brown baby." That was Selma's defense against what she once saw as her older sister's advantage: pale skin.

She sighed, picking up another, older, picture. This one was of her with her first husband, Evan, and their daughter, Jesse, at her christening. Three smiling faces all with light eyes, light hair, and pale skin posed for the camera. If she asked a stranger, "Who's black in this picture?" she knew the person would look at her as if she were nuts.

In reality, the differences between the sisters was in temperament. Selma's All-About-Me attitude vs. Thea's "Anything-to-Please-the-Parents" view of the world. After their parents died, years passed before they succeeded in patching up old wounds and becoming the sisters they were meant to be.

"Better late than never," Thea murmured and decided a glass of wine was in order to toast the news that she was getting married. There was only one other person, the most important one, to whom she needed to break the news. Jesse.

Chapter 2

Jesse checked her face in the driver's-side vanity mirror before she turned off the engine. If Kyle had given her a bruise she would have some explaining to do. Her reflection drew a big sigh of relief. No marks. Not even a love bite.

Okay, so maybe Kyle wasn't a total jerk. But yes, he was. The accidental collision of his chin with her cheek wouldn't have happened if he hadn't been trying to put the moves on her before she was ready.

Cassandra, her best friend since ninth grade, had set up this date with her cousin Kyle, who was visiting from Houston. The best friends were both smart and played soccer. Cassandra was going to Bryn Mawr while she was going to Simmons. But being younger by a year, because she had skipped the second grade, Jesse had been last in about every way with her peers: last to get her period, last to develop breasts. Now, according to Cassandra, she was the last of the virgins. She'd promised Kyle would be cool.

So, was she some sort of freak for bailing on Kyle?

Eeewu! So not!

Jesse got out of her car and then stepped back to inspect its metallic silver surface for any signs of imperfection. Just two weeks old, the Honda Insight was a graduation gift from her dad's parents. Its hybrid engine, which she'd insisted upon despite her grandparents' desire for a more powerful vehicle, made it both techno savvy and green. With the climate heating up faster than a JennAir range, a responsible person had to think ahead.

She patted the hood as she headed for the back door. Her mother would ask why she was home so early. Her mother worried too much. They were close, more like best friends than mother and daughter. Yet there were some things that a daughter didn't necessarily want to share with her mother. Some things were for girlfriends only. And after what had occurred tonight, she was about to give her girlfriend Cassandra a piece of her mind!

She found her mother with a glass of wine in hand sitting at the bar and looking positively moody. Now that was unusual.

"Hi, sweetie. How was Kendra's party?"

Jesse shrugged. "I didn't go."

"Why not?"

Jesse struck a pose, hip jutted out, an unconscious move that called attention to the curves of her sport-toned body. "I make Kendra's extended family members uncomfortable." She flipped her blond ponytail over a shoulder, notching up the attitude. "Not white enough."

The race issue had been stewed, sautéed, and flambéed enough in this household. Still, Jesse knew her mother would respond, which would change the subject of where she had been. "Did Kendra's relatives say something to you?"

"Didn't give them a chance." Jesse kept her expression as bland as possible. "Kendra told me that when they came to her graduation, her aunt and grandmother gave her a really hard time about dating a Latino guy. They said brown is not white and Latino isn't American. She should keep to her own people. Can you believe that? The twenty-first century and they are talking Nuevo Jim Crow."

The frown between Thea's eyes eased. "So what did you do instead?"

Nothing I want to share with you. A diversionary tactic was called for.

Jesse shifted hips. "In two weeks I'll be living twelve hundred miles from you. Are you going to sit up every night wondering where I am and what I'm doing?"

"No." Thea smiled the smile Jesse loved best, the one with a bit of resigned humor. "But while you live in this house, I'm still responsible."

"Not after I turn eighteen! I'll be totally independent."

"I'm going to hold you to that promise when the credit card bills come in after November 23rd."

"Okay. Bye." Jesse flipped her mom a wave and turned to make her escape.

"Wait, Jesse."

A year ago she would have argued. Tonight something in her mother's tone, and the fact that she'd been drinking wine alone, made her turn back. "What's up, Mom?"

"We need to discuss a family matter." Thea blinked and blushed.

There was only one topic that could make her mother look so weird. *Reverend Thornton.*

Jesse slid her purse off her arm and moved toward the bar to sit down. "You've set a date for the wedding."

"Yes." She looked relieved Jesse had guessed the subject. "In three weeks."

"So soon?" Despite the long engagement the announcement of a date felt sudden.

Thea leaned forward and put a hand on Jesse's knee. "I'd hoped you'd be happy for me."

"I am." She looked down at the huge emerald-cut diamond hovering above the third finger of her mother's left hand. She had been promised the smaller pear-shaped diamond engagement ring her father had given her mother when she turned twenty-one. "But sometimes I can't help thinking about Dad."

"I know." Thea's gaze shifted to the family portrait that hung nearby. "After your dad died, I didn't think I would ever want another man in my life. But then I found love again. I think your dad would understand."

Jesse nodded, not meeting her mother's eye. "I'm happy for you, Mom. Really."

"But?"

Jesse shrugged. "I don't want to lose this . . . us."

Thea scooted off her stool and put her arms around her daughter, and hugged her tight. "I'm adding to my life, not substituting people. You won't get lost."

Jesse hugged her back, glad for the warmth of a motherly embrace. At the moment she felt unsure of everything she thought she knew, especially about herself. "Can I ask you something?"

"Sure. Anything."

Jesse's gaze rose to a spot in the ceiling. "How do you know you are ready to marry Reverend Thornton? I mean, he's nice and all. . . ." Her gaze swooped down to meet her mother's. "But you haven't seen him in forever. How do you know you even still have feelings for him?"

Thea smiled. "A woman knows."

"I'm serious. Lots of women have a man in their lives but they don't marry. Kendra's mom has been dating the same guy for three years."

"Dating isn't the same as commitment." Thea scooted back onto her stool, a small faraway smile on her face. "Xavier and I both need someone to be there for us when we come home at night."

As her mother's smile deepened, Jesse noticed new faint lines form on her face. *She's getting older! That's the answer! She's afraid of being alone!*

She impulsively leaned forward and caught her mother's hand. "Listen, Mom. You don't have to marry just because you don't want to live by yourself. If you want, I can change my mind and go to U.T. instead. Austin's only three hours away. I could be back here every weekend—well, every other weekend. And you could come and visit me and we'll do stuff."

"What about when you finish college and get a job?"

"You can retire, uh, and come and live with me." *What is this? Mom's thinking I'm actually serious?*

"What about when you fall in love?" Thea gave her a wide-eyed look. "Will there be room for me, then?"

"Ah . . . sure."

Thea laughed and Jesse realized she'd been pulling her chain. "I'm not marrying because I'm afraid to be alone. I've lived alone since your dad died."

"What? I don't count?"

"You know that's not what I mean."

Her mother's smile gave away more than she intended. It was like a little electric shock to Jesse's system. *She's talking about sex!*

Jesse scrunched up her face. "Sex is overrated."

Thea sobered. "Are you trying to tell me something?"

Jesse looked away. "What makes you think that?"

"You've been home ten minutes and you haven't asked if your purchases from H&M were delivered. Something else must be on your mind. Want to share?"

Jesse tucked in her chin. "I guess I'm a little jealous."

"Of me?"

"In a way." Jesse stood up and moved a little away. "I'm seventeen years old and I've never had a boyfriend. Not a real one. And don't give me the Disney version of someday-my-prince-will-come. I don't need to meet the love of my life yet. I just want a guy to hang out with."

"But you get asked out all the time."

"Not even close. Who took me to the prom? Etienne, a friend, not a boyfriend. It was like dating my brother. Most of the guys who call or come by are friends of friends, or trying to get with someone else. They call to complain about who they can't get. No guy ever calls just for me."

"Maybe you aren't seeing what's there," Thea said gently.

Jesse's right brow arched just like her father's would when he wasn't convinced of an argument. "That's it. I'm just blind to all the great guys sliding through my life."

Thea patted the stool Jesse had deserted and she reluctantly perched on the edge. "Some women care more about going out than who they go out with. Other women care more about *who* they go out with than where they go. You think and feel deeply about things. That makes you want more from a relationship than your friends do."

Jesse couldn't bring herself to say she'd let Cassandra fix her up with her cousin Kyle because she hadn't been asked out in forever. That sounded too pathetic. "Why don't guys even want me for sex? Not that I'm easy or anything. But they don't know that, and still they don't hit on me."

"Come on, Jesse. You're smart and beautiful and athletic. I guarantee guys see you as sexy. But it takes a mature guy to step up to the challenge you present."

"Great! So now I intimidate guys." Jesse sighed. "Can't I drop the 'smart jock' label for a minute, and just be an immature boy-magnet for a while?"

Thea looked at her so long Jesse began to feel itchy before she said, "Is that what you want to do?"

Jesse shrugged. "Not exactly. But I don't seem to have much of a choice. It's hook-up or sit on the sidelines and watch."

"This business of hooking up is a mistake on so many levels."

"I agree." *Exhibit A: Kyle!* "But aren't expectations of happily ever after equally unrealistic?"

"You're asking a woman who has just said yes to a man she hasn't laid eyes on in a year."

Jesse felt the tug of a smile. "Just so you know, I think you're a little bit crazy."

Her mother waggled her brows at her and Jesse knew what was coming.

"Wait until it happens to *you!*" they said in unison and laughed. That was her mother's tag line for anything Jesse hadn't yet experienced.

It felt good to laugh. Nothing could become a huge problem between them if they could make silly jokes together. Yet, after they sobered, neither one seemed to know where to go from there. There was no point in bringing up Kyle now. She'd figured out for herself that was a mistake.

She resisted glancing at her watch. That was rude. "So? When is Reverend Thornton coming home?"

"You *could* call him Xavier, as he has asked you to."

"Okay, Xavier." As long as he wasn't angling for "Dad," or "Father Xavier" or something else totally whack she would let that awkward issue slide.

"He'll be back in Dallas next week." Thea blushed. "Jesse, do you mind if he stays with us this time? He'll take the guest room."

"Sure." Jesse looked around, hoping for something else to come into her head to say. All that came out was "Are you going to sell the house? You said before that Rev—Xavier won't live here out of respect for Dad. Has he changed his mind?"

"No." Thea's glaze slid away. "We're going to find our own place. But I'll keep this house for a while."

"What about the holidays?" Jesse didn't want to sound hard but this wasn't exactly the college sendoff she expected. *I leave then she leaves, and then our old life is really all over?*

"We'll be together, I promise. But it's important that Xavier and I have our own place where we both feel comfortable." Her mother's tone begged for understanding.

"Fine." Jesse stood up. This conversation was so over.

"One more thing. Selma convinced me it should take place in Atlanta."

"Aunt Selma's coordinating the wedding? Cool."

"Atlanta in August? I doubt it."

Jesse groaned at her mother's lame joke. "Can I have a say in what you wear?"

"Selma made the same request. Don't you two trust my judgment?"

"Not even." The buzz of her cell phone made Jesse dig it out. It was a mobile TM alert from Cassandra. "Gotta go, Mom. This won't wait."

⌘

Jesse sprawled on her bed in the dark. Her wireless laptop provided the only light as she brought up her messenger server and logged on as *Soc_R_God_S*: soccer goddess.

Cassandra was already online, waiting. Her username, *2Sxxz4U*, which read as "too sexy for you," was blinking impatiently.

2Sxxz4U: *???????????????*

Jesse took a deep breath and began to type. *Total disaster!!!*

2Sxxz4U: *What? U 2 didn't hook up?*

NO!!! Went to dinner. Then he said we should park somewhere and watch a movie in the backseat of his Dad's Escalade. He got all aggressive. Almost swallowed my earring.

2Sxxz4U: *Not the diamond studs ur grandparents gave u for graduation?*

Jesse reached up to make sure both were in place. *How did U guess?*

2Sxxz4U: *When have they NOT been N UR ears? They have soap rings on em, grrl! Ok, and we R back. . . . So????*

2Sxxz4U: *I told him I needed 2 take em off. But then I dropped one. U know how dark it is with tinted windows. Had 2 get down on my knees 2 feel for it. That's when it went so wrong.*

Did U lose the stud???

Worse . . . he says: As long as U R on ur knees, why don't U 2 have a conversation . . . and he opens his zipper!!!

What??? U never saw a dick B 4?

Jesse felt her cheeks fire with embarrassment. No, she hadn't. But she didn't want Cassandra to think she was a total baby.

I told him I didn't know him well enough to want to be on intimate terms with anything in his pants. That's when he started rubbing himself and talking about how I could at least help a brother out!!!

OH NO HE DIDN'T!!! LOL!!!

Jesse bit her lip. When Kyle had tried to coax her head toward his lap, she'd jerked away and somehow his chin connected with her cheekbone. But she wasn't sharing those details.

So? SAY SOMETHING! HELLO???

Jesse rubbed her cheek before keying in her reply.

Being UR cousin, I thought Kyle'd have some damn finesse?!?!?!?

2Sxxz4U: And this is my fault how? So, maybe he got a little aggressive. I thought U said U R tired of being a virgin. U could have changed that 2night.

Jesse bit her lip. *I might B a virgin but I'm not a fool. Some consideration would B nice. I knew him, what, 3 hours? I'm supposed 2B grateful he's got a hard on? Please!!!*

Know what UR problem is? U R N some dream world where the girl thinks the guy has 2 give a damn about her! I know for a fact Kyle was all hot 2 get with U.

An awful suspicion struck Jesse.

U didn't tell him I'm a VIRGIN???

Excuse me? Who said she was tired of being a virgin? If U can't handle it, don't go there.

Jesse took a deep breath. She couldn't think of anything to reply. The bad night had just gotten worse. She had been a pity-the-virgin date!

I got 2 go.

After they logged off, Jesse lay on her bed thinking. Cassandra and her mother were right about one thing. She was hoping for a relationship that involved more than ten minutes of sex. There had to be guys out there with more class. Sex for her needed some dignity.

She giggled at the word "dignity" applied to tonight's situation.

One thing was certain, she was tired of being labeled things like "virgin," or "biracial," or "the smart jock," or even "trust fund baby." Her grandparents loved to remind her that her Philadelphia Morgan lineage meant that one day she'd be an heiress. She wanted to be known and liked just for herself, just for being Jessica Darnell Morgan.

She couldn't wait to get to college where she would be a stranger. That was her only hope for shedding those old labels. Finally she could decide what to reveal about herself, free of the baggage of her personal history.

Chapter 3

"How's it going?"

Thea looked up from the letter lying on her desk.

Aisha, her assistant, had stuck her head in the office door and was practically dancing on her toes. But Thea was too intent on the paper before her to be social at this moment. "I'm very busy, Aisha."

Aisha nodded but half stepped into the room anyway, and lowered her voice. "You're sure there's nothing I can do for you?"

"Not at the moment." Something in Aisha's tone made Thea add, "Is there something you want?"

"No." Aisha drew out the word like a child who really means *"Of course there is! Something really important or juicy and I'm just dying to tell you if only you ask me!"*

But Thea wasn't in the mood for office gossip, no matter how juicy.

Defeated, Aisha glanced speculatively about Thea's office then shrugged. "Just another day on the job, right?"

"So it seems. But let me know the moment we get a response

from our client in Dubai. The DA's office has called twice this morning."

"Sure thing." Aisha left but looked back through the narrow glass beside the door before disappearing completely.

Uncharacteristically annoyed, Thea scanned the letter on her desk again, looking for any mistake or false sentiment or lazy word usage. Aisha, a smart, savvy young lawyer she'd hired a year ago, had proved to be a shrewd people reader. Aisha was the office gossip but surely not even *she* could have guessed what this day meant to Thea.

The Walker, Brennan, and Cullum and Associates letterhead with her name in the left-hand column as a junior partner never failed to make her heart beat a little faster. Working her way up the corporate ladder as a double minority hadn't been easy. She had sacrificed a lot to get to this point. The biggest sacrifice had involved her family. Even though Evan had readily made the decision to give up his lucrative career as an attorney in Philly so that she could accept a position in Dallas, she'd felt guilty for accepting his sacrifice. Jesse's dislike of moving from her East Coast niche to the unknown territory of Texas had tested to the max both of their parenting skills. Though, to be perfectly honest, Evan seemed to have an easier time with Jesse than she did in those days.

Thea noticed the flashing IM on her computer screen and saw that the client in Dubai had, at last, sent in the requisite paperwork. Smiling, she typed a quick thanks.

After Evan's death, she'd been suddenly thrust into the role of single parent, shouldering both the emotional battering of a child devastated by the loss of her father and the temptation of in-laws who meant well but saw the world only in their terms.

She'd lost ground for a while in her determination to be the first woman as a full partner at Walker, Brennan, and Cullum and Associates.

There were only so many business trips or late evenings she could manage with a young daughter. Her personal grief soon took a backseat to just staying afloat. All that happened before Xavier re-entered her life. Whoever said love was a private matter must never have had to deal with family.

Despite it all, she had moved up to become a junior partner last year.

Thea rested her chin in her palm and looked out on the vaguely copper blue sky of a smoggy summer day in Texas. This corner office overlooking the Dallas skyline represented the daily measure of her professional success as a woman and an African American.

Now, with a few words, she was about to hand it all back without achieving that final step up to full partner.

Xavier hadn't asked this of her. It was her idea to make this a gift to their new life together. They had met when she was sixteen. Yet they still needed time to learn each other as they were now, midlife adults with a new vision for their lives.

A second tap at her open door brought her head around. "Got a second?"

Thea smiled at her boss. "Sure, Ron. Did I forget a meeting?"

"No, no, nothing like that."

Ron Cullum was, as usual, smiling. But his big-kid face had lost its ruddy, freckled-face quality. Everyone had praised him when he started losing weight during the winter, when pounds usually pile up. But lately, the whispers had turned to how old Ron looked. Sixty was doing a number on him.

He shut her door, an unusual move that alerted her that something important was about to be discussed, and came to stand before her desk.

"I've got news I think you're going to like, Thea." His grin widened. "It's about the promotions to be announced next week. Your name is there. Under the heading 'full partner.'"

"Full partner?" Thea couldn't quite get her head around that. "You're kidding me."

Ron wagged his head. "You've waited a long time for this."

"So long I'd given up the dream," she answered before she could stop herself.

"Congratulations!"

"Thank you." She spread her fingers to cover her resignation letter, in case Ron might glance down.

She didn't think it necessary to mention the obvious, that as managing partner in the Dallas office, he was at the top. "So, what? They're kicking you upstairs to international?"

"Not exactly." Ron looked suddenly extremely uncomfortable as his gaze shifted toward the city skyline beyond her window. "It's more a permanent change."

"Ron, they didn't—ask you to take a retirement package?" She couldn't say the word "fire."

"No. I'm calling the shots." He fumbled with his hand-tooled silver belt buckle, which hung limp from a belt that even in its tightest notch was now too large. "You probably noticed I haven't been myself lately. Oh now, there's nothing to worry about," he added when she started to speak. "Only I need to take some time off to look after my health."

Thea held her breath then expelled it with dread. "What is it, Ron?"

"Non-Hodgkin's lymphoma." His expression changed, as if in saying the words he was losing a little of the battle. "But I don't want it to get around just yet. And you don't have to tell me that people recover from it every day. I've started chemo. At the end of the week I'll be checking into the hospital for a bit. Before you know it, I'll be back, spry as a jack rabbit."

"Of course you will," she responded, and it was no less heartfelt for being the only thing a person could say under the circumstances.

"And that's just it, Thea." He sat down in a chair before her desk, something he rarely ever did.

"I'm sixty years old. I have a lovely wife who's put up with a lot. And had me to deal with in the bargain." A ghost of a smile crossed his sallow face. "Now we've got three grandkids, and one on the way. I want to be able to play ball with 'em and show 'em my Texas and have 'em argue with me about everything from politics to that *gawd*-awful stuff that passes for music today. I've earned enough money for one lifetime. After I lick this damn thing, all I want is time to live peacefully with that little woman on the hardscrabble patch near Big Ben my daddy left me." He grinned. "We've turned a patch of it into a three-hole golf course so I don't have to commute to play."

Thea understood. That was how she felt about Xavier, and their future. So then, why was she even considering tearing up the resignation letter beneath her palm?

"The promotion is yours, either way. But I'll feel a lot better about things with you at the helm here when I'm not."

At the helm? In charge of the Dallas office? Was he really offering her that?

"I'm so flattered, Ron, that you think I'm ready to succeed

you. But, actually, I was about to take some time myself. I'm getting married."

Ron's expression brightened. "You and that fella of yours have set a date?"

Thea nodded. "Next week. It'll be a small ceremony. Family only. In Atlanta." She kept adding to her explanation as she realized he might wonder why he hadn't been invited.

Ron didn't seem to notice the slight. "Well, that's just dandy!"

"There's more." She let her fingers drag across the letter. "I had been thinking of resigning. My husband and I need time together. He's been away this past year."

Ron nodded soberly. "Now, I'm the last one to want to interfere in a relationship. But why not consider working after you're married? Women do that these days."

"It's what I want." As she said that, a dozen reasons popped into her head why turning down this opportunity might not be a good idea.

Acting Managing Partner! Am I nuts? The opportunity didn't present itself to every worthy candidate. There must have been wrangling behind the scenes that she didn't even want to imagine. She wasn't every senior partner's dream candidate.

The prestige! She'd make all the trade magazines, maybe a profile in *Fortune*. And lots of perks! Who said no to hard-earned success?

Reluctantly she looked back at Ron. "I may be moving away."

"Really? Where?" He looked almost impatient with her reluctance.

She shrugged, feeling foolish for not knowing the answer. "I'm not certain yet. Xavier has to find a church."

"So then, nothing's settled."

He waved away anything else she was about to add and leaned forward. "I'm not going to say you can't say no. But I went to bat for you over this promotion. There were plenty of boys with candidates of their own with reasons aplenty to question my hiring a . . . Yankee." His faded blue eyes gained a bit of sparkle. "You are kinda young and pretty for the job of SOB. But I told 'em if they didn't offer the job to the best candidate just because you look better in a skirt than any of the others, I'd have something to say about that, on the record."

Thea felt a surge of emotion threaten her usual calm. "You went that far for me?"

He shrugged. "You are my shining star. I hired you. Everything you do makes me look twice as smart as I think I am. You've earned my respect again and again. Seems a shame to pass on the payoff after all the work you put into getting it."

He's right! The certainty of that discomfited her. She did want this. Really wanted it!

When emotion threatened her in the workplace, she always fell back on formal language. "Yes, well, I must allow for other relevant factors now. For instance my new husband's position might not be in Dallas or even close by."

He gave her a long considering look. "You really are in love."

"Yes."

"Then I wish you all the best." Ron stood up a little slowly and weaved slightly when he tried to turn too quickly. Thea tightened her grip on her desk to prevent the instinctive gesture to offer a hand.

When he turned back to her, his mouth was pinched but his tone was as glib as ever. "Let's do this. Let the announcement go through. Then wait until after you come back from the honeymoon to decide. You can always resign. It'll look better to go out as acting managing partner." He paused, his jaw working. "And if you're still tempted to say no, think on this. You're so damn internet savvy you could have been working from home part-time this last year. Why not as full partner?"

Why not, indeed!

Thea nodded, grateful for his tenacity. "That's why you're still the boss of me."

"I'm just foxy enough to know a good thing when I see it." He gave her a little John Wayne salute. "Hell, I'm not going far. You get into trouble you give me a call. I know where a few bodies are buried."

Thea tore up her resignation letter the moment he left, before she could let herself think about what the promotion would mean to her plans for a cozy, intimate life with Xavier.

"I can always quit next year," she murmured to herself after she had doodled the words "full partner" next to her name on her calendar.

Chapter 4

Mrs. Hattie Patterson was on a mission from God, to find the perfect hat. Not just any hat. This hat must carry all the weight and authority of her position as chairwoman of the Pastoral Relations Committee, be suitable for her age, and still make Shirley Jackson green with envy. That was a lot of responsibility for pieces of straw, felt, silk, feathers, net, and satin. That's why she had driven all the way to Jackson, Mississippi.

"I believe that's the one, Mrs. Patterson. I do believe it is." The shopgirl's anxious expression hovered above the image of her client's in the three-paneled mirror.

"Then you are in error. I thought I had seen its like before. Now I'm sure of it."

Hattie lifted the hat from her head and pinned the shopgirl with an unforgiving stare. "I specifically asked you not to show me any hat you had sold within the last six months. Jessica Meeks, a member of my own church, has one just like this in fuchsia."

"This one's green, Mrs. Patterson. And the feathers are black. That's different."

"*Harrumph!* You must do better than that. Or I will just have to find myself another milliner."

"Oh, no, ma'am." The girl looked stricken. "I'm sure Ms. Almandine's got something that's sure to please you."

"I surely hope so." She patted her steel-gray marcelled waves back into place. "I drove a great distance in all this heat not to be disappointed. Ms. Almandine usually attends my needs herself. She knows how particular I am."

"Yes, ma'am. Only she did just have a baby last Monday." The girl took the lampshade-size hat Mrs. Patterson thrust at her. "I'ma call her and see what she suggests. Then I'll be right back with something *ex*-tra special."

Hattie gave a short sigh then, looking in the mirror, patted first one underside of her jaw and then the other with the back of her hand. She prided herself on the fact that at seventy-three years of age she did not have a slack jaw or, heaven forbid, a double chin. It took discipline and effort, but a woman retained only so many assets over time. A firm jawline should be admired. The brim of that last hat had cast deep shadows on her face, enough to hide two double chins. That's why she always wore an upswept brim.

Hattie glanced in consternation at the grouping of hats she had already rejected. Was she being difficult? No, God's work was hard work. And she'd prayed over this matter because she had a new minister to impress.

"Won't be any more lifting from the collection plate, nor the skirts of women in our congregation," she'd told the deacon just last Sunday. "We are finished with that sort of jackleg preacher. Not in my husband's church. Not ever again in my lifetime."

The fact that St. Hurricane AME Church was put to the necessity of interviewing a new minister after just one year was a source of some personal embarrassment for her. She had vouched for Reverend Samuel. And he had been a disappointment if there ever was one!

Men, especially young men, seldom got round her. She'd been reared in a minister's family and had heard daily discussions about the perfidies and weaknesses of men. She had married Obadiah Patterson at eighteen because her parents wanted her settled before temptation, in the form of the freedoms of college life, could touch her. Obadiah had just graduated from seminary. Her daddy said Obadiah was as good a man as a young woman could ever expect. And, Obadiah needed a wife. She had accepted him because he was tall and fine.

Back in those days things were done proper. A man couldn't reach a position of authority in the church until he had a wife. In fact, he needed a wife and children to get a regular stipend. After they married, Obadiah had come in as assistant pastor to her father at St. Hurricane AME Church. Later when her father rose to the post of bishop, Obadiah became senior pastor of St. Hurricane where he remained even after becoming an elder. That elevation had taken a lot of pushing and supporting, and what the young folk now call networking, to get him known in the right clerical circles.

Hattie sighed. Obadiah didn't have what her daddy called "push." He was content tending his small flock. But she was the daughter of a bishop. It was only fitting she should become the wife of one. She became a delegate to every General Conference. Served on any and every committee, under her husband's name.

She would never forget the day he was elected to represent the south central jurisdiction on one of the legislative committees at a General Conference. "That should be you up there, Hattie," another minister's wife had whispered to her. "You earned it as much as he did."

It was a compliment but it also pointed out a truth. In her day women didn't aspire to a pulpit. Obadiah's post was as close as she would ever come.

Nowadays, people like to say that times have changed. She liked to think of herself as a woman who could change with those times. So when Reverend Samuel had come with impeccable credentials, aside from his unmarried state, she had allowed herself to be tempted to ignore this lack. All because, heaven forgive her, he had reminded her of her own dearly loved and now departed Obadiah.

Sure enough, there was hell to pay.

Reverend Samuel hadn't been in the pulpit six months before there were accusations of stealing from the Sunday collection plate. It was some weeks before the deacons were able to catch him at it. By then the church elders had also heard rumors that Reverend Samuel was sticking those same thieving hands up the dresses of more than one young woman who called herself a child of God.

Well, didn't Reverend Samuel breeze out of there before they could vote him out? How he got another position over in Lafayette is still a mystery.

Hattie made a face as if she smelled something nasty. It was a bitter lesson to learn at her age, but some things shouldn't change. And that was pure D fact.

For the past month she'd prayed over their need for another

pastor until the parchment-thin pages of her Bible stuck to her sweaty hands. And then she'd prayed some more. St. Hurricane needed a real leader, someone even greater than her late husband, God rest his soul. Obadiah had been a good man but not a great one. The church needed someone who could raise up their little congregation to the level it deserved.

And then the letter came from the bishop.

Hattie fanned herself with one hand while helping herself to a peppermint from the nearby silver bowl with the other.

She still couldn't believe their luck. *The* Reverend Xavier Thornton was considering the position of pastor at her church!

There was a crash from the back room followed by a little cry of distress.

Hattie reared back in her chair and called out, "You there, child! Have you forgotten me?"

The girl came rushing into the showroom, her hair pushed up on her head, as if she'd just climbed out of bed. "Oh no, ma'am. I'm just looking for a particular hat Ms. Almandine called to say she had put back, a hat especially for you. Only I seem not to be able to find it on the shelf. I'ma keep looking though."

"You do that." Hattie carefully pushed back her sleeve to reveal the diamond watch Obadiah had given her as a thirtieth anniversary present. "I have a luncheon appointment in town I don't intend to miss."

"Yes, ma'am." The salesgirl turned and disappeared.

"The help one has to deal with today," Hattie murmured to the woman who had pushed through the front door during their conversation. But secretly she was pleased.

Ms. Almandine had put back a hat, especially for her! She

was going to need a special-order hat for Reverend Xavier Thornton.

She'd known about Xavier Thornton for years because her Obadiah—God rest his soul—was a rabid professional sports fan.

"That's putting in the 'X' Factor!" Obadiah would often shout in glee after his team scored. "That boy's got the blessing of the Almighty in his feet, I do believe that."

"He has the backing of someone," Hattie would always answer in mild reproof. "It remains to be seen whose."

For a while it seemed that Lucifer was participating in Mr. Thornton's life. While she disapproved of men playing games for a living, she read *Ebony* magazine religiously, and so knew more than she would admit about the "X" Factor's life. He was loved by the ladies a little too well. Most probably that explained why he didn't marry.

"My husband used to say, why buy a cow when you're getting plenty of milk free," Hattie said to the woman who was now trying on hats from her "no" pile.

The woman gave her a strangely offended look and moved away, but Hattie didn't even mind. She was dreaming big-time dreams for St. Hurricane.

Still, it wouldn't do for the congregation to think she was predisposed toward Mr. Thornton. Not after Reverend Samuel.

Could a man who had once inspired ungodly female fantasies worldwide have found his holy compass? That was the question.

As a good Christian woman, she didn't like to listen to gossip. That's how the Devil slipped in to trip you up. Yet she had heard things to make her wonder.

She'd learned from the deacons, who were as tickled as she was over the possibility, that Reverend Thornton had been married briefly in his post-basketball days.

Hattie sighed. She didn't approve of divorce. What God brought together, man should strive to preserve. But then some marriages, like her grandniece's, had "doubt" stamped all over them before the "I dos" could be said.

Bess Jenkins mentioned that Reverend Thornton's life had recently been touched by tragedy and some whiff of scandal. Everyone knew that was code for woman trouble.

In his letter to the church council, the bishop had mentioned that Reverend Thornton had taken a sabbatical from the pulpit in order to restore his soul. One had to hope it wasn't a sly reference to a drug or alcohol rehab program.

When Hattie called the bishop to inquire about Reverend Thornton's availability, he only said that he was reluctant to recommend her church to a man of Reverend Thornton's stature, who might find it limiting.

It was proven fact that Xavier Thornton's popularity could put any place on the map. Once he found God, that young man catapulted himself into one of the largest, richest pulpits in Atlanta, Georgia, in no time flat. If he agreed to serve them, she was going to make certain he used all his considerable charm and celebrity for the good of St. Hurricane AME Church. It was time they aspired to another bishop ordination. There must be no mess this time.

Hattie didn't like to think of herself as a woman with premonitions. God didn't like hocus pocus in his Christian flock. Still, for all her misgivings and doubts, she had a feeling in her marrow that this was an auspicious occasion.

Reverend Thornton was engaged. The bishop had been at particular pains to say that they would have a married man in the pulpit this time.

"But engaged is not married," Hattie murmured. What if his fiancée wasn't up to snuff? Well then, Hattie would find an answer for that, too.

"I found the special one for you, Mrs. Patterson." The girl, looking sweaty and flustered, staggered out of the back with a huge hatbox. She lifted the lid and then opened fold after fold of tissue paper before plunging both hands into the box to lift out its contents.

The moment she saw it, the first smile of the day lifted Hattie's stern patrician features. "Now that's what I'm talking about. That is a hat!"

Chapter 5

Y ou can't ever let a man know he's got you hook, line, and sinker," Aunt Della liked to say. "A man likes to do the chasing, and he needs something to chase after."

Thea wasn't supposed to come to the airport. They'd agreed that because it was a workday for her Xavier would catch the shuttle and meet her at her home after-hours. That was the reasonable solution. But reason lost out to anticipation two hours ago. She was about to marry a man who had not been a physical part of her life in a year. The suspense of their reunion could be shortened by at least two hours if she came to meet him.

The moment she spied him in the crowd, a thrill shot through her. The joy was chased off by a jolt of dismay as she continued to stare at him. The man who'd left her was a walking magazine ad, any time of day or night. His closely cropped black curls and Van Dyke beard were always neatly trimmed.

But today, his hair was long, practically the outsized Afro he'd worn when she met him twenty-eight years ago. His Van Dyke had grown into a bushy beard. And he'd lost weight. The linen shirt she'd sent him at Christmas hung from his broad shoulders while his khakis fell loosely from his hips. Even she might not have recognized him if she hadn't been expecting him.

As he neared her, she saw the usual smile lines about his mouth were dry riverbeds and his skin was mottled in places, as if bruised beneath the surface.

His deliberate stride and the angle of his head kept his line of vision from connecting with passersby. She knew celebrity life had long ago taught him to be self-protective in public surroundings. He was about to walk right past her.

She stepped into his path. "Xavier!"

The instant their gazes met she wondered if she had made a mistake. Then he smiled at her, a slow, dimpled smile much too sexy for a minister.

"Theadora!" His deep voice was husky, as if he'd been too long without a drink. He dropped his bags and held out his arms.

She felt a shiver of emotion rock his body as his arms closed tightly about her. When she leaned back she saw in his face raw emotions that echoed within her. He had come home, and so had she.

"Couldn't wait to see me, huh?"

She smiled and shrugged. "Don't let it go to your head."

Before he could reply, someone called out, "Reverend Thornton!"

As he released her, Thea saw a couple coming toward them. The woman, tall and regal with a chic short cut that made the most of her sterling silver hair, wore a smart sweater set and trousers despite the heat. The man, a bit taller and much broader, wore a suit and tie. Both smiled as they neared Xavier.

"Young man, I was afraid you had gotten away from me before I could introduce you to my wife." The man nudged her forward with a hand at her back. "Sharon, I'd like you to meet Reverend Xavier Thornton. Reverend, this is Mrs. Staples, my wife."

"Happy to meet you." Xavier smiled easily at the woman and shook hands. "Your husband and I had many stimulating discussions on the flight from London. Unfortunately, we were separated in customs. I had a few too many interesting stamps on my passport for them to allow me to pass through unnoticed."

"International travel these days has become tedious," the woman agreed, though her gaze wandered curiously to Thea. Thea could guess the question dying to be asked if she'd seen them embracing.

Xavier turned to her. "Bishop Staples, Mrs. Staples, I'd like you to meet Theadora Morgan. Theadora, this is Bishop Staples and his wife."

Thea held out her hand. "It's a pleasure to meet you both."

"Well then, we must be on our way," the bishop said after a short silence.

"Indeed. May you both have a safe and pleasant week." Xavier offered each another handshake and warm smile.

As they turned away Thea heard the bishop's wife's whisper, ". . . white woman?"

She had had a lifetime's experience with questions about her race. It was asked outright or implied in every encounter with strangers black or white, whenever she was half of a couple with a brown-skinned man. That isn't what bothered her. What she didn't understand was why Xavier hadn't introduced her as his fiancée.

Don't go seeking trouble, Thea. It was a small thing, she supposed, and she should simply forget it.

She reached for his computer case, the lighter of his two bags. He was quicker, and jerked the case out from under her grasp, making her stumble forward half a step. When she looked up to complain, the glint in his bittersweet chocolate gaze stopped her.

"Green eyes. I searched everywhere I traveled for a reflection of your green eyes. I finally found it in a rainbow stretched over the gorge of Mosi-oa-Tunya. I should have known. They are *African* green."

She felt embraced from head to toe, and he hadn't even laid a finger on her. Aunt Della had a point. She made it much too easy for him. Every bit of the love she felt for him must be in her eyes.

As they fell into step, she glanced at him in concern. "You look tired."

"I am."

"And thin."

One of his famous pauses ensued. They were blinking in the blazing sunlight of the 103 degree summer Dallas day before he spoke again. "You can't work in a refugee camp all day and then go back to the relative safety of your own tent and a hot meal. You find you must share, even if it's just their hunger."

It amazed her how he could pack so much emotional conflict into so few words. And, of course, there was nothing to say in answer to him.

"What do you want to do first?" she asked as he put his bags in her trunk.

He looked at her with a slow grin. "Really?"

Thea held his gaze with effort. "Really."

"I'd like to draw a big tub of water, pour in the best-smelling oil I can lay my hands on, and soak for about an hour and a half."

She laughed as they slid into the front seats of her car. "You're easy to please."

He leaned his head back against the headrest and shut his eyes. "And I'd like a deep sip of single malt Scotch. Something with a lot of years behind it."

"Can do."

"And a plate of chicken wings, fried up like my mother does them."

"You'll settle for mine and like it."

He opened one eye as he rolled his head toward her. "Truly?"

"There'll be a touch of bacon grease in the oil if you promise not to tell anyone I'm breaking your doctor's low-cholesterol rule this once. And you can use my Jacuzzi and my oils."

His brows shot up. "What about Jesse?"

"She's expecting you . . . to sleep in the guest room."

Xavier cocked an eyebrow. "Guess I'm going to lose my deposit at the Sheraton then."

"Canceled," Thea answered as she backed out of her parking space. "Things have changed. Jesse understands that. We're a family now. Or soon will be."

"She's okay with our wedding plans?"

Thea nodded. He had been privy to her worst times with Jesse. Thank goodness there were now good ones to share. "She even volunteered to help me find a wedding ensemble."

"Hallelujah!"

"What? You think I don't know how to dress?"

"Nawgh." He chuckled as he eyed her beige linen sweater

and slacks. "You have a businesswoman's way of dressing. Very nice, very classy."

She shot him a glance. "You mean boring."

He glanced at her under lowered lids. "Let's just say your outside doesn't begin to reveal your inside, Ms. Morgan."

She turned to him as they waited for a crowd of pedestrians with luggage to finish crossing the drive of the parking garage. "I'm afraid to ask what you think would match my interior."

Grinning, he reached past her to where her left hand lay on the steering wheel and lifted it. "To begin with, my ring. Why aren't you wearing it?"

"I am." She reached for the gold chain about her neck. "It's here, next to my heart."

"Hm." He tried to stick the tip of his pinkie into her ring but it was too big. "A man spends his time and consideration, and no little amount of money, on proof of the thing he's most proud of, and his lady can't be persuaded to wear it. A man has to wonder. Now, if you prefer a bigger stone, a different cut—"

She snatched the chain out of his hand. "Don't even think about it. I love this ring. It's everything to me."

"Why aren't you wearing it?"

She gave him a sidelong glance as she waited for another gaggle of crossing travelers. She'd forgotten to slip it back on after leaving work, but the oversight gave her a segue into the question in the back of her mind. "Why didn't you introduce me to the Stapleses as your fiancée?"

He dipped his head. "I owe you an apology about that. I was afraid they'd insist on taking us out to dinner to celebrate or something. And I want you all to myself."

"Is that the only reason?" Her tone was light but she needed to know.

He looked straight ahead. "I seem to remember that once you didn't introduce me to your coworkers in D.C. because you said you wanted to keep our private life private."

"Touché." Since becoming part of his very public life she had been misrepresented in the sleazoid press more than once, first as his white mistress and then his mystery baby mama. He'd told her then, "There's a different set of rules for people who live the so-called superstar life. Things will happen that will make you want to holler. But you can't, not in public. You have to learn to deal with it."

Thea smiled at him. "Just so you know. Next time, I'll be wearing my ring and introducing myself as your fiancée."

He grinned. "So then maybe it's time we tell the world officially that we are about to become man and wife. I can have it in print by the end of the week."

"You just said you'd like to keep our private life private."

"You seem in need of some public assurance. Your man being gone so long, I can see how that could worry a less than self-assured woman."

"I don't need assurance." She stole a glance at him as she pulled up to a stop sign. "Well, not public assurance."

Of course, he didn't answer that.

But he did look at her, so long and so hard that she was completely unaware of her surroundings until the driver behind her blew his horn.

Chuckling, Xavier leaned back again and closed his eyes. "*Hunh, hunh, hunh!* So, my lady's gonna fry chicken for her man. It doesn't get any better than that."

Now she didn't want to argue with someone who looked like he had not slept in a week but she was pretty sure she could do much better than that.

Chapter 6

"A rkansas?" Thea didn't try to keep the surprise out of her voice. "Why Arkansas?"

"That's where Bishop Jackson has a church with a vacant pulpit."

Xavier looked rested after his soak in her tub with a shot of Scotch as a chaser. He'd even trimmed his beard back into its familiar shape but there wasn't much he could do about his hair until he saw a barber. Still, he looked like a man renewed. The plate of bones before him attested to the fact that he had eaten his fill of chicken wings, too.

At the moment she was more interested in the fact that he had agreed to a location she didn't know about. "Didn't you tell the bishop that you're about to marry, and that your wife lives and works in Dallas?" Okay, that did sound a little selfish.

He nodded. "Weren't you the one who said it didn't matter where we were as long as we were together?"

She didn't remember actually saying that but then maybe she had. "Yes, but—"

She stopped short when his eyebrows rose. Putting a "but"

in a question about marriage wasn't perhaps the best way to attack the question.

He reached for his sweet iced tea and took a long gulp before saying, "You never said we had to live in the city."

"I thought it was assumed. We both love city life. We like music and theater and good restaurants."

"And shopping?" He sounded amused.

"Sitting there in a Ralph Lauren bathrobe your former personal assistant bought for you, I hope you don't think you have much to say about anyone else's shopping habits."

He chuckled and picked up a dry bone to suck on. "Leftover dreams, Thea. In time it will wear out. All worldly things do."

He was trying to tell her something but she wasn't sure she wanted to hear it. "What about our dreams? What about our future? They are brand-new. Shouldn't we be taking our time in making decisions about them together?"

"I thought we had. You said you were happy to do what I wanted." He tossed the lost-cause bone away. "Am I wrong?"

The businesswoman in her kicked in. "Let me rephrase my position. I'm happy to decide what *we* want to do. I know you want to pastor a church again. It's who you are, I understand that. But there are small churches in Texas. Even here in Dallas."

He looked at her, laughter in his eyes. "Let me rephrase *my* position. I need to be where I can do the most good for the least fortunate."

"Yes, but—"

He distracted her by cupping her face in his palm. "I want to make a difference."

"I know." She covered his hand with hers, uncertain she should drop into the middle of this particular argument the news of her promotion. She'd wanted to wait rather than spring it on him first thing. Now it was going to be a bit more awkward.

Maybe he saw in her expression the debate going on behind her eyes because his expression changed. "What's going on, Theadora? Something's up. Something good?"

She was amazed that he'd picked that up so quickly. "I was going to wait. I have not agreed to anything and I'm not sure—"

He put a finger to her lips. "Take a breath, lady. Then tell me your news."

She did as he suggested. "I've been offered a promotion. A good promotion."

His grin caught fire. "How good, Theadora?"

She laughed. "Full partner at Walker, Brennan, and Cullum and Associates! Ron's taking a leave of absence. And he's tapped me to be acting managing partner while he's gone. That means I'll oversee our entire Dallas office!"

He whooped and before she understood his intent, stood up and scooped her out of her chair, and twirled them both around.

"Wait! Wait!" she cried half in laughter and half in alarm. He might have lost some weight but his muscular embrace was all but crushing her and she was no small thing.

Finally he put her back on her feet. The love and admiration and pride in his expression was all she could have hoped for. "You did it! Cracked that glass ceiling from one end to the other!"

"And scrambled the good ole boy network into the bargain," she agreed.

"That's a fine thing, Theadora. I can't tell you how proud I am of you." He held her gaze a moment longer, but when she thought he would at long last kiss her, he dropped his arms from about her waist. "And I see now why my desires are a problem."

"It's not official yet, Xavier." She touched his newly shaven face and felt ridiculously pleased that something so insignificant could so move her. "The announcement isn't until Friday. I don't have to take it. I wanted to talk with you."

He shot her a surprised glance. "This is the culmination of your career. Of course you have to accept it! Unless you don't want it?" Was his tone hopeful or was it just her imagination?

Don't lie to him, Thea.

She couldn't tell him it didn't matter to her when it so plainly did. The best she could do was ask, "If I accept, can you change your appointment to one in or near Dallas?" She smiled encouragingly. "Would it be so bad to have a medium-size church?"

He drew in a long, *long* breath. "I've seen such things, Thea. Such brutality. Such ugliness. Such evil at work in the world." His expression almost frightened her. "I prayed about this, Thea. I can't just go back into my life the way it was."

She wanted to say, *You don't have to; you'll have me. We have a life to begin together. It won't be business as usual.*

But she knew he was talking about things more profound than whether or not there was a Barnes & Noble in town, or a Starbucks on the corner. They each had opportunities that they didn't want to pass up.

Xavier took her hands in his. "Let's pray about it."

Thea bowed her head, feeling okay with the idea as long as he did the praying.

"Lord, we ask you to help us to prepare for this new journey we have chosen as a life together. We ask that you help us to make the best choices in ways that will honor and serve you, dear God."

"Amen." It was a good prayer, simple and direct. She wished she had that ability. Regrouping, she asked, "How small is this small town?"

He shrugged. "I won't know until I get there."

She looked into his face hoping for a miracle. "So then, it isn't set in stone?"

"Oh no. The Pastoral Relations Committee might reject me."

"They can do that?"

"Certainly. They might not like my style of preaching, or think I can't help their congregation, spiritually or otherwise. It might not be a good fit."

She laid a hand on his chest, determined to make him kiss her without being the one to actually initiate it, and said softly, "I can't imagine anyone turning down a chance to say that Xavier Thornton is their pastor."

Something fleeting passed through his expression. "I'm done with trading on my name and my past, Thea. Completely done."

But is that the right choice? She had seen firsthand the good uses to which he had once put his money and talent, things other people might want to do but could not achieve because they lacked his abilities and his standing in the world. Yet he didn't seem ready to hear her version of his reality just now. Only time would tell which of them was right.

She reached for his hand. "This is your life, your calling, your spiritual journey. I don't want to get left out."

"You will never be left out, Thea." He turned his hand over

hers so that their fingers could intertwine. "I just thought it would be easier for you to come with me. You are a southern woman, after all, from a small town."

Thea smiled. "*From* being the operative word."

"Fair enough. If you really don't want me to consider this, I'll tell the bishop no."

"No, no. You go to the interview." If he didn't, the bishop would think her a selfish, interfering woman before he even met her. Not to mention the fact that Xavier had spoken to God about the matter. That was a one-two punch she did not know how to counter.

He brightened. "I'm not asking you to give up your dream, Theadora. You just grabbed the brass ring. You hold on to it a awhile."

"What about us?"

"Are you in need of a reminder of how I feel about you, knowing that you have agreed to be in my life in all ways from now on?"

She couldn't help but smile. "Are we going to pray over it?"

"Only if you insist." He looked away, a habit she'd learned to recognize as protective instinct. Then deliberately his gaze came back to meet hers. "I had a more earthly idea in mind."

He reached up to her neckline and slid his fingers beneath the edge of her blouse. Thea's eyes widened as she felt his warmth against her skin. He smiled at her, watching the color rise in her cheeks. And then he fished out the ring lying between her breasts and held it up. "Let's make this official, for the last time."

After she unclasped the chain, he pulled the ring free and reached for her hand to slide the ring onto her finger. "Theadora Broussard Morgan, will you marry me?"

She closed her eyes and nodded. "Yes, I believe I will."

As he leaned in to kiss her she felt something inside her release. His kiss completed the circuit of pent-up neediness and desire that had been building since she waved goodbye to him at the airport a year ago. She wanted him, needed him, and yet sought to protect him from the vulnerability she saw in his eyes whenever he gave her his full attention. She knew that wariness came from a lifetime of loneliness because he admitted when he first gave her this ring that he had never really been in love before.

By contrast, she had enjoyed an immensely happy married life. She recognized what they had for what it was: love, the long-lasting kind that became blood and bone of who you were ever after.

If it had at first frightened her to reclaim such feelings, it must surely have perplexed this worldly man of God to feel them for the very first time.

Xavier chuckled when they broke for air. "How soon is this wedding?"

"We could elope tonight." Thea kissed his nose. "Mexico isn't that far away."

"Two hours by air," he agreed. "But my sisters and yours would kill us."

"So there's going to be a wedding?"

He nodded. "Most likely."

⌘

The plaque on the door to Thea's new office was being bolted on when she arrived the next morning. When the maintenance man was done, he rubbed it with a cloth to remove his fingerprints. "All done."

"Thank you." She glanced at his badge. "Diego."

He smiled, obviously pleased she'd called him by name. "Yes, ma'am. Congratulations!"

She stared at the brass plate. Etched into it was her name and position: Theadora Morgan Thornton, *Senior Partner*. She had kept Morgan because that was how she was known in the business world. She had added her about-to-be married name because she wanted no mistake that she was equally committed to her new life.

Her new office was on the top floor of the law firm's building, in the senior partners' wing with south- and west-facing vistas that took in the downtown Dallas skyline, Los Colinas, and in the distance, the flight patterns of planes landing and taking off from DFW. It was a coveted location, position, and situation. Perks she'd only heard about were suddenly going to be hers. Use of the company jet, company lodgings in diverse places like Jackson Hole, a Madison Avenue apartment in Manhattan, private lodgings in London, Munich, and Shanghai. Memberships in country clubs and private clubs around the world were available. A week in a luxurious Japanese spa? A done deal. An idyll with family on a secluded beach in the Caymans was equally easy.

But at what price?

She had accepted this position knowing full well that Xavier would more than likely not be in Dallas.

"We'll work it out," he'd said again last night.

It was her choice. She had to find a way to make this work.

Chapter 7

"Earline, I told you to use the silver plate tonight." Hattie picked up a teaspoon and turned it handle-first toward her housekeeper. "You put out the Grand Baroque sterling."

"I thought, being that Reverend Thornton's a celebrity . . ."

"That's the very fact we need to avoid. We don't want him getting the wrong impression about his importance to us."

Earline began picking up the flatware. "Ain't nobody got the wrong impression. The man's a legend."

Hattie ignored the remark. Earline had been with her so long they both sometimes forgot they weren't related. But her housekeeper/cook did have a temper. She had been known to walk out—protest striking, Earline called it—if Hattie took too high a tone with her.

Mollified by the aromas wafting in from the kitchen, Hattie left the dining room to make certain other details were in place for her last-minute guest.

Xavier Thornton was everything she had expected, and more. He was self-assured, with the physical grace that came naturally to an athlete. He was cordial and well-mannered, too. Why, he'd even complimented her on her new hat. And, not to put too fine a point on it, he was one fine-looking man.

Even more to her liking, he was ordained. That meant that not only was he educated in the seminary but he had served an apprenticeship. And he was well-spoken. Some ministers were a trial to their congregations, mispronouncing biblical terms and misquoting God's word like a jumped-up street-corner preacher. There were doctors and dentists, schoolteachers, and nurses among St. Hurricane's congregation who would not like to see themselves poorly represented in the pulpit.

Within seconds of meeting him, there was no doubt among the Pastoral Relations Committee members that he was their man. Church attendance would be up in no time.

However, Reverend Samuel had cured her of first impressions. There were questions that, to her mind, had not been satisfactorily answered.

For instance, why would a man give up a congregation of six thousand for one of less than one hundred? His answer that all congregations were equal in God's eyes charmed the other committee members. It made her suspicious.

What about his fiancée? Why hadn't she come to the interview? Most ministers were all too happy to show off their helpmates. The committee tried to draw him out on the subject, but he sidestepped their questions by saying he did not want to presume, since she was not yet his wife. "Something there, Hattie," she had said to herself.

So then it was her duty to get to the bottom of things before the official vote in the morning. That's why she had extended to him a last-minute dinner invitation.

This disrupted the committee's plan to have him as their

guest for the dinner buffet at the Western Sizzler. A free meal, on the church's discretionary budget, had been looked forward to by all. But, as the senior member of the committee, Hattie had held sway. She would never get to the bottom of things with everyone else fawning over him.

Though the invitation was short notice, Hattie was in full hostess regalia, wearing a pink floral print silk dress, a diamond lavaliere, and rings adorning the first three fingers of each hand. She had just patted a stray curl into place when the doorbell rang.

"Good evening, Mrs. Patterson," Xavier greeted warmly when she opened her front door to him. "This is an unexpected pleasure."

"Welcome, Reverend Thornton. We are honored by your presence this evening."

"These are for you." He held out a large bouquet of hothouse-pink tulips and waxy, white, sweet-smelling stephanotis.

"Why, Reverend Thornton," Hattie gushed despite herself. "How did you know these are my favorites?"

"I inquired at the florist shop," he responded without a hint of embarrassment.

Well, she thought, he's not trying to hide his desire to impress.

"Do come in." She waved a hand in the direction of her living room.

She was particularly proud of this room with its cream walls, pale pink carpeting and drapes, and gilded French Provincial furnishings. Colorful French porcelain figurines crowded the end tables, and a multitude of crystal pieces sparkled on side tables. Some unfortunate guest had remarked that the effect reminded him of a wedding cake. The comment earned him a place on Hattie's ever-expanding do-not-invite list.

"You have a lovely home, Mrs. Patterson."

His flattery was rewarded by a slight nod. "Do have a seat, Reverend." She pointed to a side chair.

The chair crackled as he sat down.

A woman with a firm understanding of the damage carelessness can do, she had encased all the upholstered pieces in the room in clear plastic covers. They were removed only for special occasions. She wasn't certain yet that he merited the effort.

Firming her resolve not to be charmed, she said, "That is a very handsome suit, Reverend. It appears to be a designer label."

He simply nodded.

"Parishioners expect their minister to look prosperous. Some go so far as to say that their pastor's personal grooming is a direct reflection of the Eternal's beneficence toward the congregation." She paused to smooth an imaginary wrinkle from her lap. "There is, however, a fine line between appropriate and vanity."

"I would agree," he answered readily.

"And, of course, many a church can boast of full pews because its pastor is easy on the eyes. Not that looks should be the concern of a true Christian." She paused again to see how her guest would respond.

Xavier only dipped his head slightly in acknowledgment. Reverend Samuel would have offered her three flattering comments in return.

Hattie glanced around as Earline entered. "Yes, bring in

the tray. Have a canapé, Reverend. Earline's specialty is bacon wraps. She made them especially for you."

He took one of the cocktail napkins offered by the housekeeper and then lifted a bacon-wrapped cracker onto it. Grease quickly soaked through the paper, releasing the heat of the just-fried bacon into his palm.

"We know you been out of the country where you couldn't get good home-style cooking," Earline said with a broad, I'm-going-to-take-care-of-you-tonight smile. "You just go ahead and eat your fill." She did not move from his side until he placed two more on his soggy napkin.

Hattie refused the tray. "The Reverend is ready for his gin and tonic, Earline. I'll take a small Mogen David with soda."

He did not ask how she knew of his preference for gin and tonic but Hattie saw his eyes widen at her mention of it. He now knew he wasn't the only one to inquire about the habits of a stranger in order to make an impression.

When Earline had served them, Hattie nodded, an indication that Xavier might indulge. "Now then, I'd like to discuss with you my vision for St. Hurricane."

Xavier made appropriate responses as she explained her expectations. The fact that nearly everything she mentioned had been part of the day's interview did not bother her at all.

Finally she paused and sipped her wine before saying, "Now we've talked quite enough business. Why don't you tell me all about your lovely bride-to-be?"

"What would you like to know?"

"Is she a minister's daughter? Wives of pastors often are. I am. Born into the role, so to speak."

He shook his head and smiled. "No, Theadora is far from traditional."

Hattie couldn't tell what to make of that remark. "Surely your modern bride has some traditional values that will serve her well as the wife of a minister. For instance, she cooks, she sews, and she has some nursing skills?"

"Yes, yes, and I don't know."

"She sings or plays the piano? And, of course, regularly teaches Sunday school."

Hattie was certain he was about to say something else. Instead, he only said, "She is a very busy woman."

"What does she do?"

"She's just made full partner at her law firm."

"I see." *Red flag there!* "And just where is this company?"

"Dallas." Something in his tone suggested she put an end to her questions. But she was only warming up.

"I am surprised she did not accompany you today."

"I did not want to presume."

"That is to your credit. However, we would have liked to have had the opportunity to explain to her what is required of the pastor's wife at St. Hurricane. The responsibilities are numerous."

He smiled. "With all due respect, Mrs. Patterson, your last minister was a bachelor. Surely he was able to fulfill the needs of the church."

Hattie pursed her lips. "The less said on that matter the better. I am particularly charged with seeing that that mistake is not repeated, Reverend Thornton. In fact, we would not be interviewing you if you were not to be wed in the very near future. Single men do not make the most . . . let us say, *reliable* ministers to the flock."

Hattie noted that he didn't ask what she meant. Perhaps the bishop had filled him in on the conduct of Reverend Samuel.

This young man had a way with pauses that was a bit unnerving. In fact, when he spoke again, she was relieved.

Something changed in his gaze, and although he didn't move a muscle, she felt the sudden rebuff of a man whose patience has reached a limit. "Let me be frank, Mrs. Patterson. I'm prepared to offer St. Hurricane all my pastoral, administrative, and spiritual skills. Those services do not extend to my wife. She has a demanding career. If this is a problem I'll withdraw my name from consideration."

"That won't be necessary." Defeated for the moment, she moved on. "Tell me about your missionary work in Africa, Reverend Thornton."

"My congregation has always called me Reverend Xavier." He smiled then, and the intimacy of it made her troubled mouth stretch wide in delighted response. No wonder people were dazzled. She was dazzled.

He went on to talk with great passion about his experiences, and how he had not been doing missionary work but real work like manual labor and farming. "Spreading the word is easy. Living the word, Mrs. Patterson, is a much more difficult path."

He was articulate and persuasive and she knew by the end of his short speech that this was a man who belonged on the world stage. Yet something troubled him. She sensed that in his gaze. He was seeking an answer in coming to this small town. Did Miss Lawyer Lady from Dallas know what it was?

"That should serve for the present," she said finally and stood up. "I have two houseguests. I've asked them to join us for supper. If you will excuse me, I will fetch them."

Moments later, Hattie returned trailing two young people.

The young woman was more than passing pretty with a neat figure, smooth features, and hair arranged in Senegalese braids over her shoulders. First impression was that she was barely out of high school, but Xavier saw in her gaze long years of unmet promises and disappointment. If she didn't turn around soon, she would grow too bitter to love.

The boy beside her, who topped Hattie by a foot, was at that awkward age when body parts grow independent of any kind of proportion. His long, narrow body sprouted a big head and feet made cartoonishly large by the sports shoes he wore.

"Reverend Xavier, allow me to introduce my grandniece, Lola Franklin. And this is her son, Tyrell." Hattie waved the boy closer but he stopped short. "They just returned to the bosom of our family. Say hello, Lola."

Lola cut her eyes toward the relative who spoke to her like a child. But her voice was cordial as she said, "Happy to meet you, Reverend Xavier."

"My pleasure, Mrs. Franklin. Tyrell."

Hattie's gaze alternated between him and her kin. "I've assured Lola that our new minister will offer her support and advice through her trial at the loss of a spouse."

Xavier turned to Lola. "You are a widow then?"

The young woman looked startled.

"She is recovering from a matrimonial breach." Hattie spoke those words as if she were picking them up amid broken glass. "The termination of a marriage is not to be rejoiced upon. Yet an unfortunate error in judgment is now set right. I pray daily that they will find the strength to grow beyond their grief and find a better path."

"Dinner's ready." Earline stood in the archway, a broad

smile on her face. "Come on in, Reverend, and fill yourself up. Womenfolk like a man with a bit of heft to him."

"You hush, Earline." Hattie turned to Xavier. "We so rarely entertain a gentleman that the novelty seems to have gone to Earline's head."

Earline chuckled. "Ask her who was in and out my kitchen all afternoon, clucking like a hen over my preparations?"

Hattie seated Xavier at one end of the table and herself at the other, while Lola and Tyrell sat across from one another.

"Now then, will you lead us in a blessing? Something appropriate, in keeping with the return of our wayfarers." The command could not have had a sweeter delivery but the order was explicit. Sound grateful for Lola and Tyrell Franklin's return.

Xavier bent his head, his voice low and powerful in its delivery. "Heavenly Father, we come to You tonight with joyful hearts, upraised spirits, and bountiful thankfulness for Your generosity in returning Lola and Tyrell to their family. Extend to them Thy precious grace to heal and Thy strength to move forward in their lives. Nourish and sustain our spirits as You do our bodies with the gifts from Thy table. Amen."

"Amen!" For the first time a genuine smile appeared on Hattie Patterson's face.

She watched proudly as Earline served fatback with slick leaf mustard greens, then smothered fried chicken and mashed potatoes. Next came fresh sliced tomatoes and cucumber, macaroni and cheese, and corn still on the cob. With Earline doing the serving Xavier's plate soon looked like the dream of a starving man.

He sampled a forkful, murmuring approvingly. Not satisfied, Earline ladled another helping of gravy over the first. "There's plenty more where that came from."

After a few minutes of silent eating, Hattie spoke up. "Why don't you tell Reverend Xavier about your time up north, Lola?"

Xavier looked at her expectantly. "Where did you live, Mrs. Franklin?"

Lola's expression was immediately wary. "Portsmouth, New Hampshire."

"I've never been there but I hear it's a pleasant city."

Lola shook her head, her voice little more than a whisper. "I hated it."

"Northern winters are sometimes difficult for a southern-bred person," Hattie interjected smoothly.

Lola's voice was clenched but louder now. "Forget the cold. Try looking for a face of color in a crowd." She glanced at Xavier. "Tyrell was the only black child in his class. You could walk the length of Main Street and not see a single black person."

"I see how that might distress you," he answered. "My first church was in a small town in Idaho where the parishioners were mostly white."

"Did you hate it, too?"

Xavier turned his head toward Tyrell. "No. I've found people are pretty much the same, once you get to know them. They have their good and bad sides, their prejudices and their generosities." He swallowed another forkful of greens before he spoke again. "You play b-ball, Tyrell?"

Tyrell's head bobbed a nod as he continued to eat.

"You any good?"

One corner of Tyrell's mouth lifted. "The best center the Y had."

Xavier chuckled. "Who should I ask to verify that, your friends or opponents?"

"Tyrell didn't have any friends," Lola chimed in. "What he had were these white boys he hung out with. That's why I brought him home. I want him to have black friends who can teach him how to be a black man."

"I had my daddy!" Tyrell dropped his fork with a ringing sound back on his plate, his face swelling with emotion.

"Don't start, Tyrell. He was never there for either of us, and you know it!"

Hattie lifted her hand for silence. "You've more than made your point, Lola." Her tone shifted as she said, "More iced tea, Reverend?"

"No, thank you." After a long pause, Xavier said, "You have a summer job?"

It took Tyrell a moment to realize he'd been spoken to. "Me? Nawgh!"

"Then maybe you'd like to test out St. Hurricane's gym with me. Mrs. Patterson says it needs a new floor."

Tyrell's face brightened. "You are asking me to go one-on-one with *you*?"

"Afraid?"

He laughed. "I'm good, but I don't know that I want to go up against a professional."

"That was a long time ago. Of course, if you don't think you can put the hurt on an old man . . ."

Tyrell bobbed his head. "I'm good with it."

"Bring your A game. Seven A.M."

"Seven?" Tyrell blinked then shrugged and dug into his food with a new energy.

This was the sign Hattie had been waiting for. She hadn't been able to get one good conversation out of Tyrell in the week he'd been under her roof. Now Reverend Xavier had done it without seeming to strain for it.

She beamed at him as if he were her own son. "There's plenty good work to be done here, Reverend."

He smiled back. "Yes, indeed, Mrs. Patterson."

◦◇◦

"So, how did it go?"

"The position's mine if I want it." Xavier sounded less than enthusiastic.

"Do you want it?" Thea held her breath.

"I'm needed here, Theadora."

"Okay." She swallowed. "Tell me, what's Pine Grove like?"

"Why don't you come hear me preach here on Sunday and find out?"

"This Sunday? I can't. I have to be in London first thing Monday, which means I fly out on Sunday. Ron's out of the office this week undergoing chemo, so I'm going in his place. And I'm swamped trying to get Jesse ready to leave for Simmons College on Saturday. I don't see how I'm going to get it all done, as it is."

Xavier paused so long she wondered if he was upset. "How long will you be in London?"

"I'll be back in time for the wedding, if that's what is worrying you."

He chuckled then, an easy sound as familiar as the beating of her heart. "That's all I ask."

Thea closed her eyes, feeling like a sneak thief who had tiptoed past an unpleasant obligation. But that was insanity. How could she turn down a chance to veto a possible mistake in their about-to-be new life together? "What if I flew in on Saturday, after Jesse catches her flight? I'd have to fly right back to Dallas. I can only be in Pine Grove a couple of hours at the most."

He didn't hesitate this time. "I'll pick you up at the Little Rock airport."

Chapter 8

H ere we are." Xavier's tone was cheerful as they whizzed past a highway sign that read: PINE GROVE, POPULATION: 20,471.

"You're right. It is the deep south." Thea hoped her remark sounded more neutral than it was.

They had traveled an hour from Little Rock on a two-lane blacktop hemmed in by heat-weary woods trailing kudzu vines. Occasionally they passed swampy stretches of bayou warmed by the August sun into the perfect breeding ground for mosquitoes. She didn't need to roll down the window to know that breathing would be a conscious effort. Heat shimmers dancing on the highway betrayed a humidity as high as the temperature.

As the speed limit dropped, they rolled past rusted-out abandoned cars in the high weeds on the outskirts. In quick succession they passed a cemetery and a metalworks warehouse. Then, as they came upon an industrial site, a foul smell like that of roadkill in the sun invaded the car, even with the air conditioner on.

"Oh, jeez!" Thea put a hand to her nose, her eyes stinging. "What is that smell?"

Xavier grinned. "The poultry plant."

"What?" Then she saw the sign: POULTRY PROCESSING PLANT. The stink was a combination of incinerating chicken guts and feathers!

"Local people say that's the smell of money being made."

She held her breath instead of making a reply.

As they drove into the main part of town she saw whole blocks with rows of boarded-up houses. In still other blocks children ran in the streets, unsupervised. Sofas and mattresses, and in some cases what looked like the entire contents of a house, were piled on curbs, as if tenants had been hurriedly tossed out for nonpayment of rent. With an ever-sinking feeling, she noted that what remained of a once-thriving downtown was now occupied by a blue-plate-special restaurant, a discount clothing store, a pharmacy, and two wig shops. The only successful-looking building was the bank. So far she'd seen more bail bonds storefronts than fast food restaurants.

"Reminds you of home, doesn't it?"

"Hm." *Stay noncommittal, Thea!*

Which home? Not Washington, D.C., where she'd gone to school. Not Philadelphia, where she'd lived the first dozen years of her married life. Certainly not north Dallas, where tall trees were considered a luxury. It didn't even compare favorably with her hometown of Ruston, Louisiana, a small but fairly prosperous place that had turned its downtown into a historical shopping area. Pine Grove looked like a poster child for every poverty-stricken rural town of the south.

Stunned, she continued to silently stare out the window as

they drove through nicer neighborhoods and past some lovely homes. But the most generous phrasing that came to her mind was "beat down." Hard times had moved in and put up its feet. What was Xavier thinking to come here?

Finally he pulled up before a church whose sign proclaimed it to be St. Hurricane AME Church. It was an average-sized building with a redbrick exterior in the traditional Gothic style, and a large leaded window with a pointed arch. It might have been almost any small, aging church in any town any-where in the country.

He put the car in park and half turned to her in his seat, his smile broad and easy with joy. "This is the place I hope to call my spiritual home for a while."

"I see." She stared at it, trying to adjust her mindset. So this was to be Xavier's new church. "It's not St. James in Atlanta."

He nodded. "That's the point. I'm seeking the solution to megachurch ways."

"Then you've succeeded."

St. James, with its city-block-square, spectacular Jubilee Crown of Heaven Tabernacle, boasted plush stadium-style seating, and held over three thousand worshippers for each of two services on Sundays. Xavier had taped his television programs from the studio housed inside it. There had been discussion of buying a cable station or an XM radio channel before he resigned. The St. James's choir, two hundred voices strong with a full-time director and a small orchestra, sang regularly at events all over the country. Xavier once called Sunday morning "showtime," as it was up to him to energize and entertain, as well as instruct, his congregants with the Word of God.

Thea shook her head as she exited the car. St. Hurricane seemed a world away from modern worship practices. Maybe that wasn't all bad. She just couldn't imagine Xavier being happy here.

As he gave her a brief tour of the sanctuary, she was glad they did not run into anyone. She had asked that he not make plans to introduce her yet. According to him, he had not yet said yes to the post and wouldn't without her consent. Yet she could hear in his voice as he showed her around that he hoped she would agree.

"Where to next?" she asked when he came back from a quick trip to the church office.

He held up a key. "The parsonage."

✎

"There it is." They were sitting in front of a house in the middle of a residential block. "What do you think?"

Thea opened and closed her mouth. During the last week of January she'd been housebound with the flu and filled her aching feverish days watching home renovation shows on cable. She knew trouble when she saw it. And this old redbrick house was trouble with a capital T.

It had a wide front porch whose roofline sagged in the middle. Two of the dormer shutters hung crooked from their hinges. Wood trim around windows and doorways shed curls of peeling paint. The dark patches on the shingles were what every southerner recognizes as water damage. Part of a gutter had come loose and the grass and weeds had been badly cut. No one had bothered to touch the overgrown shrubs.

This was no *Fixer Upper*. Any *Good Bones* had long since

been crippled by neglect. *If Walls Could Talk* she was certain *This Old House* would complain of cracked beams, warped boards, rusted pipes, and an asthma-attack supply of mold and mildew. *Extreme Makeover* couldn't save this ugly duckling. With no possibility of *Hidden Potential* in sight, she was already *Flipping Out.*

"I know what you're thinking."

"Oh good." Thea turned to him with a look of relief.

"It needs work," Xavier said, reading her mind incorrectly.

"Xavier! It's got 'Do Not Resuscitate' written all over it."

"Nawgh! It will come around with a bit of TLC."

You can't be serious! Only a Rehab Addict *would take it on.* She had the presence of mind not to say that out loud.

Trying to be diplomatic she said, "Done much renovating?"

"Not really. But I think I could get into it. Let's look around."

Let's not! It's a disaster. Worse than any other house on the block!

Her gaze traveled down the row of homes on the street to make her point, if only to herself, and she spied a shotgun shack on the opposite corner with boarded-up windows. Okay, not the worst house. But it would take a sure enough miracle to make this parsonage a *Dream Home.*

Xavier took the steps up to the house two at a time, like a kid on an adventure. He was so obviously happy here. And she was so thoroughly miserable. She knew she needed to find something nice to say about this town. *What could that be?*

The slight breeze, warm as a breath, caressed her face and tickled the leaves overhead. She glanced around a second time. The street was lined with aging sycamores. It must have been a lovely neighborhood once. Now the sidewalk beneath her feet was cracked and broken, with sections missing altogether in places. Many of the houses that flanked the street had paint worn so thin the grain of their wood showed through. Most yards were little more than dirt patches with weed trim. But here and there a house stood proudly against the disaster of neglect.

One in particular, a modified Cape Cod directly across the street, painted a cheerful butter yellow with crisp white shutters, caught her eye. Vivid green squares of grass on either side of a trimmed walk, pink roses trailing from fan-shaped trellises, and window boxes of purple and red verbena spoke of proud ownership. It made her feel a little better. But once she entered the parsonage, all goodwill left her again.

The house looked and smelled old, a combination of dust and musty damp and the closed-up-too-long odor only really old houses have when they stand in the heat. The air was stagnant. The single weak bulb in the ceiling cast yellowish light on the contents. Old sheets covered the furnishings but she doubted they were in any better shape than the room itself. Wallpaper had come loose in the corners and curled back on itself. Faded avocado-green shag carpet looked old enough to have been laid down when shag was popular the first time.

The squeak of a faucet being turned on somewhere in the house caught Thea's attention a split second before a loud hammering began, startling them both.

"What on earth is that?" Thea cried and looked up at the ceiling where the thumping seemed about to break through the plaster.

"Loose pipe!" Xavier said loudly. "The plumbing needs a little work."

"A little?"

He shrugged as the noise ended abruptly. "Maybe a lot."

"A lot implies there's something here to salvage. This house is a teardown!"

They heard footsteps on the front porch and turned as the screen door opened.

Three women entered. The two younger women in T-shirts and jeans carried between them a mop and pail, a broom and dustpan, and a vacuum cleaner. The third, older by several decades, was empty-handed. She was perfectly coiffed and wearing a casual but neat denim pantsuit and earrings. All three stopped short when they saw Xavier and Thea standing in the living room.

"Mrs. Patterson, come in." Xavier moved to hold the door open for the women.

"Reverend Xavier?" Hattie Patterson said in a not altogether pleased tone. "I must say, this is a surprise."

"Yes," he answered easily. "I borrowed the key from the church secretary so that I might look around. I didn't wish to disturb you."

"I see. And who did you bring with you on this occasion?" The trio had been staring at Thea since they entered.

Xavier turned and beckoned Thea forward. "Mrs. Patterson, I'd like you to meet Theadora Morgan, my fiancée."

Hattie paused in offering her hand to Thea, her eyes widening as her Revlon classic matte-red lips parted in astonishment. "Fiancée?"

I've seen that look before. Even when told about her in advance, strangers almost never expected her to be so light and bright, damn near white.

Thea closed the distance between their hands and shook the woman's firmly. "Hello, Mrs. Patterson. Do call me Thea."

"Yes, of course." But she didn't.

Hattie turned away and made a motion with her hand. "Go ahead and start in the kitchen. I will be with you presently."

So this was Mrs. Patterson, Xavier's sacred cow. Thea sized up the short, compact woman who reminded her of Aunt Della in the way she carried herself. She didn't seem that intimidating.

When the young women had reluctantly exited the room, Hattie turned back to Xavier. "I hope you will overlook the state of things. The house has been closed for several months. Had I known you wished to see the parsonage, we would have spruced up earlier." Her gaze shifted to Thea, measuring. "You have caught us in an unfortunate light."

Thea smiled confidently. "I'm sure the renovations you have planned will make a great difference." She quickly calculated her timing and decided to be frank. "However, Xavier and I have been discussing the possibility of buying a house."

Hattie's glance swung to Xavier. "You did not mention this in your interview."

Thea took this as her cue. "Xavier and I are starting a new life together and I would like as part of that to organize our own home."

Hattie kept her focus on Xavier. "Of course, we can't stop you from living elsewhere, Reverend Xavier. But the Pastoral Relations Committee cannot offer an additional stipend for living expenses should you not accept the home St. Hurricane so generously provides its minister."

"We would not expect that." Xavier glanced at Thea. "And we have not made any decisions."

Belatedly, Thea realized that the woman had put her on the wrong side of the argument. "No, we wouldn't expect a penny from St. Hurricane. In fact, it would save St. Hurricane the expense of immediately overhauling the parsonage." She glanced around. "It needs a great deal of work."

Hattie's lips thinned in displeasure. "What would you recommend, other than tearing it down?"

Thea felt herself flush. Obviously, her observation had been overheard from the porch before she was aware of the women's arrival, and Mrs. Patterson had taken insult.

"I mean no disrespect, Mrs. Patterson. But the wallpaper needs to be stripped. And those water spots on the ceiling suggest that the roof leaks. Then there's the plumbing—"

As if cued, the hammering of the pipes began again.

Hattie flinched. "There are some minor repairs needed. But once the house has a good sweeping and airing, you may be surprised how cozy it can be, Miss—?"

"It's Mrs. Morgan," Thea supplied quickly.

"You're a divorcée?" No need to interpret the tone in that remark.

"Thea's a widow," Xavier answered.

At that moment Thea's cell rang. She pulled it out and heaved a little sigh. The call was from Jude Deering, lead counsel on the foreign business deal for a client that had been nothing but headaches. It was the deal that had her on a plane to London in the morning. A call on Saturday could only mean more bad news. She looked up at Xavier and Mrs. Patterson. "Please excuse me. It's business. I must take this."

Xavier nodded amicably.

She took a few steps away to be polite. "Yes, Jude. Sorry, I'm traveling and must have been out of signal range. . . . I see. Their number . . . ? Jes— Jeez, Jude!" She glanced over her shoulder at Xavier but he didn't seem to notice her near slip into blasphemy. Hattie Patterson's expression said she had.

Thea offered her an apologetic smile and walked toward the dining room, seeking more privacy. "You and I both know those terms are unsupportable. . . . If I believed that, we'd walk away. . . ."

Hattie watched until the younger woman was out of sight before saying to Xavier, "Your fiancée is not at all what I expected."

Xavier smiled. "Yes, she's something, isn't she?"

"Yes." Hattie wondered how to broach the subject on her mind. "She's obviously accustomed to the best of everything."

Xavier's tone was forthright. "Don't be fooled by her direct manner, Mrs. Patterson. She's a hard worker and takes nothing for granted."

"Yes. I see that. Always puts work first. But then young people are prone to distraction with all the gadgets of the modern world. Tyrell tells me there's now a term for cell phone addiction. No-mo-phobia."

Xavier didn't respond.

"I do so lament the loss of the old-fashioned social niceties, even in a small town like Pine Grove—" Thea's raised voice cut across her words.

"What do you mean, you can't? There's fifteen million riding on this deal for your client. Yes, I saw the news. Until there's a strike, we continue to talk. . . . When . . . ?"

Hattie turned a look of disapproval on Xavier. "It would seem that this isn't a good time to chat. Your fiancée is quite—"

"Preoccupied with international business matters," Xavier finished for her then caught Hattie by the elbow. "Let's give her a little more privacy."

"I'm not staying," Hattie answered yet resisted his effort to steer her toward the kitchen. "I just came to drop the cleaning girls off."

"Then allow me to escort you to your car." This time he urged her toward the front door.

Reluctantly, Hattie gave way. But not before she heard Thea say, "Dammit, Jude! That's not good enough!" Hattie raised her brows and gave Xavier a disapproving look.

He looked annoyed but didn't apologize as he hurried her out.

"Jude, we aren't drawing any lines in the sand. . . . No, you are the lead. That makes it *your* problem . . ." Thea glanced up as Xavier joined her in the dining room. She rolled her eyes and made a quacking-duck sign with her free hand. "Yes, yes, but there's no need to get bent out of shape. . . . What?" Her attention snapped back to the conversation. "I can't believe you said that! Why don't *you* take five and get back to me when you have something positive to offer. Right. Goodbye!"

Xavier walked over and put a hand on her shoulder. "Trouble?"

She held up a hand, too angry to trust her voice immediately. She took two breaths. "In all the years we've been doing business, Jude Deering has never spoken to me like that, as if he were dealing with a woman instead of a colleague."

"Maybe he's just caught up in the problem of the moment."

"And maybe he's never had to deal with me when I had the final word."

She shrugged off his touch and took a couple of steps away,

then paused to rub away the pain that had popped up behind her brows. "That's the problem with being a female boss. I expected some pushback when I agreed to take over for Ron. But that was uncalled for. I can never be too grateful, or understanding, or accommodating. If I am, the guys will wink behind my back and think they can get away with murder next time."

"Sounds like you've solved that problem."

She looked around. "Where's Mrs. Patterson? I hope I didn't run her off."

"Let's say she decided that this wasn't the best time for your first meeting," he answered with a sidelong glance. "Let's go."

Thea waited until they were sitting in the cool of the air-conditioned car before saying, "You're unhappy. Was it something I did?"

Xavier pulled away from the curb. "I understand you were caught up in the heat of the moment, but try to curb your speech when in the company of my congregation."

"What did I say?"

"Nothing that terrible. But even 'hell' and 'damn' coming from a minister's bride disturbs people like Mrs. Patterson."

"Oh. Sorry. I didn't think." She shrugged.

"Yes, well, I didn't expect you to meet her today, otherwise I would have warned you to be more guarded around her."

"You mean I shouldn't have complained about the parsonage?"

He kept his eyes on the road. "You didn't exactly help my cause."

"Because I said we want to buy a house?" Now she was annoyed that he hadn't backed her up. "I'm sorry but I thought we should be honest about that."

His expression told her that this wasn't as diplomatic a response as he'd hoped for, though it did sum up her feelings in more ways than one. "I thought you understood that I want to try to live within my stipend."

She stared at him. "You really expect us to live in that rundown pile of bricks?"

"If we don't live there, the entire St. Hurricane family will be insulted. It's not heaven but . . ."

But it's not Darfur.

She could almost hear him thinking that. Or maybe that was her own conscience scolding her. She was spoiled. Used to having lots of choices. Pine Grove was a shock to her system. That much was true. As far as she could tell the only place to shop was Wal-Mart. Perhaps she hadn't behaved as diplomatically as she might have.

Okay, regroup! You do crisis management well. You can handle one little leaky creaky smelly old house.

She reached for Xavier's hand on the steering wheel and squeezed it. "You're right. I'll have to adjust my thinking."

"Can you do that?" He glanced at her. His expression was one of doubt that didn't apply only to her feelings, something that totally surprised her.

"What do you think?"

He pulled onto the highway to Little Rock and released a long, slow breath. "You should know there's very little pastoral support for my attempt to simplify my life."

This was news to her. "What are they saying?"

"Both my former and present bishops tell me that many good men can pastor a small church. But few can do what I was doing before I left St. James."

Thea resisted the urge to nod. She agreed with the bishops. Even his family thought he had made a mistake in leaving St. James in Atlanta. It was from there that the Thornton Foundation, his religious-based organization, had promoted a program of self-reliance through racial pride, Christian discipline, and African American business enterprise. All his speeches about his program included "Forget the bootstrap theory. We're here to chin ourselves on the bar of individual excellence and communal economic achievement."

But that didn't matter. This was about what Xavier needed.

He looked over at her, hesitation in his gaze. "If you agree with them, I won't accept this position."

Don't put this on me! How could she tell him to give up when he so plainly wanted to test himself here? "What do you pray for, Xavier?"

He nodded as if she had asked the right question. "I'm praying that we can be happy here, really happy."

"And if we aren't?"

"Then I will have failed."

Thea looked down. It would be so easy to say no to Pine Grove, to St. Hurricane, to all that he built up in his mind as his future. But she couldn't.

She had what she wanted: her promotion to full partner and marriage to the man she loved. She wouldn't ask him to give up what he wanted.

She reached to stroke the side of his face. "I can be happy wherever you are."

He smiled and nodded. "Hungry?"

Thea smiled, grateful for the change of subject. "Starved!"

❧

"She's a white woman, Mrs. Patterson! Did you know that?"

"No, and I'll thank you to keep that to yourselves. It's no concern of ours."

Hattie had come right back to check on the cleanup. "Now do a good job in here. Reverend Thornton's bride is going to be looking for imperfection wherever she can find it. I want a spic-and-span house, do you hear me?"

"Yes, Mrs. Patterson," the two girls answered in singsong fashion.

Hattie walked back into the living room and surveyed it with a critical eye. The sheets had been removed from the furnishings. Perhaps it was old and worn, yet no other minister's family had ever had an unkind word to say about St. Hurricane's parsonage. It was good enough for them. It should be good enough for Reverend Xavier's new wife.

New white wife!

She suspected that he was hiding something. Now she knew what it was. *A white bride!* The cliché of the successful black man was still a bitter pill. Somehow she thought he'd be above that.

Hattie's mouth tightened. No doubt his money and celebrity were what tempted a woman in Mrs. Theadora Morgan's high-powered position to wed him. She'd seen that type before, all adoration and submission to her man until the ring was on her finger. Then the demands would begin. Had already begun. She wanted a new house.

Reverend Xavier was a spiritual man of purpose and power. A man like that would take care of anybody he chose to throw his protection around. She needed him to grow their little church into prominence. But now they might not get that chance because he'd chosen a wife who had no feeling for or connection with their small-town ways.

Hattie sniffed. His bride-to-be didn't even try to hide her dissatisfaction with his choice of church assignment. Perhaps she thought herself too important to be first lady of St. Hurricane.

That thought turned her heart to stone against the soon-to-be Mrs. Xavier Thornton.

Chapter 9

Jesse waited impatiently on the curb as the taxi driver removed her luggage from the trunk.

She could have taken one of the Welcome minibuses used to transport early-arrival students to campus for free, but she wanted to ease into her own impression of her new surroundings. Being thrown together with other students would have distracted her. Worse, if her mother or her grandparents had accompanied her to campus, it would have made her feel like a kindergartener.

She paid the driver and then glanced around. The original campus, expanded upon but not replaced, was a series of federal-style buildings bordering a large tree-filled park. This must be what the website referred to as The Quad.

Attending Simmons, a small liberal arts college of five thousand undergraduates in upstate New York, wasn't originally her idea. Simmons was her grandmother's alma mater, and she let it be known that the Morgans always support their own. That meant they gave generously to the college so they could guarantee family members' acceptance. While she didn't want to hurt their feelings, the patronage angle was a total turnoff. She was independent enough to want to earn her way on her own merit.

"Tradition is everything at Simmons," her grandmother had assured her. As if classic architecture was going to be useful to her granddaughter's future.

The fact that Simmons had a thriving women's soccer program did eventually make her think twice. One of her idols played on the team. Yet she didn't mention her Morgan connection on her application. She wanted to see if she could get in on her own merit. When she did, she had to think long and hard.

Simmons was tucked in the foothills of the Adirondack Mountains. Ottawa and Montreal, Canada, were closer than New York City and Philly. No one was going to just drop by. Small and unknown to any of her friends—two criteria for her college choice—didn't mean she should break her mother's bank. Tuition at Simmons put Harvard within easy reach. So, she let slip her dilemma to her grandparents. *Ka-ching!* Her tuition was a done deal. Maybe they didn't understand the distinction but she did.

"Come for the *whole* weekend?" a guy jeered as he and two friends strolled past her stockpile, which consisted of two large suitcases, a soccer gear bag, a smaller overnight bag, and a computer bag.

Ignoring them, she paid the driver.

Another of the trio gave her T-shirt and walking shorts the once-over before he said, "You need some help?"

"Not even!" Jesse stacked the overnight bag atop one of the large suitcases and clipped it in place. Then she hoisted the computer bag on one shoulder and gear bag on the other. After grabbing a large suitcase in each hand, she trotted up the ten broad steps to the front doors of her dormitory.

"I think I'm in love!" shouted the third guy as they all applauded her performance.

Winded but grinning, she pushed through the doors. Running bleachers for stamina had its uses. As for passing up a chance to chat up the guys, she'd just as soon forgo that issue for a while. It was all a little much with a new campus, a new room, and a new world to check out simultaneously.

As of this moment, no one knew her or a thing about her. As far as what the campus faculty and administration knew, she was smart and a jock. That was plenty. She was out to reinvent herself.

She was surprised to see that the interior of the building she'd entered was much more modern than its exterior would have implied. Since there was no one at the desk, she set down her bags and turned to glance out a window.

"Oh my God!" she whispered and began to giggle. At the far end of the quad stood a classic white-clapboard church with an enormous steeple. Her grandmother was right. She'd been dropped into a Currier & Ives painting!

◦∞◦

The double-room dorm suite was pretty much what Jesse expected from the diagram she had viewed on the college's virtual online tour site. But there was no way around it—it was small. The shared bath wasn't much bigger than a stall at a nice restaurant, plus a shower. There'd be nowhere to soak tired muscles after practice. A quick investigation confirmed that one bedroom was decidedly larger than the other. As in, room for desk, chair, *and* sink. Closet space was a joke in both.

"I guess I get to choose," Jesse said to the empty space and promptly took the larger room. She had gear to store, and when her shipped things came, there'd be a flat-screen monitor and books and other essentials to place. As a freshman she couldn't opt for a single, unless she had special needs. She did luck out in the room lottery with a two-bedroom suite. At least she wouldn't have to lie next to a teeth grinder or snorer, both of which Cassandra was suffering through at Bryn Mawr. According to her most recent text message, life with her dorm mate was hell.

Grrl, a cement mixer makes less noise!! Then she's got the nerve 2 say she needs COMPLETE silence 2 study. Ima havfta move!

It was only after she had changed into jeans and a fresh T-shirt and brushed her teeth that Jesse stopped to open the Welcome Kit on her bed.

"Oh crap!" She checked her watch. "Crap!" Scrambling through one bag she pulled out cleats, shorts, kneepads, and shin guards before hurrying out the door.

Soccer practice began five minutes ago.

❧

When the Simmons' women's soccer team captain was introduced, Jesse cheered with the enthusiasm of a dedicated fan.

Portia "Porsche" Wagner was her idol. All American, Liberty League. Porsche, dubbed that for her speed and agility, had been at Olympic Camp during Jesse's spring visit to the campus. But now she was here, more impressive in the flesh than in the action-shot poster on the bulletin board in Jesse's bedroom at home.

At five feet ten inches, Porsche was taller than the average women's soccer player, with a long torso, boyish figure, and rock-hard thighs and calves. It was an enviable body, a soccer goddess's body. She was known to be a scrapper, with something of a temper, but on the field she was all about the game.

Only Megan Rapinoe held a higher place of honor in Jesse's soccer world.

"I love your game," Jesse gushed when asked to step forward and greet Porsche. "You're, like, amazing."

"Really? Like *ah*-mazing?" The mimicry drew snickers from a few of the others. Porsche smirked and tossed her ponytail, scraped back so tight it gave her lean high-cheekbone face a feline look. "So, like, if you're done sucking up you can explain why I shouldn't toss your butt off this field for being late."

Jesse's cheeks flamed at the reprimand. "I'm so sorry. I didn't see my welcome packet until just this minute. It won't happen again."

Porsche rolled a shoulder. "You hear that?" She glanced at the other assembled players. "Blondie's got manners. I like manners. But they don't mean a damn thing on the field." She gave Jesse's coordinated shorts and crop top the once-over. "Are you sure you shouldn't be in the gym trying out for cheerleader? Blond hair and cute clothes may be fine in Texas. But at Simmons we play real soccer, not Barbie Dream Date soccer."

Jesse cringed inwardly as the other girls giggled but murmured, "I didn't take time to change once I knew I was late."

"If you're ever late again, don't bother to show up." Porsche turned away from Jesse and addressed the rest of the recruits.

"If a few of you impress me with your skills, I might let you dress out and sit on the bench this fall. Until then, I'm not letting you anywhere near my team." She pointed to the other end of the field where dressed-out members of the Simmons Ladyhawkes were practicing goal shots. "Those are *the* Ladyhawkes. Right now, you're just little chicken hawks. I want you to enjoy being chicken hawks." She made little *peep peep* baby chick sounds. "Because, next week, most of you will be off this field permanently."

"I thought we were recruited to play," Jesse murmured to the girl next to her.

That caught Porsche's attention. She stepped up to Jesse. "You're not on the team until you get through me."

Jesse held Porsche's unfriendly gaze. The hazing of new team members was familiar but Porsche seemed to have singled her out. It was a test of intimidation she couldn't afford to fail, even if it was her idol she tried to stare down. Still, her voice sounded hollow as she forced out, "I came to play."

For the first time Coach Brewer stepped in. "I want a show of hands of those who came to watch." No hands went up among the group of freshmen. She turned to Jesse. "Looks like you've got some competition."

"You got that, Blondie?" Porsche smiled but it might as well have been a growl.

Jesse shrugged, though her heart was beating so hard and fast she could barely hear the coach shout, "Fall in and give me fifty push-ups!"

∽∞∾

Jesse felt as if she had fallen down a flight of stairs. Her clothes were plastered to her chest and back. Sweat had left snail trails on her trembling thighs and calves. Her shoes were squishy. Porsche had been all over her, pushing, taunting, daring her to keep up if not surpass everyone else. The only thing that had kept her from collapsing on the grass at the end of practice, as several other girls did, was anger.

But anger couldn't keep her from throwing up just out of sight of the field. Or again, in the bushes by her dorm. Thank God she hadn't eaten since breakfast. Still, the Gatorade that she had gulped between workout sets was no longer her friend.

She staggered down the hallway of her dorm, eyes averted from the other girls who watched with faces of alarm or disgust. She didn't need their confirmation that she smelled of grass, dirt, sweat, and vomit. There were scrapes on her thigh and elbow from a collision with another player.

She needed a long hot shower and then rest, lots of rest.

She had one foot through the door of her suite when a snarling furry tornado the size of a mop head burst out of the smaller bedroom and attached itself to her ankle.

"What the—?"

"Fidel! Fidel! No, no!" A young woman flew out of the same bedroom in time to see her pet rip a clunk out of Jesse's sock.

"You little beast!" Jesse aimed a half-hearted kick in its direction.

The dog reacted as though she had connected. Yelping, it scurried back into the next room.

The young woman turned in fury on Jesse. "What do you think you're doing? You've upset him!"

"I've upset *him?* He bit me." Jesse pointed to her torn sock. "What's a dog doing in the dorm?"

"Fidel never bites." The girl flung back long, thick hair, the color of espresso and shiny as patent leather, to reveal a perfectly made-up face. "You will answer to me later. Fidel! Fidel?" She hurried into her room.

Curious, Jesse followed.

At first glance her roommate didn't look anything like an athlete. She was average height but with an impossibly tiny torso. Yet she had a butt made noticeably round by skinny pants that ended above the ankles. Monster platform sandals and a white peasant blouse completed her cruise-wear look. The neckline was so wide it slipped off one shoulder as she bent down to her dog, which lay quivering in its Louis Vuitton carrying case by the bed. She pulled a treat out of her purse and waggled it under his nose then jerked it back and caught him in a neat scoop when the dog jumped out after it.

"My poor, sweet little Fidel," she cooed as she cuddled and stroked him. When the dog finished chewing, she cupped its face and gave it a kiss on the nose.

Finally she looked at Jesse in the doorway and wrinkled her nose. "You smell!"

Jesse wrinkled her nose in response. "You kiss dogs!"

"Who are you?"

"Jesse Morgan. Who are you?"

"Magalys Juanita Arocha Gutierrez." She flung her hair again, just like in a shampoo commercial. "You can call me Nita. So you are my roommate." Nita's gaze narrowed. "You shouldn't have taken the larger room without considering me."

"First come, first served." Jesse smirked as she glanced back at the enormous pile of Louis Vuitton luggage stacked like Christmas gifts in the corner of their common room. She just knew the answer, but she could hope. "You play sports?"

"Do I look like a jock?" With a flourish of her free hand,

Nita highlighted first her hair and then swept the gesture downward to include her body.

Jesse rolled her eyes. "Whatever. They said we'd have a compatible roommate."

"I'm in the orchestra. I play the flute." Nita frowned. "What do you play?"

"Soccer. That's not an instrument."

"I know soccer. My people played soccer before yours ever heard of it." Nita pursed her lips as her gaze swept Jesse from sweaty ponytail to dirty kneepads. "You aren't very good, are you? You fall down too much."

"Thanks for the tip." *Her people?* Nita sounded one hundred percent American. Not that Jesse cared. All she cared about was getting in the shower before her legs gave way. "Later."

As she turned away Nita spoke again. "Where are you from?"

"Dallas."

"Ah!" Nita thumped her forehead with her palm. "Now I understand. Housing thinks because I'm a Cuban from Miami I must think of myself as Latina first, and because Texas has a lot of Mexican Latinos we should have a lot in common."

Nita's laughter was like everything else about her—dramatic. "I'm American. My parents are American. My grandparents left Cuba in 1959. But do these WASPs consider me American? No!" She narrowed her eyes. "I suppose that includes you."

"No." Jesse shrugged. "I don't fit the WASP profile. And I think you're giving housing way too much credit. They screwed up. Pure and simple."

She had checked "other" on the racial identity box on her application form, and then in the space provided listed all the various ethnic groups her family heritage allowed her to claim.

So, just maybe, it was the ethnic diversity thing that put Nita and her together. But she wasn't about to contribute that to the conversation. She wasn't interested in any *us vs. them* reality.

Nita sighed. "These Yankees get on my nerves."

Jesse smirked. "If you don't like Yankees, why come north?"

Nita checked her hair in the mirror over her dresser as she said, "Because of my parents. They didn't want me in Miami. They believe their daughter can get in 'only so much trouble' if they force her to go to a boring school in Sleepy Hollow, U.S.A."

Jesse's ears perked up. "How much trouble is 'only so much'?"

Nita shrugged. "You tell me. Sex is available anywhere. You don't even need two sexes, if you're not particular. . . ." She met Jesse's gaze in the mirror. "Or curious."

"So not!" Great, she had a sex addict on her hands.

Jesse crossed her arms and jutted out a hip then winced as her aching muscles protested. "Anything else?"

"Drugs are everywhere. Ask the Amish." Nita turned around to face Jesse. "Parents! They are in total denial!"

"So you're like in total rebellion?" Jesse hoped she sounded as uninterested as she was in this Miami Paris Hilton.

Nita smiled. "Totally."

"Don't you have to be independent to do that?" She jerked a thumb toward Nita's pile of luggage. "It's not like you're working your way through school. Your parents pick up the tab, which means they can yank you home anytime they want."

"No. I have Poppi." Nita made little kissy noises at her dog. "Poppi gave me Fidel when my parents said no. Poppi gives me anything I want."

"Like the luggage?" Jesse totaled the designer bags up to five figures, easy.

"Those are graduation presents. My parents have money. I got a brand-new *amarilla* Lexus LC 500 convertible with all the options for graduation. I drove myself up here."

"Freshmen aren't allowed cars on campus. It's the reason I didn't bring mine."

"My car isn't on campus. It's with my maid, Berta."

Jesse blinked wide. "Come again?"

"It's enough my parents expect me to live with strangers. How can I be expected to look after all my things, and Fidel, and study, and feed myself, and everything? For instance, what do they eat here? Boiled beef and potatoes?"

Jesse felt a sickly twinge in her middle at the mention of food. To shove the thought aside she said, "So you brought a maid *and* a cook?"

Nita shrugged. "Berta does both. Poppi hired her and got her an apartment in town. My parents are happy because their only daughter will get to experience dormitory life. I am happy because I will have an apartment in town whenever I like."

"Sweet. Take the mongrel with you and leave him there."

"Fidel's a purebred Bichon Havanese. The breed originated in Cuba."

"Bye, bye, *bit*-chon." Jesse made a face at Fidel and turned to leave. No doubt the dog's name was another bit of rebellion against her anti-Castro exiled parents.

"Where are you going? We are supposed to be at orientation in fifteen minutes."

"Take notes." Jesse tried not to hobble as she moved across their common room. Her muscles, once trembling, were now locking up. Practice began again at seven A.M. If she could move.

Chapter 10

The knock at her door made Jesse pull her pillow over her head. "Go away!"

"Miss Jess Morgan?" a masculine voice inquired.

"Jess-*ee*." Everybody got her name wrong the first time.

"Like the Reverend Jackson?" She didn't answer. "Can I come in for a minute?"

Jesse removed the pillow from her head. Her room was in complete darkness. She must have fallen asleep but it hadn't helped. Every muscle in her body was screaming. She didn't want anyone to see her like this. "Go away!"

To her consternation she heard the doorknob rotate and then the door opened a crack, sending a shaft of light across her bed. "Are you decent?"

"Are you deaf? Go away!"

Instead, a hand poked through to flip on the overhead light. A moment later a head full of dreads appeared, capping the first face of color she had seen on campus.

He looked surprised for just a second when their gazes met and then he smiled. "Hey. I'm Bakari Masson, your senior advisor for freshman orientation."

Jesse stared at him. "Did you say *Bacardi?*"

He laughed, his dreads doing a happy dance about his shoulders. "B-A-K-A-R-I. The resident hall team was concerned when you didn't show up for orientation tonight. Your roommate was worried, too." He checked his clipboard. "Nita said you were sobbing in the shower when she left."

"I wasn't sobbing." Jesse tried to roll away from the light stabbing her eyes but caught her breath as muscles spasmed in her back. "Oh damn!" she muttered.

Bakari came and squatted on his haunches by her bed, looking professionally concerned. "It's okay, Jesse. You're a long way from home, probably for the first time." He checked his clipboard again and nodded. "Oh, right. Dallas. Simmons must be something of a shock for a southern girl."

Jesse looked away from him. "I grew up in Philly, okay? Dallas was a short detour. I'm not homesick. I'm not scared. Or lonely. Or feeling lost. I'm fine. I'm grea—" Pain cut her off as the muscles across her rib cage protested her shout.

He frowned. "What's wrong? Are you sick?" His gaze shifted to check out her desktop. "You aren't into anything weird, are you?"

"I'm not strung out, if that's what you're asking." Jesse took two long, slow breaths before finishing. "Preseason workouts started today. I'm on the soccer team." *For the moment.*

"Ah." He smiled again, a full set of beautiful white teeth in a bittersweet chocolate face, which was enough to remind her that she must look like hell. The first interesting guy she'd seen and she had to look like something scraped off the bottom of a shoe. "Tough one?"

Jesse nodded. She pulled the pillow back over her head. "Now please go away."

"Sure I can't do something for you?"

Jesse suspected the change in his voice had something to do with the fact he might have noticed she was wearing only a T-shirt and panties. After a moment of silence she peeked out from behind her pillow to see him now standing in her doorway, arms folded and his expression serious. "Have you eaten?"

"I threw up the Gatorade special during practice."

The sound of his retreating footsteps barely registered as Jesse fell back into deep, painful, half consciousness.

It seemed as if she had been asleep for hours when she felt someone touching her forehead. Maybe it was her mom. Her mother always took care of her when she was sick. But her mother wasn't here, was she?

Half asleep, Jesse felt drugged. It was all she could do to finally open her eyes. She closed them immediately. "You're back."

Bakari nodded, his arms full. "You sounded like you needed a little first aid. I brought heating pads for your sore muscles. I had one and I borrowed a couple more."

Jesse stared at him in surprise. "I have one somewhere but I haven't unpacked yet."

"I got this covered." He dumped the pads on the end of her bed. "I'm going to have to jerry-rig them with a multi-socket plug, which is strictly against dorm policy. So don't leave them plugged in when you're not using them. If you're caught, it will be my ass in the sling."

"Okay."

He had changed from the faded Nirvana T-shirt and cutoffs he had on the first time he came to her room. Now he wore jeans and a dress shirt, tail out, collar open, and sleeves rolled, with an ugly geeky-striped sweater vest over it. And his dreads had been tied back with a strip of black leather.

Funny. She didn't expect she'd notice things like that about him.

When he had them all plugged in he handed her one. "Here you go."

Jesse tried to lever herself upright but her body was resisting all exertion.

He watched her struggle with an impassive expression. "I'd offer to help but I don't need any sexual harassment charges."

Jesse's gaze flew up to his face. "What makes you think I'd do something like that?"

He didn't answer, leaving her to speculate.

"I'm not that kind of girl." Whatever kind he thought that might be. "Jocks don't freak over a little impersonal physical contact." She tried to sit up again.

"Give me that." He took the pad, scooped up her legs behind the knees, and placed the pad under her thighs. He placed the second one under her calves. The third he wedged under her shoulders with her help.

Jesse noticed that his touch was the impersonal kind. He was like a physical therapist with a patient. Some impression she was making on her first male contact at college. She closed her eyes again. Better to pretend she was oblivious.

After a few minutes he said, "You awake?"

He was standing over her with a bottle of water in one hand and tablets in the other. "You need to rehydrate. And this ibuprofen will calm the inflammation so you can move in the morning."

"Okay," she answered.

He didn't ask her to try to sit up. He put the water down and then scooped an arm behind her shoulders and lifted her forward. To her credit, she thought, she didn't cry out, but she was gritting her teeth.

"You really messed yourself up."

He put a knee on the bed behind her and leaned her back against his thigh. Then he reached around her with both hands, offering the tablets and water again. "Take this."

Gratefully, she obeyed. "Thank you," she managed when she had drunk a little of the water.

"There's more." He picked up a tall Styrofoam cup she hadn't noticed before and handed it to her. "Drink it slowly but drink all of it. It's a whey protein powder drink. I made it myself. Hope you like vanilla."

Jesse turned her head to try to look back at him but her neck was stiff. "So what, you're a physical therapy major?"

"Government major. Minor in history and modern literature. Amateur jock."

Jesse took the drink and sipped it. "Not bad."

In fact it was just what she needed. Usually she was smarter about working out and balancing nutritional needs like electrolytes. She had a heating pad and protein powder in her bags. But she had been too exhausted to think coherently.

"Are the pads too hot?"

"No." She looked at her legs instead of him because if she turned her head she knew his crotch would be at nose level. "Why are you doing this?"

"I'm your senior advisor. It's my job."

Too tired to talk any more, Jesse leaned back against him

and continued to sip her drink. Most guys were heavy into body sprays and hip-hop colognes. He smelled faintly herbal, minty. Clean.

When his hands came up to touch her neck she thought he must be getting ready to move away and she jerked forward.

"Wait." He stopped her with his hands on her shoulders. "I'm just feeling for knots in your neck and shoulders. I can work out some of those kinks if you let me. Nothing funny. Okay?"

Jesse shrugged, not trusting herself to sound disinterested enough because she was seriously enjoying his attentions.

He moved onto the bed behind her. Slowly and firmly, he worked on the trapezius muscles of her neck and then down deeper in the muscles spanning her shoulders and back.

She had been to physical therapists many times and, having played sports since childhood, wasn't particularly embarrassed by her body. She just closed her eyes and let her mind drift so she didn't have to think about the fact that she was sitting practically in a strange guy's lap on her bed in a room alone.

"Better?" he said after a while.

She nodded, wishing he would continue until dawn. The ibuprofen had begun to relieve some of the aching and the protein drink seemed to settle her stomach rumblings.

"So? Can I give you a little advice to go with the first aid?"

Jesse came alert. "Sure."

He rested the weight of his hands on either side of her neck. "I heard some talk today about the Ladyhawkes' practice. It seems one little chicken hawk got all up in Porsche's face."

Jesse flinched. "I only said I wanted to play soccer."

"Yeah, about that." He began rotating his thumbs just behind her ears. "Things are pretty laid back here at Simmons. With less than a thousand freshmen entering per year, everyone pretty much gets to know everyone else."

"That's weird," Jess answered. "My senior class numbered over fifteen hundred."

"Okay, so this is more like a really big family. But there is a pecking order. You've gone from senior year BSOC to low woman on the totem pole. Savvy?"

"What's BSOC?"

"Big Shit on Campus."

"Cute."

"The biggest BSOC on Simmons's campus is Porsche." His hands fell to her shoulders and he gave her a little squeeze. "She's a great player. Olympic quality. But she's got a rep as a bit of a bully. If you're not into soccer as much as she is, you could become her chosen prey."

"I'm a good player."

"Good for you. But as a chicken hawk you need to think about survival. Rule one for survival: keep your head down. Rule two: don't volunteer. Rule three: let Porsche come to you. Rule four: remember rules one, two, and three."

Jesse shook her head. "If I hold back she'll think I'm scared of her."

"You should be." He swung his left arm in front of her so that she could see he was checking his watch. "I'm late."

He moved from behind her and stood up. "You can keep the heating pads for the rest of the week." He pulled a packet out of his pocket. "This is Epsom salts. There's a whirlpool in the women's locker room. I suggest you use it after your workout tomorrow. Good luck."

"Thanks."

If he heard her he didn't indicate it. He was out her door and then the suite at a trot. He didn't say what he was late for but she suspected it was a woman.

Jesse drained the last of the whey protein shake and sighed with satisfaction. It would be too depressing if she'd met someone she could really like only to discover he had a girlfriend.

Better to back up a bit.

Okay, so Bakari was nice to her. That was, as he said, his job. And he dressed like a slacker. What kind of brother would think he could rock a striped sweater vest? Only one other came to mind, André 3000 of Outkast fame.

Cassandra would say she should jump on that. But Bakari was older and seemed serious when he wasn't smiling. He reminded her of the life-size wooden sculpture of the Maasai warrior standing guard in her aunt Selma's foyer. Casual hooking up just didn't seem possible with a guy that intense.

She eased down against the heating pad and shifted her shoulders until the heat fully suffused her back. So, Bakari was good for back rubs and protein shakes, if nothing else. She'd send him a thank-you note.

❦

"This is not working, Mom. I'm stuck with the Latina version of Aunt Selma."

"It can't be that bad."

"It's bad. Nita has her own maid, more luggage than the *Titanic*, and a Bichon Havanese that bites."

"She has a personal maid?" Her mother sounded impressed.

"You don't know the half of it. Berta's in our dorm right this minute, hanging Nita's clothing on roller racks in the common room. Not that it's my room to share any longer. It's now Nita's closet."

"Oh, honey, I'm sorry. You can complain to the resident office about the dog."

"I'd rather complain about the other b-i-zitch in the suite." She was pleased her mother chuckled. A year ago she'd have gotten a lecture about language use.

"It wouldn't be nearly as bad if we didn't share a bathroom. Correction! Nita has a bathroom which, when she's not around, I get to use. Mom, there are drugstores with less beauty products on their shelves."

"Well, college roommates are the stuff of legend. I remember my first year—"

"Mom, I don't mean to be rude but this is my pity party. Okay?"

"Okay." She could practically hear her mother shifting mental gears. "How is preseason training going? Finding your niche yet?"

"Not exactly."

"Don't be so modest. The coaches have to be impressed with your skills."

"I haven't had much of a chance to show my skills. The team captain, Porsche, is all over my every move. It's like she hates me on sight because I was a couple of minutes late that first day."

"I'm sure it isn't that bad. Maybe she's just jealous of your skills."

"Mom, she hasn't seen my skills either. We just run and run and hustle and hustle, do everything but play soccer. It's like they want us newbies to quit."

"Be patient. Once you get a chance to show how good a team player you are, the pressure will ease some."

"Moving to the next topic."

"Okay. Met anyone interesting?"

Jesse sighed. This was mother code for *guy*. "It's been less than a week."

"And you're so grateful that I've been overseas so that you didn't have me checking in on you every day that you'll answer the question?"

"I haven't met any guys. Except my freshman advisor." Jesse wasn't sure why she said that so she quickly added, "He doesn't count because he has to be nice to me."

"He was nice to you? That sounds promising."

"Not even. Earlier today I passed him crossing campus with his arm around a seriously punked-out Asian girl. It was Scrummy with Yummy, as Cassandra would say."

Her mother chuckled. "So you are interested."

"Not really. He was really into the girl. So much so, he didn't even notice me. The boy's taken."

"Well, there will be others." Her mother always chose the positive spin.

"I have made two girlfriends." Toss Mom a scrap so she wouldn't think her daughter a total loser in the social department. "They are chicken hawks, too."

Jesse quickly filled her mother in. It seemed Jesse's opinion of Porsche as a bully was shared by all the chicken hawks. Emlyn Pressel and Pinky Lassiter had introduced themselves on the field after their second practice, the first day any chicken hawk had enough breath left over to actually speak.

"So now, Mom, what's the latest on the wedding?"

She launched into a riff on plans and timings to end with, "Will you still be able to come in on Friday for the rehearsal dinner? It won't interfere with practice or anything?"

"I'll be there." She wouldn't have practice to worry about if things didn't improve.

"Oh, you should know that Xavier has been offered the position of pastor at St. Hurricane."

"The church in Pine Grove, Arkansas? Sounds really country, Mom."

"I was there this weekend. Let's just say I have a bit of adjusting to do."

"What are you going to do if you decide you can't adjust? What if you hate it?"

"I won't hate it. Why would I hate it?"

"Where's the nearest Starbucks?"

Her mother laughed. "An hour away, you wicked child!"

"*Uh huh.* I hope you put down an espresso machine on your wedding registry. See you Friday."

Chapter 11

"Please tell me you're not wearing *that* to your rehearsal dinner."

Thea turned away from the mirror in the guest room to see Selma in the doorway.

She ran a hand self-consciously down one lapel of her celery-green three-piece silk suit. "What's wrong with it?"

"Everything!" Selma catwalked across the room toward her sister. Despite having had a baby, she retained her petite figure, which today was wrapped in a bright orange form-fitting sheath. Four-inch heels made her five-foot-two-inch frame statuesque. Women still clutched their men when Selma entered the room.

"For one, it's tired." She wagged her forefinger up and down for emphasis. "For another, Xavier's family has already seen you in it."

"No they haven't."

"Yes. They have. You wore it to Xavier's going-away reception *last* year."

"You're right!" All the air went out of Thea. Xavier wasn't as much of a clothes hound as Selma but she suspected he would remember, too.

"I don't have anything else. That last-minute trip to Pine Grove took up the Saturday I planned to spend shopping for tonight."

"You could have shopped in London. Hello! Couture everywhere."

"I couldn't afford the shops in London."

Selma clapped a hand to her sister's forehead. "You don't feel feverish but you certainly sound like you're out of your right mind. You're about to marry a multi-millionaire!"

Selma checked her watch. "Damn! We don't have time to shop. Xavier will be here in less than an hour to pick you up. If I hadn't pushed you about your wedding gown heaven only knows what you'd be going down the aisle in tomorrow!"

That much was true. Selma had talked her into a designer wedding gown whose price tag would have made her veto it if she'd been on her own.

Selma shook her head. "I hope you two have spent lots of time between the sheets this past week. Once Xavier sees you looking like a recycled pistachio ice cream cone he's going to need all those memories to remind him why he chose you as his bride."

"Actually, we haven't been intimate yet."

Selma's head jerked back on her neck. "Seriously? Is he sick or something? Sis, don't tell me he went and picked up one of them nasty diseases while in Africa—?"

"No—!"

"—because I hear that foreign sexual stuff will dry up a man's equipment permanently!"

"His— Everything is fine. Fine."

"That's a relief! Your new husband needs to be hitting it so good on the honeymoon you'll be thinking he's Lionel Richie." Selma lifted her palms upward and made little pumping motions as she sang, "'All night long . . . all night, all night!'"

Thea laughed. "That's no way to talk about a minister."

"He is still a man. That's what you want him to be thinking about when he sees you tonight, and praising God for that fact tomorrow."

Thea folded her arms. "It's too late to do anything about that."

"I wonder." She crooked a finger at Thea and turned toward the door.

Thea followed her sister down a long curving hall past a room with the door ajar. The voices coming from within were unmistakably those of Xavier's sisters. Cherise, Pearl, and Liz had dropped by so that the whole party could travel to the wedding rehearsal and then dinner together.

She resisted the impulse to stick her head in and say hi. Dealing with Xavier's sisters required all her wits and poise. Selma's assessment of her attire had her feeling neither smart nor composed. But as she moved past she heard her name, and paused.

"Thea's responsible? I thought Xavier said she could cook?"

"Maybe it's *what* she's cooking."

"Say what you will, I like Thea." Thea recognized this as Cherise's voice.

"Nobody's saying they don't like her." Pearl's contralto could not be mistaken for the others. "She just doesn't strike me as the type a man can't wait to come home to."

Thea winced as the other sisters shushed Pearl.

"Don't shush me. I'm just talking among us. A person can talk, can't she?"

Selma reappeared from the curve of the hallway. "What are you—"

Thea lifted a finger to her lips.

Selma sidled up to her. *Curiosity and the cat,* she mouthed, then leaned in closer to the partially open door.

"I don't suppose there's any point in bringing this up now." Liz, the youngest, paused. "But I always hoped Xavier would have a family. Do you think they will try?"

"Do you think they should?" Pearl responded. "At her age?"

"Thea's only forty-five," Cherise said.

"That's old for having babies. I wouldn't want them to have a handicapped child."

"Pearl!" the other two said in unison.

Thea could feel herself blush yet what did she expect, eavesdropping?

She turned away but Selma grabbed her arm. "You can't let them get away with talk like that!" she whispered.

"It is a private conversation," Thea whispered back. Except the conversation didn't require any passerby to strain for it.

". . . Black women have children a lot longer than other folk! Remember Great-Aunt ShaSha? She had thirteen. And Grandmother McPherson had nine."

"I'm more concerned about her suitability as a minister's wife," Pearl said dryly.

"Oh no, she didn't!" Selma's exclamation startled Thea.

"No, Selma, don't!" She made a grab for her sister's arm but it was too late.

Selma pushed open the bedroom door and marched in, waving a finger in accusation at the startled sisters. "You have some nerve, coming to a wedding I've planned, and bad-mouthing my sister."

"Hey, Selma! Thea!" Cherise's voice struck a false note as she glanced guiltily at Thea, who stood in the doorway. "I don't know what you thought you heard but no one's saying anything against Thea."

Selma didn't give an inch. "You just better not!"

Pearl stepped forward. A high school principal, she wasn't accustomed to backing down. "We have every right to discuss our brother's bride."

Selma struck a pose. "Not under my roof!"

Liz tried next. "We were just voicing natural concerns."

"You mean babies?" Selma's voice snapped with indignation. "Thea can have a child, a whole pack of them, if she wants. That's beside the point. Your brother is damn lucky to have won my sister's love again, after the way he treated her the first time."

Pearl's face pruned up. "You are hardly an impartial judge."

"You got that right." Selma walked right up to Pearl. "I say Xavier Thornton could never in this world do better for a wife than my sister. And we all know he once did a whole lot worse!"

"Selma has a point," Cherise replied. "Dominique loved Xavier's money more than she ever loved him."

"That's what I'm saying. Mistakes have been made." Selma smirked. "And, since you're so worried about who's a Christian, why don't we all do the Christian thing and join hands to offer up a blessing for Thea and Xavier's union."

Hands were linked for a general murmur of blessing from the sisters.

Satisfied, Selma smiled. "By the way, Pearl, you look great. Purple is your color." She grabbed Thea by the arm and exited like a tornado.

When they reached her bedroom, Selma pushed the door closed and leaned against it, laughing. "I guess I told them. Abusing my hospitality like that!"

"I want to—" Thea wasn't sure whether to laugh or cry. It wasn't an exaggeration to think that as little as two years ago, Selma would have been right in the middle of anyone bad-mouthing the person she thought of as her "too perfect" sister.

"You've never defended me before."

Selma shrugged one elegant shoulder. "Nothing wrong with Pearl but menopause. It's making her mean. She better flash on something else and leave this wedding alone. Now come let me work my magic on you."

Selma's closet was an extravagant space that included a sitting area, a vanity, and separate areas for clothes, shoes, lingerie, jewelry, and handbags.

"Have a seat. This won't take long."

Selma walked over, opened a louvered door, and pressed a button that began rotating one of several circular rods of clothing. "No one will notice your skirt if you're wearing the right accessories." She studied the colorful display passing before her for a few moments then plucked one off the rack, tags still attached.

"You should be able to wear this. I bought it when I thought pregnancy meant I'd go up a couple of sizes, not completely off the charts." She held up a pale gold silk chiffon halter top with a snug-fitting crystal beaded band under the bust that let the fabric flow loosely to a handkerchief hem at hip level.

Thea eyed it doubtfully. "It's not my style."

"Your style needs serious shopping therapy, remember? Try it on."

She slipped out of her suit jacket and shell and into the gold silk chiffon top.

"Too many straps." Selma reached out and unhooked her sister's bra and slipped it off. "Much better."

Thea twisted one way and the other in the closet's three-panel mirror to check herself out. The halter top held her modestly in front but dipped low to reveal a good portion of her back. "It's too revealing?"

"Girl, please! Pearl should know what you're working with. Nothing dried up about you." Selma tilted her head to the side. "You need the right shoes."

She bent over and unbuckled her four-inch T-strap sandals with chandelier-like crystal detailing strung across the instep. "Try these on."

Thea kicked off her pumps. Shoe size was the only size the sisters had in common. "They are gorgeous but I don't know that I can walk in them."

"You better." Selma watched Thea take a few tentative steps. "And don't even think about putting that suit jacket back on. You just need earrings."

She moved to another section of the closet and came back with earrings that complemented the crystals on the shoes. "Let me take your makeup up a notch."

When Thea looked at the reflection of her transformation in the dressing room's triple full-length mirror, she was positively glamorous. "This is perfect. You're too good to me."

"You have no idea." Selma ran her fingers through her shingled hair. "I've had to work miracles on the budget you gave me for this wedding. You can expect a bill."

Thea frowned. "How much?"

"Got you!" Selma's earthy laugh was one part schoolgirl and two parts foxy lady. "It's my and Elkeri's wedding gift to you."

"What is?"

"The difference on the cost of the wedding."

"Oh no. I couldn't accept. It's too much."

"Or you could just say thank you."

Thea could see that Selma wanted badly to do this for her. "Thank you."

Selma gave her a sly smile. "Good, because I added in a few extras."

Something in the way her baby sister said this reminded Thea of the self-interested Selma of old. "What have you done?"

Selma shrugged. "Xavier is a genuine ce-le-bri-*tee*. His marriage will make all the papers. I couldn't buy that kind of advertising."

"You alerted the press?"

"Do I look like a fool? I know a couple of stringers for the national papers. Your wedding is an exclusive. You won't even know they are there."

"Selma, how could you?"

Selma chose an earring and held it up to her ear in the mirror. "Can you think of someone else besides yourself for a minute? I'm trying to save my business."

Thea recognized that combative vibe. "What's wrong? Is Elkeri's business having difficulties?"

"Elkeri's got nothing to do with this." Impatience punctuated Selma's words. "This is about me, myself, and mine. While I took time off after Andromeda was born, two more designers popped up in Atlanta. One had the nerve to open doors on the same block as my showroom. Elkeri said it was to catch my spillover business. But business has slowed. I need something that will get me noticed."

"You don't need my wedding to do that."

"Don't I just? Andromeda is one demanding child. I don't have the time it takes to chase down new clients. If she gets the least bit off schedule there's no pleasing her the rest of the day."

"I seem to remember a few rough days with Jesse."

"You have no idea." Selma began surveying her racks of shoes. "Kids aren't like they used to be. I read all the books. Their little lives can be ruined before they can speak. Which reminds me, do you think Andromeda's developing a lisp?"

"No, I don't—"

"Because I can't have a lisping child. I think she should start speech therapy now, while she's in the formative stage of learning language. Speech is destiny."

"Mom?"

"Jesse?" Thea's head whipped around at the sound of her daughter's voice. She hurried out into Selma's bedroom. There Jesse was, in khaki shorts and a soccer jersey, and a heavy-looking backpack that pulled at her shoulders.

She rushed up and hugged her daughter tight. "How did you get here? Your plane's not due for another hour."

"Caught an earlier flight." Released from her mother's embrace, Jesse stepped back and smiled. "Wow, Mom!"

Thea frowned. "What do you really think?"

Jesse folded her arms and gave her mother a considering

look. "The top shows a lot of skin. And I've never seen you wear heels that high."

"Too much?"

"No. It's just that . . . you look hot!"

"Hot! That's what I'm talking about!" Selma stood framed in her dressing room doorway in another stunning pair of shoes. "And hello to you, Miss *Thang*."

"Aunt Selma!" Jesse moved to hug her. "You look fabulous as always."

"And you smell like you could use some personal time in my Jacuzzi. Dormitory accommodations are not even one star."

"True. Point me in the right direction."

Selma glanced at her watch. "You've an hour before the rehearsal starts. Tell me you're young enough to work miracles with hair and makeup in thirty minutes' time?"

Jesse shrugged. "I didn't bring makeup."

"You didn't . . . ? Never mind. You'll find everything you need in the bath. Meet me back here in twenty minutes. I'll do the rest."

"You did bring something nice to wear?" Thea whispered as Jesse passed her on the way to the shower.

"It's in my backpack."

Knowing Jesse, the backpack had been used as a pillow during her flight. She hoped Selma's steamer could work miracles.

She returned to her own bedroom to find Xavier pacing the floor. He stopped short when he saw her, his eyes widening as he took her in.

"Lady, lady, lady." He said the words softly, each a little expulsion of masculine appreciation. They made her feel his focus, his warmth, and his desire.

She did a twirl for him. "You like?"

His dimples popped. "I'm asking myself, how did I get so lucky? God is good."

She felt his flattery curl up inside her. She was in the habit of playing down her sexuality because she'd had no outlet for it. But tomorrow she'd be a married woman again with a man to love, and tease, and satisfy. No shame in that.

"God is good!" she murmured to herself as she took the arm he offered.

Chapter 12

"Who are all these people?"

Jesse craned her head to look out as the bride's limo arrived at St. James Jubilee Crown of Heaven Tabernacle. Dozens of beautifully dressed people filled the sidewalks as they lined up waiting to enter the church. "Mom, you said this was going to be a small family wedding."

"It was," Thea answered tightly.

"This is anything but small. Or private," Aunt Della answered, her praline-sweet N'awlins drawl bumped by irritation. "The whole congregation's turned out."

All three women trained their gazes across the distance of the limo's back seat to where the fourth member of the bride's wedding party sat facing them.

Selma swung her head toward the driver. "Go around to the side entrance." As the limo moved on, she met the stares still coming her way with a shrug and a fluffing of her glossy bangs. "You can't stop folk from attending a wedding at the church where they are members. Everyone knows that."

"This is about Xavier." Della nodded. "People never get tired of him."

"How did they know that we were getting married today?"

Selma met Thea's gaze with a shrug. "It was in the paper. That's why I had to change the venue from the chapel to the main sanctuary. But don't even think all these people will be at the reception."

"I surely hope not." Decked out in lavender from the tips of her peep-toe heels to the wide brim of her picture hat, Della was concerned, it was easy to see. "As it is, they'll be sucking up the air-conditioning in the church! Good thing I'm powdered down. But my hair is surely going to draw up in that crowd."

"Mom, do we have to walk down the aisle in front of all those people?"

"So it seems. But don't worry. You look lovely." Jesse sat beside her mother dressed in the strapless raspberry-pink dress she'd chosen as maid of honor. Thea took her daughter's hand and squeezed.

"Mom, your hand is like ice." Jesse frowned. "Are you all right?"

"It's just bridal nerves." Della patted Thea's knee. "I get them every time I marry. A glass of champagne always settles me."

Thea smiled vaguely in her aunt's direction. She doubted champagne would help. Ever since she woke up this morning she had to keep reminding herself to breathe.

What is wrong with me? This is what I've been waiting for, isn't it?

Xavier was so attentive last night that their families complained good-naturedly about feeling left out. When they parted with a last kiss in full view of all, she was joyous. She sat up talking with Jesse until four A.M. about old times and giggling like children.

Thea took a long, slow breath as the limo pulled up at the side entrance. She couldn't get over how sweet and thoughtful

Jesse was to have offered the first blue ribbon she'd won playing soccer in first grade as the "something blue" to tuck into her bodice. When she'd finally fallen asleep she was serene, happy, and very much in love.

But waking up changed everything.

She was vibrating like her electric toothbrush before she even got out of bed. By noon, she couldn't swallow a bite of the lunch Selma ordered for her. No one noticed how much of a wreck she was until they helped her dress. She tore two pairs of pantyhose before getting one on successfully. She couldn't decide on a shade of lipstick to wear and actually snapped at the woman doing her hair. The easy laughter of the Broussard family of women quickly gave way to an almost funereal quiet by the time they entered the limo to go to the church.

"Sis, are you all right?" Selma was leaning toward her.

Thea blinked, realizing the door of the limo was open and she was the only one still sitting inside. She took another deep breath and smiled reassuringly at the three pairs of eyes watching her from the doorway. "I'm fine."

No one challenged her as she slid out of the limo with Selma's help and that of the bridal consultant, yet she knew what they were wondering. Had she changed her mind about getting married?

No, I haven't. But . . . I need to see Xavier!

No one would let her make a call, not even send a text message to Xavier. Selma had confiscated her cell phone with Jesse's help. Aunt Della was like a watchdog who trailed her every move. They thought they were helping brighten her mood by teasing her about making certain neither of them sneaked out to see the other.

"I won't have you jinxing your marriage over a fit of nerves," Della had answered when Thea pleaded with her for just a thirty-second call. A New Orleans woman, Della believed in jinxes, hexes, and bad juju though she claimed not to.

It would all have seemed funny if she didn't feel so damn desperate.

Selma turned to the driver. "You stay right here through the entire ceremony. No buzzing off for coffee. You're on the clock."

A few minutes later the tiny bridal party was assembled in the bride's dressing room, waiting for a signal that the guests were seated and the service could begin.

Della was primping needlessly in a mirror while Jesse had mentally checked out and was playing a video game on her cell phone. The bridal consultant had retreated to a corner after Thea slapped away her hand for fiddling one time too many with her dress.

Thea paced in the dress she couldn't sit down in without wrinkling, wondering if she made a break for it if she could make it to the groom's end of the hall before they caught up with her? She caught her reflection in the row of full-length mirrors and the idea fled. Not a chance. Not in this gown.

She took a quick, short breath, suddenly convinced the gown was a mistake. Even the diamond and pearl earrings, a something-new wedding gift from Xavier, seemed wrong. She had wanted something simple, to match the wedding.

"It's a sheath. You can't get any simpler than that," Selma had assured her as she plunked her own credit card down to hold the gown until Thea gave in.

It was a sheath but it was not simple. The floor-length gown of smoky gray silk was topped by a matching bolero heavily embroidered in sterling silver. She was certain now that Xavier would think it was much too showy for a second-time bride.

She glanced again at the door. No! She was a middle-aged attorney, not some hormonal twenty-something first-time bride. No mad dash down the hallway could ever be explained as anything other than pure panic. Even Xavier might wonder if she had changed her mind.

Selma appeared in the doorway, her expression a little too bright. "It's showtime, everyone. Thea, Elkeri's here."

Elkeri came through the doorway grinning at her. "My, my, don't you look radiant!" She had asked him to escort her down the aisle because she had no close living male relative to do the honors. He offered her his arm. "You ready, Ms. Morgan?"

Thea took a long inward breath, willing her nerves to disappear. "Ready."

They made it all the way to the sanctuary doors before Selma cried, "Wait!"

She waved aside the bridal consultant to make her own last-second adjustments to the bridal gown and bouquet. "Are you holding your breath again, Thea? Breathe! We can't have you falling over in the aisle because of a lack of oxygen."

She touched Thea's hair, smoothing it above each temple. Then she cupped her sister's chin lightly. "You look gorgeous, sis." She gave Elkeri a darker glance. "Don't trip her. Remember. Slow steps and glide."

"Here we go," Elkeri said and patted Thea's hand. "Let's show them how the Broussard Sisters style it."

Breathe. Just breathe. Simple.

She was moving, watching the backs of her sister and her

daughter, who preceded her down the aisle. Aunt Della was already seated in the first pew on the bride's side. Gradually she registered impressions of cascading floral bouquets and columns of shimmering candles flanked by a kaleidoscope of colorful strangers who all but filled the two-thousand-seat sanctuary. Each image that struck her was wrong.

This is a circus! Selma promised! It is all so wrong!

Then she saw movement at the end of the aisle. First the minister in flowing robes. Then Uncle Way, Xavier's best man, stepped up. Finally Xavier appeared. With David by his side.

A gasp of pure joy escaped Thea. She knew why she'd been disturbed all day. The one fact that she could not change and so had chosen to block even from her own private thoughts was that her son, and Xavier's, had declined her invitation to walk her down the aisle.

His rejection shouldn't have hurt as much as it had. He was the child she'd given away at sixteen, too young to take care of even herself. Their reunion had been fraught with the return of Xavier to her life—a father who did not know he was one. And then there was Jesse. She couldn't choose David over Jesse in her desire to have her family together. So, she'd just pushed it so far back into the recesses of her mind that she didn't even know that was why she'd been miserable.

But now, there they were, father and son, waiting for her at the altar.

Both were handsome men, but for her there was only one who quickly filled her vision. Xavier was immaculate, so perfectly polished he literally took her breath away. This time the breathless feeling felt good. His tuxedo was fashionable yet undeniably classic. His white shirt, vest, and matching bow tie gave him a decidedly cosmopolitan, A-list movie-star look. His dark hair, dappled with touches of silver, was impeccably cut, and reflected the lights above and around him. His well-trimmed mustache did little to conceal the huge smile on his face. And it was all for her.

When she reached the altar, Xavier's warm hand closed confidently over hers, and he leaned close to whisper, "I've been trying all day to contact you."

Huddling close as if for protection, she whispered back, "They took my phone."

His eyes widened. "No lie?"

She searched his face. "I wanted to be sure . . ."

She didn't have to finish. The same question was in his dark eyes, and the answer, too. He was as nervous as she was.

"We should have eloped to Mexico," he murmured in a deep voice buoyed by humor. "But I'm glad I didn't miss you coming down the aisle in that dress."

She laughed, and he did too, so loud and sudden that it startled the minister and congregation. And then he kissed her.

Xavier might look like a self-assured and self-absorbed celebrity, but she knew the man inside. That man was dependable, solid, someone she could lean on and trust. A man who could make her laugh, and meet her in determination and dedication to whatever they set their minds to! He was the man with whom she wanted to spend the rest of her life. Xavier once said she thought too much for his peace of mind. At this moment she stopped thinking, and started to just be with him, in this kiss.

"*Ahem*. If we might begin?" the minister intoned, to bring order back to a ceremony that had decidedly strayed. "Dearly beloved . . ."

There was music and prayers and rings. She and Xavier had

written personal vows to one another but none of the trappings seemed important anymore. Two as one: that is what they were here to promise before God, and all those here to witness it, invited or not.

One of the only moments of the ceremony to remain clear to her was when Xavier asked Jesse to come forward after the rings had been exchanged.

He took her hand and Jesse's, but his words were for her daughter.

"Jessica Darnell Morgan, thank you for allowing me to share in your mother's life. You are her child and that's the strongest bond there is. I promise I will never do or say anything to come between you. That is my solemn promise to you today before God."

And then he took from his pocket a circlet of diamonds and placed it on Jesse's wrist.

There was a similar moment with David; this time a watch worth half the young man's annual salary was strapped around his strong wrist. "I share you with your adoptive parents, and your mother. And I will never not be there for either of you, ever again."

The men hugged and then David turned and hugged Thea. In the last second of the embrace she heard him whisper into her hair, "Love you, Mom."

When it came time to jump the broom, a touch Selma insisted upon as necessary to authenticate the moment as a truly African American nuptial, Thea discovered that her slinky-fit gown was not up to any kind of leap. As she hesitated, Xavier jumped first and then reached back and lifted her across it with hands about her waist. The guests applauded and cheered.

She heard only him whisper, "I love you, Mrs. Thornton."

Chapter 13

Jesse watched her mother and Xavier navigate the dance floor. It was the traditional first dance. The band played the Luther Vandross ballad "Always and Forever." Her mom's nervousness before the ceremony had vanished. She looked radiant. It was obvious her mother was in love.

She fingered her new diamond bracelet. Xavier was a nice man, in an older, intimidating sort of way. Some women craved that kind of compelling masculinity but it made her feel on the spot, as if something was expected of her that she lacked.

Her mother wasn't so easily impressed or intimidated. When she and Xavier were together, he became almost comically eager to please, bringing her cups of tea and massaging her feet while they watched TV. Her mother seemed to find everything he said worth her full attention. Yet she wasn't afraid to tease him, or tell him when he was wrong. Like just before the wedding started and they huddled on the altar like conspirators.

She'd wondered at the time if her mother was telling Xavier to call off the wedding. Then she had laughed and he had laughed, big, deep, startling laughter unexpected from so serious a man.

Aunt Della said that kind of ease together in public was proof they were meant for each other.

Jesse looked away. She was happy for them but she felt the alternate tug of being disloyal to her father's memory. Was he watching this from heaven? Was he happy that his wife had found someone else so she wouldn't be lonely anymore? Was love that broad-minded?

Then there was her half brother, David.

She spied him dancing with his date at the edge of the floor. His planned surprise for her mother was nice but, she thought, kind of mean at the same time. Why not say he was Xavier's best man instead of making an excuse that he was too busy to attend the ceremony? She remembered her mother's face when she'd told her he wouldn't be there. There was hurt. Deep hurt that made Jesse more than a little bit mad at him. But all was forgiven now. Only she felt her mother needed defending. But not tonight.

After a moment, she realized that Xavier and her mother were no longer dancing, that he was beckoning her onto the floor.

Embarrassed, she shook her head no. But he wouldn't take no for an answer and, breaking away from her mother, came right over to her.

"I'd be honored to dance with my new stepdaughter." He smiled encouragingly as the band struck up the old school tune "Celebrate."

Undecided, she looked to her mother for guidance. She was now being steered around the floor by Xavier's uncle Way, a white-haired gentleman who reminded everyone of a dapper chocolate Santa Claus.

"Show him how it's done, baby," one of Xavier's cousins

called out. "Put some new school polish on his old bebop ways."

Glad it was a fast song so that they didn't actually need to embrace, Jesse fell into step with Xavier. It would have been just too weird to be in his arms. For a few beats they were in step but then one of them missed the beat and they bumped shoulders.

"Sorry," she murmured, her cheeks flaming as she backed away from him.

"No, no, it's my fault," he answered calmly.

"Don't let his size eighteens crush all your toes," called out another guest.

Xavier laughed, and the guests joined in, too.

After only a few more beats the bandleader switched tunes and invited everyone to join the wedding party on the floor. More than half the guests immediately surged into the dance space. The hundreds attending the wedding had funneled into dozens at the reception but it wasn't intimate by any means.

"Guess you better rescue Mom." Jesse glanced meaningfully at the place on the floor where her mother was being crowded by gentlemen wishing to dance with the bride.

"I think you're right. Thank you for the dance." Xavier spoke formally as his gaze fixed on Jesse's face. "If there's anything I can ever do for you, anything you ever need, I want you to know you can come to me." He took and squeezed her hand. "We are family now. And I take that responsibility seriously."

"Seriously? Who's serious?" Selma had sashayed up to them. "Nothing can be serious tonight. It's a par-*tay!* Let me have some of this fine groom's time on the dance floor before my sister whisks him away for good."

"Groovy," Jesse murmured with a smile and faded gracefully from the dance floor. Xavier's pledge at the ceremony had surprised and touched her. His reiteration of it made plain that he wanted them to have a relationship. Perhaps, in time, they would. But it still felt strange right now.

Della came up to her, brimming with goodwill and champagne. "Why aren't you out there dancing, Sugar?"

Jesse shrugged. "I don't know any of these people and there's no one here even close to my age."

"What about that attractive young man who escorted you down the aisle?"

"James? He's Xavier's nephew." Jesse made a face. "Since the ceremony we're practically related."

"He's just married-in kin. That doesn't count." Della nodded, the wide brim of her lavender hat sweeping close to Jesse's face. "It's a lady's social duty to entertain in a pleasant manner the young man who is her escort."

"Okay. I'll see if I can find him." Aunt Della was all about the rules.

Jesse moved away with no intention of looking for James. They'd been seated together at the rehearsal dinner but he hadn't given off any "I'm into you, girl" vibe. He'd been too busy checking out every other woman under thirty who crossed his path.

Then she spied him, seated at his parents' table. He grinned and curled a finger to suggest she come over.

She lifted her brows and then deliberately looked away. Who did he think he was, expecting her to trot over like a puppy needing approval?

The trouble was he was hot, and he knew it. Tall and lanky with a Thornton head of thick curls, he had a laid-back way about him, as if the world always came knocking at his door. She might be attracted to him but she wasn't desperate to be liked.

For the next half hour she drifted about the room, lifting a glass of champagne here and there from passing waiters. Finally, after the cake was cut and the toasting was done, she was feeling more than a little boredom. Okay, she was feeling sorry for herself. Everyone, including Aunt Della, had been asked to dance. No one had asked her since Xavier.

Finally she spied James again. This time he was on the dance floor with a girl of about twelve, probably a cousin. Tall and skinny as a reed, the girl was trying out all her Beyoncé moves.

"Good evening." An older man in a vanilla-cream tux stopped her with a firm grasp of her upper arm. "You're the mulatto kid from the bride's first marriage, right?"

"Biracial, Granddad." A young woman in a sky-blue gown appeared by the man's side, smiling and shaking her head. "Granddad's a bit old-fashioned. He meant no offense."

The elderly man wrinkled his brow. "Of course I don't. *Bi*-racial. That's what I meant." He grinned a gap-toothed grin below a very thick graying mustache. "So, how you like being at a real all-soul Hotlanta function?"

"Half of me is happy." Jesse hoped her mother never heard that she said that. "Excuse me. My mother's looking for me."

She turned away, looking for an escape, and noticed doors opening onto a darkened patio lit only by the lights submerged in the hotel's indoor pool. Moving past deserted tables, she spied a pack of cigarettes and a book of matches among the remains of wedding cake and empty champagne glasses. Without stopping to think, she grabbed both and continued out into the night.

When she was far enough away so that the sounds from the party were simply background noise, she fished a cigarette from the pack. She struck a match and stuck the tip of the cigarette into the flame. She didn't put it to her lips, just watched the tobacco burn.

"Hey."

She hadn't heard any footsteps but there was James, standing a few feet away, his tux jacket slung over his shoulder. "Hey yourself."

He looked at the cigarette in her hand. "You smoke?"

"No. I just like to watch them burn." She gave each word a sarcastic spin as she held it up for inspection. She hated smoking, had never tried it, but why tell him that?

He took a couple of steps toward her. "'Cause, see, that shit will fuck you up."

"Don't tell me. With such brilliant insight you must be a med student."

He lifted both hands, palms out, and backed up a step. "Fine, be like that. I'm just trying to tell you, tobacco ain't all that. Not with its history of exploiting black slave labor to produce it."

He pulled a slim joint out of the breast pocket of his tux. "Now smoking weed, that's another thing entirely." He made a little hand motion like models do on the Shopping Network when they want to highlight a product. "This is grown by freedom-loving, enterprising brown brothers in co-opted islands and rainforests. No factories, no fuel, no pollution. Thoroughly green. You feeling me?"

"What I'm doing is legal. That's street crime, gang-related contraband."

"Nawgh." A smile came slowly to light up his attractive face. "Not weed. It's more of a free-range crop, sold in fair trade in a discreet agreement between an independent grower and a local seller. That cuts out the tax man, that's all." He leaned in close enough to make an impression but not quite crowd her. "Haven't you ever wanted to stick it to the man?"

Finally, someone was paying attention to her. Not that she was about to let on that she was flattered. "No thank you."

He shrugged. "Why is the best-looking girl at the party hanging out here alone?"

"Minding my own business." She stubbed out the cigarette. "Why are you here?"

"I was just about to ask you to dance when I saw you leaving."

"But you were having such a good time with Beyoncé the second."

"You saw me dancing?" He cracked a smile that let her know he was pleased she was paying attention. "I'ma tell you the truth. That was pity dancing I was doing. Pity dancing and family-obligation shuffling. Mom put the fear of God in me where family responsibilities are concerned. Told me that if I didn't do right by family I would go directly to hell, with her paying the ferryman. On occasions like these, it's my duty to escort the elderly, the young, the halt, the lame, *and* the blind."

Jesse examined him through narrowed eyes. "So escorting me today, that was just another pity duty?"

"Oh, *hell* no! You ever look in the mirror? You got it going on, girl." He gave her an up-and-down glance so hot Jesse felt the burn.

"That makes sense, since you worked so hard to ignore me."

He must have seen this as encouragement because he reached out and lightly brushed the back of his hand along her bare shoulder. "If it looked like that, it was just cover. If my mom had any idea what I'm thinking when I look at you, she'd take my eyesight. 'Cause, girl, you got me sprung!"

"You talk a lot," Jesse said, just to say something because he was watching her with such amazing intensity she didn't doubt he was aroused.

"So shut me up."

Maybe it was his smile. Maybe it was the champagne she'd been drinking freely. Or maybe it was just that for the first time in a while a guy she was attracted to was paying attention to her. She didn't really want to run him off.

When his soft lips first touched hers, she heard herself give up a tiny sigh of relief. She loved the way he kissed, slow and warm, with just enough tongue to keep it interesting. After a few moments, he embraced her, making her feel him from shoulder and chest to—

She jerked her mouth away as he pressed his arousal into her stomach and backed up a couple of steps. "Why are you all up on me all of a sudden?"

"Because I like you." He smiled confidently, certain of his attraction.

"Uh huh." *Never let a man take you for granted.* On that, her mother and Aunt Selma agreed. Time to slow things up a bit.

She folded her arms. "Didn't you come out here to ask me to dance?"

He blinked. "You mean you want to be on that crowded floor sweating the Electric Slide with the geriatric set?"

"I didn't say I'd say yes."

He leaned back and folded his arms across his chest like some hip-hop wannabe. "So let me get this straight. I should ask you to dance? 'Cause if that is the problem, we can be in there in a minute, doing the Chicken Dance and making it look good."

She laughed.

He moved in close again. "I got whatever you want, girl. For sure."

"My name's Jesse. Try to remember it."

"Jesse." He said it slow, letting the *ssss* hiss between his nice teeth. "I like me some Jesse." He reached out to place an arm around her neck but left a few inches between them. "Just tell me what you want, Jesse."

She wasn't certain she should just give in like this but he was kissing her again and he tasted so good and—damn! She leaned into him and this time she fit her hips against his and then did a little grinding movement.

"Oh, so now the girl's bumpin' on me." He took her face in his hands, the blunt still tucked between the third and fourth fingers of his right hand smelling greeny sweet without even being lit. "I say we need to find ourselves someplace a little more private to continue this discussion."

Jesse shook her head. "This is my mom's wedding. I can't leave."

"Okay. I see that." He gave her bare skin a finger rub along her collarbone. "How about after?"

She swatted his hand away. "You're pretty sure of yourself."

"I'm just hoping that the prettiest woman in the entire city likes me a little bit." He measured a small space between his forefinger and thumb.

"And conceited."

The space between his fingers shrank.

She giggled. "And persistent."

"I'm a man on a mission. To make you smile like that all night long."

"Show me what you got." She offered him a slow smile. "On the dance floor."

⚬∞⚬

"You all right?"

Jesse opened her eyes to see James's face hovering above hers. He looked worried. "Did I hurt you or something?"

"No." She closed her eyes again, wishing he would vanish. Wishing, really, that the last half hour would wind back to the moment before she stepped into his hotel room!

"I didn't mean to hurt you. But, damn, Jesse, you're a tight fit. I mean, that's a good thing. But it was almost like you never . . ." His eyes widened as he didn't finish his own sentence. "You're a virgin!"

Jesse shrugged. "Was."

"Shit! Baby girl, you should let a man know."

Her eyes flew open. "I'm sorry but I didn't think that a sexual status report was required for a hookup."

"Be cool. What I mean is there are things I could have done. I guess I might have done." He scratched his head. "You seemed so ready."

"I was."

"So, why are you crying?"

Jesse shut her eyes. "I'm not crying."

"*Uh huh*. I know tear tracks when I see them."

He lifted himself up a little bit, exposed her overheated skin to the air-conditioned chill of the room. Automatically she reached for something to cover her nakedness.

He grinned at her. "Still shy, huh? No need. I've seen it all. And it's all good."

She felt a blush creeping up her neck. "Don't go pervert on me. Give me the sheet."

He frowned, now suspicious. "How old are you?"

"Eighteen," she lied.

"*Hunh!* That's something I'd never have figured, an eighteen-year-old virgin."

Jesse hunched a shoulder. "It happens."

"No, it's okay." He rolled off her. "It's just that, well, I never. Not with a virgin." He touched her arm. "You sure you're not hurt or something?"

She glanced back at him, eyes narrowed. "Why? You didn't like it?"

His smile slid into place. "Oh, I liked it. Like you, a lot. And you?"

"It was okay." She looked away from him.

He slid in behind her, pulling her into him by her waist. "Maybe we should try that again, so tonight won't be only your first time."

She shot an elbow back into his ribs and pushed. "How about we don't."

"So what do you want to do?"

"Take a shower. Alone." Wrapping the sheet around herself,

she pulled it off the bed as she rose. He'd seen all he was going to see of her. She grabbed her clothes and purse and then locked the bathroom door behind her.

Once under the shower, she let her guard down. What had she been thinking?

Her head hurt from the aftereffects of champagne and there was a raw ache at the opening of her sex. She had danced off the buzz from the champagne long before she'd agreed to come up here with James. But now she couldn't defend her actions even to herself. It wasn't planned. It just happened.

Okay, so she'd lost her virginity to a guy she liked. Sounded like a plan at the time. Now it just seemed like the stupid idea it was.

She felt tears pushing at the back of her eyeballs, big hot tears that flooded her eyes without her permission then spilled over her lashes onto her cheeks.

It was stupid to cry. This is what she wanted. And James had been nice to her. Right up to the moment he penetrated her, she'd been right there with him.

Next thing, he was all hard muscle and bone and hot breath on her skin, in her ear, over her mouth. His body was pumping and pumping, like a machine that had taken control and she couldn't stop him and he couldn't stop himself. When he came, she felt it inside like a new kind of intrusion. Amazing, how a man could be so macho cocky one second, and then so completely not in control of himself the next.

Jesse wiped at the tears with the back of a hand and turned off the water. So, that was sex. She couldn't say it was better or worse than she imagined, just different. And she'd lost something. This wasn't like a bad haircut that she could just let grow out. One didn't become a virgin a second time. She was. Now she wasn't. Permanently different.

She grabbed a towel. Maybe she was thinking about it too much. All her friends said she analyzed everything to death. But she liked to understand why she felt the way she did. At the moment one feeling pushed the others aside.

She had heard how guys liked to screw and scram. Now she understood the impulse. She just wanted to get out of there.

James held up his cell phone as she came out of the bathroom. Even though she was fully dressed, she threw her hands up to hide her face. "What are you doing?"

"Taking a picture of my boo."

Suspicion took hold. "Did you take any other pictures of me, before?"

"Damn! I should have."

"No, you shouldn't have."

"What's the matter? Oh, you're still shy. So, fine, no nudie photos of my boo." He clicked several more pictures of her as he said, "I'm gonna need your email and cell phone number."

Jesse slipped on her shoes. "Just write down yours and I'll get back to you."

"Okay, okay." He reached for the bedside pad, scribbled in it, and handed a sheet to her. "That is just my user name, okay? It doesn't mean anything."

"Muf_Hown?" Jesse gave him the fish eye. "That's mature."

He shrugged. "You know how it is. You'll text me, right?"

She shrugged and checked both ears for her diamond studs and then her wrist for Xavier's bracelet. She was so not coming back here for any reason!

Something shiny caught her eye as she headed for the door.

It was the now empty foil of the condom she had been carrying around for a month. She groaned at the reminder and left without even a goodbye.

Once in the elevator she pulled out her phone and began dialing before it dawned on her that her mother and Xavier were off on their honeymoon. In fact, were probably doing at this very minute exactly what she would never guess her daughter had just done.

She veered away from that thought and closed her phone.

Chapter 14

Thea smiled at Xavier across the breakfast table laden with croissants, scrambled eggs, grits, and Scottish smoked salmon with all the garnishes. The past four days had been a paradise encompassed by their arms' reach toward one another. But tomorrow morning, the honeymoon would resolve into the real world. She had business that wouldn't wait in Dallas and he had new responsibilities at St. Hurricane.

Xavier rocked back on two legs of his chair and patted his stomach. "Selma does know how to throw down on breakfast."

"You mean her maid."

Selma had planned every breakfast and lunch for them so they had options if they didn't want to go out. A dining service was on call to bring in meals from the restaurant of their choice each evening. It was Selma and Elkeri's idea to relinquish their downtown Atlanta penthouse for the honeymoon so that the newlyweds wouldn't have to waste precious time traveling.

Thea picked up her half-drunk mimosa and looked at him over the rim. "So you aren't completely averse to the good life."

He cocked his head toward her. "I never said it doesn't have its pleasures. Selma has my undying gratitude for this time."

The reminder of her sister made her frown. "Do you think there's something wrong with her taking Andromeda on a vacation in the Bahamas while Elkeri is in New Orleans on a business trip? Shouldn't they have combined their travel to be together?"

"Why is that your headache?"

"She's my sister. I want her to be as happy as I am."

He reached out and touched her cheek. "She'll never be as happy as you are because she'll never be as selfless as you are."

"But—"

"No buts." He cupped her face in a hand that once easily snatched a basketball from the air. "Selma may be your lil sis but to the world she's a past grown-up woman who needs to take care of her own business."

He took her hand and began moving it in a slow caress down the opening of his robe. "If you're eager to make someone happy, I can think of a few ways you can please me."

She laughed and tried to pull her hand free but he wouldn't release it. A mock struggle took place until she gave up. Chuckling, he waved her hand around like a prize he'd won. And then he kissed it, nice and slow so that she could feel the bristle of his mustache against her knuckles. It was enough to tighten her inside from stomach to womb.

But then the playfulness dropped from his expression and his deep, dark gaze found and held hers with something more than passion. "I pray for your sister and Elkeri every day, Thea. Remember, I married them. But the truth is this is Selma's third try at making a marriage work. If she can't bring the lessons of her failures to bear on improving her present, then all the prayers in the world won't keep them together."

She nodded. "You're right."

"Now allow me to remind you again that as a wife you do have certain duties to your husband."

"I'm glad you didn't say lord and master."

"I surely know better than that, in taking *you* to wife."

"Reverend Thornton, you sound so *so* biblical."

"Do I? Then let's go with that."

He reached for her waist with both hands but she put up a hand in protest. "What about the maid?"

"Saw her out the door myself when I got up to refill the coffeepot."

She smiled. "In that case . . ."

He pulled her from her chair into his lap. Then he caught her face between his palms and kissed her, a long, slow, wet kiss that when it was done left them both panting slightly.

Thea spread her palm across his bare chest. The few springy hairs there tickled her palm. She had learned in Cabo San Lucas that he preferred, when it was hot, to sleep in the nude. That still surprised her. It seemed somehow decadent for a man of the cloth. However, he was giving off enough heat to prove his point of not needing covering.

His lids slid half shut as he moved her hand lower. The natural reserve in him vanished when they were alone. Even his eyes were smiling when he looked at her.

"Genesis 2:24 says 'Therefore shall a woman leave her sister and her sister's family, and shall cleave unto her husband, and they shall be one flesh.'"

"I've been reading, too," she responded, "and that passage actually refers to a man leaving his family for his wife."

He looked right and then left. "Do you see any of my kin anywhere? Do I seem content without anyone else's opinions, needs, or wants other than yours attached to my happiness?"

"Point taken."

He kissed her again. This time it seemed to Thea that the world paused.

"The next line of that scripture says," he murmured against her mouth, "'and they were both naked, the man and his wife, and were not ashamed.'"

Thea dragged her lips slowly back and forth across his. "I do like the way you quote scripture, Reverend Thornton. Is there any other pastor besides you who can make marriage sound quite so sexy?"

He reached under her gown for her naked hips. "If I have anything to say about it, you will never need to know."

A few more kisses left them ready to retire back to the bed they had left an hour earlier. He gently urged her off his lap and was about to escort her toward it when the cell in her robe pocket rang.

She offered him a little apologetic look. "I'm sorry. I have to get this."

His smile dimmed. "We agreed, no outside interruptions during the honeymoon."

"Yes, but I promised to check in this morning." She shrugged regretfully and slid her phone out of her pocket as it rang for the third time. "Hello, Thea Mor— Thea Thornton speaking."

She watched Xavier drain his coffee cup while she listened to Aisha run down a list of business matters. She tried to give

short answers because the annoyance on her brand-new husband's face was deepening with every response. "Okay, thank
you, Aisha. Yes, it was lovely. No, I'll be back in the office tomorrow. Bye."

He didn't say a word, just looked at her, but she knew what
he was thinking. Promises were hard to keep when they concerned her business life.

"I'm sorry. I should have mentioned I was expecting the
call."

He moved in very close, a man who understood that his
physical presence could be an intimidation or a persuasion,
depending on his mood. "Where were we?"

She smiled, though he did not, and closed her hand over the
knot in the belt of his robe. "You were about to say you need to
know me in the biblical sense."

His grin was slow to catch fire but it heated up her blood all
the same. "Exactly."

◦◦◦

She could hear Xavier in the shower when she came back
into the bedroom with two glasses of juice. It seemed as if
they'd exercised off all of breakfast in the last hour.

Selma had teased her about marrying a "middle-aged man"
who would not be Johnny-on-the-spot like a younger man.

Thea smiled to herself. She had no complaints! In Xavier,
the rash eagerness of youth was replaced by the deliberate control of a man who knew just what he wanted her to
feel and how much, and yet understood that something was
being withheld until she was more than ready. The fire might
catch a shade more slowly but the blaze burned just as brightly.

Chuckling, she reached down to pick up his robe from a side chair. He had always been so careful about straightening up after himself whenever they stayed together before. Since the wedding, she was finding a stray sock here, a belt there, a shoe somewhere else. It wasn't only the result of them giving in to the carnal urge to remove each other's clothing in any room they might happen to be in. It was as if he'd shed his habits along with his garments.

She cocked a brow at a pair of boxers next to the bed. If this was proof of his ease with lawful cohabitation, she'd just have to urge him to find another way of expressing his joy. Neatness counted in a marriage, too.

As she draped his robe over the end of the bed an envelope fell out of the pocket. She reached down to pick it up, and noticed it was addressed to Reverend Xavier Thornton at Selma's address. Surprised, she glanced at the return address.

Mrs. Hattie Patterson.

Xavier padded out of the bathroom, a towel around his hips.

"I see Mrs. Patterson wrote you." Thea hoped she sounded casual as she fingered the envelope. "How did she know where to find us?"

He nodded. "My church needs to know how to contact me at all times, in case of an emergency."

"Oh." She tucked the note back in his robe pocket. *His church. It was official.* "Mrs. Patterson doesn't like me."

"She doesn't know you."

"Then she doesn't like the little she's seen of me."

He stopped drying his hair and looked at her. "Somebody's feeling a little intimidated by her new life."

She nodded. "I admit it. I am nervous about this new role as a minister's wife." She swallowed, wondering how much to say about how unprepared she felt. *Keep it simple.* "I don't want to disappoint you."

He gave her a funny look. "You could never disappoint me."

"Embarrass you, then."

"Nothing you ever do will embarrass me." He came toward her, grinning. "I do reserve the right to laugh at you once in a while."

Her brows shot up. "What's funny about me?"

"For one, the way you sing in the shower." As he shook his head, the light turned the droplets nestled in his crinkly curls to diamonds. "I think it's kinda cute, you in there wailing like you think you're Aretha's little sister. But truth be told, girl, you can*not* sing."

"We can't all be Reverend 'X' with a Grammy-winning gospel CD on our vitae."

He tucked his chin in embarrassment. "That was strictly within the bounds of serving a higher cause."

"And the fact that you have a beautiful baritone while your wife can't carry a note in a basket has nothing to do with your humor at my expense?"

"Never!"

She stepped back as he closed in, shaking her head. "Let me be serious for a moment. You're such a dynamic person. I don't know how I'm going to measure up with all those who look up to you."

"You always measure up for me." He searched her face for a reaction. "After the congregation meets you this weekend, the concerns of St. Hurricane, the Pastoral Relations Committee, and those of Mrs. Patterson herself will be laid to rest."

"This weekend?" Alarm hiccupped through her though she didn't know why. "That's a bit soon."

"Why wait?" He dropped his towel and reached for a pair of clean boxers. "I'd like us to settle in as quickly as possible."

She tried not to stare as he stepped into his underwear but the truth was the sight of him nude was still very new. *Lord, but he is a lovely man. My man.*

"I understand you're anxious for us to settle but there are renovations to be made to the parsonage first." The way he paused to look at her said it all. Her heart dropped. "They aren't going to do renovations, are they?"

"Small towns move slowly." The man did put things simply.

She crossed her arms. "What are we supposed to do in the meantime?"

"Live our lives."

She didn't want to get into a disagreement on their honeymoon. But she had no intention of moving into that moldy pile of bricks.

The doorbell sounded. "I'll get it." She hurried away. *Saved by the bell.*

He was just about dressed when she returned with a FedEx mailer in hand. "It's for you."

He shrugged. "Just put it with my luggage."

"It's an overnight express from Delta Airlines." Smiling, she waved the mailer enticingly before him. "Are we going somewhere?"

"Not we. Me." He dipped his head. "I was going to wait until the honeymoon was over before I said anything."

She lowered her arm to her side, aware that something he

hadn't planned to tell her about a second ago was now about to be revealed. "Am I going to like this?"

He smiled at her wary expression. "It's nothing like that. The Thornton Foundation has asked me to sit in on the yearly planning session at the end of the week."

Is that all? "That's a great idea, isn't it?"

He sat and began tying his shoelaces. "I had hoped I'd left that responsibility behind. I did try to get David to say he'd sit on the board in my stead, to get some firsthand experience with the inner workings of a nonprofit corporation. But he's as stubborn as his mom." He slid her a seductive glance. "Wants to earn it in his own time. Yet knowing how to do something is not the same as needing to do something. I don't know that I want to get caught up in all that again."

She laid the mailer on his suitcase. "Then don't go."

He looked up. "Yes, you're right. Yield not to temptation."

"That's not what I meant. What do you mean?"

He ran a hand over his damp hair. "From time to time the urge to go back to my old life is so strong. It's second nature, what I know how to do. It would be so easy to give up on the effort it will take to commit to something else."

"Can't you do both?"

"No one can serve two masters."

She knew better than to continue along that road. It would only make him more determined to reject it. "I have an idea. Why don't you fly back to Dallas afterwards, and then we'll drive to Pine Grove together."

She could see in his expression that she had said the right thing by not pursuing his need to make a choice.

She let out a breath of relief. Being a wife again was going to take some conscious thought. It had been nearly five years since she had had to think about another adult's point of view and compromise on things she would have done differently.

So then, marriage was like riding a bike. She hadn't forgotten how to be a couple. She just needed more practice to do it well again. They were going to make this marriage of two very different people with two very different careers mesh.

Chapter 15

J esse leaned back with a sigh, letting the whirlpool in the women's locker room take the kinks out of her body. After a week of the most difficult workouts of her life, she felt that she was beginning to toughen up.

Mother Nature had taken pity on the chicken hawks in the middle of the week. Heavy rains kept them off the field for a day. Instead, they watched videos of the Ladyhawkes' last season while being lectured by the coach, assistants, and upper-class team members on classic Ladyhawke strategy and positions and stuff.

She had heard it and pretty much seen it all before. Yet the illustrated points took on new immediacy when the person with the skills on the screen was the same person in the room.

Porsche didn't stay for the full period. After holding up the wall for half an hour, smirking with her teammates whenever a chicken hawk asked a question, she'd vanished into the locker room and never returned.

Later, as Jesse had waded back across campus, she discovered where the team captain had gone. There was Porsche, shooting goals in the downpour as if it were a brightly sunlit day. Occasionally she'd pause to shake herself like a wet dog, and then she'd start again, lining up a kick and going for it as if a nine-foot-wide goalie stood between her and victory. She didn't like Porsche any better for her tenacity, but she couldn't help a grudging respect for that kind of dedication to the game.

Despite her determination not to punk out, she had taken Bakari's advice about the first law of survival: keep your head down. It worked. Porsche happily found other victims for her bullying temper. She was clever, never crossed a line that would get her in trouble with the coach. But her ugly criticisms often left at least one chicken hawk with quivering lip and unshed tears at the end of the day's practice.

"Did anybody get the tags of the bus that ran over me?" Pinky Lassiter asked as she slid into the whirlpool next to Jesse.

"That joke was old when God was born," Emlyn Pressel answered, splashing Jesse as she climbed in, too.

"They aren't bus treads," Jesse deadpanned as she glanced over at Pinky. "Those are Porsche tracks."

The three of them smothered giggles as two of the Ladyhawkes appeared. Seeing the provisional members in the whirlpool, they stopped short, exchanged glances, and then turned away.

"They're afraid Porsche will gnaw their asses if they hang out with chicken hawks," Pinky muttered.

Emlyn turned to Jesse. "She's moaning because Porsche mauled her for missing a shot Beckham would have been pressed to make."

Pinky nodded. "I love soccer but Porsche's attitude is just satanic."

"I don't know," Emlyn mused as they soaked up the bubbling heat. "If I was on the Olympic team, I'd be practicing twenty-four seven."

"You might as well pray for canonization," Pinky chimed in. "It'd take a miracle for you to be up for the Olympic team."

Jesse laughed as Emlyn made a rude gesture.

Later, when they had dressed and stopped for coffee in the student union, the talk continued to be about soccer.

"When the Ladyhawkes lineup is posted tomorrow," Pinky asked, "who thinks she is going to make the team?"

Jesse ducked her head. "No chicken hawk, if Porsche has the deciding vote. It's like she's got a grudge against us while every one of us would kill to have her skills."

Emlyn made a scoffing sound. "Who cares about Porsche? Joining the team was just a strategic move for me so I can join a sorority."

"You're going to pledge?" Jesse and Pinky asked in unison.

"Aren't you? There are frat guys that only date Greek, and I definitely want a frat man." Emlyn lowered her voice. "The sorority I've got my eye on is on probation because they got accused of prejudicial practices."

"Meaning?" Jesse asked.

"Meaning they were found guilty of recruiting only the prettiest and wealthiest." Pinky made a face. "So they're obliged to actively recruit 'well-rounded' girls now."

"That's code for fatties, geeks, and minorities," Emlyn added. "Jocks are optional. That's going to be my ticket to the pledge line."

"That's a pretty pejorative view of equal opportunity," Jesse said quietly.

"If Emlyn doesn't make the team she can always gain twenty pounds," Pinky suggested deadpan. "I'd love to make the team but I'm not desperate. I used my recruitment at Simmons as leverage against my parents' college choice. They wanted me to stay home and go locally. I need my independence."

Jesse nodded. "I understand that."

Pinky and Emlyn exchanged knowing glances. "Really? Why?"

Jesse sipped her latte while the other two waited her out.

"Come on. You never talk about your family except to say your mom says this and your mom says that. Everybody's got dirt. Divorce? Crazy boyfriend? Parental indictment? Simultaneous affairs?" As Emlyn spoke she flicked a finger back and forth between herself and Pinky. "What's your parental baggage?"

Jesse hunched a shoulder. "My dad died four years ago. My mother's remarried."

"That's right. That's where you were last weekend. You don't talk about it because the guy's a total psycho creep, right?" Emlyn nodded in sympathy. "Why do middle-age women lose their minds over these certifiable maniacs?"

Jesse recoiled. "No, nothing like that. He's a nice guy. But way different from my dad."

"So you hate him."

"No. I don't . . . I don't really know him." Jesse glanced at the guy passing their table. He had smiled at her yesterday when she came in. Today he seemed unaware of her existence. She turned back to her companions. "It's complicated. He was in her life before."

"Your mother had an affair! And so now you are standing up

for your dad who can't do it for himself." Pinky nodded vigorously. "I so totally get that."

Emlyn nodded. "My dad's second wife is a complete slut. She claims she was once a model but with those hips, I don't think so."

Jesse sipped her latte, wishing she could abandon this conversation. But that would leave the wrong impression about her mother. "It's nothing nasty. Mom knew Xavier in high school. They had a summer romance. Then she hadn't seen him since, until a couple of years ago. They sort of clicked again."

"That's so sweet." Pinky sighed. "Like one of those old Meg Ryan movies."

"His name is Xavier?" Emlyn frowned. "He sounds foreign."

"He's black." Jesse said it quickly so that she wouldn't punk out.

"Oh," they said in unison.

"That's going to change your world." Emlyn offered a knowing look.

"Not really." Jesse looked away. Why didn't she just say "my mom's black, too"? Or, "my mother's heritage is African American." Or just, "I'm biracial."

I don't get why I should have to explain myself every time race comes up in a conversation.

"People care, black and white, even if they say they don't," her mother had told her from an early age. "If they find out later, they often feel they've been lied to. Just be prepared."

Because I'm blond and blue-eyed, instead of black and brown? That's like saying that my being alive needs an explanation, or an apology.

Jesse drank deeply of her latte while she pondered what to

do. If she didn't blurt it out at every opportunity, why did she feel as if she were hiding something? It made her crazy.

Emlyn sighed. "When a parent remarries it changes everything."

"Yeah, but if you're young enough you might get showered with goodies, to make the new spouse acceptable." Pinky stirred her skinny mocha latte.

Emlyn reached for a French fry from the order they had agreed to split. "Stepmothers want to parent little kids. If puberty has caught up with you, God help you!"

"For real." Pinky nodded. "You start to remind her of all she's losing and how the best plastic surgeon in the world can't duplicate real youth, and here is her new husband looking at his daughter and comparing."

"If you play the guilt factor right, the goody bags continue." Emlyn held up her oversized leather satchel bag for emphasis. "Dad and Wife Number Three sent this—along with a blank check for new computer equipment—as my high school graduation present because they were just *too* busy to attend. It's a Fendi."

Pinky gasped. "You carry sweaty workout clothes in a twenty-two-hundred-dollar bag? I thought it must be a knock-off. How can you do that?"

"It's called revenge. Dad's wife had a stroke when I pulled my cleats out of it while I was visiting them in the Hamptons last month. Dad actually had to get between us. She pouted the rest of the weekend. I overheard her telling Dad how it wasn't right for him to choose me over her. After all, I was just passing through while he had to live with her." Emlyn faked a pout. "Guess I won't be invited for Thanksgiving."

"Xavier's not like that," Jesse said finally. "He's a minister. All about people and relationships. That kind of thing."

"Maybe it'll work," Pinky said, as if the possibility was otherwise. "Still, you've got the interracial part to work through."

"No, I don't." Jesse glanced at her companions, her heart pulsing with adrenaline. "I'm biracial."

"Yeah. Right." Emlyn laughed. "Look at you."

"I'm serious. I take after my dad. My mother's African American. My dad was white." Jesse paused. "Is that a problem?"

"For who?" Pinky asked innocently though her eyes were round with amazement.

Emlyn shrugged. "Interracial marriage and biracial children are so a Millennials issue. We are Generation Z."

"Don't you mean Generation I?" Pinky grinned. "I read somewhere we are the iPod, iPhone, Internet, I-vy-League dreamers."

"I personally am pursuing a guy with I-N-dependent wealth!" Emlyn's gaze swerved to the entrance where several members of the football team were entering, adding a few more black faces to the campus scene. When her gaze came back to the others she had a sly grin. "I dated a black guy once. His name was Mikel. But his parents didn't approve."

"Not black?" Jesse asked.

"Not rich. My dad's a public defender. His dad's a sports agent. Mikel was minted."

"Money's not everything," Jesse said reflexively. Then without knowing why, she added, "However, Xavier is rich."

Pinky nodded. "Rich is good."

"Very rich is better," Emlyn offered, and lifted her coffee in toast. The others quickly joined her.

Then because their laughter drew the notice of the players,

they turned to a very conscious attempt to show how unimpressed they were with finally getting noticed.

❧

The next afternoon Jesse sat under a tree enjoying a perfect late-summer afternoon. She had been told that the summerlike weather would soon and suddenly be replaced by a chilly upstate New York fall. Berta was in the dorm reorganizing Nita's wardrobe in expectation of the autumn weather. The big consolation was that Nita was down in the city for the weekend. When Berta left with Fidel, the room would be hers for two whole days.

"*Gracias,* Poppi!" Jesse chuckled to herself.

She'd thought Poppi was Nita's grandfather or uncle, or other older male relative. It turned out that "Poppi" was Latino slang for hot guy.

"Nice tits, Blondie!"

Jesse looked up with a scowl. Porsche had stopped on the sidewalk a few feet away. She wore workout clothes and carried a sports bag. "The pink halter's a nice touch. But didn't the surgeon warn you that implants would unbalance your game?"

Despite the snickers of a few other students on the lawn nearby, Jesse straightened away from the tree trunk and thrust out her chest. "They're mine."

"Sure they are. Like your diamond studs. Daddy buy those, too, with his *awl bid'ness* money? No, don't tell me. You think you're southern-fried Kardashian!"

Porsche started away before Jesse could form an adequately rude response. Then she turned back. "You are coming to cheer us on at our exhibition game in Albany?"

Jesse scrambled to her feet. "What do you mean?"

Porsche just chuckled and turned away.

What did she mean by that comment? Was she joking or . . . ?

The phone sounded its text message tone. It was from Cassandra.

What's shakin, grrl!

Jesse bit her lip as she typed.

Damn! Think ive been cut from team!!!

&8;

"Mom! I made the team!"

"That's fantastic, honey. But then was there ever a doubt?"

"Only every minute." No way would her mother ever understand the pressure she'd been under. "I can't talk now. I have to tell my friends. But you can come up for a game sometime, right?"

"You know it. Send the schedule."

Jesse had run to the gym to check the new team roster posted by the door to the coach's office. There were slashes through several names. Not Pinky's or Emlyn's. Or hers!

The shakiness in her knees seemed to increase with the realization that the news was good. She would be dressing out, just probably not playing in the first few games. The Ladyhawkes wouldn't start their season with a freshman in the lineup unless they had no choice. And they had choices. Nine of the previous year's team had returned.

"Someone will have to die for us to play," said one of the freshman teammates, as if reading Jesse's thoughts.

Jesse blew out her cheeks. "Maybe just catch the flu."

The girl—was her name Mari?—shrugged. "You're too nice."

Chapter 16

What do you mean 'postpone'?" The aggravation in Xavier's tone was so rare it surprised Thea. "People have made plans, coordinated events, prepared food. Can't you skip this one trip?"

"Not a chance." Thea paced her office, her door closed. She hadn't made it to St. Hurricane for church last weekend because she'd either caught the stomach flu or gotten food poisoning from something she ate on a rare late-night fast-food drive-thru. Given the extra week, the church had decided to hold an official welcome party for their new minister and his wife the following Sunday. Now, instead of leaving for Pine Grove a few days early, she had to fly to Dubai today.

"This is a critical negotiation. The opposing counsel aren't going to budge unless I'm there, in their faces, staring them down."

"You could send someone else."

Don't tell me how to run my business. She held back that reply. It wasn't Xavier's fault her life was so frantic. Ron's chemo wasn't going as smoothly as he had hoped. Travel was out of the question. As acting managing partner, she could send someone else. Unfortunately, this was her client's case, begun before Ron's illness had kicked her temporarily upstairs.

"That will send a bad message to my top client. You know how negotiations can get. Every eyebrow twitch starts to signify something. If I'm absent, the client's position looks weak."

His silence went on so long she had to stop herself twice from speaking just to get on with it. She loved the man but there were times . . .

"A good relationship between a pastor and his congregation is vital for his success, Thea."

He's talking about himself in the third person. That meant he was trying to keep emotion out of the discussion because his feelings wouldn't make it easier.

"The good people of St. Hurricane have been waiting patiently to meet their new first lady. It's time, don't you think?"

She opened and shut her mouth. When he was right, he was right. "I'll see what I can do." *Even if it means flying in and out of Dubai on the same damn day!*

"That's all I'm asking. I miss my wife." His voice had gone dark and husky.

"I miss you, too." She saw Aisha signaling her through the glass panel that flanked her door. She was late for a meeting and didn't really have time to ask how he was. "Got to go. Love you!"

⟨∞⟩

There was late, and then there was really late. Thea swallowed a cuss word as she glanced at the gas gauge on her dashboard blinking red. She was past CPT late, and now she had to stop for gasoline.

Xavier was counting on her. The entire congregation of St. Hurricane AME Church was waiting for her. If she didn't catch a break soon, she was going to miss church service altogether.

"This is not my fault." She took a deep breath. She'd been repeating those words every half hour since a four A.M. phone call from the airline woke her. Predawn thunderstorms in the Dallas area were grounding all morning flights out of DFW. When they resumed, there would be a minimum of two-hour delays.

She flew often enough to know if the airline was *estimating* two hours then three- even four-hour delays were more likely. She didn't have the luxury of time. She was due in Pine Grove by eleven A.M.

After a quick consult on the phone with a half-awake Xavier, she decided to drive to Arkansas. She hadn't considered that the thunderstorms might catch up with her in east Texas or cause flash flooding that would divert traffic from Interstate 30 onto farm roads, pushing her further and further behind. If it weren't for the fact that the Ladies Auxiliary was hosting a welcome reception for her after the service, she would have turned around and gone back to Dallas.

She pulled into a gas station off the interstate, somewhere south of Little Rock, only to discover that the pumps were so old they didn't have the credit card swipe on them. She'd have to waste time going into the station to pay before filling up.

In the distance, lightning etched designs across the face of an ugly purple cloud with a red-tinged underbelly. Yet overhead the full sun was bearing down with the prickly heat of a scorching day.

As she slid out of the driver's seat, her cell phone rang. She hesitated only one more ring before reaching for it. It was always a business day somewhere in the world.

The call failed. It was from Xavier. She tried three times to return it but couldn't get through. She gave up with a four-letter word in her mind. She was trying to stop cussing. Xavier had been very tactful when he suggested she delete even "hell" and "damn" from her vocabulary. And certainly a minister's wife didn't say "Jesus Christ" in anger.

Normally, she didn't think in four-letter-word terms but lately she couldn't seem to find any other phrasing to match her frustration on the job. Factions within her department were being territorial, testing her skills as their new boss.

"It's like the universe hates me," she said to no one in particular.

"But God loves you."

She looked up startled into the smiling face of a man in a lemon-yellow ice cream suit and white shoes, pumping gas across from her. He nodded. "Good morning, sister."

"And to you." She didn't know what else to say. It was a reminder that she was in the rural south where strangers didn't think minding their own business was polite.

As she walked to the station she ran fingers through her hair. There'd been no time to have it professionally done. Or her nails. She wanted Xavier to see the woman he had married two weeks before, not the exhausted, stressed-out, jet-lagged legal eagle she had become in the interim.

She rubbed away a trickle of perspiration from her cheek as she stepped out of the station, her credit card held hostage while she pumped gas. Two minutes in the late-summer Delta country heat and she was on simmer.

Ten minutes later she was again on her way with a cup of hot but miserable-tasting coffee and a Little Miss Sunshine Honey Bun on board. She'd packed a breakfast for the road, nonfat yogurt and a baggie of granola, but then forgot it. Her thermos mug had tipped over when she hit a rut in the detour service road near Mount Vernon. Fortunately, it had missed splashing coffee on the linen suit she'd worn, because there'd be no time to change before church services. But more than half of its contents had trickled out into the rug on the passenger side before she could retrieve it.

Half an hour later, she was off the interstate and breezing down a two-lane blacktop with no shoulder when she spied a flashing blue light in her rearview mirror.

"Damn!" She was doing sixty-five as she passed a fifty-five-mile-per-hour speed sign.

She had all her paperwork in hand by the time the sheriff, a big-gutted man with an old-fashioned marine buzz cut, mirror shades, and a brown uniform, sauntered up to her window. She was nervous. She'd gotten maybe two tickets in her entire life. But the day wasn't going well, and rural sheriffs had a reputation she didn't want to think about at this moment. She wasn't entirely successful.

Growing up in Louisiana, the last thing she, her family, or her friends ever wanted was to be stopped by the police for any reason. Alone with a sheriff on an empty blacktop in the middle of nowhere, Arkansas, that was the beginning of many a southern gothic horror story. Selma would say she'd been stopped for DWB, driving while black. She didn't look black, but she never took that for granted.

She had watched him write down her license plate number

before approaching her. Were her tags up to date? Her gaze flew to her inspection sticker on the windshield.

Okay. What had she learned from women's safety tips?

Do not lower window more than necessary to hand over paperwork. Keep your doors locked. Don't get in his vehicle for any reason. Find a busy place to pull over, in case you need witnesses.

It was too late for most of that good advice to be effective. She rechecked her door locks and hoped he wouldn't notice.

After checking out her back seat, the sheriff leaned down and squinted into her one-quarter-opened driver's window. "Good morning, ma'am. May I see your license and registration?"

She passed them to him without a word. Why hadn't she smiled and returned his good morning, like a normal person?

He didn't say anything as he perused her ID, then he went back to his vehicle.

She sweated every minute in the heat coming through her open window but decided that if she started the engine for the sake of air-conditioning, he might think she was trying to make a getaway. How would she explain an arrest to Xavier? *I'm in detention for suspicious sweating.*

Finally, after what felt like two days but was more likely five minutes, he came back to her window and looked at her carefully before speaking. "Ma'am, did you see the speed zone sign a while back?"

"No, Officer, I didn't. I'm late for church. My husband's church. He's the pastor of St. Hurricane in Pine Grove."

He glanced again at her paperwork. "Your license says you live in Dallas, Texas. That's a mighty long commute to church."

She felt her cheeks burn as if she'd told a lie, and her deodorant was definitely failing. "We are newly married and I haven't moved yet."

He never cracked a smile as he passed her license and registration back. He flipped his book closed. "I'm going to let you off with a warning this one time. I recommend you start out a little earlier for service next Sunday."

She nodded, too relieved to smile. "Yes, sir. Thank you."

⁂

An hour later she pulled up in front of St. Hurricane but there was nowhere to park. In fact, cars lined the street in all directions for several blocks. She had to park and walk back in the blazing heat. By the time she neared the church again, she was perspiring. She could hear voices swelled in song, with the verse "Lead me, guide me, along the way . . ." That was reassuring. At least they weren't about to let out. Maybe she had not missed Xavier's sermon.

Several heads turned when she stepped into the cool, dark entrance. The narthex was crowded with the overflow. She got a couple of polite nods from two elderly gentlemen standing nearby. As she moved toward the doors to the sanctuary, an usher, a pretty young girl in a white blouse and black calf-length skirt, approached her.

The first thing Thea noticed was her hair, severely swept back from her forehead and angled up in a static wave. Then she realized the girl was staring at her with hard eyes. She was accustomed to young black girls and boys scowling at anyone and everyone they passed. They thought a smile was a sign of weakness. Yet she knew instinctively that the girl's dislike was personal, for her. She just couldn't imagine why.

This is one of Xavier's church members, she reminded herself, and offered the girl her best business smile. "Good morning."

"Good morning." She didn't return the smile but offered Thea a program in a white-gloved hand.

"Do you think I can find a seat inside?"

The girl looked at her and shrugged. She turned away and then indicated with a stiff upright wave of a hand that Thea was to follow her down the main aisle.

Thea realized what the girl was about to do. Churches always filled from the back forward. The punishment for latecomers was to parade them down the aisle in front of everyone and make them sit in one of the front pews. She didn't want to embarrass Xavier by strutting to the front of the church when she was so late.

She looked quickly around. The back wall was lined with worshippers three-deep. Then she spied an empty space just beyond a woman dressed in white eyelet who sat at the end of the last pew. She leaned in and said, "Excuse me."

The middle-aged, larger-than-average-sized woman gave her a slit-eyed glance and then made a production of getting to her feet to let Thea pass by her rather than just sliding over herself.

"Excuse me, sorry." Thea said the words automatically while the usher stood watching her with lips pinched in disapproval.

A few worshippers glanced back at her. Others turned to nudge a neighbor and then jerk their heads in her direction, sharing the notice of the newcomer.

Thea sat down quickly, drawing herself up tightly, and glanced up, hoping to catch sight of Xavier between the heads in the rows in front of her. It had been a while since she'd heard him preach.

He stood on the altar with his feet planted slightly farther apart than his shoulder width. His large hands were clasped before him, fingers folded over the black leather Bible his grandmother had given him as a high school graduation present. He was robed in black silk and his sleeves rippled and billowed in emphasis of his every gesture. Three broad scarlet-velvet stripes accentuated his broad shoulders. Clerical robes certainly showed to advantage the physical gifts God had given him. The small sanctuary was as cool as a refrigerator, yet Xavier's dark face gleamed. Whatever spiritual uplift he had offered the congregation this morning was at an end.

She had missed Xavier's sermon!

They had planned the subject of his sermon together, an opportunity she was certain he would rarely offer. Yet because this would be her debut at St. Hurricane as his wife, he had asked her opinion. She had suggested that he preach about the sacrament of marriage. He thought that a fine idea. Thea felt her heart contract. He had meant his words for her, and she had missed them!

The woman on the other side of Thea leaned over and spoke. "If you're the reporter they sent from the *Democrat-Gazette*, you wasted a drive. She didn't show."

"I'm not a reporter." Though she suspected she already knew the answer, Thea asked anyway, "Who didn't show?"

"Our reverend's new wife." The woman scooted over, the gleam of the gossiper in her eyes. "After all the trouble we went to, she couldn't be bothered to show her face."

Thea opened her mouth to introduce herself but the woman cut her off. "What kind of wife makes her husband look bad in front of his congregation?"

"Mrs. Patterson did warn us not to expect too much," chimed in the woman in eyelet. "That's because she's . . ." Her voice trailed off as she stared at Thea. "I've said enough," she added under her breath and looked away.

A woman in the pew ahead of Thea half turned to join in on the conversation. "It's the children I feel sorry for. Dressed up in their Sunday best. They spent hours rehearsing. Now don't you go writing any of this, but we are most disappointed."

"Very disappointed," the woman in white eyelet agreed. "You could tell just by looking at our sweet Reverend Thornton how shame-faced he was during the ceremony."

Thea swallowed against a dry throat. "What ceremony?"

"The welcome ceremony."

The woman in front twisted more fully around and lifted an arm over the pew to point at Thea's program. "It's all in there for you to write about."

Thea opened her program. The lines in the middle of the inside page were set off by scrollwork and a different font.

Welcome of Rev. & Mrs. Xavier Thornton
Procession of the Deacons
Presentation of Flowers ____ Ladies Auxiliary
Salute _____ Junior Choir
"JOY" _____ the St. Hurricane Praise Dancers
Original Poetry _____ Mrs. Bertine Smith
Welcome to St. Hurricane __ Mrs. Hattie B. Patterson
Blessing of the Thornton Marriage
Acknowledgments __ Reverend and Mrs. Xavier Thornton

Xavier never said a word to her about a program during the service. Feeling sick in the pit of her stomach, she again looked toward the altar but he had disappeared.

"A person what don't take care of the small things won't take care of the large," said the woman next to Thea.

The woman in eyelet nodded her head vigorously in agreement yet not a single curl on her head moved. "That's a sign right there."

Great! Just great! Thea clenched her teeth. The middle of the service didn't seem the time to both introduce herself and justify her actions to her neighbors.

The soft pinging of her cell phone drew her attention. Ignoring the scowls of her pew mates, she retrieved and checked it. She had three new text messages. All were from Xavier and bearing a variation on *Where R U?* She bit her lip to keep from uttering words that should never be heard inside a sanctuary. There were whole third-world countries with better cell phone coverage than in rural stretches of the United States!

Another message arrived before she finished reading the last one. Again it was from Xavier. Perhaps that is why he had left the altar, to check on her.

Are you OK?!?

She replied quickly. *Here. Back pew. Just got your messages. Sorry.*

He answered even more quickly. *Come to altar when you see me.*

She flushed up. Now she would have to stand up at the end of a service she had all but missed and thank everyone for everything they would have done for her *if* she'd been here. Thanks to a merciful sheriff, she didn't even have a speeding ticket to wave under everyone's noses as proof of how desperate she'd been to try to arrive on time.

She glanced up to see Xavier return to the altar. He came to the edge of the altar and extended his hand. "Will my beautiful wife please come forward?"

Thea stood and turned to the woman in eyelet. "Excuse me."

The woman gave her a big-eyed stare then jerked her gaze away. But this time she stood and stepped out into the aisle to allow her to exit.

Walking up the aisle on her wedding day had been, in retrospect, a piece of cake. Every eye in the church was on her, appraising. She was suddenly aware of her hair, her makeup—she'd been in too much of a hurry to do more than reapply lipstick before she left the car—and her wrinkled suit. There were lots of comments in her wake, and to judge by the sound of them, most were not happy ones. All that kept her steady was looking at Xavier, who once again stood at the end of the journey.

Smiling broadly, he stepped down from the altar to offer her his hand.

"What kept you?" he whispered as he bent to kiss her cheek.

"Long story," she whispered back, reassured by his nearness.

He led her up the first few steps to the main stage of the altar and turned so that they both faced the congregation. "Members and guests of St. Hurricane AME Church, it is my pleasure and distinct honor to introduce to you at last, the lovely and very special lady who has so generously agreed to share my life. Will the church please welcome my wife, Mrs. Theadora Morgan Thornton?"

The applause was general but not very enthusiastic.

As it died away an older woman in a beige linen suit and an enormous pale orange top hat with a silk scarf band and rolled-back brim stood up in the front row and came forward with all the majesty of a head of state. Thea recognized her at once. It was Hattie Patterson, St. Hurricane's Sacred Cow.

As their gazes met, the hair lifted on Thea's arms.

Chapter 17

When Thea opened the driver's-side door of her car it emitted the same temperature and smells as the inside of a scorched coffeepot. It was a match for the steam coming out of her ears.

For the past thirty minutes Hattie Patterson had done everything in her power to make her feel as uncomfortable as possible. She'd done it with such a sense of decorum that Thea doubted anyone else realized what the woman was up to.

It all began with Mrs. Patterson's suggestion that she be allowed to re-recite her welcome speech for "Mrs. Thornton's benefit."

Embarrassed by her tardiness and wanting to be gracious about it, Thea had overruled Xavier's reluctance to allow it.

That was my mistake.

She should have known better. Mrs. Patterson was accustomed to the admiration and deference of all who knew her. She was not about to allow anyone to upstage her.

"Good morning, Church. It is fitting that I begin with a scripture reading. Revelations chapter seven, verse nine, says: 'I looked and saw a great crowd no man could number from every tribe, people, tongue and language. . . .' It does my heart good to see so many of you, church members and guests, today. For it is a reminder that although changes and circumstances bring new beginnings, God, by His Holy Spirit, always directs our paths within His ultimate will. And on this day we celebrate the auspicious beginning for St. Hurricane for we have been blessed above the ordinary in the selection of our new pastor."

The woman had gone on for another full five minutes about Xavier's accomplishments, beginning with his elementary years and Boy Scout badges all the way through his professional life as an athlete and businessman. She must have copied every detail from every biography ever written about him. Then she launched into his ecclesiastical accomplishments. The back wall began to lose population.

Thea had tried to catch Xavier's eye but he had stood staring straight ahead with a pleasant smile on his face. Clearly, he had mentally checked out of the ordeal. And she didn't have a leg to stand on since she'd asked him to permit this.

"Serves me right," Thea muttered as she fanned the heat from her car with her purse.

Then the woman got to her résumé.

"Mrs. Thornton is an attorney in Dallas. I don't quite know what she does but I'm sure she will tell us." Hattie had paused as if she expected Thea to respond.

Thea had smiled and shaken her head. "Another time."

This seemed to annoy the woman for she glanced at her speech and then said, "I'm sorry, Mrs. Thornton, but I was unable to gather much information about you. Your husband is so very protective of your privacy. I have no idea who you are."

She had paused a second time, Thea supposed, in hope that

she would rise to the bait. Though Xavier said something encouraging under his breath, she had merely shaken her head and said again, "Another time."

"Very well." Hattie had turned to the congregation. "Let me assure you that Mrs. Thornton is perfectly capable of expressing her opinion when she chooses." The congregation murmured and chuckled in response. That's when Thea knew that the complaints she'd heard about herself while seated in the back pew weren't just idle speculation. Mrs. Patterson had been spreading rumors about her. None of it flattering.

The woman had turned blandly toward her again. "Now, for your benefit, Mrs. Thornton, I'd like to introduce our pastoral staff."

Grumbles of protest could be heard throughout the church. It was nearly one P.M. and people had had enough of church. They had wanted to go home to an early dinner and Sunday afternoon football. The expressions in the pews before her let Thea know that many blamed her for this further delay.

Suddenly Xavier's hand had been at her back pushing her gently forward.

She had had to take the hint. "If I may, Mrs. Patterson. I'd like to stop here and thank you for all your kind words." She had turned to the dwindling congregation. "Thank you, members of St. Hurricane, for your welcome. I apologize for my tardiness. The weather delayed me. I look forward to meeting each of you individually and worshipping here with you as often as I can in the future."

"But your wife hasn't yet received her floral bouquet," Mrs. Patterson had protested. She had grabbed up a bouquet of roses from her front pew seat and brought them up to Thea, saying, "It would have been a shame to waste them. I accepted them in your absence."

"Absence, my butt!" Thea muttered. She had made every attempt to be here on time. But circumstances got beyond her control. "That's what an act of God is all about!" she murmured to herself.

"And it would have nothing to do with a stubborn woman who thinks she can manage her universe without compromise."

Thea looked up. Xavier stood there in this brain-melting heat looking as cool as homemade lemonade. And he was smiling. "I should have insisted Mrs. Patterson stop sooner. I owe you an apology, Theadora."

"You think?" She took a breath. "I know I owe you one."

He didn't speak again. He just opened his arms and all the fight went out of her. She just walked into his embrace and made herself at home.

He wrapped her up so tight she made a sound of protest. He didn't release her. "When you called from Texarkana it sounded as if you would be on time. But then you didn't arrive. I called you half a dozen times. I couldn't keep my mind on God or my sermon. I even left the altar once to text you. I began to think that maybe you'd been in an accident . . . Or worse." He heaved a sigh that made his whole body tremble. She knew then he was remembering how close they had come to losing David at a Dallas demonstration two years before. And she, Xavier.

She clutched him tighter. "I'm so sorry." She kissed his warm cheek. "By the time I realized I wouldn't be here on time I couldn't get phone service. But you didn't need to worry."

He took her face in his hands. "I need to know where you are all the time." He kissed the top of her head. "I can't afford to lose you."

Okay, he wasn't Evan, and he wasn't going to shrug off her miscalculation.

"You can't lose me." She cocked her head to one side as she looked at him. "I trust you to take care of yourself. You have to trust me, too."

He looked perfectly serious as he said, "It's times like this that I miss Jerome."

That admission surprised her.

Until he left for Darfur Xavier had had a personal assistant named Jerome superglued to his side for years. Jerome's job had been to smooth all the bumps in his boss's path and handle any ripples made by his wake. Xavier didn't have to think about anything but what he chose for himself. From personal experience, she knew Jerome had even managed the details of Xavier's personal life. If he'd been on the job today, Jerome would have had state troopers looking for her while Xavier rested easy on the altar.

Thea linked her arm through his. "I missed your sermon."

The first hint of humor rounded his cheeks, putting his dimples in serious jeopardy of popping out. "I'll give you a private reading tonight. It's all about marital faithfulness. Mrs. Patterson was very pleased."

Thea glanced away. "Did you notice how she went out of her way to make me uncomfortable in every way possible?"

"I think her irritation can be put down to the amount of effort she's put into today. She may be a bit uppity, as the old folk would say, but she merely wanted you to know how much trouble everyone had gone to, to make you welcome."

"She made her point a little too well."

He looked at her blankly. "Do you think you could be reading into the situation things that weren't there?" He checked his watch. "The reception begins in ten minutes. We should be able to make that on time."

"That's cute." She handed him her car keys and turned away, brushing away strands of hair sticking to her damp forehead.

Had he really misunderstood the woman's agenda in making everyone sit through the misery of a partial repeat of the program? Thinking about it made her mad all over again. But this was no time to upset Xavier. There was still a reception to endure.

She could just imagine what Aunt Della would say.

Theadora! Sugar catches more flies than vinegar.

Unfortunately, Mrs. Patterson seemed more like a wasp.

⌒∞⌒

Reluctantly, she got out of the car in front of the parsonage. She had done all the makeup and hair repair that was possible in a moving vehicle. Any more time in this heat and she'd need a bag to put over her head.

As Xavier pulled away to look for a parking space on the crowded street she turned up the sidewalk. Nothing had changed on the exterior. The broken shutters and peeling paint remained. The grass had been freshly mowed and a big tub of yellow mums sat on the porch by the door. She could see through the front screen a room crowded with people still in their Sunday best.

She steeled herself as she always did for difficult business meetings by reminding herself of what she had to accomplish. One, erase her poor impression of the morning. Two, make nice with Mrs. Patterson. Three, leave them all thinking she was a pleasant person. She put a smile on her face and reached for the screen door.

No one noticed her entrance. This was not a formal occasion. It was a real party crowded with people holding plates piled with Sunday food. And voices, male and female, all talking and laughing together in pitches louder than usual city voices.

"Hello there, young lady."

Thea looked down into the face of a sweet-faced woman who wore a white straw hat with a red feather in the crown. "Who are you, dear?"

She smiled back, glad for a friendly face. "I'm—"

"She's running for political office, sister." A woman looking remarkably like the first but with a wide-brimmed pink hat to match her suit turned her brown cherub face up to Thea with a smile. "I know who you are. You are running for the city council in our district. I've seen your picture on the billboard over by the highway. You are much prettier in person, dear."

"Thank you, but I'm—"

"Now, sister, you're forgetting your manners." The first of the two petite women offered Thea a thin, blue-veined hand. "Welcome to St. Hurricane. My name's Cora Brown. This is my sister, Hortense Brown. We head the Ladies Auxiliary at St. Hurricane Church. Now, of course, you must be here to meet our new pastor."

Thea nodded. "We've already met."

"Of course they have, sister. She must know every important person in town if she's running for office." Hortense shoved her false teeth forward and let them click back into place. "We got us an up-and-coming minister in Reverend Thornton."

"So I've heard." Thea held out her hand. "I'm Theodora, Reverend Xavier's wife."

The sisters exchanged surprised glances.

"Oh my. You must forgive us, my dear. We weren't at services this morning."

Cora touched her arm. "We were readying the parsonage for the reception. It certainly is a pleasure to meet you. Would you like a little refreshment, dear?"

"Something to drink would be nice. Thank you." Hungry as she was, she didn't want to be caught with a mouthful of food when Hattie Patterson approached.

"We have lime frappé and wine punch."

"Get her the punch, sister," Hortense said. "Cora makes the best punch!"

"Thank you." Thea looked about for Xavier and saw him come through the door. He was waylaid immediately by Mrs. Patterson. Now that she thought about it, the oversized top hat made the woman look like the Mad Hatter in *Alice in Wonderland*.

"Here you are, dear." Cora offered her a punch cup full of pale pink liquid. "I'm so forgetful these days. What did you say your name was?"

"Theodora." She saw Xavier signal for her. She took a steadying breath. "Excuse me, and thanks for the punch."

Xavier reached out to take her hand and bring her up next to him. He then turned to the woman in orange. "I was just agreeing with Mrs. Patterson that this has been a fine welcome from St. Hurricane."

"Yes, very nice." Thea met the dark eyes of the elder woman. The queen of England could not have been more reserved. "Nothing, I'm sure, can compete with the cultural delights you are accustomed to in a great city like Dallas. But it is the best that St. Hurricane has to offer."

"It's very nice, thank you." Thea offered her best smile. Voices around them died away to listen in on the exchange, magnifying her feeling of being on the spot once more.

Hattie gave her a searching look that ended at her right hand. "What are you drinking, dear?"

Thea smiled and lifted her cup. "It's punch. One of the hostesses served me. Would you like me to get a cup for you?"

"No, I seldom drink spirits. Certainly not this early in the day." It wasn't a question but a condemnation. "That is wine punch, is it not?"

"Yes." Thea wondered what was wrong. They'd served it to her, after all.

Hattie closed her eyes briefly, as if absorbing a blow. "Most pastors' wives find it useful to model ideal behavior for the young and weak by not drinking alcohol at all."

Thea felt her face grow warm, one of the liabilities of a fair complexion. It was not embarrassment but annoyance. "I believe drinking responsibly has its merits, as well, Mrs. Patterson. For years I attended the Episcopalian church. Even the priest and his wife will drink a toast at a wedding."

"You will find St. Hurricane a traditional community. Manners and discretion are favored over bold new ideas."

"Then I apologize if I've offended you." She almost choked on the words but they had to be said, for Xavier's sake.

Hattie turned to Xavier. "Would you mind fetching me a cup of the frappé, Reverend?"

"Gladly." Xavier looked at Thea. She couldn't read his expression but he held out his hand. She gave him her punch cup. "Can I get you anything else?"

A noose. She could not step right with this woman!

She waited until Xavier moved away to say, "I'm sorry if I offended you. I would not have you think badly of me."

Hattie did not meet her eye. "It is said that first impressions are often the truest."

She doesn't want to like me. The idea surprised Thea. Why should a woman she didn't know dislike her on the spot? Surely it wasn't because she'd been overheard making a disparaging remark about the parsonage?

Mrs. Patterson turned and signaled to the pretty younger woman who had just come through the door. "Allow me to introduce my grandniece. This is Lola Franklin."

Thea held out her hand. "Hello."

The young woman didn't take Thea's hand. Instead, she turned to her aunt. "She's white! Reverend Thornton married a white woman?" She gave a bitter laugh then turned and stalked out of the house.

Thea felt as if she'd been slapped. Even Mrs. Patterson looked a bit flustered by the outburst. They stared at one another for one long, very uncomfortable moment as the congregation about them remained silent.

Thea glanced about. *Is that it? Are they all staring because they think their precious reverend jumped up and married a white woman?*

It had been a long time since she'd had to think in those terms on a daily basis. In the metropolitan areas of the country, most people no longer remarked on interracial couples, if they bothered to notice.

When she spoke her voice was cool as ice water. "Your niece is mistaken about me." She looked beyond Hattie's challenging gaze to those behind her. "I am African American. Not that it should matter." She looked back at her tormentor. "The good people of St. Hurricane believe that tolerance is a virtue, too, don't they, Mrs. Patterson?"

Hattie's eyes widened. "Of course."

Thea glanced up as Xavier came back with a cup of frappé. He slid an arm around her, his hand curving confidently over the indentation of her waist. "I trust my wife has made her position clear?"

"Yes, she has." Hattie refused the cup of frappé. "It's been a pleasure as always, Reverend Thornton, to be in your good company. However, the exertions of the day have worn me out." She acknowledged Thea with a flicker of a gaze. "It was most interesting to see you, Mrs. Thornton."

"And you, Mrs. Patterson."

Hattie's gaze steadied. "Perhaps you'll attend a Sunday school class next week. It would be most instructive to have our new first lady lead a discussion of the scripture."

"I can't promise next Sunday." She glanced at Xavier. "But I will try."

"Oh well, I'm sure we will see something of you again . . . sometime."

Xavier squeezed her waist. "I'm going to escort Mrs. Patterson to her car."

It was pretty much a desertion by the flock after their leader left. Few made eye contact with Thea as they mumbled greetings or their goodbyes. She felt like Lot's wife, turned to a pillar of salt by her mistakes.

When the only persons left were the women in the kitchen putting away food, Cora and Hortense came up to her, each resting a hand on her arm. "We are so pleased that you're going to be our neighbor." Cora's expression was as serious as her tone. As if they knew they were disobeying Mrs. Patterson's unspoken command to shun their pastor's disgraced wife.

"That's our little place across the street." Hortense pointed an arthritic curved finger. "With the roses by the door."

Thea rallied. "You live in the lovely yellow house with verbena in the window boxes?"

"Yes. Cora is the family gardener." Hortense gave her sister an affectionate glance. "I am the cook. And tend . . . other things."

Cora smiled proudly. "Anytime you want flowers for your table just let us know. I keep daylilies and dahlias in the backyard."

"And we can get you a fresh supply of eggs."

"Thank you." Perhaps she'd made two friends after all.

∽◅◦◦▻∽

"Disaster! A complete disaster." Thea had to tell someone about her day. Xavier was at the church for the monthly vespers service but she had begged off. She couldn't face any of St. Hurricane's congregants again today even after he assured her that her mistake with the wine would soon be forgotten. Jesse was the only person she wanted to talk with tonight.

"It'll be okay, Mom." Jesse sounded so mature and calm when her mother finished her story.

"You're right. I don't think there are any more rules for me to break." She chuckled. "Enough about me. How's school life?"

"Classes are good. And I've found this new cool website called Multiplicity."

"That's nice." Thea rubbed her head, feeling the tightening sensation of a too-long day. "Listen, honey, I hate to tell you this but I'm going to have to cancel my plans to come up to Simmons on Friday night for your season opener. I feel miserable about it. I really need to spend some time here helping Xavier settle in and getting to know his church. I'm sorry."

"That's okay." Jesse didn't miss a beat. "I understand work comes before play."

"That's because you're the child of two workaholics." It was always a joy to watch her child on the field, body and soul in perfect harmony, when focused on a game. Something else she would have to forfeit to her other responsibilities.

"Congrats again on getting to play in the exhibition game yesterday. Did you get any feedback from the coach?"

"I told you, it was no big deal. I only spent five minutes on the field. If you'd gone to the restroom, you'd have missed me."

Yet a mother knows it's important to witness her baby's precious five minutes.

Thea hung up after reassurances that she would make a game soon, very soon.

But as she sat on the edge of the lumpy mattress in a house that while clean smelled faintly of mildew and Lysol, she wondered how she would manage all her obligations and promises. She wanted to see Jesse's school, meet her fashionista roommate, and watch her daughter play soccer. She wanted to sleep in the same bed as often as possible with her husband. And she wanted to catch up to her life. At the moment, it felt as if she were chasing it.

She jumped as something large and black and shiny skittered across the floor. She grabbed a shoe and squashed the roach she would later claim to Xavier was half the size of a gerbil.

"I hate roaches! And this house!" And she wasn't all that fond of St. Hurricane.

Chapter 18

Thea awakened in Xavier's arms. Despite that comfort, she felt woolly-headed and joint-locked with sleep, as if she had slept under instead of on the bed. It was this mattress. Lumpy and sprung, it was like sleeping on a sack of potatoes. She tried to turn over but the bottom sheet stuck to her back. Her skin was damp everywhere she and Xavier touched.

Unreliable air-conditioning was one more thing to add to her growing list of complaints about this house. The list was long.

There was not one comfortable seat in the entire house. She'd sat on one plump-looking cushion to watch TV only to find herself sunk so far into it that her knees were under her chin. The end tables had so many white rings from forgotten glasses that their damaged surfaces looked stenciled. The chest of drawers in their bedroom was missing a couple of knobs.

She gazed up at the bedroom ceiling and saw brownish water spots. There were matching ones in the kitchen, living, and dining rooms. Faucets in both bathrooms and the kitchen leaked. The condition of the carpeting didn't bear thinking about. Why would the church expect their minister to be content living here?

She'd complained to Xavier about a peculiar smell in the house when he came home but he seemed oblivious to things that set her teeth on edge. She supposed after living in refugee camps, any shelter with indoor plumbing would seem like heaven to him by comparison. Perhaps that's why he slept while she had been awakened before six A.M. by what she was certain was a rooster crowing!

There was really only one good thing about the place. Xavier was here with her.

Smiling, she leaned over and kissed his sleeping face. He smiled but didn't open an eye. While he didn't notice things around the house, he had no problem focusing completely on her. At least some things worked properly.

Three weeks of two-state married life and she could still count on one hand the mornings they had awakened in the same bed. But things were looking up. She had checked her calendar last night and saw that Ron was back in the office this week. It wasn't necessary for her to be in Dallas for the next few days. She could work from here, as Xavier had suggested. That way she could try to make a go of their new life. She owed Xavier that much.

He hadn't said a word about the wine punch, or her tardiness, or Mrs. Patterson, or any of yesterday's unpleasantness. After he returned from vespers, he had simply said he was hungry. They had eaten cold ham, potato salad, macaroni and cheese, green beans, cornbread, and two helpings each of Earline's peach cobbler, all left over from the reception. Then they had gone to bed and stayed there in each other's arms all night long.

Thea peeled herself away from the sheets, headed for a shower. Then she would need to make a few business calls. If Xavier was still in bed after that, she would rejoin him.

Half an hour later, she came out of the bathroom, hair wrapped in a towel, and one of Xavier's T-shirts slipped over her clean body. The first thing she noticed was the smell of bacon frying. Xavier! He must have decided to begin breakfast for them. Her stomach growled in response to the idea of food.

But a glimpse of their bed made her stop short. Xavier's long frame was still making mountain contours under the sheets. Disappointed, she sighed. Must be a neighbor's breakfast she smelled. Oh well.

As she bent forward from the waist to towel dry her hair, the rattle of a pan in the house made her jump upright. Someone was in their kitchen!

She hurriedly drew on a pair of sweatpants, glancing repeatedly at Xavier as she debated if she should awaken him with news of an intruder. She decided against it. Now that she thought about it, he had mentioned that someone came to keep the parsonage during the week.

Still, she picked up her cell phone before she left the room. Nine-one-one was on speed dial. She heard more sounds in the kitchen as she neared it, water running and the clang of pots. As protection, she picked up the empty wine bottle left on the dining room table from the party the day before. Would a burglar be listening to the *Rickey Smiley Morning Show* on the radio? She made the turn from the hall and saw her intruder.

A thin, elderly man in an old-fashioned bib apron with a frill around the neck stood before the stovetop frying bacon. When he saw her, a grin broke over his face in ripples of smiley parentheses around his mouth. "How are you doing, Mrs. Reverend?"

"I'm fine." Thea lowered the bottle and then tugged at her T-shirt to make certain it didn't cling to the outline of her bra-less breasts. "Who are you?"

"Deacon Jacobs. Didn't the reverend tell you about me?" He glanced from the cell phone to the wine bottle in her hand and wagged his head. "Oh now, did I scare you?"

"Just startled me." She put the bottle on the counter only to wonder if she should have chosen a different weapon, considering the problems of yesterday's wine punch.

Too late now.

She offered him her hand. "How do you do? I'm Thea Thornton." Suddenly alert to the possibility of another transgression she asked, "Did we meet yesterday?"

"No, Mrs. Reverend. Sunday's my day off. The way I figure it, you'd seen about enough church people for one day. Besides, feels like I already know who you are." He dipped his head, clean and shiny as a billiard ball. "The reverend doesn't talk above half about anything the way he talks about you. He'll be a better man now you're here."

She liked Deacon Jacobs on the spot. "I'm glad to be here, too. But I don't think that my being here makes Reverend Xavier"—was she going to have to become accustomed to addressing her husband as Reverend?—"a better person."

"See now, I'll tell you. He's asleep and it's going on eight thirty. Most every morning he's out of bed at five, if not before. Won't eat a thing before he goes huffing and puffing out the door and down the block, like a broke man running from a bill collector. When he comes back, he won't eat much though I try to feed him proper every morning the Lord sends. Then he's out the door on church business. Evening comes it's the same thing, more huffing and puffing, unless he's over at the gym with them basketball youngsters of his."

"Really?" Xavier never worked out twice a day when around her.

The man dipped his head as he fished crisp pieces of bacon from the grease. "Most evenings the reverend eats so little of my meals that I could get insulted. Then he reads or studies the Bible until you call." He gave her a sly grin. "Reverend smiles some smiles after that. Goes and gets himself a piece of fruit or a cup of that sour yogurt stuff he buys. Once he even ate ice cream. You don't call before bedtime, he won't touch a grape, just goes to bed. That's how I know you're good for him."

"I don't think I've ever had a better compliment. Thank you."

It was a compliment, but it also implied a great interest in the details of Xavier's life. Jerome, who knew at least as much about his employer's habits, would never have divulged so much to her. She knew that from experience. "Have you had this position long, Deacon?"

He nodded. "Fifteen years, through three pastors. Only the last didn't have a wife and that's when I moved in full-time to do the cooking. I didn't always keep the parsonage. Just since I retired from the railroad. Pension don't stretch like it once did, but I do okay. This way I get a place to sleep and meals. Only now that you're here, I'm moved in across the street with the Brown sisters. They have a room above their garage. It's a tad small but I'm a little dab of man so it's mostly about right."

"They seem very nice." They were the only church members to really welcome her besides him.

"They are. Retired schoolteachers, both of them. And they say they like having a man around the house." Squeaky laughter trailed behind as he turned away from the stove to pick up a bowl containing eggs with pale pink, brown-speckled, and bluish shells.

She stepped closer. "Those are the most unusual eggs I've ever seen."

He smiled and held up the bowl. "These are fresh, not from the store. How you like your eggs, Mrs. Reverend? The reverend is most particular about his. I fix them sunny-side up but not runny, just like he likes them."

"That will be fine. And call me Thea or Ms. Thea, if you prefer." Mrs. Reverend was something she'd never be comfortable with.

She watched him break an egg with a pink shell into a smaller bowl and inspect it. But when she saw he was about to drop it into the bacon grease she acted.

"Wait, Deacon. I brought a few things for cooking." She hurried over and pulled a can out of one of her shopping bags standing on the kitchen table. "We use this for cooking our eggs."

Deacon Jacobs put his bowl down and took the can, squinting at the label. "Olive oil cooking spray." He looked at her with a puzzled expression. "Don't seem right, cooking fresh eggs in olive oil."

"It's very healthy." She moved the greasy skillet from the fire. "I'm thinking of the reverend's health. He has to watch his cholesterol."

Deacon Jacobs frowned up. "What do doctors know? This week it's 'don't eat bacon.' Then it was 'don't eat eggs.' Now they are talking about the bottled water crisis. Next week they'll be telling a body they need pure lard to live."

She smiled. "Even so, Reverend Xavier should have what he asks for, don't you think?"

"Yes, ma'am. I suppose he's allowed." He looked mournfully at the skillet of grease before reaching for a clean pan.

"And, if you don't mind, I'd like to make my husband's breakfasts when I'm in town."

"That's your right. Only I wonder what the Pastoral Relations Committee will do about my salary if I'm not doing my job?"

Thea saw immediately where that might lead. *She threw poor old Deacon Jacobs out of his job, first thing!* "Do we need to advise them of our arrangement?"

He smiled but didn't meet her gaze. "That's on you, just so you know."

Maybe he didn't mean it the way it sounded but she was getting a little weary of defending her every action and thought.

"By the way, Deacon, I thought I heard a rooster this morning."

"Sure enough? Now that's a surprise." He looked down to stir his eggs. "It's against the law to raise livestock within the city limits, that's what they tell me." He reached out to push his bowl of eggs behind a canister. "Now sound does carry a long way in these parts. Maybe you heard a legal rooster, on the other side of the tracks."

She nodded and turned away. That was a lot of explanation for a rooster that wasn't there.

༺∞༻

She spread the contents of her legal portfolios across the dining room table shortly after breakfast. It was now three P.M. She needed a break but couldn't afford to stop just yet.

Mental note to self: buy a computer desk.

Her arms ached from the awkward position of typing on a keyboard set at too high an angle. And dial-up internet might just be the death of her. Who knew it still existed? Could anything be slower or less reliable? She'd tried unplugging the phones in the house but discovered that that did not stop them from ringing and knocking her offline.

There wasn't a single WiFi spot in town that anyone knew about. That hadn't even occurred to her when she decided to spend a few days working from here. Even McDonald's had WiFi . . . but Pine Grove didn't have one of those, either.

The cable company had assured her that they could provide the LAN line. It would just be a week or two before they could get to her to set it up. Aisha had texted to say her boss needed a WiFi router with an "unlocked" portable WiFi device that would allow her to use any SIM card, from anywhere in the world, inside it. Great idea, but it wouldn't solve today's problem.

The expense of routing her laptop through the modem on her smartphone was not an item she wanted regularly on her bottom line. And, while connected, she was unable to make or receive business calls. Unfortunately, there was a service interruption, so not even that worked today. Xavier had driven up to Little Rock for a luncheon meeting so there was no help to be had there. After wrestling with that for half an hour she gave up and went back to dial-up.

She was getting desperate enough to think about driving to Pine Bluff every day to use the public library computer facilities.

Just after she pressed the Send button to transmit a batch of emails the parsonage landline rang.

"Perfect!" She waited two more rings before picking up the phone, pissed. "St. Hurricane parsonage."

"'Bout time you answered. This you?"

"What?" She was watching the little pulsating emblem that said her email was in limbo, neither sent nor failed.

"This here is D Mo over by the prison. Where he at?"

"Who?"

"What the fuck is this?"

Thea heard a little scuffling on the other end of the line followed by several ugly curses spoken low. But her mind stayed half on the lines on her monitor. "This is the St. Hurricane parsonage. May I help you?"

"Yeah." She heard lip smacking on the other end of the line. "Maybe you can. You sound fine. Got some sweet words for a man with hard wood in his hands?"

Thea blinked, refocusing on the call. A man in prison was calling. Right! "Are you in need of God's salvation, sir?"

"Ah, it's gonna be like that. Don't get all tight ass on me. Just do your job. Get me the minister."

She mouthed a cuss word as she saw her email had not gone through before the call broke in. "The reverend isn't here. Would you please try again later?"

"This ain't a damn social call! This is my one call a week. You can take that call. Latoya ain't picking up her phone so you call her. Tell the bitch to bring me some more drawers and cigarettes, if she knows what's good for her."

"Who is Latoya?"

"What the fuck you playing at? Who is this?"

"Reverend Thornton's wife."

"Thornton? I don't know no Thornton. Where's Reverend Samuel?"

"I have no idea." Thea clutched her pen, wondering if this was a common kind of call for a minister, or just her bad luck. "If you will give me your information I'll be happy to see that Reverend Thornton gets it."

"Oh *hell* no, bitch!"

She wasn't certain which of them hung up first and she didn't care. He'd let loose with a stream of profanity uglier than any she had ever heard.

A little shaken, she got up and went into the kitchen. The room was only slightly warmer than the rest of the house. The air conditioner had died during breakfast. Xavier had gotten a promise from a church member that he would come by to check on it. That hadn't materialized. At least it was a cloudy day in the mid-eighties. With a breeze and the windows open, it was bearable. Just barely.

She jumped when the phone rang again and reluctantly answered.

"This is Shirley Jackson. I need to speak to Reverend Thornton on a most urgent matter." The woman sounded teary.

"This is Thea Thornton, Mrs. Jackson, his wife. The reverend isn't in at the moment. How can I help you?"

"Oh, that's so kind of you, dear. But it's a praying-over matter that requires a minister."

"I see." Someone was dead or dying. "I'll try to contact my husband as soon as we hang up but I need a few details first. Where are you and what is wrong? Is someone ill?"

The woman sobbed and Thea's heart contracted in sympathy. "Take your time, Mrs. Jackson. I'll wait."

"It's my dear Coobie. The doctor says it doesn't look good, and I can't afford the medication that might heal him. So I've got to prepare to accept his fate."

Thea bit her lip. "What kind of medication? Maybe there's someone we can talk with about getting a generic brand, or help with the costs. Do you or Coobie"—husband, child, relative?—"have insurance or are either of you on Medicare or Medicaid?"

"Coobie? On Medicare? My cat?"

"Coobie's a cat?" Thea's pen skidded across the notepad.

"Coobie is my best friend on this earth. Been with me nineteen years. Longer than my husband stayed. The vet says he's caught leukemia and there's nothing they can do that won't cost me a thousand dollars. Now I ask you, a thousand dollars! Might as well be a million to a woman like me. Poor Coobie."

"I'm so sorry, Mrs. Jackson." She took a deep breath. "What, exactly, would you like Reverend Thornton to do for you?"

"Come and pray over Coobie, that's what." Her voice dropped into a whisper. "Do you think it would be all right with the Lord if the reverend came and did that?"

Her heart melted. "I'll ask him. I think it would be an extra good thing if you went ahead and prayed right now for Coobie, before the reverend gets there."

"You're such a sweet person to say that. Thank you so much. God is just blessing us every day!"

Thea hung up and dropped her chin in her hands. She wasn't in Dallas anymore. That much was certain.

∽◊∾

She pulled up across the street from the Pine Grove City Hall/police station in the shade of a tree, and opened her laptop. To her joy, a WiFi network connection popped up. She was probably breaking more than a few laws, except for the fact they hadn't bothered to secure their network. She supposed a small town didn't have that much need for security.

Hoping not to be noticed, she quickly uploaded and sent all her mail and files.

Chapter 19

"Goal! Goal! Ladyhawkes! Goal by forward Porsche Wagner. Assist with a crossing pass from midfielder Jesse Morgan!"

Jesse grinned and gave her teammates the thumbs-up sign. Hearing her name over the loudspeaker was a boost she hadn't had this season. With six freshmen players finally added to the Ladyhawkes' roster, competition for field time was intense.

Porsche caught Jesse's eye in passing. "Nice play, Barbie!"

Jesse gave her a chin jerk of response as she jogged back to her midfielder position.

Blondie, Barbie, Jenna Bush. Porsche had a whole collection of names for her, all meant to be insulting. The team captain was a great soccer player but her personality was whack! But a goal was a goal and she'd assisted. That was official. It was her first assist goal of the season.

As she glanced up at the Simmons cheering section, Jesse noticed Bakari was in the bleachers. It was hard to miss his Rastafarian dreads and Lenny Kravitz plaid bell-bottoms. He gave her a one-finger wave as if he were worried someone might see him. She didn't see "Scrummy" by his side.

Still, she tossed her double-looped ponytail and turned her back. Since hooking up with James at her mother's wedding, she had taken a giant step back from the idea of looking for a guy.

After she thought about it, she decided that she'd used James. She felt bad about that. She might have liked him but she would never know. Because it certainly seemed impossible to back off sex with a guy after having it with him. And she definitely wasn't going to do that again anytime soon.

How embarrassing to discover she wasn't as blasé as her friends about sex. Not that she had discussed her weekend with any of her friends. She felt awkward. At least when on the soccer field she knew what was expected of her and that she could cope.

After two more minutes of play the whistle blew for a time-out. "Morgan! Coker! Off the field!" Assistant coach Nicco signaled to Jesse and another player. Two others left the bench to replace them.

As Emlyn ran past she cried, "Give somebody else a chance, won't ya?"

Jesse shrugged and reluctantly left the field. She was pumped, ready for action. To be taken out after a victory seemed particularly cruel. She smiled in acknowledgment of the back slaps and high fives of congratulation that greeted her return to the sideline.

"Good work out there, Morgan." Coach Brewer patted her shoulder. "Cool off."

"'K."

But she didn't want to sit or cool off. She wanted to stay on the field.

Instead, she paced behind the bleachers watching every move her teammates made on the field until the game was over.

❦

"Yeah, Mom. It was cool."

"Your first assist!" Her mother sounded so excited, even by phone. "I wish I could have been there. You see? I knew that once you got on the field you'd earn the respect of your team-mates."

"Sure." Jesse turned on her laptop. Porsche didn't insult her playing nearly as often, just her personally.

"So why aren't you out celebrating with the team?"

"I have to study for a morning class. That's the problem with playing mostly on Thursdays and Sundays. So, how are things in Arkansas?"

"Fine."

"You don't want to talk about it."

Thea chuckled. "Is it that obvious? Actually, I'm taking to-morrow off to drive over early. See if I can get some work done on the parsonage on a Friday."

"You're really going to live there?"

"Looks like it. I'm determined to make this work."

"Uh huh." As her mother related her ideas for renovating the parsonage, Jesse scanned her texts for key names. Cas-sandra had written and included a picture of herself in a string bikini and some hot guy in a banana-yellow tanga. The text said, *"Click hyperlink for video of me dancing on beach on the Caribbean TV Tempo."*

She clicked. Up came some quick cuts of Cassandra and the guy bumping on each other, interspersed with other dancers on a beach. "Oh m'god!"

"What's wrong, Jesse?"

"Uh, nothing, Mom." Jesse smothered a giggle with her hand. Cassandra had been filmed doing a body shot from a shot glass tucked in the guy's tanga. Her parents would kill her if they knew about this!

Jesse clicked replay. "So, Mom, what are you going to do about Mrs. Patterson?"

"Try to reason with her." There was a short silence. "There are things like wiring and plumbing the Pastoral Relations Committee will have to get permits for. It is their property."

"Get Xavier to talk to them. He should be backing you up."

"I don't want to put him in the middle." Her mother suddenly sounded sad.

Jesse's attention swerved back fully to the conversation. "Why not? Is something else going on between you and Xavier?"

"No, honey, nothing like that. It's everything else. This job is eating my lunch. Why did I think I wanted to be a full partner?! I should be giving it all my attention but if I want to have a relationship with Xavier's church I need to be in Pine Grove every weekend I can. In between I need to fit in meetings with clients, trips to New York and London."

"Do what you have to do, Mom. Xavier's a man of the world. He'll understand."

"You're right. But it means time away from one another. And I have to tell you, I don't like being married and still living alone half the time."

Now that was being frank! Jesse was glad her mother couldn't see her blush. At least she was talking to her as an equal. "So why can't he just find a church in Dallas?"

There was another short silence. Funny, her mother was

picking up Xavier's habit of pauses. "Do you remember all the discussions we had as a family when I was trying to decide whether to take a job in Dallas?"

"Sure."

"It meant that your father had to relocate his law practice. And you didn't want to leave your friends in Philly. Your dad practically had to start over but he wanted me to have my chance at rising to the top in a top-notch law firm. You both agreed to make sacrifices for me. That's what families do."

"So you're saying this time you're sacrificing for Xavier. You really love him, don't you, Mom?"

"I really do."

"I envy you."

"You'll find someone, Jesse. I promise." She paused again. "Oh, there's something else I have to tell you. I hate it but it looks like I can't make Parents Weekend. There's a legal conference in San Francisco I should attend that weekend."

"That's okay, Mom. I won't be here. We have an away game at Rutgers that Sunday."

"Really? Maybe I could fly back to New Jersey in time."

"Don't sweat it. I mean, how often did you see your parents when you were in college?"

"Christmas, sometimes Easter, and summers. Money was tight. I usually spent other holidays with the family of a college friend who lived nearby. Speaking of which, do you have plans for the holidays?"

"No." Jesse's stomach did a flip-flop. "Should I?"

"Absolutely. With us. In fact, why wait for the holidays. I can fly you home for a weekend anytime you'd like."

"Cool." Jesse bit her lip, almost blurting out, *Can I come home now?*

Homesickness still hit her at unexpected moments, like to-night. Emlyn's boyfriend had driven in for the weekend. Pinky was rendezvousing with her fiancé at his school. And Nita was in the city as usual. She was alone in the dorm for the week-end, again.

"Listen, baby. Anytime you feel like you could use a little TLC, you can always go see your grandparents in Philly. They still plan to come for Parents Weekend, right?"

"Oh, I better tell them about my out-of-town game." She wasn't yet ready for Simmons to know that she was one of *the* Philadelphia Morgans.

"Maybe they'd prefer to see you play. Rutgers is much closer to them than Simmons."

"Great idea, Mom!" The last thing she wanted was her grandparents walking about campus introducing themselves as the people whose name was on the new wing of the English department building. New Jersey would be neutral territory.

"Ok, honey, I need to go to bed. Call me anytime." Her mom sounded exhausted.

"Mom, things will get better."

She laughed. "They better!"

It was nearly midnight when Jesse signed on to her favorite college chat room.

Other than Emlyn and Pinky, most of her social scene was online these days with a group she'd met in the college chat room BiFace. In the beginning, the site seemed to be a to-tal screwup as members argued over whether BiFace would be about bisexual or biracial identity, with a small minority opting for both. That quickly split the site into sub-interest groups. She'd joined the BiFace subgroup Multiplicity.

In order to become a member, the moderator, CYphur, asked

candidates to define Multiplicity. They got only one chance and had thirty seconds to answer. Having had AP calculus she took a shot at it.

The word "multiplicity" is a mathematical term meaning "the number of values for which a given condition holds." However, as this site is for students with multiple racial and/or ethnic backgrounds, I guess it stands for Diversity.

CYphur: *Welcome!*

Her screen name was N_viz_able.

The group discussions seldom degenerated into the usual prelim hookup ritual of many other chat rooms because CYphur set its tone. She liked him for that, keeping the chat room from becoming just another site to troll for relationships. For instance, there were usually topics listed for discussion each day. Today's topic was: *Who is Black in a Multiplicity World?*

Judging by the few people still signed on, the discussion was about over.

She scrolled quickly through the text of the earlier conversations. Predictably, the sides had lined up with one for complete freedom to be me vs. you are what others say you are. A sample of text summed up the two sides.

Sucia_libra: *I am Puerto Rican yet I look black so to most white Americans I am black. You are what you are perceived to be.*

Esperantor: *I see that. I am Japanese and black. I even have an accent. Yet shop owners treat me like I just stepped off the corner.*

FunkUverrymuch: *F that! As an American Latina or Japanese American, the government says you're white, with all the privileges. The system is whack!*

Jesse debated a moment before she typed: *What if you don't look like what you are? I'm black but don't look it. Then what?*

CYphur: *If you got options, N_viz_able, why would you try to be black?*

Not trying.

CYphur: *You know what I mean, my half-Nubian sister.*

Jesse smiled. She'd hoped to catch CYphur's attention. *I don't think I do. Explain.*

CYphur: *You don't act black, sound black, look black. You have no half to be half black with.*

Jesse quickly typed: *How would you know how I act and sound?*

CYphur: *It's in your writing style. You're cute but you're not black cute.*

Jesse drummed her fingers on the keyboard in annoyance. She'd heard this backhanded compliment before. *Is that ghetto Black, hip hop black, or Aunt Jemima black I'm not? Just what sort of black is black to you? Obviously it's not smart, intellectual black. Sounds like you just dissed yourself!*

CYphur: *Ouch!*

FunkUverrymuch: *Can anyone join in? Or is this a private make out session between you two?*

Jesse laughed. So it wasn't just her imagination. She and CYphur often seemed to zero in on each other exclusively in the chat room. Revved for a debate, she typed: *I'm biracial like The Rock, Shemar Moore, Alicia Keys, Halle Berry, Tiger Woods, Jason Momoa, Zoe Kravitz, Vin Diesel, Barack Obama, Kamala Harris . . . the list of public faces for biracial identity gets longer every day.*

Sucia_libra: *Ask anybody, black or white, and they would say all those you named are maybe not black but definitely not white.*

What about Wentworth Miller?

FunkUverrymuch: *Who?*

Sucia_libra: *The cute guy on "Prison Break"? He's half black? No lie?*

"Gotcha!" Jesse murmured as she typed: *African and English. Wikipedia it.*

FunkUverrymuch: *What you see is what you get. He looks white, he sounds white, and he's playing white. He's white. Like N_viz_able.*

Jesse bit her lip: *What you see is what you want to see. You don't accept me, fine. I don't accept your view of me.*

FunkUverrymuch: *This is pointless.*

Sucia_libra: *Now we agree.*

Jesse watched as members of the group signed off, all but CYphur. Curious about what he would say now, she waited.

CYphur: *Looks like we're alone.*

She smiled. *Sorry if I ran them off.*

CYphur: *No, that's good. But you sound upset. Wanna share?*

Jesse took a deep breath. At least in this chat room she could be honest. *It's this requirement of either/or. I'm half black. I look all white. If I'm with black people I'm seen as the whitey hanging in the hood. If I'm with whites I feel like I'm cheating if I don't fess up. Why should I have to explain myself? Why am I always the "other" no matter who I am with?*

CYphur: *That's why we established Multiplicity. Here we can talk and exchange ideas about what it means to be us. Most people slide into the slot where they are born and drink the Kool-Aid. I enjoy the philosophical challenge of the human condition.*

Jesse nodded to herself. He was the most interesting person she had met but it wouldn't do to let him think he got to her.

Are you for real, bro?

CYphur: *How real would you like me to be?*

Jesse watched her cursor flash. That was a very good question that she didn't have an answer for yet. But! He let her call him a guy.

Just her luck. The most interesting guy she'd met so far was in cyberspace. He could be at any college on the East Coast. With her luck he was probably on the West Coast. It would be just too cliché to fall for a guy online. She was about to just sign off when he responded again.

CYphur: *You will figure it out. Bonan nokton!*

Jesse frowned at the last words before typing: *What's that mean?*

CYphur: *It's Esperanto for good night. I have aspirations for career assignments in second and third world nations as sweaty ambassador in cheap suit.*

LOL!

Chapter 20

The phone rang as Thea walked into the parsonage. She walked over and looked at the caller ID. Screen all calls, Xavier had said after her jailhouse experience the week before. Don't pick up from prisons or juvenile detention centers unless he's there. If they call right back or leave a message, it might be an emergency. Call him with the information. This, however, was an 866 number. Someone selling something she most definitely didn't want. She'd let the answering machine pick up.

She carried her weekend bag into the bedroom and then checked her watch. Xavier had been in Atlanta since Wednesday. It seemed she had beaten him home.

Home? She looked around to confirm that nothing had changed in the week since she'd last been here. Nothing had. This was not home. Not yet.

She sighed and pulled out the list she had been working on whenever she got the chance. Yes, she had added the leaking shower pan in the second bathroom. Mrs. Patterson had assured Xavier that the Pastoral Relations Committee would take up the matter of renovating the parsonage at their next scheduled meeting. So far she had filled three pages with problems to submit.

As a negotiator she knew better than to overwhelm the opposition, especially one predisposed to dislike her opinions. She had not had an opportunity to speak again with Hattie Patterson, who never seemed to be at home when she called. But she didn't doubt the woman would be her biggest detractor. So, a short list might go over better.

She walked from room to room evaluating her list. What was a bigger problem, the linoleum curling up from every corner of the kitchen or the worn-out furnishings? It occurred to her that she didn't need the Pastoral Relations Committee to replace furnishings. She could simply replace them with items from her home. Or better yet, buy new furnishings. Nothing expensive but serviceable items, appropriate for a minister. That way, she would not have to deprive herself of a kitchen table or bed in her own house.

That problem solved, she turned back to the matter of flooring. Definitely, carpeting was her first priority. It had to be the source of the unpleasant sour, musty odor that lived in every room of the house. Since this was an old house, it was possible that there would be hardwood floors beneath the carpet.

Still dressed in her business suit and heels, she pulled up the carpet in a corner of both the dining and the living rooms to discover that, yes, there were hardwood floors beneath. This was the first positive thing about the house. She preferred wood floors. Surely the Pastoral Relations Committee would prefer the less expensive alternative of sanding and refinishing existing floors to re-carpeting.

To prove her point, she decided it would be prudent to get a bid. After checking the yellow pages to discover that no floor refinishers were listed, she called the Brown sisters and got a name.

⟡

"Dogs," the hardware store owner pronounced two hours later. He pointed to the overlapping brownish rings on the pad under the living room carpet that he had rolled back. "That's dog urine."

Thea shuddered. "It must have been a big dog."

He looked at her with a little smile. "Reverend Dawson's family had four kids, two Dalmatians, and a boxer. He was always coming into my store needing a new lock or hinge or toilet plunger. Always wondered how they managed with all them dogs in the house. Looks to be at least one had a leaky bladder. When you get that happening, the others will start marking their territory, too. That's when you got a problem."

"I'll say!" Thea tried to get her head around the idea of a house where dogs, plural, peed on the carpet day after day. Cora had suggested Mr. Middleton, the hardware store owner, who also did floor resurfacing on the side. She'd dropped by his store, and as luck would have it, he was free to give her an estimate.

"Now I can't promise to get this all out." He bent over and folded back the padding to reveal huge bleached places on the wood floorboards. I'll do what I can. And you could stain them but it might take unevenly, what with the urine soaked in."

"Can you get the smell out?"

He nodded. "Taking out them rugs and pads is all that it will take. And a good airing." He looked about. "I never was in here before. You got a lot of good work to do."

"You don't know the half."

"If you don't mind my asking, what's a lady like you doing in St. Hurricane's parsonage? They hire you to redecorate?"

"No." She waited a beat. "I'm married to the minister."

"Do tell?" He blinked, his faded blue irises disappearing as his pupils expanded in interest. He looked her up and down and then again, trying to guess she-knew-what. "They got a white minister now?"

"No."

He blinked again and then a big grin broke over his reddened features. "Well, sir. How about that! He's one lucky devil, you tell him I said that."

"So am I." She cracked a smile. This is how rumor starts. "About the floors. How soon can you get in here to resurface them?"

"Let me think." He pulled at his jaw as he roamed from room to room measuring spaces with a glance. Finally he paused in the living room again. "I can do all these floors for eight hundred."

"That sounds reasonable." It was a steal, and Thea knew it. The charge would have been eight hundred dollars per room in Dallas. "When can you start?"

"As soon as next Tuesday, on account of another job I had fell through. You'll have to clear all the rooms before we start. And you'll need to let them floors dry two full days before you move anything heavy back in."

"Perfect. We'll be bringing in new furnishings." She looked

around in calculation. She would call Goodwill or the Salvation Army, or a shelter, to take the furnishings, if they would have them. "Wait. I won't be in town next Tuesday. And Reverend Thornton is away on a business matter, too. I'll have to check with someone at St. Hurricane's about letting you in. Oh, I know. Deacon Jacobs can be here."

He eyed her sprung sofa covetously. "I know a couple of people who'd take most all of this off your hands. What are you selling?"

She smiled. "All of it."

∽∞∽

Sunday school had changed. Bible in hand, Thea walked toward the classroom off the breezeway that led from the back of the church to the fellowship hall. When she was young, the morning Bible lessons were for the children. Now it seemed that toddlers through the elderly were part of Sunday school classes.

Xavier put his hand on her back when she stopped outside the classroom door. "Don't worry. Since this will be your first visit, you can sit in back and observe."

"I hope you're right." As she reached for the knob he stepped back. She turned her head toward him. "Aren't you coming in, too?"

"This is the adult women's class. The adult men meet down the hall."

Thea wondered why it was called the adult women's class, as if there were any other kind of woman. Then she stepped through the door. Gray heads greatly outnumbered heads of any other hair color. "Adult" was a polite word for "old." They sat in a circle but there was no doubting who the class leader was. Mrs. Hattie Patterson's chair was placed at the back of the room, with a chalkboard behind her. Today her elaborate hat matched a pale blue suit with rhinestone buttons that made her seem regal.

"Mrs. Thornton! This is a surprise." Thea couldn't be sure whether Hattie's tone implied amazement or consternation. Her expression said both.

Hattie didn't rise from her chair but she did turn to the large woman seated next to her. "Mrs. Meeks, would you be so kind as to relinquish your chair to our honored guest?"

Thea caught the barb. *Guest? In my husband's church? I don't think so!* But no, she hadn't come to argue but to spread the love.

She smiled brightly at the large woman she recognized as the one in white eyelet she had sat next to on her first Sunday. "No, no, Mrs. Meeks, don't move. I'll be fine right here." She spied a chair outside the circle and took it.

"Now, Mrs. Thornton, Mrs. Meeks insists that you join us. Don't you, Jessica?"

"I guess I do." It was an awkward business for the woman whose feet spilled out of her too-small shoes. Thea watched in helpless annoyance as women on either side of Mrs. Meeks offered their assistance to help her to her feet.

"Thank you. That's very kind of you, Mrs. Meeks." Thea offered an apologetic smile to the woman as they passed. Mrs. Meeks gave her a slight nod but her eyes were dark and she'd begun to perspire from her exertions.

Someone behind Thea murmured, "She didn't have much choice." She wasn't the only one who thought Hattie was a bit high-handed in her treatment of Mrs. Meeks.

Reluctantly, Thea took the chair to the left of Hattie.

Hattie cleared her throat. "Today's scripture comes from the book of Daniel chapter six, verses four through twenty-seven."

Thea's heart dropped into her shoes. Aware of her shortcomings as a student of the Bible she had asked Xavier which scripture to study for this class. He'd told her it would be the story of Job.

Hattie continued. "It's the story of Daniel in the lions' den."

As Hattie read aloud the selected passage, Thea followed in her Bible, breathing a little easier as the story unfolded. This was one she knew. Sort of.

Hattie paused, right after the verse where the king frees Daniel from the lions' den. "Who would like to start the discussion this morning?"

Thea kept her head down. *Better to be silent and be thought a fool than to open your mouth and remove all doubt.*

"Mrs. Thornton?"

Thea raised her gaze from her Bible and saw Hattie Patterson staring at her with a mirthless smile. "Would you please start the discussion, Mrs. Thornton?"

"Certainly." Thea's professional attitude of "fake it until you can make it" kicked in. She would begin the conversation then quickly hand it off to someone else.

Thea looked around the ring of expectant faces until she spied Cora's and Hortense's kindly smiles. Ah, allies. "I remember the story. My grandmother told it to my sister and me when we were children. It reminded me of a Golden Book I had just borrowed from the library. The book was the Aesop fable about Androcles and the lion. In the fable Androcles stops to help a lion who has a painful thorn in his paw. They meet years later in circumstances like Daniel's. As punishment, Androcles has been thrown in a lion's den. But the lion remembers the good deed the man performed for him and does not eat Androcles. This is seen as a miracle and Androcles is freed."

"Surely you're not comparing a child's fairy tale to God's word?" Hattie's tone implied sacrilege if not outright heresy.

The ring of women glanced from Hattie to Thea, their eyes wider than before.

"Actually, Mrs. Patterson, I was giving you the context for my memory of the story of Daniel. However"—Thea couldn't quite believe she wasn't leaving well enough alone—"fables were created as a way for many ancient peoples to better understand their world. Just as biblical passages serve as guideposts for Jews and Christians. The moral of Androcles is that gratitude is the sign of noble souls."

"Pagan myth has no place in this discussion." Hattie's nostrils flared in indignation. "Daniel is saved by angels, because of his belief in God, a very different thing altogether. We are discussing a Christian story."

George Bernard Shaw, a Noble Prize winner, managed to construct a very popular play about Christianity out of the fable! A forgotten bit of knowledge from a college lit class popped into her head. But that would be showing off. She resisted the urge to say more than "If you say so."

Clearly dissatisfied with Thea's reply, Hattie turned to the Brown sisters. "Cora, will you read the last of the pertinent passage again for us?"

"I'd be delighted." Cora peeked at Thea before she began. "'They brought Daniel and threw him into the lions' den. The king said to Daniel, "May your God, whom you serve continually, rescue you!"'"

Thea stared down into her lap, pretending to read but really tuning the whole thing out. Did anyone else besides Hattie Patterson have a say in matters at St. Hurricane? She might be respected and even revered, but at heart, the woman was a bit of a bully.

For instance, Hattie used repetition the way Thea's fourth-grade teacher taught the times tables. One did it over and over until after a while, the answer simply popped into a person's head without conscious thought. However, that method of teaching the Bible didn't allow for independent thought or interpretation. Xavier liked to say that Jesus had used example and allegory to teach because it required one to think for oneself. And that made one responsible for one's choices—the basis of free will.

Her thoughts drifted back to Cora's voice and what she heard didn't soothe her.

"'At the king's command, the men who had falsely accused Daniel were brought in and thrown into the lions' den, along with their wives and children. And before they reached the floor of the den, the lions overpowered them and crushed all their bones.'"

Thea couldn't resist speaking up. "It seems cruel to punish the wives and the children for the sins of their husbands and fathers."

Hattie's lips tightened, as if she refused to dignify Thea's concerns with an answer.

A younger woman in Senegalese braids whom Thea hadn't noticed until now spoke up. Their gazes met and Thea didn't have to be told. This was Lola, Mrs. Patterson's grandniece, who'd walked out on her at the reception after calling her a white woman. "The sins of the fathers shall be visited upon the children and the children's children!" she proclaimed in a carrying voice.

Mrs. Meeks nodded and hummed a little to herself. "And it came to pass after all thy wickedness, woe, woe unto thee! saith the Lord God."

"I know that's right! Praise God!" Lola added and waved her hand in praise.

Thea held Lola's hostile gaze. "That doesn't sound like something Jesus would have done."

"I agree." Hortense Brown clicked her dentures as she thumbed through her Bible pages, and then smiled as she pointed a finger to the passage she wanted. "Ezekiel chapter eighteen verse twenty says, 'The soul that sinneth, it shall die. The son shall not bear the iniquity of the father, neither shall the father bear the iniquity of the son.'"

Cora nodded. "Sister's right. The sins of the fathers are not to be visited upon the children."

Hattie's mouth tightened. "We must assume, then, that the families spoken of in Daniel were involved to some degree in the troubles that landed Daniel in prison."

Thea leaned forward with interest. "You're suggesting that perhaps the children referred to were not minors but possibly adult children who engaged in the same kinds of sinful activities as their parents?"

Lola leaped up. "Who can fathom the will of God but God? Only He knows what His purpose is!"

"Death isn't always a punishment, though we oftentimes think of it that way." This extraordinary speech came from Mrs. Meeks. "Maybe they were being delivered to God to be spared the troubles that would've befallen them had they been left behind." She eyed the circle. "You know how folks can be, once a big shot is brought low."

"They and theirs become despised," another woman agreed.

The women in the circle began talking all at once, as if they'd been freed for recess from Hattie's reform-school tactics. Thea smiled to herself. So it wasn't that they didn't have opinions, they just didn't have a chance to express them.

"Ladies! Ladies!" Hattie looked sternly around the circle until every voice was silenced. "It's all well and good to have opinions but we must maintain decorum." She turned to Thea. "Since Mrs. Thornton has been instrumental in today's conversation, perhaps she will summarize the lesson for us."

Thea quickly shifted through her thoughts. "I would like to emphasize this. That we must be certain when this passage is read to children that it is made absolutely clear to them that no child should ever be punished for the sin of a parent, or any other adult. They are blameless, even if the adult forced them to commit the sin."

"Well said, Theadora!" Cora nodded as the other ladies added their "amen" and "praise be the Lord."

Thea met Hattie's considering stare, as if the possibility of Thea gaining respect with some members of St. Hurricane had not occurred to her before.

⚭

The ladies of St. Hurricane, by tradition, prepared Sunday dinner for the minister's family. At first Thea didn't know whether to be grateful or resent the taking over of her wifely duty. But the chicken and dumplings were so good, she decided to be grateful. And her husband was full and happy.

"I'm very proud of you. You did well today." Xavier hunched forward over an empty plate that minutes ago had been filled with chicken and dumplings. Deacon Jacobs, Xavier confided, made a good breakfast, but otherwise was a terrible cook. That is why he seldom ate what the man prepared.

"So you heard about Sunday school?"

He nodded. "You made them question their assumptions. There is no true faith if it cannot withstand scrutiny."

His satisfaction with her performance filled in the last tiny corners of her doubt. Now was the time to tell him her other plans. "Since you think I'm wonderful, this is probably a good time to bring up something that's on my mind. I'd like to use it to make some changes here. Homey changes." She didn't want to hit him with her full agenda or he'd know how much she disliked, well, *everything*.

He smiled. "I like the sound of that. But I don't know what we can afford."

She was ready. "I keep a fund set aside for small emergencies and home repair. I'll use that."

"Isn't that for your home?"

"Wherever you are is home." She saw his eyes widen and then darken and knew she would not be refused.

But when they were in the bedroom she noticed that he was watching her as she began changing into her pj's. but it wasn't with erotic interest. He was assessing her as he often did when he wanted inside her private thoughts in a way he seldom allowed her into his. "You sure you're all right with everything?"

"Absolutely. Why?"

"No reason." He chucked his shirt before he spoke again. "There's a youth convention in Memphis the last three days of next week. I'm thinking of going."

"Oh?" She didn't want to sound eager to have him gone but the floors were being done next week. If he were out of town the timing would be perfect.

"I don't know. The more I do the more I'm asked to do." He sighed like a man caught in a dilemma. "There's no bottom to need."

Thea stopped undressing to look at him. "What's going on? You didn't say how your week went in Atlanta."

"Didn't I?" His silence stretched out until her cell rang. She didn't move as his mouth flattened out in a straight line. But then he said, "Better get that."

It was the new junior associate calling. "Monsoon? The client needs to off-load that methanol ASAP. The extra cost? If his ship is damaged in port he'll be fined, per contract, far more for contaminating local fishing grounds. But you know that because, as his contract analyst, it's your job to, right?" She noticed Xavier glance up at her tone but she couldn't help it. "You're welcome."

She put her phone down. "If they'd let me choose our new associate, I wouldn't be hand-holding an unprepared attorney through routine problem-solving."

Xavier's black gaze took her in wholly, drawing attention to the fact she was wearing only her bra and panties. "Want to talk about it?"

She shook her head and moved to lean her head against his bare chest. "We have so little time as it is, I don't want to spoil it with work."

Xavier slipped her arms about her waist, cupping her shoulders in his hands. "How can I make it better for you?"

"More of this." The only thing that would help was if she could be in Dallas full-time and he could be there with her.

That wasn't going to happen. There was no reason to torture themselves with the *if*.

He slipped one hand up the back of her neck and began lightly massaging the tightened muscles there. "So now, when do you think you'll be back?"

"Thursday, I hope. Friday at the latest."

"Fly into Memphis on Friday and let me pick you up. We'll do something special."

She lifted her head from his chest, let her palms slide up his back, feeling the heat of his skin through hers. "Really?"

He looked down at the cleavage revealed by her lacy bra. "How about I rent a room at the Peabody so we can sleep on a decent mattress for a change?"

She went up on tiptoe to kiss his chin. "You can't afford all that on a minister's salary."

He bent to kiss her on the neck, their bodies molding into one another by mutual consent. "For my wife, I will find a way."

"The Peabody," Thea murmured much later as she snuggled against her husband's back. "Isn't that the hotel with parading ducks?"

"*Uh huh.*" He was half-asleep, poor baby. She'd worn him out.

She curved her body to fit his. "Just as long as they don't have chickens."

❧

The darkness was threaded through by the music of a jazz station from New Orleans. Xavier had suggested the radio as white noise to blot out whatever sounds they sometimes heard in the wee hours before dawn. Only she couldn't sleep tonight.

As the phone rang she automatically reached to mute the radio while Xavier, suddenly alert, picked up.

"Hello. Yes, this is Reverend Thornton. When? Where are they now?" She switched on the bedside light. He reached for nearby paper and pen and began to scribble. "Say that again. Yes, I know where that is. Yes, I'll be right there. Of course. Don't leave until then."

He gave up a heavy sigh as he hung up the phone and then reached for his Bible as he sat on the side of the bed.

Thea sat up and put her arms around him. "What's wrong, baby?"

He took her hand and squeezed it. His voice was hoarse with sleep and something else. "Eighteen-wheeler hit a stalled car off Highway 69. Eight-month-old Yvonne Grant who I just baptized last month is dead. I have to find the words to comfort her mother."

There are no words for that. So Thea just pressed herself to her husband's back and offered up a silent prayer.

Chapter 21

S urprise!" Thea flung open the parsonage front door. After a simply wonderful night with Xavier spent in Little Rock, she once more felt like a newlywed.

Xavier paused on the threshold of the parsonage, surprise written large on his face. "Theadora, what have you done?"

"You like it?" She smiled as she surveyed the gleaming surface of their refinished living room floor. "I've had the bedroom and dining room repainted, too."

"It's very nice but how did you manage it?"

"Deacon Jacobs helped me."

She set her briefcase on the floor because the room was empty of furniture. It had been a week since she left instructions for the changes and she was eager to see how it all had turned out. "I wanted it to be a surprise. I haven't seen the results yet either. I'm so pleased. Are you?"

Xavier nodded. "It's wonderful."

The sound of solid footsteps of a woman in sensible shoes startled them both. Then Mrs. Patterson appeared at the front door.

"Hello, Mrs. Patterson. How are you?" Thea smiled at her nemesis. Not even the unwelcome appearance of this woman could ruin her joy with the transformation of the floors. "What brings you here today?"

"Mrs. Thornton. Reverend Thornton." Hattie inclined her head. "It was brought to our attention only today that certain liberties were being taken with the parsonage. We came over to see for ourselves."

She stared at Thea while Thea wondered if that was a royal "we" for there was no one else here. "What do you think you are doing here?"

"We decided to make a few changes, for comfort's sake." She swept out an arm. "Aren't the floors lovely? Who knew they would shine up so well?"

"Where are all the furnishings?" Hattie asked suspiciously.

Xavier looked at Thea with lifted brows.

Thea wished she could have explained herself to him first, alone, but there was no help for it. "I sold the things I could and gave the rest away to Goodwill. The money and receipts from the sales will go in the offering plate on Sunday."

At that moment Xavier's cell phone rang. He pulled it from his pocket, glanced at the caller ID, and then looked up. "Please excuse me, ladies."

He offered Thea an encouraging glance then stepped out the front door onto the porch, seeking privacy.

Mrs. Patterson took a step toward Thea, her voice pitched low. "How dare you!"

Thea crossed her arms, deliberately looking down her nose at the woman. What other reaction could she have expected? "I would seem to be perfectly within my right to rearrange furniture in the place where I live."

The older woman puckered up. "Rearrange? You admit you sold and gave away things that did not belong to you."

For the first time Thea felt a quiver of uncertainty. "The furniture was old and more than past its prime. I'm sure they gave their best to previous residents."

Hattie turned toward the hallway that led to the kitchen. "Mrs. Meeks! Please, come in here."

Today Mrs. Meeks wore a dark green dress and a red wig. She entered the living room at a slow, rolling pace. "Did you call me, Hattie?"

"I did, Jessica." Hattie rolled her shoulders in indignation. "Reverend Thornton's wife has given away every stick of furniture in the parsonage. Every piece!"

Mrs. Meeks's jaw dropped. "You gave away my grandmother Smith's china cabinet? It was precious to me."

"China cabinet?" For a second Thea was totally stumped. Then she remembered the small breakfront with the smashed glass doors and broken shelf she had found shoved in a corner of the detached garage that neither she nor Xavier used. "It suffered damage at some point. It's in the garage." Some things couldn't even be given away.

Mrs. Meeks turned to Mrs. Patterson. "I didn't see it the day of Reverend Thornton's reception and I did wonder. Who damaged it?"

The two women stared at Thea as if she stood before them holding sledgehammer evidence of her guilt.

Thea held her ground. "Since I didn't arrive in town until the day Mrs. Meeks noticed it was missing, I can't answer that."

Hattie raked Thea with a cold look. "Before you took it upon yourself to sell or give away a single piece you might have asked every church member who donated their belongings if they wanted them back. Some of the items were precious heirlooms and rare antiques. But, of course, you've already said you thought they were worthless."

Thea clenched her jaw. Most of what church members donated was ready for the trash can. Both of them knew it.

"This is my fault, Mrs. Patterson." When Xavier spoke he surprised them all for no one had noticed his return. For a large man, he could move with surprising agility.

He moved to Thea's side and put a hand on her shoulder. "I asked my wife to do a little redecorating to make this, our first home, more personal. She's a very talented woman and took me at my word."

You don't need to defend what I did. Thea didn't say that aloud because Mrs. Patterson always gazed at Xavier as if he hung the moon. And right now even she, the brass-balls lawyer, could see that she needed the advantage of a good diplomatic defense more than she needed to prove herself right.

"I'm sure, Reverend, you didn't expect to come home to an empty house."

"As a matter of fact," Thea answered, "new furnishings will be delivered this afternoon. I couldn't expect St. Hurricane to furnish the parsonage a second time."

Hattie blinked. "You are replacing a houseful of furniture?"

"That's going to be very expensive!" Jessica Meeks's expression said how impressed she was by that idea.

"I am paying for them." Thea noticed Xavier trying to catch her eye but she went on quickly. "Now that I understand how precious the things I disposed of were, I'd be happy to attempt to locate every item." Thea turned to Mrs. Meeks. "You may take your grandmother Smith's china cabinet with you. The

Reverend and Deacon Jacobs will be happy to load it into the deacon's trunk and follow you home."

Mrs. Meeks blinked. "Oh, well, now. Let's see. I don't believe I have anywhere for it. If it's damaged as much as you say . . ."

"Would you like for me to dispose of it?" Thea didn't try to hide her satisfaction.

Mrs. Meeks looked to Mrs. Patterson for guidance. "I suppose . . ."

Hattie turned to Xavier and held out a key, all sweetness and smiles. "Would you mind, Reverend Xavier, bringing my car to the front of the drive?"

Xavier glanced at Thea. She shrugged. The woman wasn't going to strangle her if he left the room. "My pleasure, Mrs. Patterson."

Hattie waited until he departed then said with a brittle tone, "I didn't wish to embarrass you before your husband, Mrs. Thornton, but this residence and all that is within it is the property of St. Hurricane. You had no right to alter it or its contents in any manner without consent."

That was one straw too many for Thea's good mood. "Perhaps you should write a manifesto so that future ministers' wives will know what is expected of them at St. Hurricane."

Hattie's eyes lit up. "Ministers' wives usually know their place. You, it seems, are the exception. Since you are expressing your ignorance, we try to patronize our own people, black people, when we do business in this town. I understand you went to Middleton Hardware to have the floors done."

"Mrs. Cora Brown recommended him." She waited a beat before making a concession. "In the future, I will consult the Pastoral Relations Committee."

Hattie glanced around. "We will expect when your husband's tenure is over that you leave as many pieces of furniture as you have seen fit to deprive us of."

"You can be certain we will leave things in better condition than we found them."

The two women eyed one another, taking measure before the next match, which both were certain would occur.

∽∞∾

"Precious antiques, my Aunt Fanny!" Thea stood hands on hips in the middle of her shiny new floors. "That was just an attempt to embarrass me."

Xavier wagged his head. "You move a little quick, Thea, even for me."

"I wanted to surprise you. I should have counted on Mrs. Patterson snooping. But I had no idea they'd be so hateful about it!"

"*Nawgh*. They just want to be respected. They know those things weren't worth much. But they gave them, and they didn't have to, and they want that acknowledged."

"So, I've failed again." Thea puffed out her cheeks in weariness. "I can't seem to step right in this town."

"Some of it is small-town southern ways of thinking. It's like this. Every item has value when you don't have much."

"When you put it like that, I suppose I should reimburse them for the furniture."

"I wouldn't do that. We'll have a newly furnished parsonage to leave them. That will satisfy." Xavier closed the gap between them and touched her cheek. "If you send each member of the committee a homemade dish, they won't even remember the problem by Sunday."

She made a face at the idea of baking. She barely had time to breathe. "How about flowers?"

He took her hand. "I should have explained this before. You can't toss your money around here, even if you earned it. People work very hard for what little they can accumulate. They don't begrudge others that have more, if they earned it fairly. But it grates when those with more make that apparent by buying things and giving gifts they can't afford to give in return. If we make the parsonage look better with our own money, they start to think it's our way of saying they can't provide adequately for their minister."

"That's not true in your case. Everyone already knows you're worth millions."

He grinned. "These days I'm just a lowly pastor living on a monthly stipend. You can appreciate the difference."

She nodded reluctantly. "Now what?"

"You need to keep a lower profile with the things you do, that's all."

There went her plans for a new oven. "You make it sound like I drove through town in an Escalade with diamond grillwork."

"Now that might impress them in an entirely different way." He chuckled and hugged her shoulders. "Try moving a little slower, that's all. And ask for advice from Mrs. Patterson and the rest. Even if you know the answers."

Thea resisted voicing the complaint that as long as she lived here not even her home was her own. Renters had more privacy and freedom than those who lived in St. Hurricane's parsonage.

She was good at some things, like her job in the barracuda

corporate world. However, the scheming of small-town life seemed beyond her. "I've messed up again, haven't I?"

"You're doing fine, Theadora. You were trying to help. And I appreciate it. But you are going to have to win over Mrs. Patterson. You must surely find a way."

Thea shook her head. "It could be easier just to find and relay that horrid carpet."

"The floors look good." He grinned. "Did you happen to throw out our mattress, too?"

She looked sheepish. "I did."

He nodded. "All right then! My shoulder and back owe you a debt of gratitude. Now let's see, how can I repay you?" His eyes sparkled.

She laughed. "I was hoping the furniture I ordered in Little Rock would arrive today. Are there any hotels in this town?"

He sent her a glowing look from under his lashes. "A reasonable facsimile."

Her cell danced in her pocket. "Hold that thought."

She answered and listened for a moment. "When? How serious is it? Yes. I understand. Yes. Thank you."

Thea looked up at Xavier, tears forming in her eyes before she could fully comprehend what she'd heard. "It's my boss, Ron Cullum. He collapsed and was rushed to the hospital this morning. He's in intensive care and not expected to live."

Xavier nodded. "I'll call the airline and get us on the first flight out of Little Rock."

Chapter 22

N ever in all my born days!"

Hattie felt a complete fool. The Pastoral Relations Committee had just voted to accept the Thorntons' offer to renovate the parsonage. Despite her very-well-thought-out arguments against it, written in her fountain-pen script on notepaper so that she could refer to them in case she forgot one or two points.

She had tried unsuccessfully for years to get the committee to allocate funds to fix up the parsonage. It was an eyesore. Everyone said so, but no one had been willing to spend a dime toward changing that fact. However, they were happy to allow an interloper like Theadora Thornton to walk in and take over. More than that, they voted to make plumbing repairs and even replace the air conditioner, because she had given the committee the monies she made on the furnishings and then offered to share the cost!

Just because she was Miss Big City got bling didn't mean she should be tossing it in the faces of the good, hardworking people.

"Disgraceful! Completely unacceptable!"

Lola looked back over her shoulder as her aunt walked into the room. She was stretched out on the sofa in the TV room in curlers and pajamas with a glass of iced tea in her hand. "What's wrong, Auntie?"

Hattie surveyed her niece in distaste. "Don't you ever get dressed, child?"

Lola swung her legs off the sofa and sat up. "What for? Nowhere to go."

"I'm sure you could find plenty of good works to do if you sought them out. What happened to that position as teacher's aide at Tyrell's school?"

She screwed up her face. "They don't pay. And they expect me to keep regular hours. I'm not that kind of fool."

She eyed her grandniece with disappointment. "If God had seen fit to present Obadiah and me with a child, I hope I would have done as well by her as I have tried to do by you and your son. But the time has come when you must fend for yourself."

Lola's head snapped away from the reality show she'd been watching. "What do you mean?"

"I mean you need to find a job that brings in at least as much as you use up living here. Tyrell's about to eat me out of house and home."

"He's a growing boy. He needs to eat. If his no-account father would just send us some money."

"No-account, did you say? Tyrell's father has a job. You could still be living with him and enjoying all the benefits of his labor."

"He doesn't want me."

"How do you know?"

Lola looked down. "He filed for divorce this week."

Hattie thought about that. In her experience there was only

one reason a man filed for divorce first. "I've never pushed for an answer before but I think it's time I insist. Exactly why did you leave him?"

"I didn't." Lola hung her head and mumbled low, "He put me out."

Hattie sighed. "Please don't tell me another man was involved."

"Fine. I won't."

"You gave up a marriage to a good man with a regular income for what? Sex?"

Lola reared back. "The way you say that makes me think you don't know what you're talking about. Back in the day, didn't women ever want to get some just because it's that good?"

"You fool!" Hattie dropped her purse on a chair as she came forward. "Women have been making fools of themselves forever over some man claiming what he's got is *that* good. Let me tell you something! It's not that good. It's never that good! Look at where you are and what you've lost, and tell me it was that good?"

Lola rolled her head back on her neck and glared from the corners of her eyes but she didn't deny her aunt's words.

Satisfied that she'd made her point, Hattie said, "Do you still love your husband?"

"That doesn't even come into it."

"Because if you do, you need to start thinking about how to show him that you are worth taking back."

Interest flickered in Lola's expression. "How would I do that?"

"First, show some responsibility for yourself and your son. Get a job."

"I tried all the beauty shops. They are full up."

"Do you type?"

"Yes. And I can operate a computer. Tyrell showed me how."

"Excellent! Mrs. Jenkins has been our church secretary for years but her eyes are getting bad. Reverend Xavier is so much busier than Reverend Samuel ever was. She can't keep up and would like to retire."

"How much does it pay?"

"More than you make at present. You need an income to show your husband that you're serious about working things out."

"I didn't say that I want to keep him. In fact, I don't." But Lola's words didn't convince even herself. "So if I was interested in a job, what sort of job is it?"

Pleased by this concession, Hattie walked over and sat down next to her niece. "I need a trustworthy person to be my eyes and ears into Reverend Xavier's life at the parsonage. There are things going on that the Pastoral Relations Committee should know about."

Lola crossed her arms. "You got Deacon Jacobs for that."

"Unfortunately, Deacon Jacobs is so taken with Mrs. Thornton that he's of little use to me—us. How would you like a part-time position at the parsonage, too?"

"Doing what? And don't think I'm going to be a domestic."

"Deacon Jacobs will continue to see to the housekeeping, laundry, and shopping. But meals have never been Deacon Jacobs's strong suit. I'm certain Reverend Xavier would appreciate a woman's touch in the kitchen. He has allowed several times how much he misses his wife's cooking when she's out of town."

Lola's eyes lit up. "For real? I can work for Reverend Xavier and get paid twice?"

"The church doesn't have money for two part-time jobs." Hattie considered her next words carefully. "However, I'd be willing to continue to house and feed you and Tyrell to make up the difference. That way what you make as church secretary will stretch a bit further. I will, however, expect results."

Lola reached for her glass of iced tea. "What kind of results?"

Hattie was shrewd enough to know that her grandniece was the kind who would blab whatever she knew to others. And Lola's dislike of Mrs. Thornton was, if anything, stronger than her own. What she was considering attempting she couldn't share with anyone, not even with Earline.

"The Pastoral Relations Committee needs to know what changes Mrs. Thornton is making to the parsonage. We are accountable for these things at tax time."

"That's all?"

Hattie ignored the question. "You can begin tomorrow."

She didn't trust Mrs. Thornton. She suspected that fixing up the parsonage was just the first step in her campaign to show her husband how unappreciated he was at St. Hurricane. He was seldom in Pine Grove during the week. He must be spending his days with her in Dallas.

For a town that didn't even have a movie theater, the spiritual lives of its community could take up an extraordinary amount of a minister's time. There were births and weddings and funerals, visits to the sick, even trips to hospitals in nearby counties. There were marriages to be refereed, teen counseling to be done. The prison load alone took up two days of many a pastor's week. When Obadiah was alive, bless him, he went once a week to the city and county jails and once every other week to the state or a federal facility where parishioners had incarcerated family members. And once a week he spent time at the county juvenile detention center, where mostly boys who should be in school getting ready for their real lives were already caught up in situations likely to end their time on earth before they were of legal age.

Reverend Xavier wasn't tending to half those duties.

Hattie's perfectly arched brows knitted in irritation. That was his wife's fault, drawing him away from the very people who needed him most. Playing Delilah in her short skirts and expensive clothes! Spending money like water because she had it! And then, coming into Sunday school with tales of pagan ways while flouting sound Christian doctrine. The woman was a menace. She had to go!

She passed Tyrell's room on her way to change from her street clothes into something appropriate for working in the garden. Curious about why a healthy boy should be closed up inside on a bright afternoon, she stepped in to see what was going on.

He was folded up like a pretzel on his bed, peering at the screen of the laptop balanced on his crossed legs. She didn't know a thing about computers but she knew it was just foolishness for Lola to spend money she didn't have to spare to get him a computer. "What are you doing, son?"

"I'm checking out the Pine Grove Instagram page. They got pictures of Reverend Xavier on here."

Hattie nodded and smiled. "Yes, Reverend Thornton is having a positive influence on the souls of Pine Grove, and so quickly."

"They ain't talking about him on account of their souls," Tyrell snickered. "I'ma tell you true, Auntie. Way some of these girls talking in this chat room! 'Reverend X' is what they call him. As in X-rated. That's 'cause he's got them thinking about more than prayers in their beds at night! *Ow!*" He ducked but he'd already been popped on the back of the head.

Hattie scowled at him. "You better pray God doesn't strike you dead for talking about a holy man that way."

"No minister true to his calling ever kissed a woman like he's doing in these pictures." Tyrell called up some informal shots from Xavier's ball-playing days. In them he has his arms around a series of hot-looking women. "Wait, now, here's the one you'll like. He's all up on her, too."

The photo showed the new Reverend and Mrs. Thornton sharing the traditional end of the wedding ceremony kiss. That was not what shocked Hattie. It was the poor judgment that allowed the photo to be taken, considering that the groom was her new pastor.

"My husband, God rest his soul, and I never so much as held hands in public."

"He sounds punked," Tyrell muttered low.

Unsure of what her great-nephew meant, Hattie ignored him.

"Now look here, Auntie, at salaries for corporate lawyers." Tyrell pointed to a new screen he'd brought up. "I can see why the rev's with Miss Light and Bright. With that kinda money coming in, I'd be all up in her shit! *Ow!* Damn, Aunt— *Oww!*"

He seemed as surprised by the second shot to the back of his head as he was the first.

"You know I don't allow profanity in my house, Tyrell!" Hattie shook her hand to stop its stinging. In more ways than one, that boy had a hard head! "I don't intend to repeat myself again. Understood?"

Tyrell scowled at her but nodded.

Hattie gave him a long look. She prayed and worried over the child. She truly did. Angry all the time, seldom speaking, holed up in his room on this computer, he had all the makings of a hoodlum. There wasn't much she could do about his mother's attitude, but he needed a male mentor and role model.

Lola stuck her head in the doorway. "It's eleven forty-five. I gotta do a friend's weave at noon. Tyrell, turn that computer off for a while." She started pulling rollers out of her hair as she hurried on down the hall.

Hattie watched as Tyrell, instead, pulled up a video game called *Gangbanging*. Once the trailer began, thugs talking X-rated trash popped up on the screen, jamming automatic weapons in one another's faces and pulling the triggers.

"Oh no!" Hattie leaned over and placed both hands over the screen. "Turn that off this instant!"

Tyrell glanced up at her as if to gauge whether or not she was serious. Realizing that she was, he rolled his eyes, sprawled back on his bed, and hit the exit button.

"Tyrell, you worry me." All she knew to do with her worry was to put him to good use. "Now you come help me with the lawn. I'll have Earline set out glasses of lemonade for us for when we're done."

Tyrell grumbled something too low for her to hear, but Hattie suspected it had to do with the fact that she owned an old-fashioned push mower and expected him to use it.

"It's forward-thinking to be green," Reverend Thornton had said in approval when he'd dropped by and noticed Tyrell cutting her lawn two weeks before.

She didn't know about green. What she knew was that

young men needed ways to work off their excess energy until they were too tired to get in trouble. Tyrell, in particular, had a lot of excess energy.

Later that afternoon, she made a call on Mrs. Meeks, then Mrs. Rafferty, and then the town gossip, Mrs. Clark. With each she casually mentioned the fact that while Mrs. Thornton did seem a good sort, one had to judge by what she did more than what she said. She was free enough with her spending "for St. Hurricane" when it benefited her as well. But where was the proof of her tithing when it didn't?

As for Sunday school, did one really think it appropriate to quote other texts as if they were equal to the Bible?

A seed dropped here and there . . .

Chapter 23

Emlyn wandered around Jesse's dorm room, glancing at various items. "What's this?"

Jesse shrugged, her eyes not leaving her European lit textbook. The Ladyhawkes had played ten games in the past three weeks, three of them on the road, and her studying was suffering. "It was shoved under the door when I came in this afternoon."

"Why didn't you open it?" She picked up the elaborate invitation that unfolded like an origami creation. "Oh my God! You're being rushed!"

"Hm?"

"Gamma Gamma Mu! You've got a special invite to them!"

Jesse kept her head down. "So what?"

"To be considered Gamma Glamour Girl material?" Emlyn made it sound as if Jesse must be stupid. "The dorm must be flooded with them." Jesse's voice dripped sarcasm. "You got one, didn't you, Pinky?"

"In my dreams." Pinky unfolded from her Lotus position on the floor just outside Jesse's room. "Not everyone gets dirty rushing invites."

Emlyn frowned. "What's dirty rushing?"

"When a sorority or fraternity indicates to a potential rushee that they want the person before the official rush season begins. It's a sort of preemptive strike. The person has to be really popular."

Emlyn stared at Jesse. "Gamma Gamma Mu is like the hottest ticket on campus. How did you rate?"

Jesse ignored the question.

Pinky plopped down on the bed beside Jesse, causing her book to jump and close. "It's all the goals she's assisting. They must see her as a potential rival for Porsche's position as team captain."

"No one's a rival for Porsche!" Jesse and Emlyn answered as one. It had been announced this week that Porsche had made the U.S. women's national soccer team, prelim to the Olympics. End of argument.

Jesse flipped her book back open.

"Why you?" Envy curled through Emlyn's words. "Why Gamma Gamma Mu?"

Jesse closed her book, giving up the effort to study. "Who knows how they think?" She wasn't about to admit that her grandmother was a member of the alumni. The campus chapter wouldn't know about that, either, and she didn't want them to.

"That's the point. No one knows why they choose who they choose." Emlyn eyed Jesse with envy. "I'd snap it up in a second if I was invited. Think of the men available to you if you're Greek!"

Pinky nodded. "Gamma Gamma Mu has major Ivy League connections. You'll be set."

"Parties," Emlyn chimed in.

"Better. Access to their computerized bank of Simmons's

course exams and intercollegiate term papers!" Pinky pointed to Jesse's textbook. "Your college success will be practically made."

Nita appeared in Jesse's doorway. Despite the cooler temperatures she wore a vibrant Bape pink-and-blue camo-print hoodie unzipped to reveal a black bikini bra, four thin gold chains with charms, skinny jeans, and lipstick so shiny her lips looked simonized. Fidel yipped in greeting from the circle of her arm. "I'm going Lambda Theta Alpha."

"Lambda who?" Emlyn turned to her. "I never heard of them."

Nita's shrug made her long dark mane ripple. "It is a Latina sorority."

"There is such a thing?"

Nita's smile dissolved. Jesse ducked her head for she knew from experience what was coming.

"What? You didn't think we had our own sororities? That we must suffer being neglected by most WASPy sororities, then beg for the token brown-skin position in them and black sororities so they can both march in the diversity parade?"

"What*ever*." Emlyn tossed her head, her finer hair no match for Nita's. "I only said I didn't know about them. I didn't say I wanted them Gitmo'd."

"That is a joke? Because I'm Cuban?" Nita's usually all-American accent had gone south. All the way to *Coo-ba*.

Jesse hopped up. "Okay, everybody take a chill pill. Freudian slip, Nita. Emlyn, don't even speak."

"Emlyn? Auto-edit?" Pinky made a flip-the-switch gesture with a finger.

Emlyn answered with a different finger gesture.

Nita scratched Fidel behind the ears. "So you know. There are dozens of Latina and Latino Greek organizations in the States. I've been rushed by the Gamma Phi chapter— 'The Ivy Fortress.' That's the Lambda Theta Alpha chapter at Cornell."

"You can do that? Pledge at another university?" Pinky's interest was piqued.

"Yes, because there is no Latina sorority on Simmons's campus."

Jesse smiled. "I think that's cool, Nita."

Nita gave her a funny look and then shrugged. "So then, you are invited to my party in the city next weekend."

Emlyn's antenna went up. "Party in Manhattan?"

Nita looked right through her.

Jesse shook her head. "I have a game on Sunday. In Philly."

Nita nodded. "We'll take my car and I'll get you there in time for the game."

"It doesn't work like that," Emlyn interjected. "If Jesse doesn't travel with us, she can't play. If she doesn't have a really good reason, she'll get suspended."

Jesse faked a cough. "I think I'm coming down with something."

Nita nodded once, turned on her Miu Miu heels and left.

Emlyn made a face at Nita's back. "Why do they have to act like that?"

Jesse frowned. "Who's 'they'?"

"All minorities. They act like someone is always trying to insult them."

"Ix-nay on the ace-ray," Pinky murmured, and tried to be

subtle by blocking the finger she pointed at Jesse with the palm of her other hand.

Usually Jesse let this kind of mess slide. But today everything was working her last nerve for reasons she hadn't had time to put into words. She slammed her book closed.

"Those once-called minorities you refer to now make up a majority in almost one-third of the most-populous counties in this country. And not your traditional border areas of the country. Last year Chicago edged out Honolulu in Asian population. Washington, D.C., moved ahead of El Paso in the number of Hispanic residents. As for black populations, Houston overtook Los Angeles. Non-Hispanic whites are the new minority. So get *freaking* over it!"

Pinky whistled. "When did you become an urban anthropology major?"

"This is an institute of higher learning. I read. Go figure."

Emlyn shrugged. "You can be so weird sometimes."

Jesse nodded. "I know."

⌒∞⌒

Jesse tried to keep her tongue from hanging out as she looked around Poppi's two-story penthouse on Manhattan's Upper East Side. It looked like a layout for *Architectural Digest, South Beach division*. The dominant color was white, walls, drapes, soaring ceiling, so white it blinded. The gleaming floors were sand pale. The sofas and chairs were sleek and modern with wood or metal trim. It was the kind of space that needed turquoise sky and azure beachfront views to balance its starkness. Instead, custom lighting bounced and reverberated off all surfaces while white sheers hid the rainy autumn skyline.

"Leave your shoes at the door." Nita pointed to a fancy basket inside the entry. "Poppi hates heel prints."

Jesse didn't bother to reply that her sneakers weren't about to leave a mark on the high-gloss flooring. Nita's wooden-heel sandals were another matter. Maybe Poppi was the reason Fidel hadn't joined them. "Where's our host?"

"There." Nita pointed to a photo printed on canvas in a twenty-four-by-thirty-six-inch silver gilt frame near the entry.

Jesse paused, her eyes going wide at the picture of a shirtless man at the prow of a large gleaming yacht. He was handsome. Strikingly so. And very tan, the old-fashioned kind of tan one got from lying in the sun until skin browned like a roasted turkey. He had a decent shape. Must have a personal trainer to keep pecs like that. But his hair seemed too thick. And his teeth were a little too white. He looked a tad too perfect. Botox, definitely. Face-lift?

Nita came up to her, clearly in love with the view. "What do you think?"

"He's ah . . . mature."

Nita's eyes narrowed. "He's only thirty-six."

"*Only* thirty-six?"

"You don't approve."

Jesse shrugged off her duffel bag and let it drop to the floor. "I don't have to."

"Look at George and Amal Clooney, Beyoncé and Jay-Z, Leonardo DiCaprio and any model/actress under thirty—"

Jesse folded her arms. "And your point is?"

"Lots of younger women date older—*mature* men. They have style, sophistication, flair." Nita checked her makeup in the mirror she'd pulled from her bag. "Best of all, they have and know how to spend money."

"Okay."

"You are thinking sex."

"Not even!" Not after gazing at Poppi. It would be like having sex with a girlfriend's father! "Only, what do you bring to the table?"

"I don't understand."

"The women you named in relationships with older guys have careers. They are independent. My mother says that a woman should know she can be okay on her own. Live an independent life before she becomes part of a permanent couple. How do you hold your own in this relationship?"

"I am a woman. That is enough." Nita glanced at her with resentment. "You know what your trouble is? You have never been in love."

"True."

"I love this man. I love him more than anybody I ever met and that scares me. That's why I need some distance, you understand?"

Jesse folded her arms across her chest. "So you invited a bunch of strangers to his apartment while he is out of town so you can get your freak on?" This tidbit about the weekend had come up on the drive down to the city that morning. Poppi was out of town. The guest list was strictly college and twenty-something friends of friends. "That's some kind of distance. He may just kick your butt to the curb when he hears about it."

"You don't understand a woman's power over a man."

Jesse decided this conversation was pointless, as most of theirs were.

Nita reached for her phone. "Make yourself at home. Choose any bedroom upstairs. I must check with my party planner about the caterer and the DJ."

Jesse glanced again around the very expensively decorated apartment. "Are you sure this party is a good idea?"

Nita smiled. "Don't ask."

Jesse shook her head. Not a good answer.

Chapter 24

Guests came in waves. The twenty-something city dwell-
ers arrived first from points uptown and downtown.
Later on, according to Nita, college students from up
to a hundred-mile radius would begin dropping in. It quickly
became clear that while a few Anglos, black and white, were
invited, this party represented the United Nations of Latino
culture. More impressive, Nita seemed to know each and every
person by name.

When the crowd reached critical mass, the hired DJ pumped
up the volume to a level that turned the penthouse into a sky
club. Pink was first up to "Get the Party Started." Beyoncé's
perennial "Single Ladies" flowed into Redman, Christina
Aguilera, Cardi B, Bad Bunny, and assorted Spanish language
hip-hop artists Jesse had not heard before. The sole directive
was the beat, solid, percussive, and addictive. Soon the guests
were breaking down with hips that didn't lie but would jump
and bump and grind on whoever was front, back, or on either
side of them.

Well into the evening, a particularly conspicuous group of

ladies appeared. When Nita spied them she cried, "Sucias!" and grabbed Jesse by the arm to drag her along as she hurried toward them.

They greeted one another with a lot of squealing and rapid Spanish. The only phrase Jesse caught was "The Lambda chicas be here!"

They were all pretty with lots of hair, and even more attitude, wearing tiny, ruffled skirts that barely covered their hips, or skin-tight minidresses or skimpy low-riders. Representing every Latina skin tone, they looked like Bratz come to life.

"Leave your shoes at the door." Nita pointed at the three large woven baskets she had set by the door for this purpose.

"You expect me to drop my Via Spiga heels in there?" The one in a baby doll dress reared her head back. "I hope you got security up in here. If they show up missing, you owe me two hundred and seventy-nine dollars, plus tax, and pain and suffering."

"Please! This is not an East Harlem barrio scene." Nita pushed Jesse forward. "Everyone, meet my roommate from Simmons, Jesse Morgan. Jesse, these are the Lambda sorority sisters from Cornell."

"Hi. I'm Colibri." Colibri was a sparkle-gloss-and-cami kind of girl.

"Bianca, here." She wore a short bubble skirt with a colorful and nearly transparent ruffled halter top.

"Hola. I am Avivi." Tiny as a bird, with a head of frizzy curls balanced on her long, narrow neck, Avivi was the only one of the four with a pronounced accent.

"Tanisha." Tanisha was nearly six feet tall and one foot wide.

"Tani modeled during fashion week for both Savage x Fenty and Kerby Jean-Raymond," Nita inserted for clarification.

Tanisha's gaze slipped down Jesse's body. "You got it going on in that tank. Great arms and abs. You play sports?"

"Soccer."

"Houses look for sporty types for their activewear collections. Send me your headshots. Could be something for you. The blonde thing is hot again."

"Natural," Nita contributed. "I peeked."

As they slipped back into Spanish, Jesse melted away. Headshots! As if everyone had them, just in case. Still, it was nice for Tani to say she had modeling possibilities.

Jesse wandered over to where the catering service offered assorted spicy tapas while two bartenders kept the partiers supplied with Miami Cocktails and Spiced Pear Martinis. Nita's only directives of the night were that there be no drugs and no smoking of any substances that might be absorbed into the furnishings or leave telltale residue. The party swirled around her. People smiled but moved on to someone they knew. She was in it but not of it. Not a happy thing at a party.

She had nibbled her way through a generous plate of hors d'oeuvres and just about decided that the night was a bust for her personally when she saw a guy standing not ten feet away, staring at her.

It was shocking how absolutely good-looking he was. He had black hair and a dark, penetrating gaze from a wide-cheekbone face. Lashes so thick and long it looked like he was wearing eyeliner. But there was nothing swishy about him. He was too casual, in slouchy jeans and a dress shirt with collar open and sleeves rolled up.

"Un Mujeriego," Colibri murmured in passing by Jesse and nodded in the guy's direction. "Careful."

Jesse shut her mouth. Playa. No translation needed. Women wouldn't let him be anything else. Too bad. He was one sexy beast! Without speaking she turned her back.

All at once, the music stopped. Surprised by the abrupt pause, conversation died along with the dancing. For a moment, the air seemed to vibrate with the instant stillness.

"Lambda Ladies are in the house!" Tanisha cried and let loose with a high whooping sound her girlfriends picked up and repeated. Delighted, guests clapped and backed to the walls, clearing a space in the middle of the room. The four women strutted out onto the dance floor and struck poses.

The DJ had obviously been cued for he announced, "Lambda Theta Alpha women present the Lambda Stroll!"

Rihanna's "Break It Off" filled the air but the vocals had been remixed with lyrics the Lambda sorority sisters sang as they began moving in unison to the beat.

It took Jesse a few seconds to recognize their coordinated dance moves as comparable to African American Greek Stepping. The women on the floor infused their line dancing with Latin American, Caribbean, African, and salsa dance moves. They were wonderful, athletic, and sexy at the same time.

Jesse caught Nita's eye and gave her a thumbs-up. So these were sisters of the sorority Nita hoped to join. They certainly knew how to have a good time.

The guests erupted in whistles and cheers and applause when the ladies finally trained off the dance floor with giggling and sashaying appreciation.

"Que pasa?"

Jesse turned around to find "un Mujeriego" standing right behind her. "Hi."

"What is that?" He nodded toward the red cocktail in her hand.

She looked at the drink she had chosen strictly for its presentation. "Some kind of a martini called Dragon's Breath. Dry ice makes it smoke."

He reached for it and she handed it over. He took a small sip. "Interesting."

She shook her head. "Actually it's pretty nasty."

He grinned and nodded. "I'm Edgardo."

"My name's Jesse—Jessica."

"Would you like to dance, Jesse-Jessica?"

Jesse felt herself begin to panic but another part of her readily answered, "Okay."

He took her drink and handed it off to a passing guest. Then he took her by the hand and led her to the dance floor, something the guys she knew in high school had never done. And he didn't release it when they found space. The top-chart music of earlier in the evening had changed. What was playing now was classic Tito Puente.

He must have noticed the look on her face as couples around them began to dance. "Can you salsa?"

Jesse shook her head, hair sliding forward to half cover her face. "I'm really bad at partnering. I always try to lead."

He laughed. "How about I show you how? It's really quite simple."

Jesse rolled her eyes. "That's what people always say before they try to teach the impossible."

But watching his feet move to the rhythm—one, two, three,

pause, five, six, seven, pause—it didn't seem that difficult. Copping peeks at the way he rolled his pelvis wasn't bad either.

"Now you try."

Jesse swept her hair from her face and tried to match his steps. He watched her a moment then nodded and took her by the waist.

It was weird, being partnered with a guy. It reminded her of the old-fashioned dancing her mother and Xavier did at their reception. But this was nothing like that. The rhythm was irresistible. The liquid undulating of Edgardo's movements met the suggestive beat without effort. Latin guys had that going on, she noticed, as partners all around her moved easily to the complicated rhythms. Unlike so many men who thought they had to show off on the dance floor, these guys had subtlety and finesse.

Edgardo suddenly pulled her into his arms, grabbed her hand and pushed her away into a spin. She was amazed that her body seemed to know exactly what he wanted her to do. And though her steps might not have exactly matched his, she came back into his embrace as easily as if they had practiced it a hundred times.

He smiled at her. "I told you. Simple."

Grinning, she added a little hip roll to her steps and he laughed in appreciation. One melody tracked into another and they stayed on the floor until they were both breathless.

"You want to sit?"

Jesse nodded. But then the music slowed. Instead of walking her off the floor, he stepped up closer to her and pulled her tight against his chest. "One more, for now," he said against her ear as they began to sway in a sexy clench. Jesse willed herself to just let go for once of concerns about what he was doing and what she was feeling. After all, they were in public and nothing was going to happen she didn't want to have happen. Anything else she'd worry about later.

Finally he leaned into her so that his mouth was next to her. "I want to be alone with you. What do you want?"

Boy! He didn't waste time. A little shudder of disappointment rippled through her. He must have noticed since they were plastered together from face to hip but he didn't understand the reason behind it.

He tightened his hold on her. "Is that a yes?"

He leaned in to kiss her but she backed a little away. "How about we get something to drink? Cool down?"

He shrugged and released her, all but her hand.

As they moved toward the bar, Tani passed them, winked and fanned herself with a hand. "Muy caliente!" she whispered to Jesse and laughed.

Then while Edgardo ordered for them, Colibri came up, her eyes flashing. "Your roomie's acting like she's never before seen sex on two feet." Jesse followed her nod to the dance floor where Nita's partner was leaning over her in a very urgently sexual way. "Makes you wonder about what old Poppi's like in the sack."

Jesse looked away. "Maybe I should say something to her? She's had a lot to drink. She might make a decision she will later regret."

Colibri shook her head. "Nita needs to get her freak on. It's just a dance."

Jesse looked back at the couple on the floor. Nita had unzipped her leopard-print romper to the waist so that her wispy bit of bra was on full view. Her partner, now shirtless, hauled her in for a little bump-bump. *Just a dance!* It looked like sex standing up. Just watching them made her sweat.

When Edgardo had collected a couple of tequila shots for them, they moved to a far corner of the room where it was a fraction quieter, and they could talk about nothing and everything. The night mellowed out into a very warm, fuzzy cocoon. She learned he was a junior at Dartmouth and a business major. He was from L.A. and had come east to go to college to get "cultured." He said everyone called him Onyx. He'd tell her why the next time they talked. He was impressed she played soccer. It turned out his sister played for Marquette so he knew what a big deal it was for her to make the Ladyhawkes.

When he finally leaned over and tried to kiss her, this time she let him.

She checked her watch when he suggested moving on to a club downtown where he and several friends he came with were planning to finish out the night. She was tempted but it was already one thirty A.M. and she had to be up by six if she was going to make Rutgers on time. She would not be able to play because she wasn't with the team tonight but she wanted to cheer them on just the same.

One moment the room was like the inside of a heart, dark, hot, humid with the pulse of blood and the rhythm of life. The next it was noon on Miami Beach.

No one had seen or bothered to notice the door opening and several men in suits arrive. The coming and going had been too casual. But the moment Jesse's eyes stopped blinking against the brilliant light that suddenly flooded the room, she knew these men weren't on the party guest list.

The last of the chatter of the startled guests ceased as one of the men walked into the middle of the deserted dance floor. He was familiar to Jesse though she had never met him. *Poppi!*

"Nita! Where are you?"

Nita came forward slowly, looking every bit like a six-year-old who'd been caught raiding the cookie jar. The man from the portrait was all too real and he didn't look amused by what he was seeing. Maybe that was because Nita's hair was a mess and her romper was not quite zipped to a respectable level.

He took Nita by the upper arm and pulled her to his side, not roughly but with enough force so that without a word his position in her life was clear. He surveyed the crowd, who seemed to know instinctively that this was not a man to be ignored. "This is my home. You are not my guests. Get out!"

Watching the reaction, Jesse thought it was like in a movie where the bad guys walk in, cock semiautomatic weapons, and the room scatters. It didn't matter that there were no weapons here or that the only threat was their uninvited host. The room cleared so fast the doorman below must have thought the fire alarm had sounded. Fascinated yet repulsed like a bystander to an auto crash, she didn't even consider herself part of the action until Edgardo squeezed her arm hard. "Come on. This party's over."

Jesse looked into his beautiful eyes. "I can't. I'm Nita's guest."

"You're sure?" He stared at her with such longing she almost changed her mind.

"I'm sure."

He leaned and kissed her hard, like he wanted her to remember him. "Another time."

Jesse retreated to a bar stool while the DJ and the caterers packed up. On second glance, the men who came in with Poppi appeared to be ordinary middle-aged businessmen. After offering them a drink, which they all declined, Poppi saw them to the door. Only then did Poppi seem to remember that Nita was still there.

He walked over to her. "What do you think you were doing tonight? Who was that *chico* pawing you?"

Nita had had time to collect herself. She had retreated to a white leather chair where she was sipping a glass of champagne. "No one important, Poppi." She smiled at him over the rim. "We were just partying. Fun."

One second they were talking, the next Poppi had walked up and knocked the glass out of Nita's hand. As it shattered unnoticed on that very expensive floor, the screaming began in English then switched to Spanish.

Amazingly, Nita did not give ground, but shoved her chin up into his face and attacked with equal abuse. Then he slapped her. A full open-handed slap that snapped Nita's head back.

Shocked, Jesse jumped to her feet. "Don't you dare hit her again!"

His head swung toward her in surprise "Who are you?"

"I'm Nita's roommate—and friend." Heart pumping, Jesse began to wonder, a bit late, if her choice should have been about safety, not loyalty.

He took a few steps toward Jesse. "I don't know who you are, young woman, and I don't care to." His voice was very cultured, surprisingly so. "Leave my home at once."

"I will. But you must let Nita leave, too."

His eyes narrowed. "Nita doesn't want to leave."

Jesse glanced at Nita. She shook her head.

He shrugged. "There, you see? This is a private matter. I think I've been more than fair by not calling authorities on you and your friends. I could have you arrested for unlawful entry and underage drinking. For all I know, they might discover narcotics on the premises. I advise you to leave now."

Nita made a pushing movement with her hands. "Go, Jesse. Get out now."

Jesse stood indecisively. Her mother had always told her if she got into trouble to save herself first, then get help. "I—I have things upstairs."

He nodded, indicating that she could go get her things.

Feeling sick in the pit of her stomach, Jesse ran upstairs and shoved things into her bag and then hurried back down. One glance showed her that Nita was now sitting on the sofa sulking while Poppi leaned over her talking earnestly.

She left without a word.

When she was in a cab hailed by the building doorman, she pulled out her phone and dialed 911. "An illegal party, yes. There's an underage girl still there. The man wouldn't release her. He hit her before I left. And he said something about having drugs." She had to give the address twice before the dispatcher got it right.

When she hung up she was shaking all over. She didn't know if she'd done the right thing. But at least the police would check to see if Nita was okay.

"Where to, lady?" The cabbie had swiveled around to stare at her.

"Times Square." She couldn't think of any other Manhattan address. And now she had nowhere to stay.

She didn't need permission to come into the city, just to

spend the kind of money a midtown Manhattan hotel would cost. And her mother would have questions about why she hadn't made plans before two A.M. Think! Cassandra had friends in the city.

Jesse texted her friend. *Party in NYC. Lost bed. Help.*

Luckily, Cassandra was still awake to answer. *Oh my God! NYC party? Envy U. Cousin on 135th will put U up.*

Jesse made a face. *Safe?*

Damn, grrl. Even Clinton's up there!!!

Chapter 25

"Yes. Yes, that's very good news. Give him my best and tell him I will be by again after work. Okay, only fifteen-minute visits. I understand. Intensive care regulations."

Thea hugged her arms to her body as she stared out at the late October skyline of Dallas. Ron had suffered a series of heart attacks, brought on in part by the chemotherapy he had begun months before. After two surgeries, due to unexpected complications, he was still fighting for his life. And that had to be a good sign. But it meant she no longer had the luxury of working away from Dallas during the week.

The other partners were beginning to question Ron's thinking in making her, the newest partner, acting managing partner of the Dallas office. They weren't alone in that thought. She had never worked harder and felt less capable. But she wasn't going to give up, not when Ron was counting on her. He'd never let her down. She would go to the mat for him.

But it was costing her, in so many ways.

Xavier had flown back to Dallas with her to go directly to the hospital the day they found out about Ron's first attack.

He had been so good with Ron's wife and grown children. Even though he was a stranger to them, they gladly received him as a minister and as her new husband. Whenever her first husband Evan's name came up in conversation, as Ron and Sarah had known Evan well, Xavier had shown no signs of unhappiness or annoyance. He just kept squeezing her hand reassuringly.

She wished for his kind of calm right now in her own personal storm. She had been feeling little of it during the past few weeks while business kept them apart. Except for Sunday mornings, when she sat alone and lonely in the front pew as first lady of St. Hurricane, they did not see each other.

Thea turned from the window, fiddling with her ring as if it were a good luck charm against the pileup of lonely days. At least they had Sundays. Each and every time she heard him preach, it was still a revelation.

Xavier became a different entity when he delivered God's word. She closed her eyes, recalling how his robes accentuated his gestures as he paced, an impatient, often-interrupted athletic stride in shoes polished to patent brightness. His voice rose and fell in rhythmic intonation until it was as hoarse as a lover's in the grip of a passion stronger than his natural caution. By sheer physical will he dared the congregation to look away, be indifferent, or be bored.

The members felt his intensity and passion. Yet she knew from experience many of the women misinterpreted the source of his fervor. She'd noticed the Sunday congregation getting younger and prettier. Some of their newest visitors filled out membership forms with addresses as far away as Monticello, Pine Bluff, Star City, and Dumas. Visitors included guests from the surrounding three states. She knew what they did not. It was not the man her husband wanted them to hunger after, but his words of salvation.

Their desire to know the new minister did not extend to her. The moment the service was over, she remained marooned in isolation by those who craved the attention of her husband. Her triumph at the adult women's Sunday school class had eroded. This was Hattie Patterson's doing. She didn't know how or even why, but a person didn't have to see the wind to feel the breeze.

Thea picked up and drained her third and final cup of coffee of the morning.

While Xavier preached sermons on charity and forgiveness, she received neither from his congregation. She had grown to dread the moment when a church member would approach with a request. Inevitably her answer became etched in the asker's face as disappointment or resignation or resentment. Overheard comments that she was "too preoccupied," "too important," or just plain "too stuck-up" to participate in their lives could not be fought when she didn't have the time to prove otherwise.

Yet how could they expect her to cope with choir practice on Tuesday evenings, or chair the annual autumn bazaar fundraiser set for a Friday evening, or even host a women's Bible study class on a Wednesday night when she worked in Dallas?

It was slowly beginning to dawn on her that what she had chosen in becoming Xavier's wife was more than she could cope with gracefully. Loving him was easy. Understanding the dedication he had to a place and people whose ways she did not understand, and who seemed not to understand or even like her, was much *much* harder.

Aisha knocked at Thea's office door and entered. "The gentlemen from Kobayashi are here. I put them in conference room A."

"Thank you. See that they are offered refreshments. Oh, Aisha, would you see if you can get me on a midday flight into Utica, or Syracuse, or Schenectady for Friday? I'll need a rental, too. Oh, and check the drive time to Simmons from each of those airports before you book."

"Going up to see Jesse play?"

"I hope so." Thea looked back at her computer. "I think they are at Simmons. But you better check my calendar, just in case. I have her schedule posted. Oh, and I'll need a return flight out on Saturday afternoon via Little Rock. Hm, better make the ticket open-ended. I don't know when I'll be back."

Aisha smiled. "Your plate's full."

Thea nodded absently. "Things are starting to slide off the edges but I'm taking as many bites as quickly as I can."

She picked up her portfolio to head for the meeting and her phone rang. Though she was late, mother-instinct kicked in to make her check it. It was Xavier.

"How's my favorite lady?"

"Rushed."

"Then I won't keep you. I just wanted you to know that you've received mail from Mrs. Patterson."

"What kind of mail?"

"Hold on, I'll open it. Now isn't that nice? It's an invitation to tea at her home this Saturday."

"Saturday's no good. I'm going to surprise Jesse by showing up for her game Friday night. I plan on spending the weekend with her. I don't suppose you could?"

"How many times in the past few weeks have you said you

wished you could find a way to make peace with Hattie Patterson?"

"Is Mrs. Patterson really going to kick if I ask for a rain check?"

Xavier's silence said it all.

"Okay. I just really want to see Jesse. I'm not even sure of the date for the game yet. I'll call you back after lunch."

Thea hung up and met Aisha in the hallway.

"The Ladyhawkes play on Thursday and Sunday this weekend." Aisha checked her notes. "Thursday's game is in West Virginia."

"I'm in L.A. until Thursday." Thea straightened her shoulders. "Okay. Change of plans. Book a flight to Little Rock on Saturday morning. I'll just have to make Jesse's game the following weekend."

Aisha's smile dissolved. "You're scheduled to be in Chile next week."

Thea stared at her. "That can't be right."

Aisha nodded. "It's the conference on international environmental law as it concerns halting fossil fuel expansion. Ron's oil and gas clients want the firm to hear firsthand what is being proposed to deal with global warming. After Ron went into the hospital, I rebooked the conference for you. Jack and Lacey are flying into Dallas from the New York office to meet with you for the longest leg of the trip." She flipped through her calendar. "Yes. You're booked to leave on Tuesday."

Thea couldn't think of which cuss word she should use.

Then she found it. "Shit!"

She moved down the hall, leaving Aisha with mouth agape.

Everything was messing with her mind.

⤜∾⤛

There were eight missed calls on her cell when Thea checked at the end of the day. She had accidentally left it behind in her office, and back-to-back meetings had kept her from retrieving it until now. In a real emergency, Jesse and Xavier knew to call Aisha. All but one were from Xavier. The only message was his.

"Didn't want to leave you a phone message about this but I have to catch a flight. I know you don't keep up with the music business but maybe you've seen the headlines. You remember Bazz Azz, the rap impresario I persuaded to become involved in the Thornton Foundation? He was arrested earlier in the week. Things have gotten a little out of control in ways I don't want to talk about here. I've been asked to intercede. That means I won't be in Pine Grove this weekend. But you should still come and visit Mrs. Patterson."

Bazz Azz! Her least favorite of Xavier's associates! Best known for producing thug rappers with misogynistic lyrics and lewd videos, Bazz Azz had come under Xavier's influence through his Black Man's Master Plan Crusade. Xavier thought he had reached the young urban millionaire. She always had her doubts. Now they seemed to be justified. Why was Xavier on his way to Atlanta? Surely not to put his face in the tabloids next to a man like Bazz Azz?

Grinding her teeth, Thea went to her computer and googled Bazz Azz. Photos of women in skintight shorts that only covered half their rear ends came up first. Then she saw the beginning of a headline: *Bazz's Azz in a Sling: Hip-Hop Mogul Arrested in Shooting of Rival Music Executive.*

"Oh my God!" *Attempted murder!*

Thea opened the news story and read quickly, slowing down only when she noticed Xavier's name in a sentence.

In his formal statement to the police, Bazz Azz loudly proclaimed his innocence, citing Reverend Xavier Thornton as his character reference. The former NBA sensation known as The "X" Factor, Reverend Thornton was named by Bazz Azz as his "personal spiritual guide who understands how a man can be profane and still holy."

"Great! Just wonderful!" The heat of anger roiled through Thea. This would explain Xavier's concern. His name was being dragged into the investigation of a felony by a man he once knew, and she disliked. "That is so unfair!" Her gaze skimmed down through another headline article.

. . . at his court hearing this morning, Bazz Azz again proclaimed his innocence while openly boasting about his multimillion-dollar contribution to the Thornton Foundation as proof of his spiritual worth. This has led to new eruptions at the Thornton Foundation, already undergoing internal strife. To quote board member Ed Spearman, "The morning's revelation shocks and enrages many of Reverend Xavier's more conservative supporters . . ."

Thea shook her head. Xavier hadn't said a word about any of this. She googled Thornton Foundation to find news stories she had somehow missed. Some of it was weeks old, except about Bazz Azz's connection to the Thornton Foundation.

Aisha stuck her head in the door, her eyes going to Thea's monitor. "Oh, so you've seen it."

Thea whipped her head around. "Did you know about this?"

"It was just on the national news."

"What?"

Aisha nodded. "Your husband was on CNN at five. My girlfriend called to tell me. I was coming to tell you in case you hadn't heard."

"No, I hadn't." Thea glanced at her watch. It was after six P.M. She could stream a newscast on her computer, but she preferred to be alone when she listened.

Once at home, she no longer had to wonder where Xavier was or what he was doing. The cable news shows were doing their usual overkill of not-enough-information-so-keep-looping-what-we've-got news. News-bite interviews with Xavier's allies and opponents, as they square off to make political hay out of the controversy, filled the half hour between top and bottom of the hour news. She surfed among the various news channels until she had pieced together enough information to make her mad and scared.

In between she called and left messages on Xavier's cell. It was after ten P.M. when he finally returned them.

Instead of apologizing to her for the situation he found himself reluctantly pulled into, he went on the defensive. He launched into an explanation of how Bazz Azz was being framed, and that in all likelihood charges would be dropped by the end of the week. She listened to his explanation with growing impatience. But she waited until he finally took a breath.

"I just don't see where you fit into the mess he's made of his life."

"I got him involved with the Thornton Foundation. I have to defend that action."

"You mean you have to defend yourself because Bazz Azz betrayed you by going public. He was supposed to be an anonymous donor to the foundation, right?"

"He's young and hotheaded and—"

"And not above using your good name when it suits his needs." Thea was amazed at how angry she was on her husband's behalf. "He's a user, Xavier. He's worse. He's been arrested for attempted murder!"

"It's not quite like that, Thea. You don't know where a guy like Bazz is coming from."

"I know he's a thug. I know that when things got tough, he didn't uphold his own honor or street cred. He traded on your public esteem for his own purposes."

"Thea, I haven't got time to argue about this."

"My God! He tried to kill a man!"

Xavier's abrupt silence struck her like ice water, chilling her anger. But she didn't apologize. How could she? For what? She was right. He knew she was right. He was just too stiff-necked to admit it.

"The charges won't stick. In fact, the real shooter was arrested along with Bazz. His name just made for more sexy headlines. You'll see it in the morning papers."

"Even if that's true, the damage is done. He betrayed you."

This time his silence seemed more patient and thoughtful. She was remembering a time before their world exploded in headlines and pain and mistrust. But she couldn't find her way back.

Back to peace.

"Trust me." The words, said low and quietly, hooked her back into their world.

She rubbed the tension locking up her neck. "It's not you I don't trust, Xavier."

"I'm a big boy, Mrs. Thornton." She could hear a smile curl through his words.

She shook her head and immediately regretted it as pain shot up from the back of her head to throb in her left eye. Was this in response to their conversation or the entire frustrating week?

"When will you be back?"

"Early part of the week. I have to speak to the foundation board on Monday. They've called a special session."

"And they require the services of a minister because all hell may break loose?"

"Something like that." He paused. "I'm sorry to put you through this. It shouldn't come up, but if it does, don't answer any reporters' questions. Oh, and good luck with Hattie Patterson."

Great! Tea with Hattie should round out a perfectly awful week. Battling reporters would be preferable.

Thea hung up the phone with a growing sense of anxiety over the number of things in her life she couldn't control. The life they had chosen for themselves had them by the throat. Right now she had to manage the one thing she could: her head.

After going months without them, migraines were again becoming a regular part of her life. There was no point in waiting to see if this was the beginning of another. Once the real pain hit, the meds would only be able to do so much.

She moved gingerly into the bathroom to the medicine cabinet. Medications her doctor had suggested she take daily to prevent migraines made her feel stupid and slow. If there ever was a time when she needed to be sharp and smart it was now.

Chapter 26

Thea ignored the discomfort of her stiff plastic-covered chair as she pushed the hem of her skirt down over her knees. She was having tea with St. Hurricane's first lady.

Iced tea, that is, served with slivers of fresh lemon, sprigs of mint, homemade lemon ice-box cookies, and a dish of salted nuts. These were displayed on the two-tiered brass and glass serving trolley pushed into the room by Mrs. Patterson's housekeeper.

"There's fresh lemonade, too." The housekeeper sounded pleasant enough though she stared at Thea as if she were a selection on the cart. "We aren't citified but I can serve up most anything plain and simple."

"Perhaps Mrs. Thornton would prefer something . . . stronger." Hattie's lips lifted in a sly smile. "Sherry, perhaps?"

"No, thank you." The reminder of her blunder set Thea's back up. Just as she had suspected, this was to be an interrogation, conducted this time over fine bone china, sterling silver, and footed crystal iced tea glasses.

She had promised Xavier that she would be cordial and accepting of advice even if she later ignored it. She promised herself that she would do her flat-out best to make the woman like her. But it was a fact that Hattie Patterson got on her last nerve, and it was already shredding under the pressure of the last twenty-four hours.

After the housekeeper served them and left the room Hattie looked at Thea. "Will you bless the food?"

Who blesses cookies?

Thea swallowed the crumbs in her throat, put her half-eaten cookie back on her plate, and bowed her head. "Gracious Lord, who in your bountiful magnificence spoke the world into being. We honor you, Lord, give you all the glory, and ask that you bless this humble repast and all those who partake of it. Amen." She had been practicing the prayer Xavier wrote for her for such occasions.

"It was kind of you to invite me into your home, Mrs. Patterson."

"Yes, that is the point of the invitation, to become better acquainted." Hattie passed her guest a glass of tea and then picked up her own. "Why don't you tell me about yourself, dear?"

Thea smiled. "What would you like to know?"

"Something about your background. Was your father a minister?"

"No. Both my parents were college professors at Grambling College."

"I see. Then perhaps you had a grandfather in the ministry? An uncle?" Her eyes widened each time Thea shook her head.

"No relations at all with a calling to the ministry?"

"We are drawn more to academics. My sister has a degree in interior design. I took the business route."

"How interesting. I am the daughter of a minister, as well as the widow of one. As a rule, a minister chooses very carefully the woman who will share his life's work. The church is a consuming vocation. Many women find they are not up to the job. That's why most often a minister is best served when he marries within 'the fold.'"

No doubt that was meant as a slight but what had she expected, really, but more of the same? "I'm surprised you did not go into the ministry yourself, Mrs. Patterson."

"Oh no. In my day women were encouraged to be helpmates, not seek the spotlight. I had no further ambition than to serve at the leisure of my dear Obadiah." Hattie frowned slightly. "He never quite achieved all he deserved. Still, I like to think I had a hand in his elevation, such as it was."

I'm sure you pushed him uphill all the way! Thea took a sip of her tea to hide her expression. "Did you have no career of your own?"

"Not as young women think of careers today. I taught in the public school system for nearly forty years. Nothing as grand as being an attorney." Hattie smoothed a doily on the arm of her pink silk chair.

This prompted Thea to say a second time, "You have a lovely home."

"Thank you. I understand you have quite a large home in Dallas."

"I've been fortunate to make a very good living." *So I'm not attached to Xavier for his money.* "I work very hard for what I have."

"So hard that it's impossible for you to be here often." Hattie pursed her lips. "Did you work as hard during your first marriage?"

She knows about my first marriage. Perhaps Xavier told her.

"Until recently I thought so. Two promotions within the past eighteen months are proving me wrong. Fortunately, my daughter is in college so I can travel and keep late hours without neglecting family."

"Is that so? You have a daughter?"

"Yes." Thea couldn't be certain this was news to the woman for her question did not contain surprise.

"Do you carry a photo?"

"Yes." Thea reached into her purse and pulled out her favorite of Jesse, taken after she'd made the all-star Texas soccer league team last spring. She brushed away a bit of lint before handing it over. "Her name's Jessica Darnell Morgan."

Hattie took the picture and lifted her reading glasses, which hung from a thin gold chain about her neck. Thea saw her brows rise and rise and rise up her forehead.

"She takes after her father."

Hattie looked up. "Does she?"

"Evan was blond and blue-eyed, too." Thea said this with a defiance that brooked no argument.

"I see."

I'll just bet you do. She wasn't about to open that discussion today.

"You've led an interesting life, Mrs. Thornton." There was no denying the censure in Hattie's tone. She and Xavier's sister Pearl were cut from the same fault-finding cloth.

Her gaze shifted to Thea's extravagant diamond ring and

her mouth primmed. "I've had the pleasure of knowing Reverend Xavier only a short while but have come to believe we share a love of the Lord that surpasses that of common understanding."

Thea chuckled. "You make my husband sound holier-than-thou. Yet everyone comments on how he is as much at home in the world as he is in the church."

"Yes." Her gaze flickered to Jesse's picture again before she returned it to Thea. "It's most unfortunate that Reverend Xavier has been in the news this week. Consorting with a man accused of shooting another. It's quite disturbing."

"Xavier knows how to handle himself in public."

"I don't doubt that. Yet, aren't you concerned about the possible damage to his reputation by being involved in this unsavory business?"

Thea's first thought was to defend Xavier. Her second was to tell the truth. "I do not like Bazz Azz—" Hattie shuddered at the name. "Nor the music he is best known for producing. However, he is well respected in the music industry. And he's far from a street thug, whatever his early years. He and Xavier have had a long personal association during which Xavier has served as his spiritual counselor."

"It is an association that Reverend Xavier would have done better to sever."

"Don't you think he should be the judge of that?" Hattie's brows took flight again so Thea tried for a more conciliatory tone. "After all, Xavier was once a celebrity himself and understands all the temptations that wealth and fame bring with them."

"Yes, and old habits are so easily stirred."

"I beg your pardon?"

"You admit you are an outsider who lacks an understanding of the delicate balance of responsibilities and constraints required in a minister's life. You cannot know that it is not enough for a pastor and his family to be above reproach; it must also appear that way."

"And I would take exception with anyone who doubts my husband's devotion to his calling."

Hattie nodded. "I have no doubt of his dedication to his ministry. But one cannot overlook the adage that one is known by the associations he or she keeps."

Don't let her get to you. "Reverend Xavier has never been intimidated by what others may think. When he is right, he does not need to appear right."

"Nevertheless, I urge you to call your husband home at once."

Is she serious?

The idea that she could call Xavier to heel like a puppy made Thea laugh. "You don't know my husband if you think I can persuade him to abandon anything he is bound and determined to do."

Hattie didn't see the humor. "That doesn't speak well for the prospects of your marriage, Mrs. Thornton."

"I disagree." Thea picked up a cookie and stuffed it in her mouth before something came out of it she would later regret.

Hattie deliberately set her glass and plate aside then folded her hands in her lap. "Let me speak frankly. You occupy a place of honor in our beloved St. Hurricane Church. Yet it has been repeatedly remarked upon that you do not attend a single Bible study class, women's auxiliary meeting, or even choir practice."

She held up a hand for silence when Thea tried to speak. "Please allow me to finish. I am aware that you are a big-time Dallas attorney. Your husband has gone to great pains to defend your actions. But it troubles us that he should be put to that task when it is your place, as his wife, to make his path easier. We have many professional women within our congregation who manage to do both their jobs and still tend to their spiritual needs, and give service to the church."

Thea had promised Xavier to listen to what this woman had to say. But it was hard to sit still under her high-handed tone. "Is that all?"

"Regrettably, no."

Thea stared woodenly at her. "Go on."

"As a minister's wife, you represent your husband, at all times and in all places." Hattie moistened her lips with her tongue. "It is written in Matthew 6:24, 'No man can serve two masters: for either he will hate the one, and love the other; or else he will hold to the one, and despise the other. Ye cannot serve God and mammon.' If you are not prepared to give up your life for your husband's ministry, Mrs. Thornton, then you are not the right wife for a minister."

A chill snaked down Thea's backbone. *Somebody just stepped on my grave.* Her aunt Della would say that about an unpleasant sensation. Now she knew what it meant. The God-fearing Christian woman sitting before her so composed and cool wanted to get rid of her. She had been insulted in every way possible. Yet she didn't want to give the woman the satisfaction of seeing how much she affected her.

She came slowly to her feet. "Let me be as frank as you,

Mrs. Patterson. You do not know me. You do not really know Xavier. Or else you would not dare to say such things."

Hattie's eyes shone with indignation. "I have a right to speak my mind. I've devoted my entire life to St. Hurricane through first my father's and then my husband's ministries here."

Thea gripped her hands together, trying to do the Christian thing by not verbally attacking an elderly woman. Oh but it was hard! "That is commendable. But Reverend Xavier is pastor here now."

There was no hint of repentance in Hattie's tone or her expression. "St. Hurricane is my life!"

"But it's not *your* church! It's God's church."

The housekeeper plunged through the swinging door from the kitchen, eyes as wide as her ears had no doubt been while listening on the other side. "Did you call, Mrs. Patterson?"

Thea answered first. "I am ready to leave, if you will please get my purse for me."

The housekeeper's gaze swung to her employer, who offered the slightest nod of agreement.

Hattie rose to her feet with great dignity. "I can see that I've upset you, Mrs. Thornton. That is regrettable. I do hope when your mind settles that you will think on all that I have said."

Thea didn't reply though she doubted she'd think of anything else.

ॐ

Hattie continued to sit in her living room as Earline cleared the dishes. She felt no satisfaction in what she had done. She had thought to speak the truth and shame the devil. Instead, she was left with the feeling that she had let zeal lead her to prideful acts.

"Perhaps I said too much, Earline."

"Yes, Hattie. Perhaps you did."

Surprised, Hattie turned to her housekeeper but she had walked away. Never, in all their twenty years together, had Earline ever called her by her first name.

Chapter 27

Oh no, she didn't! And you didn't read her?"

When Selma got angry, she got angry enough for two. "I'd like to see her try to say half of that to me. I'd have gotten all ignorant and acted a fool. Why are you just now telling me about this woman?"

"Because I thought she would go away. What am I going to do?"

"Tell Xavier. The woman's after you."

"No, I'm not going to do that."

"Why not?"

"It will put him in the position of defending me, again. The Pastoral Relations Committee hired him. If his wife becomes a problem, they can certainly fire him."

"Fire Xavier? They have better sense than to lose him because of one heifer's big mouth! It's a good thing he married you. I'd have lost my mind up in there the first day."

Thea felt better letting Selma field the anger and frustration tying her up in knots. The expression of those emotions had never come easily to her. Selma thrived on drama.

She had called Aunt Della first, seeking advice. But she wasn't her usual shrewd self. Perhaps that had something to do with the fact that she had a head cold and said she had taken something for the stuffiness that made her light-headed. She'd mouthed pieties about Thea's inner light shining through. She was certain Thea could simply charm the woman into submission.

"Just let her see the delightful, capable, lovely person you are, Theadora. Who could not like you?"

Mrs. Hattie Patterson, that's who! At least Selma understood that much.

"She's after you," Selma continued. "You need to figure out why."

"I know why. She adores Xavier. She sees him as some sort of savior of her little-patch-of-ground world called St. Hurricane. It was her father's church and then her husband's church. She thinks she's got first claim on any minister in that pulpit."

"And you think I'm freaky? Oh, Thea!" Selma's voice dropped into a whisper. "What if she wants to get rid of you, permanently?"

"Your imagination is running away with you. I'm the wife, remember?"

"And you know what they say about women who see ministers as God's answer to their prayers. I wouldn't ever set a foot over her threshold again. And don't eat or drink anything she ever offers from her hand."

"What are you talking about?"

"You know. We grew up in Louisiana. She's not that far from the state line. You don't know what kinda potions she might keep tucked away."

"You're starting to freak me out, Selma. The woman's a pain but she's a normal pain."

"You just better watch out! Bye!"

Maybe calling her sister wasn't such a good idea after all.

Then there was Jesse.

She had not yet made a single trip up to see her daughter. Her team was going into the Big East Conference Tournament next weekend and even the possibility of her making a game was slim. But more than that, something was up with Jesse. She could feel it in her voice.

Jesse had tried to palm her off by saying that despite their differences, she was missing her roommate, who was away from school for a few days. When Thea asked why, Jesse had been evasive and then quickly got off the phone.

But then she had called back within the hour to ask about Xavier being in the news, and why her mother had not called to tell her about it. She said it was all over campus, about Bazz Azz and Reverend Thornton, although only her closest friends realized that that man was her new stepfather.

Thea sipped the single malt Scotch she had poured herself to calm her temper and stave off a headache. She had tried to play off Jesse's concerns, saying it was no big deal. Xavier's role as spiritual advisor was being blown out of proportion because this was a slow news weekend. Yet she felt that in so many ways, as a wife and a mother, she was failing.

She had thought she was prepared to answer every charge Hattie Patterson might make against her. But in the end, Hattie had caught her in her most vulnerable spot. She had accused her of not being the wife Xavier deserved.

She picked up her drink and checked the doors of the

parsonage, certain they were locked. The list of who had access to the keys to all church facilities changed by the week. That's why she had installed deadbolts to use when they were in residence. Xavier might not mind waking up in the morning to Deacon Jacobs humming in the kitchen but it unnerved her.

It was only when she was locked up and safe in her bedroom that the thoughts she'd been trying to outrun ambushed her again.

She sank down onto the brand-new mattress and let out a shuddery breath. The conviction had been coming on for weeks, yet she hadn't wanted to admit it even to herself. Was the choice between God and mammon, as Hattie put it, really between what she loved and whom she loved?

That should be simple. But it wasn't.

She loved Xavier. She wanted to keep her career. She thought they could live two lives. But the truth was she only wanted part of the second half of the bargain they had struck. She wanted Xavier. She wanted to keep her job. She did not want the life they led at St. Hurricane.

But how could she tell him that when she'd encouraged this? How could she ask him to give up what she was not willing to sacrifice? Or was it now her turn?

Can I give up my job? Don't I love Xavier enough to do it? Is that what it means to love him enough? What if I can't adjust to life as a minister's wife? Then what? I can't fight God for Xavier.

Once the questions were asked, they swirled about in her thoughts like the leaves skittering across the pavement outside her window.

She pressed her forehead against the cool surface of her glass and stifled a sob with a fist. She had one more call to make tonight.

Thea steeled herself for Xavier's questions about her visit with Hattie Patterson as she punched the program button for his cell.

It rang five times before it was answered. A woman's voice said, "Yeah?"

Thea jerked. "Hello? Who's this?"

"Who are *you*?" All the urban attitude in the world went into the question.

"I'm Reverend Thornton's wife."

"Oh." She could hear music thumping in the background, as if the woman who answered was at a party or in a club. There was laughter and then another woman's voice in the distance said, "Grrrl! Just hang up!" Then the first woman came back on the line. "He's busy. Call back later." She hung up.

Thea stared off into space. There was a strange woman answering her husband's phone at ten P.M. Selma was right.

They, whoever *they* were, were ganging up on her!

❦

She was up and packed just before six A.M. The days were so much shorter now that she could see Venus shining like a spotlight in the midnight-blue eastern sky as she stepped out of the parsonage. She stopped to make certain the door locked behind her. She wanted to be out of town, preferably across the state line into Texas, before St. Hurricane realized that neither their minister nor their first lady was gracing them with their presence this Sunday morning.

A rooster crowed as she slung her bag into the car. Thea swung around.

"I heard you!" she said to the empty street and waited. The second crow was cut off in mid-voice.

She got in the car and closed the door. No one else in the neighborhood admitted to ever hearing that bird. She folded her arms on the steering wheel and rested her head on them. Either they were all lying or . . . "I must be losing my mind."

Chapter 28

"Challenge! Challenge!" Jesse screamed as an opposing team member headed down the field after winning a cleared ball.

The Ladyhawkes were one goal behind the Rutgers Scarlet Raiders. It had been a close game. Her team was feeling the heat of the closing minutes that might shut them out of a tie that would put them into sudden death overtime.

Jesse watched, teeth clenched, as the Ladyhawkes' shift-and-sag defense was left to freshman teammate Mari Gioia, first defender. She ran forward to intercept the breakaway ball only to be outmaneuvered by a commit-the-defense play by her opponent. That miscalculation caused them to collide, and both players went down.

Jesse winced. It was as if she could hear knee tendons tearing in the fall.

Coaches and teammates flew out onto the field. Within minutes it was clear that only one girl was seriously injured. Mari had to be helped off the field to a waiting ambulance.

The rest of the game was a blur. Even when it ended with,

"That's the game! Ladyhawkes 3. Scarlet Raiders 2!" Jesse could not regain her former joy in the play.

By the time she reached the locker room, she was furious. Injuries were a hazard of the game. She was nursing shin splints and had a whole line of raspberries and turf burns on each leg from the day's play. But serious injuries on the field always affected her like a blow to her stomach.

"That was a stupid rookie mistake!" Porsche stalked through the room with an expression of rage on her face while the rest of the team scurried past in silence.

"You can't forget for one second your training on the field. Everybody knows that! Mari has no future on this team. Can't remember basic strategy! Never should have started. Dumbass bitch!"

The rest of the room remained silent but Jesse was feeling much too much to just let it go. "Mari gave us everything she had today. What, you can't take the sight of someone besides you giving it all out there?"

Porsche swung around. "Are you talking to me, Miss I Had To Buy My Way Into Everything? I know all about it."

Jesse blinked. "What are you talking about?"

Porsche smirked. "I'm saying I know you're a trust fund baby. The heiress to the Morgan banking fortune. Your family paid for the new English department wing here on campus." She put her hand up to her mouth in mock horror. "Or was that supposed to be a secret?"

Jesse's heart lurched as she glanced around the room. Everybody stared at her or looked away. The secret was out.

Jesse's gaze came back to Porsche and, seeing her grin of triumph, she remembered why she disliked her so much. She was a bully. And she, Jesse Darnell Morgan, had had enough.

Arms trembling, Jesse tucked them beneath her bosom, feeling none of the casual attitude she tried to adopt. "My family has money. So? Paris Hilton and I aren't best friends, in case you were thinking I could get you an autograph."

That made a few of the team snicker.

Porsche's face reddened. "I know more than you think. You're a sham. You've been hiding the truth about yourself because you're ashamed for everyone to know that your family had to buy your way into Simmons and onto the Ladyhawkes team while the rest of us had to earn it on talent."

Jesse gasped. "That's a lie!"

Porsche stuck out her chin. "Is it? Everybody in this room knows you didn't have the skills to make it onto the team on your own."

The accusation was so outrageous Jesse didn't even try to answer it directly. "So what if my grandparents can buy and sell this college twice? That has nothing to do with me."

"Or maybe you're just embarrassed for people to know the truth that the Morgans buy what they can't earn. I saw the letter they wrote Coach."

Jesse's face burned. "I don't care what you say you saw. But I'll wear that letter like a badge of honor on my chest the day you slap *I'm a bitch* on your back!"

Porsche charged her so fast Jesse only had time to ball her hands into fists before she was right up in her face. "I've had enough of you!"

Jesse braced herself. "I wish you would!"

Coach Brewer stuck her head out of her office. "Wagner! Morgan! Knock it off!"

Neither moved. Jesse could feel Porsche's hot breath and wondered, as the milliseconds whizzed past, how many blows they would have to trade before their teammates pulled them apart. She hadn't been in a real fight . . . ever.

"Wagner! You deaf?" Coach Brewer barked. "Get your Olympic-caliber butt in my office. Now!"

Porsche blinked, as if coming out of a trance. "Don't think—" She wheeled around in midsentence and marched into the coach's office, slamming the door behind her.

One of the Ladyhawkes' upper-class women whistled. "You must have good insurance, Blondie."

That made the rest of the team chuckle and the brick wall of tension crumbled as they joined in with comments and opinions about the outcome of the match that didn't take place.

Jesse didn't move at once. Her stomach clenched and unclenched, and then she knew she was going to be sick. She turned and ran for the lavatory.

❧

"I can't believe my grandparents would do that to me!" Jesse was holed up in her dorm room with Emlyn and Pinky.

"So they did write the coach?" Pinky asked in wonder.

"That's what Porsche is telling everyone. She said she saw the letter." Emlyn was watching Jesse intently.

Jesse jumped up from her bed, adrenaline powering her around the room. "Even if it was true, how would Porsche possibly get access to something like that?"

"She's a work-study student. Parents are blue collar so she's on scholarship and works in the athletic department. She does filing and stuff."

"So much for ethics!" Jesse kicked a stray shoe out of her way.

"She's just jealous because you're loaded," Pinky offered.

"So how rich are you?" Emlyn asked.

But Jesse's thoughts were elsewhere. "Okay, Porsche saw a letter from the grandparents. It wasn't about how they paid my way into school. My SATs were in the high thirteen hundreds." She saw Pinky and Emlyn trade glances. "What?"

"The letter said something about how pleased they were that their granddaughter was playing so much, particularly since she was just a freshman."

Jesse's face fell. *Implication clear.* "How am I ever going to prove I had nothing to do with that? Didn't even know about it!" She let out a shuddery breath. "What if everyone believes Porsche? They will think that I bought my way into college and onto the team! How do I fight that?"

Her two best friends looked away.

❧

CYphur: *If anyone's interested they can watch you play. Just keep making those assists. No one can say money buys your game on the field.*

Jesse smiled, more grateful than she could say for CYphur's support.

She had sent Emlyn and Pinky away, annoyed because she wasn't even certain they believed her. She was too mad to call her mother just yet. Besides, with Xavier in the news and all the controversy surrounding that, she had enough to deal with at the moment.

As for her grandparents, she didn't dare call them. Not until she could decide how she felt about them writing her coach in the first place, even if it was all aboveboard.

CYphur was a safe bet because he didn't even know who she

was. They were now doing their own private chats, outside of Multiplicity. It had grown out of the fact that they liked to discuss things the other members didn't find interesting. Still, neither one had yet revealed their name, or even where they attended school.

You believe me then?

CYphur: *I've seen you play.*

Jesse jumped as if she'd been goosed. *What?*

CYphur: *Online. Clips of all women's college soccer games go up on websites immediately after the matches. I must have seen you play, even if I didn't know which one was you, right?*

She typed: *Sound logic.* Only he'd hesitated a moment before replying. Was he lying about knowing who she was? Or just trying to cheer her up? *Okay. Thanks.*

CYphur: *You mad because you thought I knew what you look like?*

Jesse grinned. *Only if you're better looking than me.*

CYphur: *Not a chance.*

∞

Nita did not return to campus for nine days. By then, rumors of every kind were circling about her absence. The most popular one was that she had fallen down the steps going to the subway after a wild night of partying in Manhattan and injured herself. She was staying with a friend to recover and would be back on campus soon.

Jesse suspected it was all a lie because Nita didn't email her. And Berta had a furtive look in her eyes when she came to the dorm to pick up a few things.

When she finally arrived by limo that afternoon, Nita

emerged from the depths of the private car with every hair in place and lips glossier than usual. She also sported two black eyes half hidden behind enormous designer shades, a sling on one arm, and Fidel in the other.

"A wrenched shoulder and two bruised ribs," Nita accounted to the gathering. "But I am on so many painkillers that I really don't mind."

"Oh my God!" Jesse muttered as she watched the spectacle from the second-floor landing of the dorm. "He beat the holy hell out of her! How can she lie for him like that?"

Emlyn and Pinky, whom Jesse had confided in about her weekend in Manhattan, kept glancing at her. "Aren't you going to call her on those lies?"

"No." Jesse swallowed the bile of guilt. She had left Nita and this was the result! She felt sick with cowardice. Her mother's advice to always save herself first didn't seem so clever now that she was face-to-face with what she'd abandoned Nita to endure.

She turned away, pushing past girls who didn't get out of the way fast enough.

A few minutes later, Nita arrived in their dorm room, accompanied by her maid, who clucked and fussed and hovered over her employer until Nita finally sent her away on an errand to find some item of clothing stored at the apartment in town.

When she was gone, Jesse opened her door.

Nita swung around with a smile. "Dios! She means well, that woman, but she has been driving me mad!"

Jesse's lip quivered as she looked at her. "Oh, God! I'm so sorry, Nita!"

Nita brushed aside Jesse's anguish. "These things happen."

"You don't have to be nice! I know I ran out on you. But I'm not afraid. I'll testify against the bastard if you want me to."

Nita tossed her head. "I don't know what you're talking about."

"I know Poppi did this to you."

Nita peeked at her over the tops of her shades. "What? Poppi never hurt me."

"I was there, remember. I saw him slap you."

"Oh that. It was nothing."

"Come on. I know you didn't fall down steps into a subway. You're always boasting about how when you're in Manhattan you never use the subway."

"So, I tried it. You see what happened."

Jesse took a deep breath. "You are afraid of him, aren't you?"

Nita dumped Fidel onto her bed. "You want to know the truth? We were having a very civilized conversation when suddenly there are police at the door. Some idiot called them with claims of domestic violence. Who do they arrest? Me!" She cursed in Spanish until Fidel began to bark in distress.

"Why were you arrested?"

"The police searched the apartment and found a tiny bit of cocaine." She rolled her eyes. "Poppi uses it for an edge in certain high-powered meetings."

"Purely medicinal, right?" Jesse was too shocked to be anything else but glib about the drug discovery.

"But the police did not take that into account. So I said it was mine."

"You what?" Jesse got mad all over again. "How stupid can you be!"

Nita's eyes flashed. "You sound like my parents. Poppi said

it was best if I called them to bail me out of jail. If he did it, the police would think he'd put me up to lying about the coke."

"Unlike the fact that it was your own dumb idea?"

Nita turned to move Fidel off her bed but winced in pain.

Jesse scooped up the dog. "Who beat you, Nita? And don't say no one. You've got bruises back and front."

Nita lowered herself carefully onto her bed. "My parents are so unreasonable! Once we were back in Miami I told them about Poppi and the cocaine. They went loco! Mami took a broom handle to me."

"Your mother beat you?" Jesse couldn't wrap her head around that. She could barely remember being spanked by her own parents. Losing TV privileges was major punishment. Beatings with a broom handle, it didn't compute.

Nita reached up to adjust her shades. "She thought I was on drugs. I tripped trying to get away from her and smashed my face into the doorjamb." Nita felt gingerly about her glasses. "The doctor says my nose isn't broken, thank God."

"Oh yeah. Everything's just great." Jesse mechanically stroked Fidel. "You only have an arrest sheet for drug possession, missed your midterms, and your mother tried to kill you."

"She never did!" Nita's gaze narrowed as she watched Fidel's enjoyment of Jesse's attention. "Mami was so contrite when they brought me home from emergency. She offered me anything to stay in Miami. But I told them I have to live my life."

Nita fiddled around a moment and then swept a hand from behind her back to reveal a ring with a brilliant pale yellow stone the size of a dime.

Jesse gulped. "Is that real?"

"Canary-yellow diamond. Four carats. Harry Winston." Nita

played her hand under the overhead lights so that the stone shot tiny rainbow refractions all over the ceiling. "I saw Poppi yesterday when I stopped over in the city on my way back here. I told him that I need more time to be certain about us. That's when he gave me this. He said he doesn't want to lose me."

"It's big enough to choke on." And that would shut her up about drugs and everything else.

"We are engaged to marry next June."

"You're a fool, Nita!"

Nita gave her a smug look. "You're just jealous."

"This is hopeless!" Jesse turned and walked out.

∽∾

Can you even believe it? The price of a beating and a drug rap is a four-carat diamond.

CYphur: *That will buy a lot of Icy Hot.*

Jesse smirked. *Not even funny!*

CYphur: *Maybe the diamond's enough to keep her warm.*

No. It's cold and a weird color, like he is.

CYphur: *LOL! A man wouldn't have to buy diamonds to win you?*

He only has to act like a man.

CYphur: *What? You don't want a hottie with a basketball butt who "makes me laugh, has a car, can pay my bills"?*

Jesse giggled. *If he's cute but doesn't act like he knows it, that's okay.*

CYphur: *What about love?*

Jesse hesitated a second. *What about it?*

CYphur: *Don't you want to be loved?*

I haven't figured out what that is.

CYphur: *Sounds like someone's been hurt. Guy break your heart in high school?*

No guy.

CYphur: *No guy? Ever?*

How much to tell? *Nothing serious.*

CYphur: *I see.*

I'm not a virgin but I'm celibate, for the time being.

CYphur: *That's a bold move.*

It's all that makes sense these days. What about you?

CYphur: *I'm solo. Again. Looking to make a meaningful connection this time with someone.*

Jesse made a face as she typed: *Some poor unsuspecting woman has no idea you're circling?*

Long pause.

CYphur: *I guess not.*

Chapter 29

"You must be very happy to see someone you can identify with win the vice presidency," Tom Grant said loudly.

Thea lowered her newspaper. Seated facing her, Tom pointed at the front page. She folded the paper and looked at the group photo of presidential candidates and smiled. "Yes, I'm very happy to see a qualified woman winning one of the country's highest offices. We can do anything, haven't you figured that out by now?"

Tom's left eye twitched. He couldn't correct her without making it plain he meant the black vice president. That was too un-PC in public even for him.

Tom was so predictable!

Usually she didn't bother to use the VIP lounges at airports but her flight out of LaGuardia had been delayed two hours and she needed a comfortable spot to unwind, even if it meant sharing space with her old nemesis Tom Grant. A dyed-in-the-wool pain in the ass, he was one of those professional colleagues she kept finding herself doing business with. Thankfully, he didn't work at Walker, Brennan, and Cullum and Associates. Despite his attempts to keep it otherwise, the playing field had leveled.

He'd never forgiven her for outmaneuvering him two years earlier while they both served as counsel for a client testifying before a congressional subcommittee. At the time, he was a senior partner while she had yet to make junior partner. Now she was acting managing partner of the home office in Dallas while he ran the firm's Houston office. Technically, she outranked him. It must stick in his craw, as her father would say. Maybe that's why he was knocking back bourbons.

Thea reached for her soda with lime—she never drank liquor while traveling—and looked again at her watch. Flying had long since lost its glamour along with its comforts and on-time scheduling. The appeal of the lounge was the quiet and sense of solitude.

She seldom paid attention as other passengers came and went. Yet something made her glance up as the doors opened in the lobby. To her surprise she saw Xavier enter.

He had on an expensive charcoal-gray suit, like the kind he wore when she first met him, and mirror-bright dress shoes. And he wasn't alone.

As the party of four paused at the counter to check in, the apathy of the lounge's seasoned travelers evaporated.

Xavier's companions included Bazz Azz, in baggy jeans, a diamond-encrusted belt buckle no one could overlook, and a black silk shirt completely unbuttoned to expose the triumph of a personal trainer. Two attractive young women, one on each arm in suede hoodies, skin-tight capris, and stiletto heels, completed his ghetto fabulous look.

As they moved into the lounge, Thea caught Xavier's attention. A genuine smile quickly chased away his surprise. He turned to Bazz Azz and said something. The younger man gave her a look she couldn't read and then a nod of acknowledgment before steering his companions off in the direction of the bar. As Xavier came toward her, she closed the distance.

"What are you doing here?" they asked at the same time.

Xavier grinned but didn't touch her. "We're headed for D.C."

"I'm catching a flight to Dallas." Thea didn't reach for him either. Ministerial reserve in public places.

They sounded like casual friends who'd just bumped into one another after years of being out of touch instead of newlyweds of several months. Maybe that was because they hadn't seen each other since her tea with Hattie. The phone calls they'd exchanged during the week were brief and less and less intimate because they didn't have time to get into a discussion of things that were really on their minds. Now wasn't the time, either.

Thea finally leaned in and kissed him on the cheek, saying in an undertone, "I didn't know you were coming to the city."

He dipped his head and brushed his lips across hers. "It was last minute. I came up because Bazz asked. I was just about to call you." He held up his cell as evidence of his sincerity. "But this is better. Cancel and come to D.C. with me."

"Can't. I have meetings in Dallas in the morning." Thea's gaze kept going to the bar where people were gathering around Bazz Azz or ogling the women by his side. She looked back at Xavier's disappointed expression and wanted to ask when he'd be home. But that would sound like a stereotypical question from a lonely wife who suspected her husband of not wanting to be at home.

"I'm Tom Grant, Reverend Thornton." Tom had come up

behind her and now stuck out his hand. "Your wife and I are longtime business associates."

Thea grimaced because Tom made it sound like they'd been more.

"Yes, I remember you. D.C. Two years ago?" Xavier shook hands.

"You remember me?" Tom was genuinely flattered.

Xavier smiled and glanced at Thea. "I remember it as the night I introduced Thea to my family. She didn't know it yet but I had already decided I wanted to marry her."

"Isn't that romantic?" Tom sounded about as thrilled as if he'd been told about an appendicitis operation. "I'm going to go freshen up my drink." He pointed to Thea's soda and grinned. "You want another one? Vodka, was it?"

"No thank you. I've had enough soda with lime for one night." Oh, he was so funny she forgot to laugh.

Xavier took her hand. "Can't you cancel tomorrow? I need to be with you."

She nodded, feeling the current that always ran between them when in the same room. "I need to be with you, too. Can't you just come home with me? We need to talk."

"I can't." His black eyes searched her face. "Bazz is going to make the morning news talk shows to try to nullify the events of last week."

Thea stiffened. "And you need to be there to hold his hand?"

"I need to be there to remind him to sound repentant even if he's pushed by the press."

"Doesn't he have a manager for that kind of thing?"

Xavier's voice dropped. "His manager was the one finally charged with the assault."

She backed up a step. She kept her voice low but suspected

that anyone watching them would know the conversation had taken on a chill. "This is what you want to be caught up in? After all your talk about wanting to back away from the limelight?"

"Thea." He said her name so softly, only she knew it was a rebuke. *Not here,* his eyes told her.

She looked away. "I think they're calling my flight. I'll see you back in Dallas tomorrow night."

"No, I have a wake tomorrow in Pine Grove and then the funeral." His expression pleaded for understanding. But she was suddenly angry.

"Fine. Put me in your calendar for Saturday. In Pine Grove." She glanced over at Bazz Azz. "Good luck with your babysitting gig. He looks like a handful."

❧

The minute she opened the door to the parsonage she realized she was safe from confrontation for the moment. Tyrell Franklin had Xavier's full attention as they sat at the new dining room table talking.

"We got to get us some ballers on the court, Rev."

She saw Xavier writing on a pad. "How about Donte Hawkins?"

"Nawgh. He's about as wide as he is tall. He can't move no ball."

"Let's give him the chance. What about John Leonard and Frisco?"

"What kinda name is Frisco?"

"Hispanic. We have two new families in the church."

Tyrell chuckled. "Mexicans play ball?"

She walked quickly through the living room, glad to have a moment to collect herself from the six-hour drive.

"This is a chance for kids who won't make the school teams to play basketball."

"We're going to lose every game." Tyrell reared back in his seat and noticed Thea. "Hey, Mrs. Reverend."

Xavier looked over his shoulder at Thea. "Evening, Mrs. Thornton." Even the way he said her formal name had a caress in it.

"Hey yourself." She tried to smile but it felt like a mistake. "I'm just going to go in and change."

She stripped off her silk suit and stockings and tossed them together in a knotted heap in the bedroom corner. She had taken a day off on Friday and driven in directly from her office. By the time she pulled on jeans and a long T-shirt, she had decided on a course of action. She fisted her hair back into a ponytail, twisted it, and clipped it to the back of her head with a hair claw.

She would not be a hypocrite by sitting in the front pew at St. Hurricane on Sunday mornings. She no longer cared what Mrs. Patterson or the Pastoral Relations Committee would make of her absence. Things had changed. She was no longer willing to try to please or appease.

Xavier had once said that Hattie Patterson wanted to take her under her wing. It was clear now that the woman wished she could smother her in some dark place!

She'd had two more hard days of thinking about their lives and how it wasn't working. But she didn't want to tear Xavier's world apart until she had decided how she could put it back together.

She slipped into the kitchen. The first thing she noticed was that Xavier had eaten. Two plates were in the sink. He must have served Tyrell, too. She heard a chair scrape in the dining room as she opened the oven door and discovered a dish she had not made. Then she heard Xavier saying goodbye to his guest.

She waited in the kitchen until Tyrell was gone. Then she came to the dining room doorway with a half-eaten casserole in her hands. "What's this?"

Xavier looked up from his reading. "Chicken with rice. Mrs. Jenkins brought it by earlier in the week. We have a freezer full of casseroles. Church ladies certainly like to cook." He patted his middle. "Help yourself. You won't need to make a meal for the next month. It'll be like being a guest for dinner in your own home."

Thea's smile wouldn't come. *A guest in my home. No, in Xavier's home.* He didn't leave much more than a toothbrush at her home in Dallas these days.

She went back into the kitchen and pulled open a drawer to get a serving spoon. But there were no utensils in the drawer. She was looking at neatly folded tea towels and a pair of oven mitts she'd never seen before. Biting her lip in annoyance, she pulled open another drawer, and then another. Nothing was in the place where she had put it.

Suddenly the room felt too small, the walls were crowding in. Someone had been in her kitchen. Some woman! This was nothing Deacon Jacobs would have done.

Several gallon cans of paint stacked in the corner by the kitchen door caught her eye as she turned away from the cabinet. She went over to look. Each can contained a different color. Caribbean blue, coral, and primrose yellow. She would never have chosen those hues for a home.

Snatching up a gallon, she marched back to the doorway separating the kitchen from the dining room. "What's this, Xavier?" She held up the can.

He looked up again. That's when she noticed he was reading his sermon, which he always printed on yellow paper. "Since you said you wanted to paint the other rooms, Mrs. Patterson had Deacon Jacobs pick up paint from Walmart. She said he got a good price by buying colors that had been returned."

A guest in her own home. "These colors would make the parsonage look like a Caribbean bordello."

Xavier laughed. "We can find a more diplomatic way to say no."

"I don't want to find a more diplomatic way. I don't want to have to apologize for every thought I have." She turned to leave when his voice stopped her.

"Thea, what's wrong?"

She turned back. "Who's been in my kitchen moving things?"

He half turned in his chair with an I-knew-you'd-hate-it expression. "That was Lola's doing. She said you had things in all the wrong places and rearranged them while I was out of town."

"You let another woman come in here and change things after I had them exactly where I wanted them?"

The look on his face said he knew he'd done something wrong. "Okay, Thea. You're right. But I didn't let her. She volunteered. It's just a few knives and spoons. It won't take a lot of time to put it back."

"I don't have even a damn minute to mess with this!"

She went back into the kitchen, Xavier following her, and put the paint back in the corner. Then she pushed a drawer to close it but it was stuck. She jerked it hard and it came unstuck so quickly that she lost control. It slid all the way out, dumping flatware onto the floor. The clatter made a funky backbeat for her anger. "She had no right! My home! My things!"

Xavier stepped forward to take the drawer from her. "Come, Thea. What's bothering you?"

She swung around on him. "Me? I can't turn my back without someone sneaking in here making changes. Last week it was those ugly curtains someone put up in the guest bedroom. Now I've got paint I don't want, and a kitchen arrangement I don't want."

"I see your point." He nodded and set the drawer on the countertop. "But, come on. You're overreacting just a bit."

Why do men ever use that sentence! She jutted her chin out. "I don't want to come home to *my* house and find out some other woman has rearranged *my* things or is feeding *my* husband because she thinks I don't know what I'm doing!"

He held up both hands in defeat. "I'll ask everyone to just back off and leave us in peace for a while."

"Why should you have to do that? Why can't we just lock our doors and feel safe that no one will change the color of the walls while we're out?"

He chuckled. "Come on, Thea. We live in a parsonage. It doesn't belong to us."

A guest in her own home.

She swung away from him. "This is not working. I need time to think. I need time at home, in my home."

"Okay, I see that. Why don't you take a week's vacation and chill? Go see Jesse. Visit Selma."

She knelt and began picking up forks and spoons. "No, I mean I'm not coming back here."

His voice changed. "For how long?"

"I don't know."

"Okay." She could feel him thinking, calculating, though she didn't look up. "I can take time off—well, a short while. I'll come back to Dallas with you for a while."

"No!" The force of her own voice startled her. She glanced up. He looked as if she had slapped him.

She stood up. "I'm sorry, Xavier. I want to be alone for a while. There are things I have to think about, and I don't need any pressure."

She saw him tense with the realization that she was talking about more than tea towels and paint. "Is this about me? Something I did or should have done? You're angry because I went to the aid of Bazz Azz. Is that it?"

"No. It's not about you or him. It is about *us*. There's a difference."

"You need to tell me what's wrong with us so we can fix it."

I'm not sure that the fix is one I want to make.

She looked away. She couldn't talk when he was all she could see. That's when she thought she could do this, make it happen, try a little harder. He did that by just being there. "I shouldn't have come back."

She moved past him quickly and went into the bedroom. Her overnight bag was still packed. She picked it up but when she turned he was filling up the doorway.

"You can't just leave like this!"

Hurt and shock had stripped his mellow bass and changed his easygoing expression into hard lines. "You owe me some sort of explanation. I am your husband." He said those words with all the ancient power of possession.

"You don't own me."

The second she said that, she regretted it. This wasn't supposed to turn into a fight. Though, God help her, what else could it be? She wanted out—at least as far as the door for now.

"Talk to me, Theadora!"

She put her hands up when he came toward her. "Don't make me say things that I'm not sure I believe."

For God's sake, don't let him touch me!

If he held her and kissed her, she knew she would cave in for now, to stop his pain and hers. Then they would just have to do this all over again tomorrow, or next week, but they would. Loving each other wasn't the problem. It just couldn't solve the problem.

She could tell him what Hattie had said but it wasn't really about her mean-spirited, spiteful lecture. It was something she had known all along and ignored in the hope it would work itself out.

I do not want the life we lead at St. Hurricane. But how could she tell him that after she had encouraged him in this undertaking? *Can't fight God for him.*

He changed direction, stepping off to the side, his head half turned from her. "Just talk to me. Tell me what you're feeling."

"You want to know how I feel?" Something burst inside her. "I feel that I can't do this!" Frustration and hurt set in motion words she'd wanted to hold back. "I made a mistake thinking I could be a minister's wife. I don't want to become what it means to be a minister's wife. I don't pray enough. I don't know the Bible. I can't quote scripture and I don't want to teach Sunday school."

Why did men always look so surprised when the women in their lives blew up?

He shook his head. "That can't be the problem. What do you want from me?"

"Nothing. I want nothing from you." She reached the doorway then turned toward him. "*I* want to do better, Xavier. But I can't do that now. I can't."

He made a sound like a grunt and dropped onto the edge of the bed. He was angry. She could see him struggling to contain it. Finally he looked up, challenge in his expression. "You can't what, be my wife?"

"I don't—" She shook her head. "I need time to think."

"Let's sit and pray over this, Thea. Come and kneel here with me. Anything can be set right by prayer."

She recoiled. "Maybe for you. But not for me. I can't lie about that anymore. I don't feel it, Xavier. I do believe in God. But when I pray I don't feel a thing. Not the peace you preach about, not the solace, and certainly not the answers."

He held out his hand to her and she saw that it trembled slightly. "I love you."

Coming from a lesser man that might have been an easy play. But she knew he found those words hard to come by.

She was cracking inside, her heart splitting right across the middle. "I love you, too. But . . ."

"But what? It's over?" He was watching her with big eyes full of pain.

"I don't—" The more she said, the deeper the chasm between

them seemed to grow. She wanted to explain but there was a weakness creeping over her. And, the desire just to be done. At bottom, the dread of having to keep trying was greater than the pain of escape.

The words tumbled out of her. Not in any coherent order but from the pain and passion of holding them in too long.

"I thought I could make this work. I thought I could fit our two lives into one life. But, no matter what I'm doing, I feel guilty about what I'm not doing. I'm not twenty. I can't bend and adapt and change my ways as I once could. I'm not a bad person because I like to be able to buy designer coffee on the corner. I'm not some hard-nosed bitch because I love my job and want to keep it. I'm a problem solver. I'm a doer. I'm good at finding the middle ground and compromising for the best for all concerned. I'm trying to find one for us."

That seemed to relieve him. "We haven't been married but three months. It takes time to sort out problems in a new life."

She blew out her breath. "It's not about time. It's about whether I want to try to sort them out."

This time he didn't have anything else to say.

She picked up her overnight bag and stepped out into the hall.

It took him a moment to understand what she was doing. "Where are you going?"

"To sleep in the guest room."

He came after her, filling the narrow hallway. "You don't have to do that. I won't touch you. You need to sleep in your own bed."

She looked at him. "That's the trouble. Nothing in this house feels like it belongs to me."

He put his hand on her shoulder, as much a caress as a command to stay with him. "Nothing?"

She knew what he was asking. But after he'd told her often enough he'd prayed for this undertaking, she wasn't even sure Xavier belonged to her, either.

Can't fight God for him.

She backed out from under his touch. "Let me go, Xavier. Let me have some time to get myself together. I don't want to make any mistakes I'll regret."

Tears stood in his eyes. "Are you leaving me?"

"I'm trying to save myself. Don't force me to choose anything else right now."

⊶⊷

She hoisted her bag and moved toward her car. She was carrying back more than she had brought because the weather was changing. The dark early November morning held a whisper of a chill that had yet to reach farther south into Texas. Xavier was still asleep. She'd heard him walking the floor and knocking around in the kitchen until after two A.M. Now at a quarter of six he was dead to the world. She didn't want to fight anymore so she was leaving before that could happen. The note she'd left said as much.

The crowing of the rooster sounded so loud and so close Thea dropped her bag on the sidewalk. And then she felt something brush past her leg. She let out a yelp and leaped up onto the hood of her car.

"Mrs. Reverend. Is that you?"

She hadn't noticed anyone approaching but suddenly a figure stood a few feet away. She didn't recognize him at first in the darkness though he seemed to know who she was. "Deacon Jacobs?"

"Uh, yes, ma'am."

Another figure came up beside him. Dressed in droopy pants and a hoodie, he held a big sack. "What's she doing out here?"

"Now don't get upset. It's nothing." Deacon Jacobs turned to Thea. "Is something wrong, Mrs. Reverend?"

Thea steadied her breath. "No. I—I was just leaving." Her hands trembled badly as she tried to find the keypad to unlock her car. "Was that a rooster I just heard?"

Deacon Jacobs's smile was like that of the Cheshire cat, and all she could see distinctly. "Now, Mrs. Reverend, don't be asking about that just now. All in good time. You just shouldn't be out here like this, in the dark. It ain't safe."

The young man had backed into the shadows of a tree. Deacon Jacobs moved to come between her and her view of him. "I'm asking you to go back inside."

"I'm just leaving." She opened the car door, tossed her bag on the passenger seat, and slid behind the wheel. She locked the door before starting the engine. Yet she didn't throw the car into gear.

Instead, she watched through the rearview mirror as the deacon and boy walked back across the street and around the Brown sisters' house into their backyard. Were they about to rob Cora and Hortense? Surely the deacon wouldn't be involved in anything like that?

Then the silhouette of the younger man tumbled into place in her mind.

"That was Tyrell!"

She put the car in gear and drove down the block to knock at the Brown sisters' front door.

Chapter 30

Jesse was annoyed with herself as she walked back across campus to the dorm from sorority house row.

She had just been to the party Gamma Gamma Mu gave for its most wanted rushees. It was a last-minute decision that wasn't worth the effort. It consisted of a dozen nervous freshmen women who didn't want to make eye contact with one another. That was part of the drama. A girl could not afford to bond with another, in case they were chosen by a different sorority, or dropped altogether. Until the lines formed, this was strictly an every-girl-for-herself situation.

Most of the Gammas didn't even bother to show. The rushees were left to deal with lukewarm champagne, crudités, and caviar that no one in her right mind would take a second bite of.

As she was leaving another rushee came up to her. "It's obvious this is a last chance for sorority sisters to look over the unchosen. Want to bet we are all also-rans?"

Jesse saw a Gamma girl standing nearby. The soror met her eye but didn't smile. And so that's that, Jesse thought. Since meeting the Lambdas at Nita's party, the idea of belonging to a sorority had gained in appeal. But if it wasn't meant to be, that was okay, too.

After a phone call to her grandparents a few days ago, at her mother's suggestion, she wasn't certain she could ever trust them again. They admitted writing her coach, but only to commend their granddaughter's performance on the team. They swore they hadn't tried to influence the coach in any manner. But then she remembered that her grandmother was a Gamma Gamma Mu. So now even the prospect of being rushed was tainted. In fact, she felt her whole college career at Simmons was under a cloud of suspicion, ruined by the specter of her father's family legacy having bought her way in. Maybe the only thing to do would be to change schools.

The only good thing to happen all week was that Edgardo had called her out of the blue the night before. He said he'd gotten her number from Nita. A complete miracle in itself, since they still weren't speaking. And he wanted to see her again.

Jesse smiled to herself as she walked up the steps to her dorm. She'd said she wanted to see him, too, but didn't know how that would happen since she had no reason to go back to NYC again soon. Going up to Dartmouth was out of the question while soccer season was in full gear. That's when he said he'd most likely see her at the Big East Conference Tournament. His sister's team at Marquette and the Ladyhawkes were ranked to meet in the semifinals. Small world!

She saw Nita coming toward her across the dorm lobby, wearing a short white skirt and really high heels though it was definitely jacket weather north of the Finger Lakes. Makeup hid what was left of her bruises but it seemed nothing could heal the rift between them.

Jesse decided to take the high road. "Thanks for giving Edgardo my number."

Nita ignored her as she plowed out into the chill night.

Jesse shook her head. They had had words again just last night. She had tried to reason with Nita, reminding her of her dreams of a fine arts degree, and her desire to start a chapter of Lambda at Simmons. Was she really willing to abandon all that for marriage to a drug user who beat her? Because whether she wanted to remember it or not, Poppi had struck her in front of Jesse. Once a man crossed that line, statistics showed they almost never backed off. Nita had told her in gutter Spanish what she could do with her opinions.

Despite all that, some things were looking up. She was playing more and playing better soccer than ever before. CYphur was right. Her skills were dampening the accusation that she wasn't Ladyhawke material.

And, she'd become something of a persona on campus after standing up to Porsche. The reason for the fight also got her some curious stares that usually ended in some guy coming over to talk with her. But she wasn't really into any of those guys. They wanted to hook up with the woman who dared stand up to Porsche, as if being with her made them look daring or strong or something.

Most of her social time was spent online with CYphur. He was funny and could argue well. He said he was on his college debate team. She liked that, too. Her dad had gone to nationals as a member of the Georgetown debate team. They talked politics and movies, real-world things that had nothing to do with being hit on and hooking up.

Emlyn said liking a guy because he could argue made her weird.

Jesse had defended her opinion by pointing out that her parents were attorneys. Defending one's point of view well was communication in her household. She loved her grandparents but she didn't understand them because they defined themselves in terms of who they were—the banking Morgans—and who they associated with. Her parents had taught her to be proud of herself for herself and what she accomplished on her own. That's where CYphur came in.

She was certain in the beginning that CYphur must be the biggest geek on his campus. He was probably short and skinny or twice her weight with bad posture, a gross complexion, and in need of adding a daily shower to his regimen. And his taste in music! He was a hipster, liking bands she'd never heard of with names like Death Cab for Cutie and TV on the Radio.

But lately none of that seemed to matter. Well, yes, good hygiene would always matter. But she was ready to risk finding out where he was and who he was, just as soon as soccer season was over.

As she reached her room, two senior Ladyhawke teammates stopped and handed her a ribbon. "You need to wear this discreetly at all times to all events on campus, including classes, for the next two weeks."

"Why?"

"You have to finish the rush but you belong to us." Jesse watched as one of them touched the small enamel pin on her sweater. The initials were Gamma Gamma Mu.

"Wait!" She hurried after them. "Is this about my grandmother?"

The two girls exchanged glances. "If you must know it's

about your chances of following Porsche as team captain when she graduates next year. You've got guts and skills on the field."

The second girl nodded. "We've never had a Gamma Glamour Girl as a team captain before."

Jesse held their gazes. "You know I'm biracial?"

"Is that supposed to be a pro or con for you?"

"It just is." Jesse turned and walked away, her smile so wide she wondered how she'd be able to fit in her door.

⚭

"Are your parents here?"

"Half," Jesse answered a teammate as she laced up her cleats for the Ladyhawkes' semifinal game. "My mother's new husband."

"Interesting."

"Yeah." Jesse hadn't seen Xavier yet. But he'd called to say since her mother was in Chile on business he wanted to come up and root for her team. That surprised her. He had never before called her, and her mother hadn't said a word about him coming up. She didn't mind that he would be here. In fact, it helped to think that someone out there in the bleachers was thinking only of her. Edgardo was bound to be cheering for his sister.

"Where's your buddy, Blondie?"

Jesse looked up to find Porsche standing before her. "You mean Emlyn?"

"That's the one. Your freshman girlfriend disappeared into the bathroom half an hour ago and no one's seen her since. If she's puking up her guts in fear, tell her that's okay. Half the other team is, too. But we need her on the bench."

Porsche swung away without waiting for a reply. That was fine by Jesse.

Since their almost-fight Porsche seemed to forget she was alive unless they were on the field. Then Porsche was all about the game. Rumor said that the threat of a poor-conduct flag in her file for violation of the character clause of the athletic department had been enough to cool Porsche's temper. Calling an injured teammate a "dumbass bitch" wouldn't go down well with Olympic officials.

Jesse found Emlyn in the last stall. She could hear her crying. "What's wrong, Emlyn? Cramps?"

"Cramps are a breeze." Emlyn lifted the latch and the door swung open. She was sitting on the toilet in a hunched-over position, her face streaked with tears.

"You're sick. I'll go get Coach!"

"No!" Emlyn's voice was ragged with desperation. "Nobody needs to know. Okay?"

"Then tell me what's wrong?"

Emlyn sucked in a breath. "Herpes."

"Oh!" Jesse moved in closer and put a hand on her friend's head. "You know how—" Emlyn gave her a look. "I mean who?"

Emlyn shrugged. "There was a private party for Greeks a couple of weeks ago at the frat house. The little sisters put it together. We all got wasted."

Jesse fidgeted as blood heated up her cheeks. "Oh." Fill-in-the-blanks time.

"If you're going to criticize—"

"No, just oh."

"I'd had my eye on this one guy in the fraternity whose girlfriend is Greek. But he said something about how he couldn't poach a fraternity's little sister without the frat's permission. So there was a toll charge." Emlyn sounded so ordinary, as if she was talking about a cab ride to the airport. "I did two guys."

Jesse squatted down and began wiping her friend's face. "But you're like the most gorgeous girl. You could have any guy. Why would you want to be a frat sluttie?"

Emlyn glared at her. "What?! Are you suddenly Mother Theresa? Everybody does it. I just got unlucky." She hugged herself tighter. "It's the price of a party. Not all of us get to be a Gamma Glamour Girl."

Jesse couldn't think of a thing to say. She had heard the lectures since she was twelve. Who hadn't? But sexually active and sexually transmitted diseases finally made a hardwired connection in her head. "Okay, so, what can I do? What do you need?"

"Ice bag. And I borrowed some medication. It's in my bag."

Jesse got to her feet. "You can't play today."

"Duh!"

Jesse went to Emlyn's locker and rifled through her bag until she found a medication bottle. She gasped softly. The prescription was for Porsche!

As she came from the lavatory, having gotten Emlyn an ice bag, water, and meds, Porsche came tearing through the locker room, clapping her hands and shouting, "Come on, Ladyhawkes! Move it! We've got a championship to win!"

Chapter 31

The crowds at Union College were much larger than those Jesse had played in front of before. Not that she had much time to think about crowds.

From the beginning of the game, it was clear that the Ladyhawkes were on the defensive, with one of their best players, Tanya, benched by an ankle injury that had occurred during practice the day before. It spooked the team, even with Porsche out front shouting encouragement and invective.

Within the first ten minutes of the game a midfielder delivered a brilliant pass to set up UNC's first goal. By halftime, the Ladyhawkes were in serious jeopardy of being knocked out of the first round of the tournament.

When Jesse took the field just after the half, the Ladyhawkes were down by one goal. In no time she was bottled up on the right sideline, with her back to the goal. She was in this position when she saw an attacker coming toward her with the ball. She spotted Porsche blazing diagonally across the field. Jesse challenged the ball and with a sweeping kick fired a slicing rocket to Porsche all in one continuous motion.

A fraction of a second later, Jesse felt the pain of cleats digging into her thigh as her opponent's kick went wide of the mark and she lost her balance. And then she was tumbling, too, pain searing through her leg.

⸎

"Gramma and PopPop, what are you doing here?" Jesse had been wheeled back from having stitches to find her grandparents in her emergency room cubicle.

"How are you feeling, sweetheart?" Richard and Shirley Morgan asked in unison.

"Okay." Jesse sucked in a breath as the orderly helped her from the gurney back into the bed. "I hurt my leg. And I got a bunch of stitches. That's all."

"That's all?" Jesse thought her grandmother sounded as appalled as if she'd said her face needed complete surgical restructuring. "Soccer is such a rough sport for a young woman."

Jesse looked out the window of the hospital room. "The one time I get to ride in an ambulance and I can't really remember it."

"You were in a lot of pain from that gouge in your thigh."

"Cut, Richard," Shirley corrected. "Your grandfather likes to exaggerate the gore factor. The other girl was injured, too. Strained a tendon, I'm told. But you are both going to be just fine."

"They gave you something for pain before they put you in the ambulance." Richard checked to see if his wife would interrupt again. "You're going to be fine."

Jesse looked back at them with a new thought. "How did you get here? Did the coach call you?"

"No, dear." Shirley patted her hand. "We were at the game."

Richard nodded. "Your grandmother's had a cold all week. We didn't want to promise to be here and then disappoint you. But she was better this morning so we decided to drive up and surprise you."

Jesse smiled. "Nice."

Shirley patted Jesse's arm this time. "We wouldn't have missed it for the world. We had no idea your mother wouldn't be here. The coach told us she's halfway around the world at a legal conference in Chile." Shirley's tone said what she thought of that. "Now I'm doubly glad we came since you'd have had no one here to look after you."

Jesse didn't rise to the bait on that one. She loved her grandparents dearly but there had always been a bit of a competitive ping-pong match between them and her mother. It had only gotten worse after her dad died. She'd given her mother her blessing for the South America trip, saying it was okay as long as she was back in time for the finals at Texas A&M. Even her busy mother could make it from Dallas to College Station.

The nurse stuck her head inside the curtain and smiled at Jesse. "How are you doing?" Jesse gave her a weak thumbs-up. "Okay. They'll be coming in a few minutes to take you to X-ray before they set that broken leg."

"Broken?" Shirley's voice rose an octave. "But Jesse said she only needed stitches."

Jesse dodged her grandparents' gazes. "Didn't want to worry you."

The nurse stepped in for a moment. "She fractured her femur. They need to be certain it's a clean break. If so, she'll be put in a traction splint. Her doctor will come in and explain."

"Buck up, Shirley." Richard put an arm around his wife. "Jesse's a star athlete. They can't just stitch her up like an old blanket. She needs special care."

The nurse smiled at Jesse. "There's a minister out here who wants to see you. He says he's a friend of the family. A Reverend Thornton."

"Xavier?" Jesse tried to nod but that didn't seem to be a good idea because her head already seemed to be floating. "He's my mother's . . . my stepfather. Let him in."

Jesse was surprised by how glad she was to see Xavier. "Have you called Mom?" were the first words out of her mouth.

He smiled. "Not yet. Knowing your mother I thought I'd better have a direct sighting report to give her." He glanced at the two other people in the room.

"These are my grandparents, Richard and Shirley Morgan. Gramma and PopPop, this is Reverend Xavier."

Jesse watched curiously as they all shook hands and exchanged the kinds of pleasantries older people do when they meet. How awkward that her dad's parents should meet her mother's new husband without her mother being there. She suddenly felt sorry for Xavier. He'd told the nurse he was "a friend of the family," as if he thought she might not want to claim him directly. Yet now he seemed completely at ease.

"Thea talks most warmly about Evan." He held Shirley's gaze as he spoke. "She tells me that he is to blame for half of Jesse's brain and all of her athletic abilities. I'd say she inherited some of the Morgan good looks as well."

Her grandmother's returning smile seemed genuine. "How charming of you to say so, Reverend Thornton."

"Xavier, please. We are connected by family now."

"Yes, we are." Shirley turned to her husband. "Let's get a cup of coffee and let these two have a moment alone." She bent and kissed Jesse's cheek. "We've already decided that you can come home with us to recuperate, since your mother's not here." She glanced at Xavier as if expecting a contradiction.

"We'll see," Jesse answered for him.

Richard offered his hand to Xavier again. "You must come to Philly with Thea and Jesse sometime so we can get to know you better."

Xavier inclined his head. "I would be honored."

When they were gone, Xavier pulled out his phone. "I'm not supposed to use this in here but I think you should talk to your mom."

Jesse shook her head slightly. "If she hears how doped up I am, she'll freak. You call her." She reached for his hand. "Will you be here when I come back from getting my cast?"

"Nowhere else, Jesse." He squeezed her hand hard. "Now what do you want me to tell the two very anxious young men pacing the emergency waiting room?"

"Two?"

"A young man by the name of Edgardo Terranova from Dartmouth. And another named Bakari from Simmons." He waggled his eyebrows at her. "You're very popular."

Jesse felt her smile go lopsided. "Not really."

"Oh, and there are several of your teammates out there, too. What should I tell them?"

The orderly pulled back the curtain at that moment. "Ready for another ride?" He checked his clipboard. "Jesse Morgan? X-ray?"

She nodded then looked at Xavier. "Tell Edgardo to call me when he gets back to Dartmouth. If they want, the others can wait."

He smiled and nodded.

"Xavier?" Jesse bit her lip. "After I'm released, can I go home with you?"

She saw a shadow cross his face but he only said, "I'm sure your mother will want you with her."

Her cell phone chimed and she reached for it.

Text from Porsche: *Nice rocket, Blondie! But U missed the best part. I split 2 defenders, juked the goalkeeper & knocked N the game's winning goal. C U @ practice!*

⁕

Jesse looked at the ceiling. She'd dozed off again. The medications they had given her in order to set her leg were making her world slip-slide in and out of focus. The chair Xavier had been sitting in was empty. The curtain rustled then opened a crack. "You decent?"

Jesse tried to adjust her eyes to the person who slid inside. Then she knew who it was. Only one person she knew wore dreads.

"Bakari? Why are you here?"

He came over to her bedside with a big grin. He wore a red T-shirt that read "Black Rock" under a black leather biker jacket and jeans. In one hand he held a single chocolate candy rose on a stem. He presented it saying, "I'm your biggest fan. Did you know that?"

Jesse took the rose but didn't look directly at him. "You have a girlfriend."

"Had. Over. A month ago. Found I was more interested in someone else."

She kept her gaze on the rose. "If that's true, why haven't you ever talked to me?"

"Jesse, we chat all the time." He rolled back his sleeve and there, on his forearm, was a small, colorful symbol. It was oval-shaped with a curve above and four lines in the center.

She cocked her head to one side. "A football?"

He shook his head, setting his dreads dancing. "It's the Mayan symbol for zero. They were the first to systemically use the zero as a place value."

"I'm feeling kinda spacey . . . can't do riddles tonight."

He grinned and pushed down his sleeve. "Spacey, huh? The ancient word for zero is cipher."

Jesse blinked. "But that's . . ."

He nodded.

"You're CYphur?" Jesse's brain suddenly kicked into gear. "All this time you knew who I was and you didn't say anything? That's cheating!"

"All you had to do was ask me who I was. You never asked. But that's cool. We've gotten to know one another without the posturing."

Jesse channel-surfed her mind for the essentials of all the confidences she had exchanged with CYphur over the past three months. Some of them made her stomach flip-flop. Some of them embarrassed her. But the bigger part of them excited her. He knew about her background, her mother and Xavier, about her grandparents and her fears of not fitting in. And she knew lots of personal things about him. Better yet. CYphur was someone she was already attracted to. He dressed kind of like an upscale dumpster diver but clothes were so external to the man. He was cool, and interesting, and on campus!

She smiled to herself as she fingered the paper enclosing the rose. "So?"

"So, we can dispense with all that awkward getting-to-know-you stuff."

She knotted her arms under her breasts but her movements were awkward. Must be the painkillers. "You think I think you're the guy for me?"

He leaned on the bed railing, bringing his face down on a level with hers. "Why don't we test your theory?"

She looked at him. "My theory?"

"I once asked you what you were looking for in a guy. You said, 'A man only has to act like a man. Hold down a job, and like it. Think more about "us" than "I." Understand that I'm not going to dissolve into his plans just because we are together. And respect my mind.' Those are your words. Do I qualify?"

She felt a smile tugging at her mouth but held it back. "You have a job?"

He grinned and reached for the end of her ponytail, which hung over her shoulder. "I'm your senior advisor, remember?"

∞

Her mother was coming to take her home. Her grandparents had gone to the airport to pick her up.

Xavier, who had also stayed in town overnight, was pacing Jesse's hotel room as they both waited for her mom to arrive. It was sort of fascinating to watch him all tensed up, except the reason for his anxiety wasn't happiness. She didn't need to know him well to know that. His expression had a flat, blank look to it, as if he had been Botoxed all over. But his mouth was tight, as if he had a pain he didn't want anyone to know about.

"What's wrong between you and Mom?"

Xavier stopped pacing and she could see that he was trying to decide what to tell her. Her parents always seemed to be trying to shield her.

"You don't have to say everything's fine. I'm not a child. I want to know."

He started pacing again. "You'll have to ask her yourself, Jesse. Your mom won't talk about it."

"Don't you know?" Jesse rolled her eyes. "She doesn't want to quit her job."

That stopped him in his tracks. "She told you that? I'd never ask her to quit."

"I know. But she thinks she should, in order to be a good minister's wife."

"She told you that, too?"

"No, but I've lived with her for eighteen years. I know her pretty well. You have to read between the lines with Mom."

"Amen to that!" His face came to life with an extremely interested expression. "Go on."

"She hates your church. That Sacred Cow lady? She's a beast." Xavier didn't argue.

"She's been giving Mom hell—ah, heck. But she didn't want to complain to you. That would be wimping out, you know?"

Xavier frowned for a while. "Anything else?"

"Mom wishes you were pastor of a church somewhere else. But she won't ask you to change your mind. Because of Dad. Because of what happened."

Xavier sat down. "Tell me about that."

Jesse pulled the teddy bear Xavier had given her close. "Did you know Dad gave up his law practice in Philly for Mom?" He shook his head. "She never said much about it later on. But the first few days after he died, she kept asking everyone, the hospital, the doctors, Gramma and PopPop, everyone, whether things might have been different if Dad had stayed in Philly. She was like crazed with the idea that maybe she was responsible because she had forced us to move to Dallas because of her job. And Dad was working too hard trying to reestablish the practice he left behind in Philly and so it killed him. The doctors told her that wasn't the reason. Aneurysms just happen." Jesse shrugged. "But sometimes Mom takes on responsibility for things that aren't her fault."

Xavier nodded. "She's always been that way, shouldering all the responsibility when she should have shared it."

"That's what she does for people she loves."

They exchanged glances of understanding.

It was some time before Xavier spoke again. "So you think your mother won't ask me to leave St. Hurricane, even though this is what's best for her, because that would be the same as asking me to give up something as important to me as your dad's law practice was to him?"

"Yeah. Only Mom got it wrong. Dad didn't mind. He never minded, and I would have known. I missed my friends more than he did Philly. I was once complaining to him and he said, 'Your mom did us a big favor, Jesse. You just don't appreciate it yet.'"

She looked down at her leg cast covered in a black net with gold Ladyhawke lettering along the side. "I think he meant he got to be just himself in Dallas, not a Philadelphia Morgan. It's important to be allowed to be who you really are, isn't it?"

Xavier didn't say anything for a long time. So long, Jesse decided she must have insulted him.

Then he suddenly got up and came over to her and kissed her forehead. "Thank you, Jesse! I think you just answered a prayer."

"Really? How?"

He sucked in his lower lip and nodded to himself before replying. "I'll tell you after I talk with your mom."

Jesse smiled. "Cool."

Chapter 32

"We need to talk."

Thea looked up. Xavier stood in the doorway of her home office in Dallas. He was dressed in a sport coat and slacks with a thin knit sweater underneath. He was leaving. Beyond him she could see his black leather flight bag standing in the entry. He said he had a wedding to perform in Pine Grove on Saturday.

Thea shook her head. "Not now, Xavier. I'm not really prepared for—"

"Now. You made it crystal damn clear what you were thinking the last time we really talked. Now I want to talk. And you need to hear me out before I catch my flight."

Without a word, she waved him in.

Her chest tightened up as she watched him move into the room with that familiar stride. It shifted something in her too deep to be called mere sexual desire. He pulled at her heart compass, shifting the needle each time one of them moved.

He was going back to Pine Grove because she couldn't speak the words to make him stay.

He had been amazing since Jesse's injury, arranging a limo for the three of them to the airport, finding a first-class, front-row seat for Jesse so that her cast and crutches wouldn't be an issue on their flight to Dallas. He'd even hired movers to rearrange the first-floor den of the house into a bedroom for Jesse, complete with all the things she wanted from her upstairs bedroom. Thea had balked at him buying Jesse a new iPad when she had left a perfectly good one behind at school. He'd said, "She deserves a little pampering. She's got some things to get through."

Soccer season was over for Jesse. Maybe her soccer career.

Xavier had arranged for an orthopedic team in Dallas, renowned for their sports medicine practice, to take Jesse's case. There were perks in being a former NBA player, and he had tapped into many of them for Jesse. After more tests, the doctors said that Jesse could go back to school at the end of the week, but that she'd need to be evaluated again after Thanksgiving. She might be facing surgery for a meniscus tear in her knee.

Thea tried to smile as he sat down on the loveseat in her office but the effort failed to make her mouth. His expression gave no hint of his thoughts.

For the past five days they had behaved as if the fight in Pine Grove had never occurred. For Jesse's sake, she supposed. Xavier had seemed to be in a remarkably good mood, renting and watching movies with Jesse while she went into work, and barbecuing anything he could find at the grocery store for dinner.

Only when he kissed her good night, before turning his back to her in bed, did she see the hurt and frustration and longing on his face. He must have seen those same things in her expression but she just couldn't invite him into her body when she didn't know what the next step would be. Now he was leaving and she didn't know when, or if, she'd follow him.

He watched her silently for so long that Thea found herself crossing and recrossing her legs just to have something to do.

She noticed that he noticed and so she stopped.

"I have some things to say, Theadora."

She nodded.

He didn't begin at once. A person could grow old in the lull of one of Xavier's famous pauses.

"When we married, I thought our tough times were behind us. We've been through some things, Thea. God knows we have. But I never would have considered you a coward."

She frowned. "What do you mean?"

"I'm talking now. You'll get your chance. I thought I married a woman who knew what she wanted, and how to get it and hold on to it. You stood up to everybody in your world when you were sixteen, including me. And when it all came down on you, you took that, too. I have never to this day heard you blame anyone for the problems in your life. God knows you could have, and no one would have said a word against your complaint."

He breathed in through his nose so strongly she noticed his chest expanding to accommodate it. "So, for you to just up and walk out on our marriage of less than four months—"

"I didn't—"

"You gave up on us!" He didn't raise his voice. He didn't have to. The force came through in his deep timbre.

"Can I speak now?"

He shrugged a big man shrug. "If you've got something useful to say."

That dig brought her chin up. She never let anyone back her into a corner for long, not even him. "I didn't give up. I just let a lot of side issues get in my way because it made it easier for me. I wanted an excuse not to come back to Pine Grove."

"Did you need one?"

"Yes." She looked at her fingers knotting and re-knotting. No other way to say it. She looked up at him. "I can't be the wife of the minister of St. Hurricane Church, Xavier."

"Don't waste my time, Thea. You've already said that."

"Then let me be clear." He was pushing her harder than she expected.

"I can't be what they want and expect, and probably deserve. I think I knew it the day you told me about that church. But I was so sure that we were meant to be together that I began bargaining with myself. I thought if you got what you wanted then I could have the promotion I worked for all my professional life, and everybody would be happy. But I was fooling myself. I wish I were able to be all you and they need. But I can't even try to do that without giving up my job. And I won't. That sounds awful. Selfish—"

"Honest." He cut her off without heat. He rubbed his chin, picked at a bit of lint on his cuff, and looked off toward the window before his gaze came back to her. "So, this is only about St. Hurricane?"

"It's about what you need, to be able to have the life you are meant to have." She exhaled a long, bone-weary breath. "You told me you asked God for this church. I can't fight God for you. I won't even try."

He tapped a finger on the shiny surface of the shoe of his crossed ankle. "Funny you should put it that way. I've begun to think I've been doing the very same thing, fighting God."

Thea swallowed carefully. "Why?"

He shifted his ankle off his knee and leaned forward, resting his forearms on his spread thighs. "I've been holding out on you. Keeping secrets. Sneaking around behind your back."

Her stomach did an express-elevator drop. "I see."

"No, you don't. So, I'm going to tell you. I've been sneaking over to Atlanta or up to D.C. when you've thought I was in Pine Grove." He laughed at the surprise in her expression. "There have been indications that I'm needed back at the Thornton Foundation ever since I returned from Africa. At first I ignored them, thinking it was just temptation to test my resolve. But the Black Man's Master Plan Crusade has fallen off without me. The hip-hop artists who signed on for the Macon Project have backed out. Bazz Azz's troubles just put a public face to what had been months of boardroom bickering."

This was news to her. "Why would they abandon the Thornton Foundation?"

He dipped his head. "Contrary to public persona, any artist who can hold on to the millions he or she makes has to have a good business sense. They say because I'm not involved, they don't trust the Thornton trustee board. And frankly, the board doesn't give much respect to the brothers and sisters whose money they so badly want."

"Can you blame them?"

"Yes. If you invite a person into your house, you can't criticize the shoes that brought him there. The board is full of do-gooders who don't want to be associated with the image of some of our contributors. But if you remember, anonymity was part of the benefactor requirements. Bazz Azz slipped up. Even so, we won't take money from just anyone. There are potential men and women of influence among the entrepreneurs of the entertainment world. If they can be made to understand their power for good, their potential is unlimited. Respect and self-lessness need to shake hands."

"But even after you went to the meeting, you told me you didn't want those responsibilities anymore."

"That's just it." He dipped his head. "I do, Thea. God help me, I want back in my old life."

Something like hope began to flicker inside her. "Go on."

He sent her a glowing look from beneath his lashes. "When we ran into one another at LaGuardia, I didn't tell you the whole truth. I'd been in New York City at a gala for the Thornton Foundation. I'd begun a conversation with a couple of the board members about how I might move back into the position of CEO, and I wanted to feel out the rest of the trustees."

"Reverend Thornton, you barefaced lied to me!"

He nodded, the first quiver of a smile flitting on his mouth. "I've been holding out on you because I made a promise to you not to go back to the limelight. You said you hated being a public person. Up till now you've been holding me to it."

"That's because I thought it was what you wanted."

"True. I thought it was. Even the bishop said I was so convincing that he appointed me to St. Hurricane against his better judgment. I can't prove it, but I suspect he hoped that dealing with Hattie Patterson would bring me to my senses pretty quick. When it didn't, he started pushing."

"Pushing how?"

"He's been calling me. Checking up. Mrs. Patterson's been calling him, too. She has peculiar ideas about me and my future." He smiled at some joke he didn't seem interested in sharing. "He said he didn't want to make it seem that he was forcing me out of St. Hurricane if that's where I wanted to be."

"I wish he had."

Xavier chuckled. "I think the bishop is as afraid of Hattie Patterson as anyone. I'll have to resign myself. He won't pull me out. But we've had some interesting discussions. Last time he reminded me about the book of Matthew and the 'Parable of the Talents.' He said what I was doing by taking a lesser role was burying my talents, and that that is a sin."

Conflicting feelings pulled at Thea until she didn't know whether to be relieved or hurt. "Why didn't you tell me about all this?"

He paused again. "I once told you that there had never been anything in my life that I couldn't walk away from." He made eye contact a contact sport. "I remember how you looked at me, as if that was a great failing in my character. I was worried that if I walked away from St. Hurricane, you would see it as evidence that I hadn't changed. I didn't want to fail to keep my promises to you."

"Oh, Xavier." She said it so softly she wasn't certain he heard her. But he was rising from the loveseat as she was from her chair.

They met in the middle of the room, arms out, then locked

about one another. *Home.* Her heart compass *twanged* to correct itself toward the man in her arms.

He took her face in his hands, cradling her head as if it were the most precious thing in the world. "Did you notice how easy it was for me to arrange things for Jesse?" She nodded. "I can use my power for good. But I need someone to keep my head from inflating over that fact. I need you, Theadora."

"So, will you go to Atlanta?"

He shook his head. "I won't have to be any particular place to do what I do. The bishop says he'll assign me as an assistant where I can be affiliated with a church without accepting the full responsibilities of pastor. Taking back the helm of the Thornton Foundation means I'll be traveling a lot of the time. I can live anywhere. All I need is an airport nearby."

Thea didn't let herself smile. "What about St. Hurricane?"

His smile was one of triumph. "Can you live with not being their first lady?"

She nodded. "I've never been more uncomfortable in my life than when I'm being addressed as the minister's wife. People call the parsonage and ask for prayers or advice about things I don't understand. They expect me to know where to find a line of scripture in the Bible without a moment's hesitation. Which prophet said what and on what occasion? One woman called to ask how to cure a wart."

"Do you think I know the answer to that?"

"No, it's more than that." She placed a hand on his chest. "I feel incompetent as a minister's wife. I'm not even comfortable praying in public."

"I see you several times a day with your head slightly bowed and your eyes closed."

"I'm not praying, I'm thinking."

"What are you thinking?"

"Oh, things like, how am I going to make such and such happen? What do I do next? Who or what did I forget to do? How long is this infernal meeting going to last? Did I turn off the hose in the yard?"

He laughed. "About fifty percent of those are prayers. You just don't address the Lord directly. 'Oh Lord, how am I going to make such and such happen?' 'Dear God, what do I do next?' You see what I'm saying? You don't have to call His name for God to know you're talking to Him."

"But it would be more polite to address Him directly."

He nodded. "Him or Her. The more I've thought about it the more I've come to suspect that God is a She. Who else but a mother would put up with the foolish, ignorant, backsliding, willful ways of humans and still at the end of it all be willing to forgive?"

Thea laughed with him.

Dear Lord, but it is good to be with this man. He made her feel right.

"You're going to be late." She backed out of his arms, willing to let him go, for now. He didn't try to hold her as he knew there'd be a plane leaving without him if this lasted five seconds more.

She followed him to the door but when he picked up his bag, she remembered. "Why did you call me a coward?"

He grinned, dimples in full effect. "My mother used to say, 'You can run away but your problems won't get stolen while you're gone.'"

"What?"

He just kissed her again, long and hard, the kind of kiss that promised there would be many more.

When he set her away from him again he said, "You do what you think you have to do. But I'd hate to think Theadora Thornton would back down from a little old lady in a big hat."

Chapter 33

Hattie sat in the first pew. It had been a while since she had had the pew completely to herself. But for three Sundays running now, she had not had to share it with Reverend Xavier's wife. He'd not given any explanation why she wasn't here for those Sundays, and no one dared ask.

"Disgraceful," Hattie murmured to herself. What kind of young woman was Mrs. Thornton to simply abandon her duties to her husband and his church?

Certainly, she had been hard on the woman. But the more she thought about it, the more certain she was she had done right. She hadn't actually expected her to leave her husband, however. Young women nowadays couldn't face any adversity or sacrifice.

Just look at Lola, sneaking behind her husband's back because she'd felt neglected! She had nerve enough to show up penniless on a relative's doorstep but not the courage to beg her husband's forgiveness. That's why she'd written him just this week, telling him that his wife had confessed all, and seemed repentant. If he could find it in his heart to take her back, she was certain Lola would behave properly in future. Tyrell needed his father. And she needed back her peace and quiet.

"Let the church say amen!"

"Amen!" Hattie stood and raised her right hand in supplication as the choir swelled in song. This is where she belonged. This is how things should be. Daughter of a bishop, widow of a minister, she had always known her place at St. Hurricane. She had literally been reared within these walls.

As she swayed in time to the music she remembered how she had once crawled about her mother's knees while she played the old long-gone upright piano for the choir. In that corner where today stood a beautiful electric organ. The brass plate on the front told anyone who cared to look that it was donated in the name of her late parents. She'd done that.

As a youngster she'd helped polish the communion cups and silver collection plates that were passed around each Sunday. Nowadays most churches, even St. Hurricane, made congregants bring their tithes to the altar because too much stealing went on when the plate was passed. Lord, Lord, what was this world coming to when His people stole from Him beneath His roof?

She'd sung in that very choir loft and been kissed for the first time in the robe closet by John Deshazer after practice when she was thirteen. Then five years later she had walked down the aisle of this church to marry her sweet Obadiah. The only thing lacking in her world was children. But God had other plans. She had come to understand that these last years, living without Obadiah. God had put her in charge of His temple, St. Hurricane AME Church.

Yet lately, she hadn't been able to pray right. The words just wouldn't form themselves in a reasoned fashion. She'd start off praying for one thing only to find herself lost in phrasing that didn't make sense to her even as she was saying the words. She was sleeping fitfully, too. Not even the wearing of her favorite fall hat, a turban covered in the autumn colors of quail feathers, lifted her mood.

There's something on your conscience, her mother would have said. Her mother was always looking for ways in which the devil might be slipping temptation into her children's paths.

But she didn't have any reason to feel badly. She'd done the righteous thing when it came to Reverend Thornton's wife. If it was distressing to her, then sometimes that's what God expected. Right wasn't always easy. Sometimes right was hard.

If only she didn't feel so badly about doing right.

Her gaze moved guiltily to where Reverend Xavier sat, looking so proud and upright in his robes. Yet, there was no light in his eyes this Sunday. He was no doubt missing his wife. Did he know what had happened between her and his bride that ran her away? It would be like her to blame someone else for her own shortcomings.

Hattie compressed her lips and looked away. That wasn't on her head! The silly girl should return immediately so that they might all see that she had learned her lesson.

What was the choir singing now? She had lost track of the melody.

Hattie sat down and turned to the young woman sitting in the pew behind her. "Is it warm in here to you? It seems remarkably warm for November. Pass me a hand fan, child." She reached for the fan then paused.

At the back of the sanctuary a group of women had arrived. They were strangers, all but Thea Thornton. Hattie suppressed a smile. This was more like it. The prodigal wife had returned.

The party of seven came straight up the aisle. They were dressed in the height of fashion. One in particular was a striking young woman with a one-year-old girl on her hip dressed in the same coordinated colors, hat, purse, and shoes, as her mother. The youngest of the women was on crutches. Hattie frowned. She'd seen that long blond hair somewhere. Oh yes, this must be Thea's daughter. Thea and her daughter, she noted, were the only ones not wearing hats.

The eldest, a woman much of her own age, led the procession to the front of the altar and turned left, into the front pew opposite her.

Reverend Xavier came immediately off the altar though the choir was in full throat in a hymn of praise. She saw him bend to his wife, their heads so close together that they touched. Their whispered words were too faint for her to catch.

When Xavier glanced in her direction, Hattie looked away with an innocent expression and began rearranging her purse on her lap. So then, the wife was back. Things would settle down now. Her conscience was salved.

As the choir ended on a note of exultation, Xavier went back up to the altar. He clapped his hands, suddenly animated. "Praise God for He is good! Brother Edmond, you gave us some fine music today!"

The church responded with rousing "amens" and clapping for their choir leader.

"All right now. All right now." Xavier held up his hand for the church to quiet down. Hattie particularly liked this about his style. Reverend Xavier did not seek to whip the congregation into a frenzy on Sunday. He liked the church happy but not shouting in the aisles. He was old school and she preferred that.

His face radiated pride as he looked out at his flock. "I have a surprise for you. My wife has asked to address the church this morning." He paused to gaze out at Thea. "I do not know what message she brings but I know this much. Her heart is good. And her spirit is great." He lifted and held out his hand toward his wife. "Mrs. Thornton?"

You could knock me over with a feather! Hattie liked to say when something surprised her. The tips of a dozen heavenly wings seemed to flutter about her as Thea moved to the lectern just left of the pulpit.

⁂

Thea rose slowly to her feet, slow enough to feel both Aunt Della's pat of encouragement on her right arm and Jesse's tight squeeze of her left hand before she let go. She had called Aunt Della to tell her what she proposed to do this morning and her aunt had offered to come up and lend her emotional support.

Jesse, whom Thea planned to take back to school tomorrow, had invited herself. Aunt Della, it seemed, had taken it upon herself to call Selma. Selma had called Cherise. And Cherise had called her sisters, Liz and Pearl. Come this morning, the assembly of her family outside St. Hurricane had grown from two to seven, plus her niece, Andromeda.

She wasn't certain whether this was a good omen. Or that Xavier would approve of what she was about to do. But she had something to say.

Her left leg was shaking as she climbed the low step to reach the lectern. She headed Xavier off with a tiny shake of her head when it looked as if he was about to come and offer escort. This was her moment, for good or ill.

She opened her papers, adjusted her mike, glanced at Hattie Patterson sitting not more than ten feet in front of her, and took a breath.

"Good morning, Church."

"Good morning." The response was polite but not enthusiastic.

"I am a stranger to most of you. It has been said that I have preferred it that way." She glanced at Hattie. "That is not true. What is true is that I had hoped to serve as your first lady without offering you much of myself in return."

As murmurs of agreement reached her ear, Thea glanced at Jesse, who was holding Aunt Della's hand, and took courage. "I often told my daughter when she was a child that to have a friend you must be a friend. So today I want to share with you a little about myself, so that we may part as friends."

New murmurs pulsed through the congregation.

"Did she say 'part'?"

"Is she leaving?"

Thea looked down at the speech she had written and then turned the pages over. She didn't need notes to tell the truth.

"I was born Theadora Maxine Broussard in Monroe, Louisiana. My parents both taught at Grambling University. My father, David Broussard, was head of the science department. My mother, Camille Broussard, was head of the English department. I'm named after my daddy's father, Theodore. Mom said the doctor wasn't sure she could have more children after

I was born. So, even though I wasn't a son, I carry the family name. For ten years I was the center of their lives, an only well-beloved child. I liked it that way. I had all the attention all the time. And then my sister, Selma, was born."

Selma, being Selma, took this moment to rise and turn and wave at the congregation. Andromeda, in her arms, waved too.

Thea smiled. "You see what I've been up against ever since. Upstaged and outdressed from the beginning."

The parishioners clapped in appreciation.

"We grew up attending St. Luke AME Church in Rustin. We sang in the choir, gossiped in the back pew on children's Sunday, and spent summers in vacation Bible school. As I look back, I understand that St. Luke is where my character was formed. The ethics I use in my career and the morals that guide my personal life come from being there. And, when I reflected on it recently, I realized that so many of the important things that have occurred in my life began there. I have not always lived up to those standards, but I have always known what the goal was."

"Amen, sister!"

Thea swallowed the urge to skip the next, the hardest, part. "During the summer I turned sixteen I met an exceptional young man from Chicago after service at St. Luke. He was fated for the church even then. He told me so. But it wasn't what he wanted for himself at the time. We fell in love. That was right. We conceived a child. That was wrong."

She paused to let that thought register with her listeners. No breath of response stirred the air. It was as if they were a theater audience waiting for the next plot twist. She stole a quick look at Hattie, who had a gleam in her eye. Okay, this truth wasn't pretty but it was real, and she owned it. Always would.

She lifted her head, chin tilted a little higher. "I never told my parents the name of my child's father. Pride got in my way." She stole a glance at Jesse, who was staring at her with love. "And so, I went to live with my aunt Della until my son was born."

Aunt Della stood up and faced the congregation with an expression of matriarchal pride. "Theadora always was a good person. Even a good person can make mistakes."

"You told a truth there!" shouted a voice from the back.

"I gave my son up for adoption because I thought I was protecting those I loved, both the father, who never knew I was pregnant, and my family, whom I had shamed. I am not proud of that. But I own it."

She had not heard anyone come up behind her but suddenly a hand was on her shoulder. "Can I speak now, Mom Thea?"

Startled, Thea glanced around and up into her son David's face. He bent and kissed her cheek. "Jesse called me and told me what you were planning today so I thought I should be here to support you, too."

Rather than allow her to step aside, he held on to her shoulder as he faced the audience. "This is my birth mother. We didn't meet until two years ago. But it turns out we remained in the same family all along. No one has ever loved a child more than my adoptive parents love me. But I am doubly blessed to have two sets of parents now. And, an annoying little sister who I suspect has grown up a lot in the past year." He winked at Jesse.

Then Xavier was by Thea's side, sliding his arm around her, his voice deep and steady and confident in her ears. "Many of you know that two years ago I learned of a son I had not known I fathered. Thea's son, David, is my son. I did not know of my son until Thea told me two years ago. That was my failing. I had abandoned a young woman and her unborn child without knowing what I'd left behind. Recently God saw fit to bring them into my life for a second chance with both. A grace so precious to me. I will not abandon either of them again."

A shuffle of a pair of feet could be heard in the silence.

"This is like a play," someone said in a voice that carried from the back.

Xavier smiled at his wife. "You were speaking, Mrs. Thornton. Continue." Father and son backed up behind her.

Thea's voice shook a little as she continued. "I won't bore you with my college years except to tell that that is where I met my first husband, Evan Morgan. He was white. *What* Evan Morgan was," she said a little louder, to quiet the swell of whispers, "was never important to me. *Who* he was was everything to me."

The whispers dropped away.

She looked over at Pearl, who sat ramrod straight at the far end of the pew, her dark gaze narrowed on Thea. "Some might not agree with my choice. I would say to them that happiness is too precious to doubt."

Thea could feel her heart beating as if she were a hurdler in a flat-out race for the gold. "We were blessed with a child." She held out her hand. "My daughter, Jessica Darnell Morgan."

Jesse stood up on her crutches, looking a little embarrassed.

"After fourteen years of marriage, I lost Evan suddenly. One morning I was a loving wife with a wonderful husband and teenage daughter. By noon I was a widow with a child to care and provide for."

That earned her more amens.

"Some of you at St. Hurricane have felt slighted by the demands that my career in Dallas makes on my life. All I can say to that is I have been grateful for it every day and for my ability to provide for my child. I am sure I am not the only woman here today who has headed a single-parent home."

She was answered by a chorus of women voicing agreement.

"It is not easy to feed, and house, to care for and provide for family alone. It is not a simple matter to be both nurturer and breadwinner."

Applause rippled through the congregation.

"I do not ask for your praise, only your understanding that I am no different from many of you. Women work hard every day. That is nothing new. But we no longer expect a woman who works hard to lay her work aside because a man comes into her life."

"I know that's right!" said a choir member.

"A bird in the hand, praise the Lord!" cried someone from the Mommies' Room.

Thea directed her gaze straight at Hattie Patterson as she said, "I'm good at my job, and I love it. I will make no apologies to anyone for that fact."

Applause erupted again, some of the younger women coming to their feet.

Thea had eyes only for Hattie, who seemed to shrink a little in her pew. That's when she realized it wasn't this elderly woman she had been fighting, but her own fear that she could not have what she needed and wanted. Yet love is about being fearless. And now, in this holy place, she was no longer afraid.

Thea looked back and stretched out her hand toward Xavier, letting the strength of having survived flow back into her. He nodded slowly, as if he could read her mind and her heart.

She turned again to the congregation who were still clapping. "Sometimes, through the grace of God, a person who has lost something precious gets a second chance. I love my new husband. I believe that we have earned our second chance to be happy, and that only we can determine how our lives should be lived. So now you know me. I hope we can be friends. But whatever our futures hold, I wish for you all the peace and grace that is God's blessing. Thank you."

Once more Xavier had come to stand beside her. He raised a hand in praise. "Let the church say amen!"

"Amen!"

Amid applause a sudden swell of chords from the organist cued the choir to fill the church once more with song.

Xavier took her hand and leaned in close to whisper, "If I'm not careful, my wife's going to do me out of *my* job."

Thea squeezed his hand tight as he escorted her from the podium to her pew.

Jesse sprang to her feet and threw her arms around her mother. "Mom, that was so honest and so brave!"

Pearl came up to her, her expression as unreadable as any Xavier produced. "Theadora, you know I've had my doubts about you. It's because my brother is precious to me." Her face cracked. "But, sister-in-law, that was before I heard what you had to say today!" She enveloped Thea in a big hug. "You and Xavier will be in my prayers every day for the rest of my life."

The rest of the service became a blur to Thea, wedged within the comforting protection of her family, until just before the benediction when Xavier announced that he was leaving St. Hurricane.

He ignored the protests that met this announcement. "I am going on leave from the pastorate in order to take up my duties as head of the Thornton Foundation." He smiled at Thea. "My first task will be to move the headquarters from Atlanta to Dallas."

"Mom, did you know?" Jesse whispered.

Thea shook her head.

"In a few weeks, a young minister and his wife, along with three small children, will be interviewing with you. I hope you will show him all the hospitality and Christian charity you have shown me in my time here. Let the church say amen."

"Amen!"

After church was over, Hattie approached Xavier and Thea as they stood among the members offering them best wishes and laments that they were leaving. "If there's something I've done"—she looked uncertainly at Thea—"or said to make you, or your wife, feel you need to make a break with St. Hurricane . . ."

Xavier let her hang so long Thea felt sorry for the woman. "Speaking for myself, I can't say that I recall a thing. And if there were, on Thea's side, I don't think you'd want me to know, would you?"

Hattie lowered her gaze. "Just so."

Thea watched her walk away before making up her mind and catching up with Hattie. "We would really like it if you and your family would come to the parsonage for dinner at two P.M."

Hattie stared at her. "I believe my dinner is already prepared."

Thea eyed the woman she would never really like. "I'm sure it will keep until tomorrow. Because, Mrs. Patterson, I wouldn't like to leave you thinking that I don't know that everything you did—even the hurtful things—you did for St. Hurricane. I respect that kind of loyalty, if not your methods. Maybe we've both learned something about how to deal with people we don't understand."

Hattie eyed the young woman before her for so long Thea thought she was about to be shut down again. "You think you know what's right every time, don't you?"

"No, Hattie. I know I don't. That shouldn't be the difference between us."

This time humor thawed Hattie's gaze. "If I was starting out now, I'd be a bishop before my life was over."

"Hattie, if you were starting out now, you'd end up my boss. I think our dinner's getting cold, don't you?"

☙

Cora and Hortense insisted on making Sunday dinner for the entire Thornton family. They served smothered chicken with rice, oven-baked chicken, and fried chicken, with the usual assortment of vegetables, deviled eggs, and egg custard.

When Xavier had blessed the table, the Brown sisters brought in a crispy baked hen on a platter surrounded with hard boiled eggs still in the shell.

"What are these? It's not Easter."

Cora stood proudly. "They're genuine Araucana eggs. Some call them Easter eggs." She held up a blue and a pink egg. Those about her *oohed* and *aahed*. "I first learned about them watching Martha Stewart on TV. The eggs were so pretty I just had to have some. Our mother used to keep chickens. They take up no space at all. So Sister and I bought a pair." She simpered like a little girl.

Hortense stood up. "Any of you who thought you heard a

rooster these last months. That was our cockerel. You must have a cock if you want the hens to lay."

"Keeping chickens in the city limits is illegal," Hattie announced in a severe tone.

Thea nodded. "You're right. Or rather, we thought you were right. As you must know by now I believe in women in business. I thought that two of St. Hurricane's oldest members had been involved in a clandestine operation. What I discovered by going to the county courthouse is that raising chickens within the city limits is not illegal. It's a loophole left over from the Depression era. What one cannot do is slaughter chickens within the city limits for sale without a license."

She glanced at Xavier. "Cora and Hortense have been to the agricultural department and sorted out a method of sale that has every potential to make them very successful businesswomen. Miss Cora and Miss Hortense will shortly be open for business, on market days, selling fresh eggs and free-range chickens."

"We don't need the money for ourselves. Our profit will go first to fix the leak in St. Hurricane's roof. After that, I'd like to see us get new carpeting for the sanctuary."

Xavier came up behind Thea as the others gathered around Cora and Hortense to congratulate them. "You amaze me."

Thea nodded. "They were doing it. Now they have more than before we came."

EPILOGUE

Thanksgiving dinner at Cherise's home in Alexandria, Virginia, was everything an American family could want. Two turkeys with giblet gravy graced the sideboard for the thirty-something family members gathered there. Three kinds of dressing surrounded them: Thea's cornbread, Liz's sausage and apple, and Cherise's crabmeat stuffing. There were casseroles of candied sweet potatoes, green beans, whipped potatoes, mac and cheese, Jell-O molds, ambrosia, corn soufflé, spiced peaches, and cranberry sauce. Pearl provided rolls so light and rich, diners scooped them up in twos and threes. The dessert table looked like a holiday bakery window display.

As Uncle Way said when it was his turn to add a blessing at the table, "Lord bless the fool who can't find something to satisfy both soul and stomach at this meal!"

David and his girlfriend were due in Friday, after enjoying Thanksgiving with his parents. A few weeks earlier, he had lost his first election, but by a close enough margin to impress state party officials. And he was happy enough with that, as a beginning.

"He's got a future in politics, that boy," Aunt Della declared. "Nobody to somebody in his own hometown first time out. Mayor, you watch. He's going to be mayor. Then governor."

After eating enough to keep them full for two days, nearly all the men and most of the women had drifted into the media room to watch the Dallas Cowboys Thanksgiving Day game on the new LG GX 77 inch smart TV. Santa had come early.

Thea cuddled up next to Jesse on the family room sofa and watched her daughter pick the nuts out of a brownie. The initial doctor's report about Jesse's leg was encouraging but not stellar. She would heal completely. But collegiate sports might not be in her future.

Thea hugged her. "How do you feel about the prospect of not playing soccer next year?"

Jesse shrugged. "I don't have anything else to prove on the soccer field. I'm thinking about joining the debate team."

"Really? You know your dad was on the debate team at Georgetown?"

"*Duh*, Mom!" Jesse took a bite of her brownie.

"It's your eighteenth birthday tomorrow. What would you like to do?"

Jesse smiled to herself. "Somebody wants to take me out. A guy from Simmons. His name's Bakari."

"He lives in D.C.?"

"No. He lives in Boston but he's going to take Amtrak down for the day."

"I've met him."

They looked up to find Xavier in the doorway with a slice of sweet potato pie in one hand and a fork in the other. "Nice young man. But what happened to Edgardo?"

Jesse blushed. "I told them both I'm not ready to get serious. And I'm practicing celibacy. Bakari said he could hang."

Thea glanced up at her husband. "I'm impressed."

The sound of the doorbell sent Xavier to answer it.

A moment later he appeared back in the doorway, his brows raised and a funny look on his face. "Selma's here. I think I'll go see what the score is." He trotted away as Selma arrived in the doorway behind him.

She was stunning in cream leather pants, thigh-high boots, and a fox fur jacket. Après-ski, if she skied, which she didn't.

"Selma!" Thea rose from the sofa. "We thought you weren't coming."

"I wasn't but then Elkeri went and lost his mind! One minute we're getting ready for bed. The next he's packing his bags."

"Where did he go?"

"The Negro went home to his South Carolina, collard-green, stew-meat, ham-hock-cooking, fish-frying mama!"

Thea resisted the urge to say, I knew something like this was going to happen. "Where's Andromeda?"

"He took her, too."

"Xavier told me you had arrived," Cherise said as she came into the room. "Selma, *grrl*! What has happened?"

Selma dumped her fur jacket on a chair and struck a Naomi-at-the-end-of-the-catwalk pose. "He wants me to stop working. Can you even believe that?"

Thea put a finger to her lips. "Don't let Aunt Della hear you. She's taking a nap."

Cherise nodded. "Why would he want you to do that?"

"He says he can provide for us. And that Andromeda needs me. *Huh!* Last time I checked it took two incomes per family just to keep the American dream alive."

Thea frowned, watching her sister closely. "I'm surprised Elkeri would suddenly just decide something like this out of the blue." Selma gave her a wide-innocent-eyes look. "Or is there another reason? Selma?"

Selma perched on the arm of the chair next to Jesse. "Hey, baby girl. You healing okay?"

"Selma, where's Andromeda?" Cherise asked.

Selma gave her a sour look. "I told him if he was leaving, he was taking his daughter with him."

Cherise gasped. "You let him take her? But you say he's terrible with her. Aren't you worried sick about your baby?"

Selma looked at her newly manicured nails. "Honestly? It's the most peace I've had since she was born. I slept until noon, had my hair done, packed a bag, and caught a flight to D.C. And I didn't have to feed, talk to, or think about anybody but me. I don't know why I thought I needed to be married. Men will make you do some dumb sh— stuff!"

Thea folded her arms. "Are you going to get to the real point anytime soon?"

Selma held up a hand. "I may be pregnant."

"May be?" the other three women chorused.

Selma glanced at Jesse. "You might want to go get some dessert."

"Not on a bet!"

Selma looked from her niece to her sister and best friend. Both women crossed their arms and gave her the fish eye. "I'm just not ready to go through all that again."

"That's why they invented birth control," Jesse answered solemnly.

Selma jerked her head back. "Just what would you know about that, *Miss Thang?*"

"PE sixth grade, Aunt Selma. So, why weren't you using protection?"

Cherise snapped her fingers. "I think you've been busted."

Selma shrugged. "So, maybe I was thinking Andromeda needed a little brother or sister, sometime soon. So they can be close. But that doesn't mean I need to give up my business to have a baby."

Jesse nodded. "I'd never give up my career for a man. He'll have to love me for me."

"You are so right!" Cherise offered. "Wait for love."

"I did." Selma shrugged off the surprised looks directed at her. "Okay, so maybe I got a little nervous in my twenties and made a couple of mistakes."

"You once married a married man, Aunt Selma," Jesse confirmed.

"Did I know that at the time? I did not!"

Cherise and Thea looked at each other and broke out in laughter and high fives.

"Men!" Selma scoffed. "Can't live with them, but I don't intend to live without mine."

"But you just said—" Jesse objected.

"Elkeri is a patronizing, old-fashioned, country-acting fool. But he's mine. I'll forgive him, eventually. After I get a little more rest time."

Cherise clicked her tongue. "Shame on you, Selma, worrying the man like that."

Selma smiled her slyest, most seductive smile. "He's done me a favor, taking Andromeda off my hands for a few days. Now, I'm hungry. Eating for two is so much work!"

She turned toward the kitchen. "Where's that turkey? Somebody had better have left me a slice of breast and some dressing! And some cranberries!"

Jesse shook her head. "Aunt Selma's a trip!"

"Always was. Always will be," Thea answered. "More dessert, anyone?"

⤷∞⤶

Later, when the Cowboys game was over, Thea and Xavier put on jackets and went for a walk in the chilled night air.

Xavier hugged her close. "There's something on my mind, Theadora. Selma's situation got me to thinking about it. Just thinking."

"Hm?"

"You aren't too old to have a child. But I'd hate to put you through that unless it's something you really want. However, we could offer a wonderful home to a child in need. I'd like to think I could do no less than David's father did. There was a man who took in my son and loved him as his own because I wasn't there to do it. I'd like to be able to do that for another man's child in need."

"You're talking about adoption? I think that is a wonderful idea, Xavier. But can I be very selfish and ask that we give *us* a year before we decide?"

"That's fair. We have a lot more adjusting to do."

Thea bit her lip. "And if we don't have a child?"

He grinned. "I've seen a couple of Jesse's boyfriends. One day she's going to give us some fine grandchildren."

"And we will spoil them."

"Absolutely."

"And we will be happy in the meantime."

"Always."

"And forever."

When he broke their kiss, he held on to her so that she could feel his warm breath on her chilled cheek. "There is one other something, Thea. I hope you will agree to do this a bit sooner."

Thea held her breath. "What?"

"I'd like to rehire my personal assistant, Jerome, if he's available."

She laughed in relief. "He would certainly make our lives easier. He can coordinate our calendars, remind us of our obligations, and see that we have free time together."

"Now if he could just cook!"

Thea felt touched on the quick. "Are you saying I can't cook? I thought you liked my cooking?"

Xavier just kissed the foolishness out of her. Then he took her face in his hands and rubbed his cold nose on hers. "I love everything about you, Theadora Broussard Morgan Thornton. I always have. I always will."

A+

AUTHOR INSIGHTS, EXTRAS, & MORE...

FROM

LAURA CASTORO

AND

AVON A

BOOK CLUB GUIDE

Laura is available for book club interviews
in person or via phone
For more information contact: *laurawrite@aol.com*

1. What do you know about the nature of the relationship between Thea and Xavier from their first phone conversation in Chapter One?

2. What do you think of Thea's sister Selma and her Aunt Della? Why are they essential to Thea's life?

3. What is the relationship between Thea and her daughter Jesse? Does that relationship affect the decisions they each make in their own lives?

4. Is Jesse's reaction to her mother's remarrying typical for a teen?

5. Does Thea handle her daughter's ambiguous feelings about the marriage in a positive way?

6. Once Thea realizes that Xavier wants a small church in another state is she honest with herself about how she feels about that? Is she too quick to decide to "just make it happen?" Does this decision cost her anything?

7. Thea's and Xavier's first meeting after a long separation is awkward. Why do you think they each behave as they do?

8. Xavier's reputation and his sacrifices—his willingness to walk away from his mega-church in Atlanta, his year of service in worn-torn Darfur, his putting his multi-million dollar estate in trust that he's unwilling to touch—make him appear to be a totally sympathetic even "saintly" person. Is he too good to be true? If not, where are the cracks in his

armor? In running away from prideful things, instead of accepting the honors and problems that come with them, is he demonstrating another kind of pride? Can even a good man make decisions that hurt others?

9. Are Thea's expectations that she can walk away from her career reasonable? Whose decision is it? Who should rightly weigh in on this, Xavier?

10. Just as she is about to resign, Thea is offered the promotion she's worked toward her whole business career. Is she torn for the right reasons, or for reasons she has manufactured for herself? Does it matter that the decision to resign her position was a private decision? After all, she's been operating as a single parent and career woman for several years. So when she changes her mind, should she tell Xavier she was even considering resigning before the promotion came along?

11. When Thea tells Xavier about her promotion, is he really happy for her? Is she really happy for Xavier, too, or is Thea doing some wishful thinking when he announces he wants to pastor a church in another state? Are there other choices they might have or should have considered?

12. As more and more modern couples face the challenges of two-career families, the dilemma facing Xavier and Thea is compounded by the possibility of working and living in different states. In what ways does this portrait of a long-distance two-career marriage ring true to you? In what ways not?

13. Thea feels that she must put Xavier's desires first because he is called by God. Is that a realistic attitude? She says she can't argue with God if that's where God wants him. But should she have voiced her opinion of moving to Arkansas anyway?

14. Do Thea's feelings of inadequacy as a future minister's wife play a role in her decision not to leave her job? Is she aware

of that, or is it something only the reader knows at this point?

15. Some of Jesse's experiences in high school have left her feeling uncertain of how she is perceived by others. Discuss how the following issues seem to have impacted her life:

    A. Being biracial
    B. A jock
    C. Her age, being a year younger than her peers
    D. Her grandparents' wealth, which will one day make her a trust fund baby

16. Why does Jesse not use her connections to get into college? Is this a wise choice?

17. How do her experiences as a biracial child affect her relationship with girlfriends? Guys? Her grandparents? Her decisions about her future?

18. Sex is always a huge issue for a young person. What do you think of Jesse's decision to rid herself of the label "virgin" before she goes off to college? Is this a real issue for young women? Is it motivated by society's pressures?

19. Jesse's desire is to meet the world on her college campus on her own terms without labels like: "biracial," "only child," "jock," or "trust fund baby." She tells herself that this is because she wants to be judged only for herself. Is this a sign of maturity? Insecurity? Independence?

20. What other things may be motivating Jesse? Do you think she is aware of all these motivations?

21. What motivates Hattie to form an opinion of Xavier before she actually meets him? How does she see him fitting into her plans for St. Hurricane's Church?

22. How do Hattie's life experiences as the daughter of a bishop and later the wife of a minister shape her views of life?

23. Thea's uncertainty about what it means to be a minister's wife

begins before she meets Hattie. How does this affect her feelings about Xavier's choice of a new church? Should she have a say-so in his choice? After all, Xavier's life's work is not just a career choice but God's work.

24. Thea says she envys Xavier's ease with God and the spiritual life. She is a Christian yet she is uneasy with her own relationship with God. How does this affect her relationship with Xavier?

25. What is Xavier's reaction to her admission of a shaky relationship with God? Does it help or hinder Thea's decision?

26. Is Xavier behaving selfishly by not putting Thea's career needs ahead of his own?

27. Is the tug of war between Thea and Hattie one of social (city vs. rural), generational (forty something vs. seventy something), cultural (Hattie thinks Thea is white when they first meet), or personal difference? Or is it some or all of the above?

28. Why do many of Thea's attempts to cope with the parsonage home backfire with the members of St. Hurricane's congregation? Is it a matter of pride, control, other things?

29. Is Xavier unaware of the extent of his wife's struggle, or is his faith in her ability to overcome them rooted in his desire to keep things the way that are?

30. Do their ages play a significant role in how Thea and Xavier respond to their problems? Would a younger couple, in their twenties, react differently? How so?

31. What changes in Thea's job after she becomes VP? How do these changes affect her relationship with Xavier? With Jesse? With St. Hurricane?

32. How do you see the ages of the women in the story contributing to their attitudes about relationships, husbands, marriage, and a "woman's place" in public/church life?

Jesse—18
Thea—40s
Hattie—70s

33. Does Xavier's search for his place in the world cause him to discount the seeming abundance of gifts God has given him? Is his rejection of his charisma the same as, in the old expression, hiding his light under a bushel barrel?

34. What do you think Xavier is afraid of, in rejecting his fame and fortune?

35. When Thea accidentally bumps into Xavier at an airport lounge and discovers he is traveling with Bazz Azz's entourage, should she feel betrayed?

36. How does Xavier explain himself? Do you believe him? Do you think he might be lying even to himself? Why?

37. How does he come to reconcile the use of his talents with his desire to serve God selflessly?

38. How does Jesse's injury help to bring her closer to Xavier and, indirectly, with her mother?

39. Do you feel that Thea and Xavier have successfully found a formula for their lives that will allow both of them to thrive in their public and private lives?

REFLECTIONS OF AN
INVISIBLE SISTER

My mother tells the story of what happened when visitors came to my Negro-college-based elementary school in Pine Bluff, Arkansas, in the late 1950s. The visitors spied me and another student, a boy, and remarked in surprise, "Oh, you're *integrated*." They may be forgiven their mistake. I was naturally blonde with green eyes and freckles, while the boy had blue eyes and what we used to call "nice" hair. We were both so fair we burned in the sun. Yet we were "colored," as our birth certificates read.

I grew up in the segregated South, in a town where three generations of my father's family had lived, and everyone knew me as Dr. Parker's daughter. My father was a dentist and a leader in the AME church and the Boy Scouts. A one-time state president of the Arkansas branch of the NAACP, he organized civil rights boycotts and rallies in our hometown. I didn't have to wonder what I was. I knew what I was, and I'd always been proud of it.

When desegregation came, things changed. Patronizing places formerly closed to us, such as the main floor of the movie theater or the soda fountain at Woolworth, made me conspicuous to Whites who hadn't known I existed. They would stare uncomprehendingly at me and my friends. I later learned that one reason I wasn't asked out much was because Black male friends were afraid they'd have to deal with ignorant Whites assuming some uppity Negro was trying to date one of their own.

In 1966 I went to Howard University on a scholarship, convinced that here, at last, would be people who understood my

...on and thought nothing of it. But Black Power reached ...pus the same year, and reverse prejudice came into full ...om. I was again an outsider—this time among my own.

I met and married my husband while at Howard. He is second-generation Italian-American. As I tell people crass enough to ask why I married White, I didn't. I married a man with no racial agenda. But marrying Chris did plunge me for the first time into the White world. From my new vantage point, I learned that nearly every White person carries innate prejudices about my people. For instance, many Whites can't accept Black as a label for me. They believe I should "pass." I always ask them why I should be ashamed of who I am. To pass would mean giving up my family—because we run the gamut of the color spectrum. It embarrasses Whites to confront the truth that it is *their* attitudes that make it a liability to be Black.

That word again: *Black*. Applied to me it's confusing, yet both my parents and all my grandparents are African-American, although there is also Native American and European blood in our lineage.

People who know my heritage are careful of what they say around me. But there have been lots of opportunities to observe people with their guard down. Whites, not knowing what I am, have repeatedly told demeaning jokes about Blacks in my presence. On the other hand, I've also been snubbed, ignored, and made the object of crude remarks behind my back by African-Americans who thought I was White.

When I was younger, I railed against such arrogant stupidity. Now I pick my fights. But I can still speak up when pushed too far. Last summer my husband and I were at a party where a White friend of the host spent most of the evening proving he was an equal-opportunity bigot. As he drank steadily, he insulted every race, creed, and color, every religious and political view. At first I kept my opinions to myself. But late in the evening, he announced that White Americans are at the top of the heap and that's just where "we" belong. I decided to set him up.

I asked sweetly, "You can't mean *we* deserve everything *we* have simply because *we* are White?"

"Yes, you and me," he boasted through his fog of liquor. "You're successful because you're superior."

"Excuse me," I said, "But *I'm* an African-American. Yes, I am successful as you are. I earned it through education and hard work, just like the rest of my family." As I launched into a recital of my family's background, the bewildered man turned to my husband and said accusingly, "Is she really Black? She doesn't look Black."

Chris smiled and answered, "She can't help that."

First published in *Essence* magazine in April 1997

Laura Castoro

Bestselling author **Laura Parker Castoro** loves being a writer. "It's the best thing in the world. You spend your days working only with people, your characters, who you like, while making them do things you think they should do. If you're lucky, they listen. If you're even luckier, you get paid. Now that's a dream job!" Laura lives in Pine Bluff, Arkansas, with her husband Chris.